THE AGENT

THE AGENT

CREATED BY
Bill Adler

WRITTEN BY
David R. Slavitt

DOUBLEDAY & COMPANY, INC.
GARDEN CITY, N.Y.
1986

Library of Congress Cataloging-in-Publication Data
Slavitt, David R., 1935–
    The agent.
    I. Adler, Bill.
PS3569.L3A75   1986   813'.54   85-16038
ISBN 0-385-23007-9

THE AGENT

PROLOGUE

He was running. He was a fat man, running, and he was trying to remember what son of a bitch had said that the saddest thing in the world was to see a fat man run.

Said? Written, more likely. One of his clients, no doubt. And in any event, it was untrue. The saddest thing was to be a fat man running. From a crazy person.

There was another sharp little pop.

A crazy person with a gun.

Leonard Castle had had little experience of guns, and wasn't even absolutely sure that he'd seen and heard right. Shots, according to the conventions of cheap literature, were supposed to "ring out." Maybe they did, indoors. But outside, on the streets, the sound had been more like a cork popping. No reverberation at all. A small gun, then? A small—what was the word—caliber?

But even a little bitty gun could kill you, could hurt you badly.

And it's always safer to assume the worst.

Castle cut in front of a parked car, ran into the street, and then cut back behind another car and returned to the sidewalk. Crouched down, he tried to zigzag. He was by now puffing considerably.

He wasn't really obese, but portly, a carefully groomed man with custom-tailored clothing and custom-made shoes, he looked sleek and had an authoritative air of gravity and power that wasn't at all accidental. He was in good health too, for a man of his age and his size, but fear and flight do not bring out the best in anyone.

It wasn't just a mugger or serendipitous loony, either, no random piece of insanity that had just happened to attach itself like a burr to his trouser cuff. This person had sought Castle out, had followed him, and had been waiting for him in order to make this attempt . . . It was personal, intended. A mistake, maybe, one of those bizarre errors the Mafia make in movies? Unlikely. But then the only other explanation was that it had to be one of Castle's clients, dissatisfied and looking for redress, not from the world or some publisher, one or another of which had done him wrong, but from his agent, his own representative. There was nobody else Leonard Castle could think of who would want to kill him.

Who else cared enough?

It would be his instinct to try to talk it out, to negotiate, but how do you negotiate with a crazy person who's armed? You don't even dare slow down. These small guns were supposedly inaccurate except at very close range, but Castle wasn't sure how far to trust that. He was, at any rate, large, making a deplorably easy target. Even as he ran, he could imagine the bullet, could all but feel its pain, a kind of searing that would at any instant streak through him. The only thing he couldn't quite predict was where he'd feel it. The gut, no doubt. That was the biggest, the most central, and therefore the likeliest place.

Another of those deplorable little pops.

Still running, doing a kind of fat man's shuffle, he was making, it appeared, quite reasonable progress along West Seventy-second Street. If he kept on weaving this way among the parked cars and taking advantage of whatever cover offered itself, he might yet get away. Presumably, this nut wouldn't want to kill innocent bystanders. If he could just get to Columbus Avenue and turn the corner . . .

Maybe, Castle thought, it was the building he lived in, the goddamn Dakota. Ever since that other fruitcake had shot John Lennon, there'd been a threat hanging over the place. First Rosemary's Baby and then Lennon, and it was like living in a haunted house. Or haunted condominium. But the convention of spookiness had established itself and the dark gray stone structure was now famous and menacing, and therefore an invitation to the deranged to carry on in the established tradition.

But literary agents don't get shot at. That was just dumb. And there was no opportunity to make that clear to the person whose footsteps he could sense more than hear, maybe fifty yards back.

Castle had in fact been aware for some time that he was being followed, or he'd had the unusual sensation of being watched, feeling the attention that was focused on him. Even now, as he crouched down so as to hide behind a parked Buick and at the same time wave his hand to attract a cab, he was convinced that his pursuer wasn't a stranger. There was malevolence here, something furious . . .

There was also the gun, of course. And Castle realized that there might be something intentional in the slow pace of his pursuer, as if the object weren't to catch up but only harry, to keep him going just this way, maintaining and increasing the menace as the slow and exquisitely drawn-out chase continued.

Impossible? Not if it was a client. Castle's clients weren't always the brightest people in the world, but they usually had some cleverness, some caginess to them. Some of them were weird but they were—he certainly hoped—a point or two above the typical Manhattan thug on the old Wechsler-Bellevue scale. They could surely be tricky. It wasn't impossible that the whole idea was only to scare him into calling for a policeman who would then make a report of the incident. And in the New York Post, *there'd be a piece about a prominent agent going around the bend, claiming what twenty paranoids a day come in to report—that he'd been followed and was being shot at . . .*

Did that make sense? Anything was possible in this city and in this business. And almost anything was better than being wounded or even killed by a nut with a handgun. The first order of business was to get the hell away from this guy.

Castle was tempted to descend into the areaway of an apartment house and try to hide below the sidewalk level, but he was also afraid of being stuck there in what would turn out to be a cul-de-sac. He saw a doorman standing at the building's entrance and he made a dash toward that open door.

"There's a guy following me," he said. "I think he may have a gun."
"No kiddin'!"

"Can you call a cab for me? You've got one of those lights, don't you?" He tried not to sound panicked and not to puff too hard.

"No, that don't work," the doorman said. "I got a whistle only." He was wearing dirty khakis under the maroon greatcoat with the brass buttons. He was a kid, really, with acne marks on him, so that his face looked like that of the man in the moon. The night doorman, probably, or just a temporary.

"Try the whistle, then. For five bucks?"

"A guy with a gun? No shit!" The kid grinned, flashing white teeth.

The five dollars had been too much. For two the young man might have been willing to humor a crazy fat man, but for five he was halfway to believing that there could be real danger.

"Is there another way out of here?"
The doorman shook his head.
"You've got a phone, don't you? You could telephone for a cab!"
"Look, mister . . ."
"Five bucks, and you don't even have to go outside. Call for the cab. Do a guy a favor, why don't you?"
He was considering it.
Thinking fast, Castle realized he had to recoup lost ground and make

up for his earlier errors. The guy wasn't sure whether to believe him or not, couldn't decide if he was a nut or not, and if a nut, harmless or not. Castle had to take all that out of consideration and bring his attention back to the money. He reached into his pocket and found his money clip. He peeled off a five-dollar bill and put the rest back. He held out the folded bill between his second and third fingers. "Five bucks," he said, "or nothing at all. You decide." And then he turned and took a couple of steps toward the door.

There was nothing in the world he wanted to do less than go back outside. But he couldn't let this doorman know that. He couldn't appear to hesitate. He couldn't even look back. He had to put one foot in front of the other, and keep his head facing front.

"Okay, mister. I'll call you your cab."

"Thanks," Castle said.

"They'll want to know where you want to go. What should I tell them."

"The East Seventies," Castle said.

He caught a glimpse of his image in a smoked mirror on the wall of what had once been a fairly glitzy lobby. It looked bedraggled now, and so did he. His white sport coat had a smudge running down one side, where he'd rubbed against some filthy car. His tie was askew, and his hair was a mess. He tried to smooth the hair down, but it did no good. Portly people have to be neater than anyone else, or else they look like slobs.

"Okay, I'll make the call," the young man said. He took the bill and went off to a phone.

Castle realized that there hadn't even been an instant's hesitation about it. He had known without question that he would go to Susan Flowers' place and that she'd take him in.

She might not like the idea. She might not even like him any more. But she had loved him, which was something else altogether. And at a time like this, when he was in trouble, she'd take him in.

There was another perfectly good reason for going to Susan's apartment. He and Susan had broken off, and it was therefore unlikely that anyone would make a connection between him and her. Her apartment was an unlikely place for him to go, which meant it was safe. And Castle needed time to think about what to do. Report this? Hire a private detective? Get himself a bodyguard? It was outrageous how modern life had turned medieval, with security guards all over just as if each office building and apartment house were one of those old walled towns. It was even worse in Europe. In Italy, some of those industrialists and *movie stars couldn't go anywhere except by helicopter for fear of kid-nappers and terrorists.*

But, no, this was different. This, Castle felt sure, was personal. The worst-case scenario was that it turned out after all to be one of his clients, one of those people for whom he'd worked and schemed to turn their life stories into dollars. "The new Rumpelstiltskin," People maga-zine had once called him, "who turned facts into gold." Still, the public-ity was always welcome, and they'd spelled his name right.

Usually, his clients were happy. Some were delighted. Most of them were tough enough and experienced enough to understand the rules of the game and to separate themselves from the books and magazine articles, movies and miniseries that resulted from his negotiations on their behalf. But some of them, men and women who had been in the public eye for years, took it personally, which was always surprising and also risky. Worse yet, some even began to believe the stories they'd been telling their interviewers and ghostwriters.

"Cab's coming," the doorman reported. "You want I should call the cops too?"

"No, no. I'll be okay."

"I didn't think there was no gun, man." The kid flashed a knowing grin, and advised, "You shouldn't fuck around like that, man. Another guy, he might get nervous and put your lights out with a nightstick just out of jittery nerves, you know?"

"You're probably right," Castle agreed.

The kid opened his coat to show the club that he'd been holding on to for his jittery nerves.

Castle nodded, acknowledging that he was impressed by the size of it. They waited together, just inside the front door, until, in a matter of minutes, a cab pulled up and came to a stop.

"You'll open the door for me, like a good fellow?" Castle asked, holding out a folded dollar bill.

The kid obliged, taking the bill and telling him, or maybe warning him, "You be careful now, man, you hear?"

From the relative safety of the cab, Castle looked back to see whether he could spot anyone trying to follow him. There was still a remote chance that he'd misinterpreted all these little pieces of sense data. Maybe he'd even imagined the whole thing? He was tired, had been working too hard for too long, and needed a vacation. His nerves were raw.

But there had been a figure, its face hidden by the brim of a fedora but with a memorable glint in the right hand. A figment? It seemed to have appeared out of the shadows near the entrance to the Dakota. Almost certainly it had been male, but it could have been a woman trying to look like a man. And there had been those three little popping noises—shots, he had been sure. Castle had taken off as quickly as possible, which was the only sane thing to do.

He supposed he ought to call his sister, Lisa, and warn her. She too had an apartment in the Dakota. It was unlikely that any assailant would know this. Still, the fact of an assailant was, in itself, so improbable that Castle had no idea how to figure the odds on what kind of person that could be. Calmer, now that his breathing and heartbeat were returning to normal, he realized that the stresses and their consequent risks had always been there, for he was more than an agent, after all. He was a broker of fame, a glitter merchant, speculating and trading in reputations. And fame does funny things to people. It builds them up and tears them down. It affects their sense of what the world owes them and blurs their vision of the limits of the human condition. They start to think that anything they want is possible and even probable, and that what they want, they ought to have just because of who they are. They get the peculiar notion that they are creatures of special grace, the darlings of fortune, and that the whole purpose of each day's sunrise is to warm them. Sometimes, for a while, it even works out for them, and they read in this run of good luck an entire lifetime's destiny rather than a single extraordinary chapter.

Worst of all, the public agrees with them, believing even more devoutly than they do that there is something special about them, something wonderful and worth standing out in the rain for hours just to get a glimpse of. They are surrounded by adoring headwaiters and attentive television cameramen and they begin to take it for granted that this is how existence is going to be for all time. But their moment ends, their series is canceled, their films have a rough time at the box office, or their records fail to go gold and platinum, and they get crazy and look for someone to blame.

Until now, they had looked elsewhere, but there was no reason for Castle to suppose himself immune. He was dealing with volatile people, interesting but not always admirable or even likable, and with a fair number of them the circuits weren't wired in any too well.

The police were a last resort. He thought he ought probably turn first to more discreet kinds of protection, at least for a while, in the hope that he could get some confirmation of his guess as to who it was that wanted either to kill him or else to scare him to death.

1

Leonard Castle and Susan Flowers had first crossed paths a couple of years earlier, having been brought together by their interest in ex-President Harlan T. Farnsworth, who was one of Castle's clients.

Farnsworth was one of those villain Presidents, a son of a bitch like Lyndon Johnson or Richard Nixon, one of those men people love to hate. And like Johnson and Nixon, Farnsworth had a soft spot in his heart for dogs. Johnson had had those dopey beagles, and Nixon had had Checkers and then King Timahoe, and in the same way, Farnsworth had his brace of bloodhounds, which gave the cartoonists almost as much of an opportunity as the President's famous bald dome.

Everybody knew about the bloodhounds, of course, but only Castle had figured out how to use them, how to contrive an introduction for himself and, more than that, how to earn the ex-President's confidence and gratitude. Politics aside, the talk on the street was that Farnsworth's memoirs would go for a couple of million, and you don't need a calculator to figure out that 10 percent of that is still a nice piece of change. The question was how to break out of the pack, how to distinguish himself from the other able literary agents in town. Nothing wrong with any of them, of course. Their reputations were solid and well deserved. But there is always room for an honest hustler. Castle wasn't going to sit there behind his desk hoping that by some stroke of luck Farnsworth's hatpin might fall on his name in the list in the yellow pages.

What he wanted was a way to meet Farnsworth, and the dogs were the way to do it. An old trick, of course. Young men learned to pick up women—or other men, for that matter—following each other around with their little poodles or Yorkies and their pooper scoopers. What Castle wanted was something like that but with class, a little bravura even, to which Farnsworth might react in just the right way.

It was a challenge to which he responded as he might have with a chess problem. He checked with Effie to make sure that there was nothing obligatory on his calendar, gave her some instructions about a couple of phone calls that might come in, and left the building. He liked to walk briskly, not in the park, which was where muggers and perverts hung out, but along the busy streets with their windows of invitation or blandishment or even defiance—a lapis lazuli washstand and toilet bowl set, for God's sake?—so that he'd be diverted and his subconscious would be allowed to work its magic on the problem at hand. He walked just fast enough to get his heart going but without working up a sweat. That was the optimal pace, with the rhythms pounding and the circuits humming agreeably. He was a big man but much of his bulk was muscle. He'd been a big kid, which was quite a different thing from being a thin guy carrying around a lot of fat cells.

Pushing fifty, Castle could still keep up a brisk clip that would gobble up the twenty-block Manhattan miles so that he could start out in midtown and wind up in So-Ho or even down at the Battery, if the problem he'd set himself was complicated enough to require that much processing. The odd thing was that if he'd broken his rule and gone to the park, he might have seen the solution even sooner than he did. As it happened, there was a life-sized porcelain bloodhound in the window of an interior decorator's studio which seemed to call out to him, to demand that he stop, stare, and try to puzzle out its cryptic suggestion. Send the President a porcelain bloodhound? No, of course not. One couldn't bribe a President, not even a terrible President like Farnsworth. One had to use a little subtlety—but not so much that it couldn't, in the end, be seen through.

What if . . . ? He began to see it, in rough outline at first but then in clearer detail. It was dumb, but so dumb as to approach brilliance.

He stuck out the walking stick that was partly decorative and partly a protective weapon, using it to hail a cab. He returned to the office to ask Bobo, his office boy and gofer, whether he knew anything at all about exercising dogs.

"You getting a dog, boss?"

"No. I hate dogs. They are mostly stupid machines for turning food into shit, like some people I know. It's somebody else's dog. Or actually, two of them. You know how to exercise dogs?"

"What's to know? They walk. You hold on to the leash. When they stop, you stop."

"It's not very complicated, I guess."

"No, boss."

"I may have some dog exercising for you to do," he promised. Bobo didn't look all that enthusiastic, but then Castle paid him well. It was a dumb economy to try to squeeze office help. Castle knew he needed their best efforts and their loyalty, so he was generous both to Effie and to Bobo. It was a justification for what was his inclination anyway.

"Whatever you say, boss."

Castle went to work designing the brochure that would best present that deluxe service to which someone like Harlan Farnsworth would suppose himself and his famous matched bloodhounds entitled. Not just any old exercise service, but the grand treatment with the armed security guards for pets of the rich and famous.

Wrexham Livery sounded good. It was a sign he'd seen on the side of a panel truck on the way back to the office. It took him the better part of an hour to do the brochure, and most of the next morning to arrange with the printer for the right typeface and stock. The printer's minimum order was for 500 copies. Castle knew he'd throw away 499 of them, but his investment in bait would still pay off handsomely if the one big fish bit.

The President had just bought a triplex apartment in a Park Avenue building, and his bloodhounds would be needing exercise. It was a job that Farnsworth probably assigned to his Secret Service agents, but they'd be doing it reluctantly without caring for the dogs. The special attention that the Wrexham Livery Service could offer might just be attractive enough to pique Farnsworth's interest. That, at any rate, was what Castle had to play to, as he did both in the printed brochure and in the accompanying note—on his personal letterhead. He declared in that document his long-standing admiration for Farnsworth, his delight and pride that Farnsworth had chosen to settle in New York, and his concern as a dog lover that the President's bloodhounds would not have the same comfortable opportunity for exercise in a secure setting that they had formerly enjoyed on the lawns of the White House. It was in pride and in friendliness that he offered to the ex-President the enclosed description of a service he might find convenient. The number on the brochure was Castle's unlisted home telephone, where the answering machine simply recited the seven digits.

It was strange how these bad-guy Presidents preferred canines to

human beings—or not so strange, consitering how they were all sons
of bitches.

At the worst, Castle figured that he would have gambled a few
dollars and lost, but he would have more fun with the play than any
sucker at the tables in Atlantic City or Vegas. Every evening, when he
got home from work, he played the tape on the answering machine.
This was something he did out of habit, almost as mechanical as the
machine itself. But now there was the extra interest, a special anticipation. Each day he wondered whether there might be that message from
someone on Farnsworth's staff, the inquiry about the Wrexham exercise service. Castle never expected that Farnsworth himself would be
on the line, but there it was, that famous gravelly voice, asking for
more information, leaving a number, and inviting someone from
Wrexham Livery to return the call.

That was Effie's job. The next morning, Castle briefed her, explaining exactly what she was supposed to say, and even played the part of
the ex-President as they ran through the conversation a couple of
times for practice so she wouldn't be too nervous when she spoke to
Farnsworth. The trouble was with the prices. Castle hadn't listed the
charges in the brochure because he hadn't been sure what his costs
would be. From his inner office, he called a security agency to find out
what an armed guard would cost, either by the day or by the week.

He set a schedule of prices for Wrexham Livery that wasn't cheap
and would reduce his own net loss. More important, he figured he
would have to charge Farnsworth enough to make the operation look
legitimate. Figure in the cost of taxicabs and Bobo's salary. At the
worst, he figured it would run for maybe a week.

"Okay, go ahead and make the call," he told Effie, and he went out
to the men's room to wash his face. He didn't want to be in the office,
didn't want Effie to be rattled by his own nervousness. A little cold
water, a splash of bay rum, and he could saunter back to get the
report.

"He'll try us for a week," Effie announced. "The daily service." She
had no idea why it was such a good thing, but Castle was pleased and
therefore she was pleased. Castle sent Bobo out to Hammacher
Schlemmer to get himself an impressive-looking whistle that he could
hang around his neck, and to a uniform company to pick up a chauffeur's cap. He called the security agency back to arrange for the guard.

"Would you tell me what's going on, boss?" Bobo asked when he
returned with the whistle and the cap. He wasn't at all happy about

wearing the cap and wanted to be reassured that Castle hadn't taken leave of his senses.

"What you have here," Castle told him, "is what they used to call in the movies a 'cute meet.' They used to spend all kinds of time and energy getting the main characters together. There'd be a psychiatrist and a madame and they'd meet at the complaint window at Macy's, and it would turn out that each had ordered a couch but the couches had been delivered wrong. And by the time they'd straightened out their little difficulty, they were more than halfway to being in love."

"President Farnsworth's going to fall in love with me?"

"Not with you, Bobo. With me."

A blank look gave way, after a moment, to a smile. "Okay, boss, whatever you say."

"You only have to wear it when you pick the dogs up and then when you bring them back. Okay?"

"Okay, boss."

"I figure it will only run a couple of days. At the worst, we'll do it for two weeks. I promise you!"

The question was whether Castle could stand it himself for a whole week. But then, there might be a way to speed things up, a way of letting the President know that there was no such thing as Wrexham Livery and that it was only an eager agent hustling him for his business. If it hit him the right way, and if he was any kind of a sport at all, he'd be flattered by Castle's exertions and impressed by the efforts he'd put forward. It was also possible that he'd be offended, that he'd feel he'd been used or bamboozled. That risk was unavoidable. But Castle was optimistic, mostly because he couldn't believe that Farnsworth was such an absolute and thoroughgoing prick as most people said he was. There had to be some redeeming feature somewhere. For starters, the man liked dogs.

He wrote the initials HF on his calendar and boxed them. Then, in a demonstration of almost Eastern serenity, he put Farnsworth almost entirely out of his mind. At the end of the day, he telephoned his sister, Lisa Barr, the gossip columnist, to feed her the item about Farnsworth's dogs.

In the morning, when Castle woke and looked out of his window, he was dismayed to see that it was raining, no downpour but a persistent and depressing drizzle. He regretted his ridiculous plan, but then he had already invested too much thought and effort in it to abandon it now. Besides, as he thought about it over coffee, there were possibilities here that might be exploited. It could be fairly amusing, actually.

And the point of the exercise was to keep it light and graceful, to keep Farnsworth smiling, even though he'd been taken.

He dressed with special care, an off-white suit and a Panama hat. And he tucked a pastel handkerchief into the pocket of his jacket. He put on his raincoat, took a couple of umbrellas, and went out to wait while the doorman found him a cab, which wasn't so difficult at this early hour. Castle checked his watch. It wasn't quite seven o'clock yet. Everything was right on schedule.

At the office, he found Bobo waiting for him. And the uniformed security guard arrived on the dot at seven-fifteen. On the way over to President Farnsworth's building, Castle explained what he wanted them both to do. It wasn't very difficult. Whether or not he thought it was funny or even just nuts, the guard didn't react. That was acceptable, Castle decided. This charade wasn't being mounted for the guard's benefit.

Bobo put on the chauffeur's cap and he and the guard went up to the doorman of Farnsworth's building to announce themselves as the Wrexham Livery people and to ask for President Farnsworth's bloodhounds. Castle stood out on the street, waiting, imagining how it was going. The doorman would be calling up. There'd be someone upstairs who'd been told about this and, after a moment or two, would be coming down with the dogs. And about now, they ought to be coming out of the building. But there was no sign of them. Had something gone wrong? Had the President thought better of the arrangement? Had someone tipped him off?

Keep calm. It's just a joke, just a little piece of foolishness. It's nothing to get excited about, Castle told himself. But his artistic sense had been engaged, and he wanted it to work, not even for any practical result, but as a maneuver, as a pure piece of manipulation.

And there they were. The two men and the two dogs. Bobo approached with the dogs and turned them over to Castle, who took the leashes and felt the sudden tug from the dogs, which were bigger than he'd expected and very powerful. Jesus, they were strong animals!

He opened one of the umbrellas and held it out over the dogs. Bobo held the other umbrella over Castle. They made an odd-looking group as they paraded across Fifth Avenue and into the park, where the reporters and photographers would be waiting for them.

The dogs weren't much upset by the flashbulbs. They were used to such things. They were friendly beasts and wanted to greet the reporters, and they kept tugging on their leashes, which made it hard for Castle to answer some of the reporters' questions.

"What are the dogs' names, Mr. Castle?"

"Mac and Ike," he said.

"And which one is which?" the reporter asked.

"I haven't the vaguest idea. I'm doing this to make an impression on President Farnsworth, to show him how far I'm willing to go on his behalf."

"You don't think he'll object to having his dogs used this way?"

"They don't look to be in too much discomfort," he said. "It's a dog's life, having to go out into the park like this. I don't think they mind much who is on this end of the leash."

"You really think they need an armed guard?"

"I don't know. I hope not. But I didn't want anything to happen to them while they were in my care. I am counting on President Farnsworth to be a sport about this. I figure he's had a lot of practice with more serious things. But there's a limit to what a man can stand. I wanted him to understand that his dogs would be safe."

"What if he's not amused?"

"Then I've guessed wrong, haven't I?" Castle admitted. "But I won't have lost much. I don't really think I'd have been the first agent he'd have called. Up there among the top ten, maybe, but not the first or even the second. So I wanted to call his attention to myself and the extra effort I am prepared to make on his behalf. Even if he doesn't get the message, there might be other people who do."

"So you're using us, isn't that what it amounts to?" another reporter asked.

"Sure, but you knew that. If you don't think this is funny or newsworthy or whatever, you don't have to write about it, do you? You've been had before. What's one more time?"

He grinned. He could afford to. The television crew was coming into view. And if it was a light day, he was a lead-pipe cinch to make the noon news. Between that and the photographs showing him and Bobo and the two umbrellas, the piece would be irresistible, if only for the caption.

In fact, he had to call a halt to the reporters' questions to get the dogs back home to Farnsworth's apartment. He sent Bobo up to deliver the dogs, and the accompanying note that he'd worked on the night before, assuring the President that this elaborate prank had been fundamentally good-natured and motivated by Castle's desire to enlist him as a client. He offered to continue the dog-walking services until there was an indication that they were no longer required. He certainly didn't want to leave the President in a position where he'd have to walk the animals himself.

Castle went back to his office, worked until noon, and then turned on the television set to watch for himself and see how he'd been treated. Within the week, Harlan Farnsworth was a Leonard Castle Literary Agency client. Within the month, there was a check for half a million dollars—the first of four such checks in a complicated step deal—on Castle's desk. When it cleared, 90 percent of it, or $450,000, went to Farnsworth. The rest was Castle's to keep.

*

The announcement of the Farnsworth deal was in all the papers. But something about it caught the attention of Jack Ditson, at *Periscope*. Ditson was the associate producer, an old newshound who had put in his time at *Newsweek* and had started out as a United Press reporter in Springfield and then in Chicago. He was a rumpled-looking man who prided himself on his dumbness. He insisted that in this business there was no shortage of brains. What his writers and unit producers had to do was keep their stories simple and clear, so that even a guy like him could understand what they were saying. In fact, he was only playing at being dumb, and they all knew that, but they went along with it, kept the material as simple and as clear as they could make it, and took his suggestions seriously.

Susan Flowers could have ignored the page torn from *Publishers Weekly* with the item about Farnsworth circled in red grease pencil and the scribbled note asking, "Why does this bother me?" She had learned that Ditson might be dumb but he wasn't stupid or frivolous, and he certainly wasn't unshrewd. She wondered what he might have read or heard or seen to be bothered by this bland announcement. Two million dollars was impressive but not bothersome. Leonard Castle? He was just the agent. Still, she went to the morgue and looked up his file. A few old feature pieces from *The Village Voice*, from *Publishers Weekly*, from *Women's Wear Daily*, from *New York* magazine. A fair number of little clippings, odd bits of information about some celebrity or other. She took the envelope back to her desk and pored over it, making notes to herself on a yellow pad.

The name, originally, wasn't Castle but Rook. And before that Baruch. And his sister was Lisa Barr, the columnist, who'd taken the first syllable for herself. Born 1935. Erasmus Hall. NYU. Went to work for MCA, then with Perry Gilman, and then, when Gilman died, kept the business going and ran it himself. More connections with celebrities and appearances at parties.

Nothing disgraceful, nothing criminal, nothing even faintly aromatic. She puttered around, reading back issues of newspapers and magazines, trying to get snagged by the same piece of information that had lodged somewhere in Ditson's mind. Three hours produced nothing at all.

She went to Ditson's office and asked if he had a minute.

"For you, sweetheart? Any time! What's up?"

"That's what I wanted to find out from you. Can you give me a hint? What is it about Farnsworth? The book? The money? Castle?"

"I wish I knew. But you know, it's just a feeling."

"Lisa Barr is his sister. That's all I've been able to pick up so far." She explained about the Barr/Rook business.

"Maybe that's it."

"That Lisa Barr is his sister?"

"No, no," Ditson said. "Something I read in Barr's column. Not too long ago."

"I'll take a look," she said.

"Let me know if you come up with something. It really is a nuisance. Like having your teeth itch."

"Teeth don't itch," she told him, maybe for the hundred and fiftieth time.

"So you keep telling me, sweetheart. I know better."

He was right too. She found it in five minutes. The bit about the dog service and the hungry agent. Of course! That had to have been Castle. And he had fed the item to his sister.

She typed out a memo to Ditson, letting him know what she'd found and agreeing with him that it was a cause for dental itch. The operational paragraph was the concluding one in which she asked, "It sounds like fun. Is there enough for a segment on Castle? Shall I open a file?"

She was not at all surprised when the memo came back with Ditson's scrawl at the bottom: "Open the file. Worth back-burner attention. Keep me informed. Thnx. JD."

*

Farnsworth was no dummy. Any man shrewd enough and tough enough to scramble close enough to the top of the heap where he could make a grab at the presidency of the United States of America was no fool. One could discount a lot, attribute a fair proportion of the achievement to luck and timing, but Castle knew enough about how the world worked to understand that when nickels fell out of the sky, you had to be there first of all, and it helped if you also had a hat to hold out to catch them with. Farnsworth usually had a gunny sack.

They didn't have occasion to meet very often. Farnsworth generally kept to his triplex, busying himself with work on the book. Every now and then, he'd make one of his occasional television appearances. And once in a great while, he and his Secret Service entourage would take off for some lecture or even just a seminar at Yale or Princeton. Like any snob, Farnsworth was a sucker for such requests if they came from the right places. (It was more complicated than that, of course. Castle suspected that Farnsworth was negotiating about which institution would get his papers or which of them was prepared to do the most in return for being honored by the Harlan T. Farnsworth Memorial Library.) Still, the former President enjoyed going out to these Ivy League places and showing up their tweedy professors as innocents and dreamers. You'd never catch him at a place like NYU.

Mostly, he worked on his book, talking his recollections into his little Lanier every morning, pausing only to check a date or a diary entry, and in the afternoons editing the typed transcripts of earlier sessions. As far as Castle could tell, judging from those three or four occasions when he called on the ex-President, Farnsworth put on a jacket and tie even when he was all by himself, just sitting at his desk and correcting typescripts. The man appeared always to be wearing the same suit but it was always immaculately pressed, so that Castle supposed he had a whole closetful of them all in that same cut and that same deep blue serge.

Their meetings—or audiences, really—were brief and businesslike. Farnsworth welcomed Castle, invited him to be seated, reported on the progress he'd made since the previous visit, and then invited Castle's views on the manuscript's prospects.

He wasn't at all interested in hearing Castle's literary judgments. The President made it clear that Castle was welcome to his opinions, whatever they were. Farnsworth wanted to hear only about money and deals. The first and only time Castle tried to urge him to be more personal, to let readers know what he thought and, even more important, what he felt, Farnsworth raised a hand like a traffic cop and stopped him dead. "When I call a broker to sell a piece of property, I expect him to do that job, not to be an interior decorator or a landscape designer or an architect. Just take what there is and sell it. Or bow out and let me find someone else who's willing to do the particular job I'm expecting him to do for me. You're welcome to think whatever you like. The only question is whether we can sell this, and for how much. Is that unreasonable?" And then he had stretched his lips horizontally in what couldn't really be called a smile but was more a piece of facial punctuation. It was an expression the cartoonists had used, and they hadn't been his friends.

"Yes, Mr. President, that's reasonable enough. But there are places where the two areas overlap. Just a touch here and there of personal connection, of personal emotion, and we can do better on the first serial rights. And those will help us on the book contract, which is where the major money is."

"First serial rights. You mean magazines and so forth?"

"That's right. Excerpts that we place early to demonstrate what the public interest is, how deep it goes, and what the sales of the book can be."

"It seems to me that there'd be a risk in that. What if the magazine sales are disappointing? Your scheme could backfire, couldn't it?"

"We'd make the deal with a magazine and announce that. Then, before the magazine appeared, we'd make the book deal. We'd have the magazine hold off until an agreed date that was close to the appearance of the book so that the magazine appearance would help the book, whetting readers' appetites."

"I see," Farnsworth said. "And each time, each deal is a little different."

"Absolutely. It's a matter of getting people to jump on a bandwagon. You have to persuade a couple of people at first that there is one, and they've got to put up some large dollars to get on first, but then it gets easier. The general public are the last ones in line, and by then most of the decisions have been made."

"And they're the ones who decide whether those earlier guesses have been right or wrong. It's not altogether unfamiliar."

"A lot depends on those excerpts, though. People will be making large bets on the basis of just a few pages. And the better we start out, the stronger the material, the better our chances are down the line."

"I understand what you're saying. I'll give it some thought."

"That's all I ask, Mr. President."

There was that odd expression again, somewhat like a gas pain but with menace to it. This time, Castle had the sense that it meant he was dismissed. He took the sheaf of pages Farnsworth had prepared, put them in his attaché case, ostentatiously locked the case, and then took his leave.

He didn't go back to his office but home to his apartment in the Dakota, where he put a Brandenburg Concerto on the stereo and calmed himself with a cup of tea. Only then did he open the case and skim through the typescript, impeccably prepared on heavy rag bond, of the ex-President's memoirs, his account, self-serving and exculpatory but informed and often persuasive, of those turbulent years in the White House.

It was a quick look only, and he turned the pages in a regular rhythm as he scanned for proper names, occasionally slowing to take in a sentence or a short paragraph. He went back, to read through a second time what Farnsworth had written, seeing how the man had settled scores, held grudges, paid off debts of loyalty, and in general behaved himself—not so much as an author but as a politician and a human being. This was the question people would be asking, the reason they'd be wasting their time and money on this bastard's account of his downfall . . .

Castle found himself getting angry at the guy all over again. And then he leaned back, picked up his teacup, and took a sip of the nearly cold Earl Grey. He was pleased. If Farnsworth could still get his goat, there were other goats, whole flocks of them, vast herds that would all come stampeding, eager to be shorn.

Do you shear goats? he wondered. Angora goats maybe.

He checked his watch. There was just time to take the President's manuscript to the bank and put it into the safe-deposit box. That was what Farnsworth had insisted on, and as far as he was concerned advice was tantamount to an executive order. He just didn't think Castle's office safe was safe enough, not for this.

Castle had been willing to humor the man. He'd rented a safe-deposit box in which to keep the manuscript pages the former President entrusted to his care. He wondered, though, what would actually happen if someone were to steal this little bit of manuscript. Would it be so terrible?

Might it not even be a good thing?

It was a ridiculous idea, but it wouldn't go away. He'd been fighting it for weeks, every time he went to the bank this way. It kept coming back and buzzing infuriatingly around his head like a mosquito in the middle of a hot August night.

*

The cab slowed to a stop for a red light. It was in the park, and darkness and menace glared from the vapor lights that made the road-

way garish and exaggerated the darkness beyond. What if Susan wasn't home? he asked himself. What if she was home but had company, another man? Or what if she was home alone but still unwilling to let him in?

It wouldn't be surprising. Their relationship had seemed to flourish and then it had gone off, for no good reason. That happens sometimes, and sometimes people resent it and try to fix blame, if only to exonerate themselves. He didn't suppose that Susan would do such a thing, but people do what they have to do, to avoid discomfort. It's hard to blame them. He was guilty too, he had no doubt.

But there was no point in anticipating. You could beat yourself that way in any meeting, any time with anyone. Let the dealer deal and then play the hand. That was the only way to go.

2

The helicopter outside was shiny black with the silver logo of Rorschach, Inc., which was Bart Blackpool's production company. It was waiting at the Billings airport, just as Blackpool had promised. But the pilot had explained to Castle that there were two other passengers he was supposed to take back. "Mr. Blackpool apologizes, but he didn't think you'd mind. One of them is a vet. Mr. Blackpool found this wounded eagle, and the poor critter was halfway starving to death. He's got a vet coming in from UC Davis to set its wing and help figure out a diet for the bird until it can fly again. You want to go into the bar and have a drink or a bite to eat—as Mr. Blackpool's guest, of course?"

"No, no. That's all right. They fed me on the plane. And I don't mind waiting for the vet. It's a kind of a good deed, I guess, and I wouldn't want to stand in the way of that."

"I wouldn't want to stand in the way of anything Mr. Blackpool wanted, actually," the pilot said. He was one of those people who looked like a pilot, with the wrinkles around the eyes but a square jaw and a full head of salt-and-pepper hair and not an ounce of fat on him anywhere. A Vietnam pilot, probably. And, Castle rather supposed, more than just a pilot for Blackpool. A bodyguard too? It was possible, surely. He had been waiting at the gate at which Castle had arrived from Denver.

"And the other one?" he asked. "You said there were two people."

"Oh, he's just a screenwriter. If he gets in before the vet does, we'll take him along. Otherwise, he can rent a car and drive. The vet's the important one."

Castle nodded, as if that order of priority were self-evident. "Pretty country around here," he said. "I got to see some of it, looking down. It's a nice clear day."

"Oh, yeah. Pretty country. Out that way, not too far, is where Custer was massacred." The pilot grinned as if the massacre were one of the more attractive features of the region.

It figured, though. Castle remembered that Blackpool's spread was somewhere in the Big Horn range, and it stood to reason that the Little Bighorn came flowing out of those mountains. He'd just never made the connection before. What he'd been thinking about was how to handle this prima donna, this superstar, whose inability to write his life story was coupled with an odd reluctance to have anyone else help him. Pride and sloth? And a couple more of the seven deadly sins, as likely as not. The trick was to be open and receptive, ready to pick up the hints that might be there waiting for a shrewd or merely sufficiently attentive and sympathetic observer. If Blackpool had the idea that he was being "handled," he'd resent it and, as likely as not, throw Castle out on his ear. Maybe from the shiny black helicopter.

Blackpool's talents were mysterious. He wasn't a bad actor and sometimes showed a spooky kind of intelligence and an attractive energy that had helped his screen career. But it was something else, the delicacy of his features, the small frame and the almost feminine modeling of his nose and lips, that made him so appealing to audiences—to young girls especially. One thought of Michael Jackson or Robert Redford or, if one was a little older, of Alan Ladd, and the fragility their looks suggested. They could play against that delicacy, as all of them had done. It was interesting to men but irresistible to women. And for Bart Blackpool, it had opened the door to serious money and power in motion pictures. He called his own shots—in several senses. Certainly, he picked his own properties, chose his co-stars and directors, or even directed, himself, if he felt so disposed.

And most of the time, he lived out here, just south of the Montana line on a huge Wyoming ranch, in the foothills of the Big Horn range, a little bigger than one of those small European countries.

"You sure you couldn't use a cup of coffee?" the pilot asked.

"I'll join you if you want one," Castle said.

"I don't mind. Name's Frank," he said, holding out his hand.

"Leonard Castle."

"Yeah, I know."

There was a coffee shop with a fountain on one side and booths along the opposite wall. They sat and had coffee. "It shouldn't be long now," the pilot said, checking his Rolex. "Mr. Blackpool sent the jet to Sacramento to pick up the veterinarian. I'd guess they'll be touching down in ten or fifteen minutes."

As he spoke, two men appeared at the entrance of the coffee shop, one of them wearing exactly the same outfit as the pilot—the black cowboy boots, the blue jeans and matching denim jacket, and the red bandana at the throat over a cream-colored western shirt. Castle realized that it was a kind of uniform. The other man, then, a shorter fellow running a little to fat and wearing oversized spectacles with black plastic frames and Photogray lenses, had to be the screenwriter. He had a briefcase with him, but it was the worried look on his face that gave him away.

Castle had as much reason to worry as this guy did, but he hoped it didn't show so clearly. His guess turned out to be correct, though. The writer, Stu Rosenthal, was up for a conference with Blackpool. The pilot introduced the writer and the agent, sent the other man from Rorschach over to the baggage claim area to pick up Rosenthal's bag, and excused himself to go and check with operations about the jet from Sacramento.

"You been working for Blackpool for long?" Castle asked after the writer had had a chance to order a Diet 7-Up.

"Six months," Rosenthal said. "Maybe a little more than that." Rosenthal was wearing a blue velour shirt, khaki pants, and Nike running shoes in an awful purple.

"What's he like?" Castle asked abruptly.

"I don't know. I've never actually met him. We've talked on the phone a couple of times. He sounds reasonable enough. Smart, that's for sure."

"Oh, yes."

"You represent him?"

"Just on one project. I've never met him either. Like you, I've talked to him on the phone."

"Well, I guess this is something. Progress maybe."

"I hope so," Castle said.

The waitress brought the writer his Diet 7-Up. Apparently he now felt either enough trust in Castle or else enough discomfort to ask her to bring him what he really wanted, which was an Alka-Seltzer.

*

The vet arrived from Davis, a surprisingly young-looking fellow in mirror sunglasses and a pale blue business suit. He'd gone directly from the jet to the helicopter. The pilot had sent his associate to the coffee shop to round up the other two, less important passengers. Still, they were being invited into the presence, and as the screenwriter had said, that was something.

The helicopter was loud and it rocked and yawed distressingly. Castle didn't trust the vehicle altogether, not this particular one but any of the species. He looked down at meadowland and the occasional glint of river water reflecting sunlight, and thought back to the beginnings of this business with Blackpool.

He'd been sitting at a poolside table in the Four Seasons, having lunch with Sy Kroloff of Helicon House, and Sy had been giving him a hard time, saying no to every goddamn proposal. He just sat there eating his assorted wild mushrooms, probably aware that Castle was more than half wishing the mushroom gatherers had screwed up and plucked something that was deadly poison and was waiting to be speared by Kroloff's fork.

"Come on, Sy, you're being a pain in the ass, you know that, don't you? It's no way to do business. You're wasting your own time as well as mine."

"I'm not wasting my time. I'm eating mushrooms," Kroloff said. "They're terrific."

"But what would you like? I mean, if you could have whatever you wanted?"

"Besides the mushrooms?"

"Besides the mushrooms. Like a book. To publish. You remember publishing, don't you?"

"If I could have whatever I wanted, it'd be . . . some star's autobiography. Somebody presold. Somebody who could move a hundred thousand copies just on the pictures. Somebody we wouldn't have to promote but just schedule, letting all those bastards from *Time* and *Newsweek* and *Today* and *Good Morning America* call us for a change with their goddamn tongues hanging out."

"Okay, fine. That's progress. Whom would you want?"

"That's progress? You're a funny man."

"Maybe. Give me a name."

"Burt Reynolds."

"He's been signed. Give me another."

"I don't know. How about Bart Blackpool?"

"Okay. For how much?"

"You're kidding."

"I'm dead serious. How much?"

"For Blackpool? Gee, I don't know. Half a million?"

"Not enough."

"Maybe not. Look, are you sure you're not just horsing around?"

"Absolutely. Make it a million."

"Okay, a million."

"I'll get him for you."

"You're out of your mind."

"We'll see whether I am or not."

And Castle had gone back to his office to compose a telegram to Blackpool describing the offer he'd received for a hardback advance of a million dollars for an autobiography and inviting Blackpool to call if he was interested.

A million dollars is interesting enough for a phone call, even to someone like Blackpool. That's what Castle had bet on, anyway. That, first of all, and then his own abilities as a salesman to find out what Blackpool really wanted and then offer it to him. In Blackpool's case, it hadn't been so very difficult. When the call came through, as Castle had been all but certain it would, Castle had pitched him on the wonderful things he could accomplish, not only with the money but with the book too, in promoting conservation and the protection of wildlife. It was a cause dear to Blackpool's heart. He'd agreed to do the book.

Now, a year later, Kroloff was restless, wanted the manuscript or wanted his money back. And it seemed impossible to get Blackpool to produce. That was why Castle had flown out here to Wyoming to talk to the star and see whether there wasn't some way to work around the problem. It did not look as though it would be easy, but then Castle figured he owed this project a little work. It had been too easy until now.

The helicopter lurched in one of those sudden downdrafts or whatever they were, and the screenwriter in the seat beside Castle let out an audible groan.

Castle issued mental memos, one to the pilot: Pay attention and don't crash, and one to the screenwriter: For God's sake, don't vomit. But he didn't say a word. He just smiled and nodded, as if he were serenely confident that everything would be all right. It was a perfectly useless thing to do, but as often as not, it worked.

"Down there," the pilot announced, "you can see some of Mr. Blackpool's buffalo herd."

"What does he do with them?" the writer asked.

"Do with them?" The pilot laughed. "Nothing. He just owns them.

He likes to own things." There was a pause, and then, as if he'd realized that his remark might have been misunderstood, he added, "It's the best way Mr. Blackpool knows to protect things he likes, owning them."

"That figures," the writer said.

"If you can afford it," the pilot said, "it seems to work out pretty well."

Castle listened and sopped it up as he stared down at the buffaloes. It was impossible to say what tidbit might prove to be useful later on as he tried to persuade this odd man to behave reasonably. There were hundreds of those animals dotting the sloping uplands. If they were all Blackpool's buffaloes, then it stood to reason that this was also Blackpool's land, empty of any roads or buildings, or signs of human presence for that matter, for as far as the eye could see. Tough to get to a fellow like that, or to expect him to respond to the ordinary blandishments. He hardly needed any more money or fame or even the power that those could convert to. What could a fellow like Blackpool want?

The vet asked the screenwriter what the movie was about, and the writer was delighted to explain it. Apparently, there was some kind of feud that had gone on in the late nineteenth century between a couple of paleontologists, one from Yale and one from the University of Pennsylvania, and they'd come out West to dig for dinosaur bones but they'd each had spies in the other's camp. And General Custer had been on the scene at exactly the same time, getting wiped out by Sitting Bull.

"What Mr. Blackpool started out with was the one scene, an image really, of this bearded professor named Othniel Marsh—he was related to the department store people who owned Jordan Marsh in Boston—coming through with his wagon trains and telling the Indians that he was from Yale and was looking for old bones. They just let him on through. And then they fought the Battle of Little Bighorn and wiped out that whole company. And then back comes Professor Marsh, and the Indian chiefs wave at him and instruct their people to let him go on through, and he thinks it's because he's from Yale and they respect that, but actually it's because they think he's crazy and they have a kind of awe for crazy people."

"It doesn't seem like much to go on," the vet said.

Rosenthal grinned, agreeing. "On the other hand," he said, "there's a tone, a hint of what he has in mind. That's more than you get with a lot of these people."

"There it is," Frank announced, pointing down below.

The house was not large but it was impressive, a futuristic structure made mostly of poured concrete and glass. There were tall projections for cathedral ceilings and huge glass-curtain walls to take advantage of the view of the small lake in the foreground, the foothills behind it, and range of snowcapped peaks in the distance. It seemed to expand as the helicopter descended to the concrete landing pad off to one side of the house.

Blackpool, surprisingly small in person, had come out to greet his guests, first the writer, then the agent, and finally the veterinarian, whose hand he took and hung on to as he led the way from the pad toward one of the outbuildings where, presumably, the eagle was waiting for help. Castle watched them and noted how Blackpool leaned toward the vet as they walked, communicating attentiveness in body language. A film actor's trick? Or was it a spontaneous and unselfconscious expression of Blackpool's inner feelings?

"If you'll follow this way?"

Another one of Blackpool's denim-clad minions had appeared to grab Castle's bag and was leading the way to the house. Rosenthal, carrying his own bag, followed along behind. Castle wondered whether the writer wouldn't have done better renting a chicken suit and trying to pass himself off as a specimen of endangered wildlife. It would have been risky, but at least he'd have captured Blackpool's attention.

A room had been set aside for Castle, but there had been no instructions given about what to do with the writer. Out in the bunkhouse with the hired hands, perhaps? It wasn't necessarily a slight. Castle supposed that Blackpool might be eager to have Rosenthal whisked back to Billings and hurried home to his word processor to churn out screenplay pages while the ideas of their conversation were still fresh —or the inspiration of their audience was still glowing.

Castle accepted the invitation to go to his room and freshen up, leaving Rosenthal behind in the entrance hall with the bizarre chairs made from the horns of animals, Texas longhorns most likely. Castle followed down a long carpeted hall passing a series of closed doors that were not in themselves ominous. But he found himself a little intimidated. He'd dealt with famous people before and was used to them. But this guy was spooky. It was a carryover from the films, no doubt, that trick of Blackpool's of seeming not to be there, even in love scenes. There was a reserve, a vacancy, something about the eyes or the way the head tilted, and those adolescents who made up the bulk of movie audiences wanted to reach out to him and rescue him from some abyss. Here, in the man's house, Castle felt the full force of that negative pressure.

He tried to fight it, dredging it up to a conscious level and then making fun of it. It was just a coincidence that the vet had been summoned on the same day and that Blackpool had been so concerned about the health of that eagle. It wasn't a slight, either to Rosenthal or to himself. In a matter of minutes, there would be a welcome, an apology, some sort of exchange of more or less frank talk. But even as his mind formed the excuse he was aware of its flimsiness. He wasn't convinced.

The room he'd been given turned out to be a small suite, a sitting room, a bedroom, a bathroom of impressive size with plants growing in tubs and an assortment of sybaritic devices that included a Jacuzzi and a Thermasol steam bath as well as the sunken tub, the bidet, and the marble vanity with double sinks. There was a refrigerator, stocked with beer and soft drinks, on the chance that someone might come out of the steam bath or the Jacuzzi with a thirst. But none of that was Blackpool, particularly. It was only money, lots of it, but impersonal and anonymous.

Presumably, those doors in the corridor all opened on similar guest suites. There could be dozens of people here doing all kinds of business with Blackpool, and all of them filed away in these suites. For hours or even days. Weeks? Castle couldn't remember being jumpy in quite this way with any of his other clients. To prove to himself that this state was nonsensical, he opened the door and retraced his way to the large public rooms. Rosenthal was gone. Castle walked into a library and stood there inspecting Blackpool's shelves, most of them filled with matched sets of standard authors. He took down a volume of Bulwer-Lytton, opened it, heard the binding crack a little, and put the book back.

He turned to the magazines on a large polished library table, hoping that one or another of them might hold some clue about Blackpool's own interests or personality. But they too seemed to have been picked by a decorator—*Time* and *Newsweek* of course, and *Atlantic* and *Harper's,* but *Architectural Digest* and *Arizona Highways* and *Town and Country?* Maybe these were for the staff or for visitors. Maybe there was another, smaller room where Blackpool kept his own books or magazines or videotapes, or whatever it was he read or watched.

Castle looked up. He had the impression that a figure had passed by the open door, a blur of pink flesh. A naked figure? He thought so but

wasn't sure. He wasn't even absolutely sure he'd seen what he thought
he had. He went to the doorway, looked left and right, and saw nothing.

This time, he didn't try to argue himself out of his conviction that
this was a peculiar place and Blackpool a strange sort of fellow.

Another of Blackpool's people dressed in the denim with that red
bandana came in to ask if Castle was hungry.

"No, thanks."

"If there's anything at all I can get for you?"

Castle shook his head. "Do you suppose Mr. Blackpool will be tied
up much longer?"

"Impossible even to guess, I'm afraid. I'm sure he'll see you as soon
as he can."

It turned out to be almost an hour later. Castle had wandered
through three different living rooms, one more or less Spanish, one
high-tech and aggressively modern, and one rather smaller that looked
to have been brought over from some eighteenth-century English
country house. Castle had also been outside, where he'd explored pa-
tios and terraces and a sculpture garden, and had passed a pool, outdoor tennis courts (one clay, one grass), an indoor tennis court, and a
dressage ring for riding and jumping. He'd seen half a dozen different
young men in those denim outfits but he hadn't bumped into any of
Blackpool's other guests. He hadn't even seen Stu Rosenthal. He had
accepted, finally, a ham sandwich—which turned out to be Westpha-
lian ham on San Francisco sourdough bread with a couple of leaves of
fresh limestone lettuce and a dab of grainy Moutarde de Meaux—and
a beer. The young man had asked whether a dark Beck would be all
right.

What was weird, he decided, was the way it sent a double message,
implying at the same time both concern and indifference. When Blackpool at last appeared, he was—of course—apologetic but so smooth
about it, so artfully offhanded, that Castle had the feeling he was being
handled by someone's executive assistant. It wasn't as though he
didn't know the nature of the pressing business that had kept Blackpool occupied all this time—watching a hurt bird get treated by the
Davis veterinarian. Blackpool's laconic "Sorry" was tantamount to
admitting that. He grinned, shrugged, and lowered himself into a
leather club chair in the small English parlor.

"That's perfectly all right," Castle said, relaxing into the matching
chair across the fireplace apron. "I've been well looked after."

"I'm glad," Blackpool said. "But I'm sorry, I guess, that you've come all the way out here. What I told you on the phone still holds good. There is just no way that this book is going to happen."

Castle observed that Blackpool was wearing the same denim outfit that his household staff wore. It wasn't that they dressed like him, but that he was dressing up as if he were one of them, as if he too were a servant to some mysterious invisible creature whose name he happened coincidentally to bear and some of whose power he could occasionally wield.

"The Bart Blackpool story is going to be told," Castle said. "Sooner or later, one way or another, with your cooperation or in spite of your objections, somebody is going to write that story. And my message to you is exactly what it was when we first talked about this project— that it makes sense for you to keep as much control over it as you can and to participate in the earnings too, for that matter, although that's obviously a secondary consideration."

"You're right," Blackpool said. "Leonard . . . May I call you Leonard? You're a hundred percent right. I agree with every word you say, with every syllable. But that doesn't change the fact that I can't do it. It's just more than I can manage to deal with. You understand? It isn't *won't* but *can't.*"

"Perhaps if we found exactly the right collaborator for you, someone you could work with comfortably . . ."

"I'm up to my ass in writers, Leonard. It's what I *do.* That's not the real difficulty."

"What is the difficulty, Mr. Blackpool? If you were to let me see exactly what the difficulty is, then I might have a better chance at doing something constructive to solve our problem and extricate us from this impasse."

"I'm not sure that's any of your business, Leonard."

"Mr. Blackpool, I have a ten percent interest in this book. Your ninety percent may not be significant to you, but I assure you my ten percent is of considerable significance to me. If there's a problem somewhere, it's my business."

Blackpool's eyes crinkled up a little but hardly in a smile. He seemed to be squinting into sunlight, even though the lighting in the room was artfully subdued. "If you have a problem with money," he said in a voice just above a whisper, "that's your business, not mine. What I'm talking about here has nothing to do with dollars."

"The publishers thought it did. And you signed their contract . . ."

"You know as well as I do, Leonard, that those contracts are not

enforceable. There's no such thing in this country as indentured servi-
tude. All I have to do is pay back the money, and that's it. I walk
away. I'm a free man. We're all free men and women, aren't we?
That's America!"

Castle was getting nowhere. Worse, he was losing ground, for Blackpool was getting bored, losing patience and filling the time now by
posturing. When the pleasure of that game began to pall, then Blackpool might throw Castle out. Or just disappear in search of that blur of
pink flesh Castle was almost certain he'd seen running by the open
door of the library.

"Well?" Blackpool prompted, letting the edge of his impatience
show.

"Is there something you're afraid of having come out," Castle
asked, "something unappealing perhaps that you don't want to include
but can't omit? I'm just guessing, of course, but could it be something
like that?"

"If it were, do you think I'd admit it? Or if I did, do you think it'd
be to you, Leonard?" Blackpool grinned at the absurdity of it.

"Of course not," Castle said, feeling better now that he had the
man's attention again. "Because if that were the case, then the project
would be twice as important. Then you'd be thinking not of keeping a
secret, which is impossible over the long haul, but of getting your side
of the story out first, keeping on top of what gets out and to whom and
in what version."

"Oh, I know all that. That's what everybody says."

"What everybody says is frequently true," Castle said. And then he
tried a different tack that Blackpool's put-down had suggested. "You
don't seem to trust me, Mr. Blackpool."

"I don't distrust you more than another man."

"That's not quite the quality of relationship I have with most of my
clients."

"Maybe so. Maybe they're finer human beings than I. Or maybe
they're dumber than I am. Or maybe they've just been luckier. I don't
trust anyone much. And as we established from the get-go, you and I
have different objectives, maybe. Yours is to keep your ten percent of a
lot of money. Mine is not necessarily going to fit in with that. So
there's no reason for me to trust you, is there? And a hundred thousand reasons not to."

He stood up for punctuation. And then, perhaps because he realized
with his theatrical training that he'd uttered a decent exit line, he
exited.

Castle was resigned. He'd taken his shot. He'd tried. And if he'd failed, it was only because Blackpool was a hard case.

At the worst, at the bottom line, he'd had the use of fifty thousand dollars of Kroloff's money for more than a year, at no interest. He'd always known that it might have to be paid back. And it was there. He could get such a sum together and cough it up if he had to.

If only Blackpool had given him a little more time, he might have been able to find some angle, figure out the right bait to use. In this short time, he'd had to fly blind . . .

And then he remembered the bird.

He chased out after Blackpool, looked for him, but couldn't see him. He wandered through rooms, opening doors, calling out from time to time, not quite shouting but loud enough to be heard a room or two away, "Mr. Blackpool? Mr. Blackpool!"

"Can I do something for you?" One of his people in those denim outfits was barring the way.

Castle said, "I have a question for Mr. Blackpool. There's something I meant to ask him, but he got up and left in a hurry."

"Yeah, he does that sometimes."

"I've got to find him."

"That's what a lot of folks say. It doesn't work that way, I'm afraid."

"Is there some way of getting a question through to him?"

"Well, you can try."

"How?"

"Try me," the man said. He was smiling but he was exercising his fingers into a fist and out again.

"And what's your name, if I may ask that?"

"I'm Tim. I'm Mr. Blackpool's executive assistant."

"Would you ask him, Tim, how his eagle is doing? I meant to inquire, but we got onto other subjects, and then, all of a sudden, he was gone."

"Eagle's going to be okay, I think."

"Is there any way I could see it?"

"I'll go and ask. You wait in the library, would you?"

Castle thought about that. "I'll be in my room," he said. He hadn't quite been ordered to leave yet. His bag was still in that room, which made it, at least in a manner of speaking, his room.

This silent treatment was a double-edged sword, maybe. One could interpret silence however one pleased and until proved wrong—or

thrown out—one might be able to play a little. He wasn't out on his
ass, or not quite yet.

*

The vet had gone, but there were lists of what to feed the bird and
what medicines to give it. There were a couple of wranglers who wore
the same denim outfits as the staff up in the house, but their clothes
looked different. Maybe these were the real items, bought off the rack
and from the piles on the shelves of tack shops and army and navy
stores. The custom-made numbers on the people up at the house fitted
too well and looked too good to have been worn in a barnyard. The
wranglers were feeding baby rabbits to the eagle, which was picky
about its food and wouldn't take carrion. It had to be live meat that it
had killed itself and knew was fresh. The vet had shown them how to
get the bird to take its antibiotics, by giving the rabbit an injection just
before they put it into the eagle's cage.

It was all reasonable enough, and yet nasty, Castle thought. Still, he
showed nothing but admiration, and even fascination, as he watched
these people playing God. Or playing at being God's henchmen and
messengers. Blackpool was the one who was playing God.

There'd been no actual message from Blackpool, but the report
from Tim was that it was "all right with the boss" if Castle wanted to
go down to the stables to see how the eagle was doing.

So Blackpool knew he was still here. Maybe he even liked the idea
that people hung around to see him, waiting for the chance of an
audience just like the dukes and counts and princes used to do at
Versailles. Not a conversation or an interview, but an audience, after
which Bart the Terrible would either shake his head, or maybe nod, or
perhaps just look away or even bolt from the room the way he'd done
earlier in the day. A crazy way to do business. But there was a pattern
in it, a coherent kind of message. All Castle had to do was figure it out.

He watched as the eagle struck at the bunny with the talons of one
of its feet. There was a sickening squeak and then, mercifully, silence.

"He's gonna make it," one of the wranglers said quietly.

"Could be," the other allowed.

"Does Mr. Blackpool come down here himself much?" Castle asked
as he watched the big bird tear the carcass apart.

"Hours at a time. He's been doing most of the work, as a matter of
fact. He's just tired, I guess. He's been feeding the bird by hand, or
trying to, for three days now."

"Is that so?"

"Oh, sure. I'd begun to think he didn't trust us to do it right," the wrangler said.

"It looks as though you two are doing just fine."

"What matters is whether the bird is doing fine. And it looks as though he's maybe going to pull through."

"What happened to him?"

"He got shot. There are guys out there that shoot them for their feathers. For Indian headdresses mostly. One bird wears two or three hundred dollars' worth of feathers."

"That's against the law, isn't it?"

"So are a lot of things, mister."

Castle shook his head in unfeigned regret at the nastiness of some people's behavior. "I appreciate your talking to me," he said, and he headed back toward the house. As he passed the pool area, he heard a splash and he turned off the path to see who was out there swimming. It was possible that only the sheer size of the place had kept him isolated from the other guests, both temporary and permanent. It was also possible that this was some bizarre game of Blackpool's, something he liked to do for its mysteriousness, or to show off, or maybe just for the hell of it.

It was Rosenthal who emerged from the pool, wiping the water from his eyes.

"Stuart! How's it going?" Castle asked, genuinely pleased to see the writer.

"Can't complain. How's it going with you?"

Castle held out a hand in front of him, palm down, and yawed it back and forth. "At least one of us made out okay. He likes what you've done?"

"Actually, what I meant was that I can't complain because I never expected much to begin with. A guy doesn't like to whine."

"There may be a way we can help each other," Castle said. He paused and waited for Rosenthal to ask, "Oh?"

"You know anything about nature? Conservation? The great outdoors?"

"Some. I guess I could pick up what I needed. What's the project?"

"I'm not sure that there is one. But there's got to be something easier to sell to Blackpool than what you and I are trying to peddle. My guess is that it'd make more sense to pitch what he's already interested in buying."

"Sounds reasonable."

"Why don't you go down to the barn and take a look at that

wounded eagle? Talk to the guys down there. That's what Bart Black-pool cares about. That eagle and its wilderness. That's what we've got to work with."

"Why not? I can't do much worse than I've been doing up to now."

"Give it a half hour. Who knows what might come out of it?"

"A book, you mean?"

"A book by Bart Blackpool on conservation and the wilderness and our precious heritage. All that wonderful whole-grain stuff. In collabo-ration, of course, with Stuart Rosenthal. And photographs by some-body like Ansel Adams, but alive and cheaper. Coffee-table book for Christmas."

"Fine. Great," Rosenthal said. "I'll go down and look at the eagle."

Castle made a circle with his thumb and forefinger. He was comfort-able now that he had a fall-back position. But before he fell back to it, he thought he might risk a foray forward. He went up to the house and into his suite, found his briefcase, and extracted from the locked case a manila envelope on which Blackpool's name was written in large black letters. He went back out to the public rooms and wan-dered aimlessly until he found one of the denim-clad staff to whom he could hand the envelope, asking that it be delivered to Mr. Blackpool at the earliest possible moment.

*

"What the hell are you trying to pull, Castle?"

Blackpool was furious. He had come bursting into Castle's room with Frank and Tim behind him. He had the envelope in his hands. "I don't appreciate this one bit. And I think you'd better get the fuck out of here before I have you thrown out. Or shot for trespassing."

"Hold on, Mr. Blackpool. I was simply trying to make a point . . ."

"I think you've made it. And I'm going to stick it up your ass in another twenty seconds."

"Will you listen to me for a minute? I'm just trying to show you that this kind of stuff isn't so hard to get hold of. If I can find it, anybody else can find it, if he's got half a brain and takes a little trouble and time."

"Don't shit me, Castle. This is blackmail. This is extortion and blackmail, and I think it stinks."

"It isn't. I'm not going to use any of that. I'm just showing it to you to demonstrate that it can be found. It can be got hold of. People can put two and two together and come up with a pretty accurate guess about what the answer might be."

"Where did you get this?"

"The photographs?" Castle asked.

Blackpool nodded.

The photographs were of Blackpool, of course. They were unusual in that they showed him without a shirt. There were two shots, both of them from the rear, with Blackpool looking around so that one could see his famous profile. What was less famous—hardly known, in fact —was the pattern of scars on his back.

"I got those from a photo service file. They were taken a few years back, apparently in the locker room of some country club where you appeared in some celebrity golf tournament. They ran in a paper in Columbus, Ohio, with a caption about how you got the scars in your early days as a rodeo rider and Hollywood stuntman. I showed them around to a couple of doctor friends of mine. They weren't convinced by that explanation."

"And what did your friends tell you?"

"They thought that it looked more like child abuse. So, just for fun, I tried to find any reference in any of the stuff about you to your father, and I couldn't do that. It cost me a few dollars, but I put somebody to work finding out where you grew up and digging up whatever he could about your father."

"That was an accident," Blackpool said.

"Maybe. I believe you. Look, I'm your friend. I don't guess you're convinced of that right now, but it's true. I'm just trying to show you what the wrong kind of guy could do with this. I mean, supposing that somebody else had found this stuff and then jumped to conclusions about you and your younger brother. Suppose that somebody figured how maybe your father beat the two of you up once too often, and that you were both crazy with fear, and in self-defense you and your brother killed him . . ."

"That's enough," Blackpool said. He turned away. He walked out of the room. The door slammed behind him.

After a minute or so had passed, Castle tried the door. He wasn't at all surprised to find that it was locked.

Until Blackpool settled down a little and decided how to react and what his next move ought to be, Castle was his prisoner.

It wasn't comfortable, but Castle didn't suppose he was in much greater danger than he would have been going out for a walk any evening on Columbus or Amsterdam.

The Xerox copies of old newspaper clippings from Blackpool's early days in Omaha lay on the dove-gray carpet where the actor had dropped them. Castle picked them up and put them back in the envelope.

The old man could have fallen accidentally into the threshing machine, just the way the newspaper reported. Out alone in the field with his two sons, something like that could have happened. Freak accidents do happen sometimes.

But the suicide of the brother the following year, that was a hell of a coincidence. It made a man wonder whether there might have been some connection, or what else might have happened—and apparently it wasn't altogether a wild speculation to imagine it some other way and ask whether the two brothers hadn't done their old man in, hitting him on the head maybe and then throwing him into that threshing machine.

It was a hell of a burden to be carrying around. But it explained a lot about the way Blackpool needed to keep control, had to be in a position to exercise power, had to call the shots himself and have things his own way. Here and in L.A. in his dealings with the studios. He was lucky to be in a position to be able to do that, of course. The alternatives were mostly disastrous, dangerous either to himself or to the people around him.

How dangerous? Well, that was a question that Castle was about to learn the answer to. He took off his jacket, folded it, and laid it carefully over the back of a chair. He took off his shoes and stretched out on the queen-size canopy bed. He unbuttoned his collar button and loosened his tie. He didn't expect to be able to fall asleep but he supposed he might as well be comfortable as he waited. It could be quite a while.

He must have drowsed off at least for a while, because when he heard the sound of the lock in the door and looked at his wristwatch, he saw that a couple of hours had elapsed. The door opened. Castle didn't move.

"Mr. Castle?"

He turned and blinked as if he were just waking. "Yeah?"

"Mr. Blackpool wants to see you." It was Tim, Blackpool's chief honcho.

"Right away. As soon as I wash my face." Castle went into the bathroom and took his time about splashing water on his face and drying off. He went back to the bedroom, put his shoes on, put his jacket on, and then followed Tim, whose impatience was showing, back down the long hall to the other wing of the house.

Blackpool was waiting for him in a billiard room he hadn't seen before. There were two tables, one with pockets and one without. Blackpool was running a string on the table with the pockets. Rosenthal was leaning against one of the paneled walls, a cue in his hand.

"I've got to hand it to you, Leonard. You're a sly one," Blackpool said. "Very slick indeed."

"What do you mean?" he asked.

"You know damned well what I mean. I heard your idea from Rosenthal here."

"What idea is that?" Castle asked.

"Doing the book about conservation and the wilderness. The thing is that I've actually got some of that written. On the other project, what I started with was a description of this house and how I live most of the time. And I've got seventy or eighty pages done about the mountains here and the birds and animals that I'm living with out here. I've got a copy for Stu. He's going to take that back with him."

"Good. Terrific."

"It's what you had figured out all along, isn't it?"

"No, not at all. It crossed my mind only when I saw the eagle down there and heard how you'd been up for most of three days and nights taking care of it. I figured that this was something you care about. I figured that there was enough of Bart Blackpool in this that it might be a way to go if a conventional autobiography didn't work out."

"And that other business was just bullshit, right? A little shock treatment? Or a little blackmail?"

"Neither one. I thought of it as a demonstration of what could happen. And it still could. I'd think about that long and hard if I were you."

"But in the meantime, this is better than nothing, right?" Blackpool suggested.

"Oh, yeah. Something is always better than nothing. I expect I'll get some flack from Helicon House, and we may have to make a few adjustments on the money . . . ."

"We've got to cut old Stu in for some of that, surely," Blackpool said.

Rosenthal grinned. Castle nodded and smiled. "But I think I can work those details out. We'll also need a photographer. And if you don't mind, we can have him come out here and you can show him around. Or her."

"Be happy to," Blackpool said.

"So it's agreed then," Castle said.

"Fine with me," Blackpool said. "You want to shoot a little pool?"

"If it's okay with you two, I'd just as soon get back. I've got to talk to Sy Kroloff, and I've got some other business that needs tending to."

"Frank will run you over whenever you say. You want to go now?"

"If that's not a nuisance. And maybe Stu could come with me so that on the way we can work out the pitch I've got to make to Kroloff."

Blackpool shrugged. "Sure, whatever," he said, and he turned his attention back to the pool table.

On the ride back to Billings, Rosenthal was bubbling over with gratitude and admiration. "What really knocks me out is those pages of his. How did you know that he'd have part of it already written?"

"I didn't. That's just a bonus. All I knew was that he wasn't going to go with what we'd agreed to. And there was no way to force him. So I was looking around to see what he might find more acceptable."

"Terrific. Just amazing!"

"Terrific is right, but in the root sense. That guy is not easy. You keep your distance, you hear? Everything by mail. And as little of that as possible. You got that?"

"Oh, sure."

"I'm not kidding," Castle said. "Any questions, any problems, you get in touch with me. Who's your agent?"

"Gary Mull, of Pacific Talent."

"I'll give him a call tomorrow and we'll work this out. Okay? But if you have any communication of any kind from Mr. Blackpool, you let me know about it."

"You got it," Rosenthal said. "By the way, what was it that you and he were talking about, that shock treatment or blackmail or whatever it was?"

"Forget it. Forget you ever heard those words mentioned. I'm serious. A guy could get himself into deep caca messing with that stuff. Just . . . wipe it from your mind."

The helicopter lit like a huge bug on the big painted circle of the Billings airport. Frank got the bags out of the luggage compartment and handed them over. "Have a safe trip, gentlemen," he said.

*

These people were flaky. That was a given, and he had accepted it long ago. He even prided himself on the skills he had developed, the dexterity with which he could handle the complicated, the cranky, or the damned near crazy client, coming out most of the time with a result that the client might or might not understand was in his or her best interest.

But all it took was one dissatisfied nut, one out-of-whack person who was convinced, rightly or wrongly, that he'd been betrayed. It didn't have to be true. The truth was altogether irrelevant. What counted was the perception of one unstable mind . . .

That it was an unstable mind was fairly obvious. Sane people don't go around shooting guns off in Manhattan. The junkies ask for money first. And the others let you know who they are.

Blackpool? Castle didn't think so. Farnsworth, maybe? Or some gunsel that one of them had hired? Some fanatic attendant acting on his own?

"Cut down Fifth a few blocks," he told the driver. "I want to make sure I'm not being followed."

"Whatever you say."

3

Susan woke and reached out but Mike was gone. He did that sometimes, taking off in the middle of the night without so much as a
goodbye kiss. They'd argued about it years back, but he'd always had
his answers ready about how he'd kissed her but she didn't remember,
or how he took off so she'd wake up and miss him, desire being better
always than satiety. He was always good with intricate explanations.

What he wasn't good at was being there.

She stretched and remembered the workout of the previous night.
She was just barely able to get up and stagger to the bathroom, turn on
the hot-water tap, and sit down to pee while she waited for the tub to
fill. She felt like a rag doll with most of its stuffing gone. All fucked
out.

It would have been a fine sensation if he were there to share it with
her, if he cared enough to hang around. But that wasn't Mike. He was,
as he'd told her often enough, a good pal and a good partner, but a
loner. And there were—as in the song Pinocchio sang—no strings.
Still, there were times when it was reassuring to have him there, available and eager and so damned expert as to turn their lovemaking into
an athletic contest. He was proficient but so unemotional, and occasionally she was in the mood for that. There were also times when she
hated him for the way he made everything so mechanical. She'd re-
solved often enough not to see him again, but it had been like a heavy
smoker's attempts to swear off cigarettes. She could go a week or two,
sometimes even a month or two, but then she'd get to feeling sorry for
herself, feeling sorry for her body and what it was missing. It deserved

a little exercise and even some fun. It deserved the kind of workout only Mike could give it.

So she'd call him, and he'd swear, every time, that he'd been just on the point of calling her, and that there wasn't anything he'd rather do than see her. And they'd make a date for that very evening—always at her place so that he could get up in the middle of the night and maybe even give her that kiss before he tiptoed out.

The blindfold and the vibrators were on the hamper, where he'd left them. He had known that she'd come in here and take a bath. He was good at figuring out how she'd respond and what she'd be feeling and what her next move was likely to be. But it wasn't with caring and tenderness. He was thoughtful, the way a poker player is thoughtful or a quarterback, trying to figure out what the defense is going to expect.

She flushed the toilet and went to test the water. As she bent over the tub, she saw the Walkman he'd left hanging from the shower-curtain rod. It was another game.

She was more than a little weary of these games of his but she wasn't incurious. She put in the earpieces, hit the play button, and waited while the leader ran and the few seconds of silent tape, and then she heard the moans, hers, from the night before.

He'd recorded the noises she'd made, and here they were for her to listen to again so that, even as she resented him, she'd remember how good it had been, how many times she'd come and how violently.

And he had known she'd be here in the bathroom, getting into the bathtub, and that she'd be horny in the abstract way one can some-times be after a night of strenuous sex with that irritation and conges-tion down there, and all the nerve endings raw and sensitive. And he'd even known that she'd get into the tub, touch herself, and jerk off, hating him for making her do it to herself one more time and at his command, just the way she'd had to do it the night before in order to get him to give her what she wanted, what she had begged for, what she now heard herself beg for, and had to remember as wonderful when he had joined her at last.

She heard herself whimpering, imploring him to fuck her, and then she heard her reaction as that series of cascading orgasms began. And she felt the new one, tingly like bells under the surface of the water. She let out a slow sigh, took the Walkman off, and put it on the bench beside the tub.

Clever, and typical, and altogether manipulative and bastardly.

It was—almost certainly—designed to keep her away from him, to make her try not to call him again. That way, he'd have a rest, or opportunity to light on the other flowers in the garden he maintained of unattached career women who liked a civilized dinner and a barbaric bang every now and then. And all the time, he could rely on the fact that she'd be thinking about him, resenting him but also missing him, and mostly missing how good he could make her feel if it amused him to do so.

She supposed it could be worse. There were lots of women who were obliged to pay for this kind of thing, not just in humiliation but in money. Or learn to go without.

Maybe paying for it would be easier, more honest and straightforward.

Maybe Mike would make her do that someday, the way he'd made her pick up that stranger and go to bed with him on the cruise they'd taken years ago.

That was when she had finally realized that her fantasy of his settling down one day and their working out some kind of sane and loving relationship was just a fantasy. That was when she'd figured out that along with her admiration for his intelligence and her lust for his body she also felt hatred for him, for how he had used her—and how he used himself too, for that matter.

Giving him up, of course, was something else.

What she really needed was someone to take his place, someone nice and loving and decent, the kind of man three million other women in New York were also fantasizing about. Those kinds of men were only in Harlequin romances, which was why those dumb books sold so much.

She got out of the tub, wrapped herself in a big velour towel, and padded into the bedroom to write herself a note about those Harlequin books and one or two psychiatrists or sociologists and the piece that could make about the end of romance in the real world.

She dressed, fixed herself a cup of coffee in the one-cup Melitta, and toasted an English muffin that she ate with just a tiny dab of Elsenham's orange-and-tangerine marmalade on each half. She fetched the *Times* from her doorstep and glanced through it as she ate her breakfast. An article on the lower half of the front page caught her attention. Evidently, Scott, Snair, and Bryce were charging that *Vista* had obtained their copy of the Farnsworth memoirs illegally and that the article about Farnsworth in the current issue was prima facie evidence of theft. Susan turned to page 23 for the continuation of the story, where there was a whole column explaining how the auction for first serial rights had gone, how *Time* and *Newsweek* had been bidding

against each other, and how *Time* had eventually won with a sum said
to be well up into six figures.

The story went on to say, "Clarence Eames, the publisher of *Vista,*
not only denied wrongdoing on the part of his staff but accused *Time*
of practicing 'checkbook journalism.' According to Eames, 'The memoirs of President Farnsworth are news, and the news is out there for
anyone willing to work hard to go and find it. You just can't buy and
sell information that is vital to a democratic society. It has to be in the
public domain.'

"Leonard Castle, who is President Farnsworth's literary agent, denied that anyone was trying to keep the news from the public. '*Time*
was going to publish these excerpts,' he said, 'and I hope they still will
do so. Scott, Snair, and Bryce are going to bring out the whole book.
So the public's right to know doesn't come into it at all. The only issue
is the timing, and the question of property rights. My client has been
injured. *Time* has been injured. And I can't see where anyone has been
helped except *Vista* magazine.' "

She took a clean knife from the flatware drawer and cut the two
pages from the paper. She popped the last bit of muffin into her mouth
and hurried back to the bedroom to put on her face and get down to
the office.

Her hunch turned out to be correct. Jack Ditson's memo was waiting for her on top of her desk. He asked, "Anything from the Castle
file? Need soonest."

She added the clip from the morning paper and took the file in
herself.

"I don't know about this guy," Ditson said.

"What's the question?" she asked. "I don't know a lot either, but
maybe I can help you guess."

"He's holding us up for a shitpot full of money."

"I don't understand."

"That bullshit about how nobody's helped but *Vista.* You read
that?"

"I read it, yes."

"It's a crock. Farnsworth is helped by it. And Leonard Castle is
helped. He's got a starting price of four hundred thou for a two-part
interview with Farnsworth, pegged to the book publication. You like
that?"

"We pay them?"

"You got it, sweetheart. That's what they're asking. And if we don't
pay it, *60 Minutes* will, or *20/20.* There are three vice presidents up

there in the executive suite wringing their hands right now and sweating into their custom-made underwear."

"You think he's going to get it?" Susan asked.

"Oh, yeah," Ditson said. "After all, it's front-page news. And it's an ex-President of the United States, even if it isn't exactly Abe Lincoln. Somebody will pay it. It might even be us."

"Amazing. You have to admire his nerve."

"I'm wondering, thinking about that fancy stuff with the dog-exercising service, whether he might have had something to do with *Vista* getting hold of that manuscript."

"With him, nothing is impossible."

"Work on it, would you?"

"Even if we don't get Farnsworth?" she asked.

"Especially if we don't get Farnsworth," Ditson said. There was a mischievous little smile on his face. As she left his office, Susan could see, reflected dimly in the glass pane of his door, a similar smile on her own face.

*

There were just three of them in the spacious office of Melvyn Dodge, editor in chief of Scott, Snair, and Bryce, Inc. Georgina McKittrick, vice president and director of publicity, sat at one end of the large tufted leather sofa. Dodge sat at the other, holding his coffee cup well away from the kidskin vest that covered his sizable paunch. Susan had the easy chair on the side that faced the large marble coffee table. From time to time, she checked the ruby light that indicated that the power pack was in good shape and that the cassette in her Sony was operating properly.

Her inquiry was about the security arrangements that SS&B had made, and more particularly those special precautions that had been taken—almost as though the house had known ahead of time that someone might try to steal the ex-President's memoirs.

"There are certain books that are sensitive and that require special care," Dodge told Susan. "Most of the time, the kind of book we have to protect that way is a work of fiction, some surefire best-seller. Movie and television people will try to get their hands on it before we're ready to entertain bids."

"Why?" Susan asked. "What's the advantage in getting an early look? They still have to bid, don't they? They still have to buy the rights."

"Oh, but it's much more complicated than that," Ms. McKittrick explained. "If you have a jump on the rest of the industry, even of a week or ten days, you can go out and hustle, line up a cast, maybe get a director, do a lot of the packaging, and then you can go to one of the studios with all of that in place. The studio is going to reward that kind of initiative and they're the ones who are putting up the money. So there's a terrific incentive for hustlers out there. And the hustlers aren't always the people who are the best for a project as far as quality is concerned. Even with a commercial book, a best-seller, that's a consideration."

"I can see that," Susan said. "What kind of precautions do you take with books like that?"

"There are usually only two copies of the manuscript," Dodge explained, "and there's a very limited number of sets of galleys. Each of those is kept in a safe to which only certain people have access. They have to sign them out and return them personally. And those are all people we trust, people who aren't going to run off a copy on some Xerox machine after hours."

"What about the copy editing?" Susan asked. "It's my understanding that you have free-lance copy editors. They're not always overpaid. One of them might be vulnerable, perhaps?"

"On these special books, we do the copy editing in the house. It's expensive to do it that way, but if it's what we have to do, then we do it," the editor in chief said.

"You mean the book editor does his own copy editing?" Susan asked.

"Sometimes. Or we set up an office and have the copy editor come in and do it here in the office rather than at home," Ms. McKittrick explained.

"And at the printing plant, we have our own security people," Dodge said, putting his cup down on the table. "It's always worked before. I can't understand what went wrong this time."

"We've got people investigating, of course," Ms. McKittrick said.

"Could the theft have been from President Farnsworth?" Susan asked. "Could someone have got hold of one of his copies?"

"Anything's possible," Dodge said, "but that just doesn't seem likely to me. For one thing, he's got Secret Service protection, which means it'd be awfully tough to break into his apartment. And then, for another thing, he's sore as hell about this."

"Would it be possible for me to talk with him, just for a few minutes?"

"I'll be glad to ask," Ms. McKittrick said. She was one of those

tweedy women who verged deliberately on the dowdy, as if to pro-
claim that she was all business and that the success she had achieved
was based entirely on competence and hard work.

"I'd appreciate that," Susan said. "And what about Mr. Castle?"

Dodge shook his head. "He's Farnsworth's agent. It's not likely that
he'd do something like that behind Farnsworth's back. In his place, I
don't think I'd have the nerve."

"Still," Susan said, "the publicity that has come out of this has been
considerable."

"They've lost substantial amounts of money," Dodge said. "*Time*
has renegotiated their price downward by a lot."

"They've also gained substantial amounts of money," Susan said. "I
don't know what the final price was, but we dropped out at half a
million. So whatever *60 Minutes* paid, it was more than that. Which
makes up for whatever they lost from *Time,* I'm sure."

"You talk to Farnsworth," Dodge said. "If I can't convince you, I'm
sure he'll be able to. That's an angry man there."

"Would you have any objection to my talking with the people down
at the printing plant?"

"None at all," Dodge said.

"I'll be happy to set that up for you," Ms. McKittrick said. "Will
you be going down with a crew?"

"Later on, perhaps," Susan told her. "I'd like to go down and look
around and talk to people first."

"Of course."

"And I suppose I ought to talk with Mr. Castle too."

"I'll let him know you'll be calling on him," Ms. McKittrick volunteered.

"It used to be different," Dodge said. "Back in Mr. Bryce's day, it
was a gentleman's business. Back in those days, the very idea of manuscript security would have been laughable. Now, it's a different world.
A different world!"

"That's why we're interested in the subject, Mr. Dodge," Susan
said.

He was absolutely convinced. Susan was less sure of Ms. McKittrick, but then she didn't suppose the woman would actually warn
anyone that something odd might be going on here.

*

Vista was Clarence Eames's toy, which made it right that the magazine should be published in an old building on Twenty-third Street in

the heart of the wholesale toy district. Eames was one of those Maserati socialists, a left-wing millionaire who acted out his oedipal drama in public in political ways, not just in atonement for the sins of his tycoon grandfather, who had very probably exploited the workers and kept all the surplus value for himself, but in defiance of his conservative parents. Their shock and dismay at his behavior delighted Eames, or at least that had been a part of his motivation years ago. Now, it was mostly habit.

Still, when *Vista* had been about to go under, an old Trotskyite review with most of its readers dead or disillusioned, Eames had picked it up, paid off some of its creditors, and given it a new lease on life. He had even managed to find remedies for the fiscal hemophilia that always plagued it. Now, *Vista* was no worse off than *The Nation* and *The New Republic*, or, on the other side, *The National Review*. He had beefed up the back of the book, hiring some sprightly book reviewers and a highbrow guttersnipe theater critic whose printed insults to certain actresses were sufficiently outrageous as to attract a certain kind of readership, more mauve than pink perhaps, but Eames seemed not to mind. He also liked to do startling things in the front of the book, and this theft of the Farnsworth memoirs had exactly the right combination of naughtiness and flair.

Susan Flowers knew all that. She knew, too, that Eames would enjoy playing games with her. One of the reasons for his having bought the magazine was to become an instant celebrity. It wasn't just owning a magazine, but having people from other magazines and newspapers and television networks sitting in his living room or in his office, listening to him the way his students had once sat and listened when he'd been an assistant professor of political science at Dartmouth. He just ate it up.

He received her alone, as if to show off that he didn't need media experts and advisers. He was a media magnate himself after all, despite his turquoise running suit and his duck-billed workman's cap with the John Deere logo. "Now, what can I do for you, Ms. Flowers? You want some carrot juice?"

"No, thanks. I wanted to ask you about the Farnsworth papers . . ."

"Well, as I said on the phone, there isn't a lot I can tell you about that. It's all *sub judice*, as they say, and my lawyers tell me that it isn't a hell of a good idea to be talking about that. I'm sure you understand."

"I appreciate that. But when we were on the telephone, you did

volunteer one terribly interesting comment. I wrote it down, actually."
She opened her little leather-bound notebook from Mark Cross and
read what she'd written. "You said, 'We didn't do anything illegal or
unauthorized.' Did I get that right?"

"Did I say that?"

"That's what *I'm* asking you. That's what I heard."

"Well, then I guess I must have said it."

"Is it true?"

"Would I call myself a liar?"

"It's the 'unauthorized' part of it that I find interesting," she said.

"In your place, I guess I would too. But I can't help you out any
more than I've already done."

"Without trying to push you, it seemed to suggest that you had
authorization from somebody, and because of that whatever you
might have done to get hold of the copy of the memoirs was legal."

"I have no comment to make on that."

"You don't seem worried, though."

"I try never to worry. It's not good for the circulation or the diges-
tion. You sure you wouldn't like a little carrot juice? I extract it myself
with one of those terrific machines."

"No, but thanks anyway. Would this be an example of your rich
man's revolution?"

"The carrot juice or the Farnsworth papers?"

"Either one," Susan said.

"No, I don't think so. I think the carrot juice is relatively cheap.
And I think what we did with the Farnsworth papers is just an example of enterprising journalism. It isn't fair for the big guys, the press
lords who own the big chains or the mass-circulation magazines, to
control the news the way they do. This is an alternative, just one
among many, but it's what I try to do the best with that I possibly can.
It isn't just a matter of grabbing attention, which isn't a bad thing by
the way, but of holding that attention and using it to good purposes.
You know perfectly well that the best segment you can turn out is no
good unless it gets out to an audience. It's the same with print, only
the numbers are smaller."

Susan did her number about the possibility of a segment on Eames
and his magazine, and how it was iffy but there was real interest. He
was obviously willing to cooperate in any way he could.

"Do you have photographs of your top people? That might be useful."

"I can get them together. It'll take a while. You need them right away?"

"Whenever it's convenient," she said, hiding her satisfaction as best she could.

"I'll get them over to you this afternoon or tomorrow morning at the latest."

"That'll be fine," she said. "I'll set up appointments with some of your editorial people early next week, assuming that everything works out."

"Sorry I can't do more for you on the Farnsworth thing."

"I understand. You've done what you could."

" 'One hand washes the other,' as my grandfather used to say, and didn't mean it as a joke, even though he was in the soap business."

"I'll be in touch," Susan promised, lying through her teeth. "And thanks again."

"Next time, try the carrot juice," he told her, and he held up a V for victory or peace or whatever it was.

Back at the office, Susan dropped by the photo lab for the blowup of the photo of Castle. That was the likeliest bet. But from what Eames had said, it would have been Castle and someone from *Vista* together. If she could get that and then confront him with it, she might get him to level with her, and it would be a hell of a piece.

Either he'd done it with Farnsworth's knowledge and approval, which would make a hell of a story, or he'd done it without even telling Farnsworth—and that was even wilder. Assuming that she could connect Castle with what had happened, which was the only way she could make any sense out of it, Susan just didn't see how she could lose.

The photographs came over from *Vista* late in the afternoon, but there was still time for Susan to arrange to rent a car to drive down to Pennsylvania—a convertible, because the weather was nice and the leaves were turning.

She had no idea how long it would take to get what she hoped to find down at the printing plant, assuming that something was there to be found. If she was lucky, a couple of days might do. And then she could fly to L.A. on Friday. She had the travel department book her a flight, just to be safe. They could cancel if they had to.

And after the weekend out there, if everything broke right, they might begin to think about Castle himself. She was looking forward to that. Pursuing him this way, she was beginning to think of him as some kind of mythical beast.

*

She was blindsided. She'd had all the angles figured or all the likely ones, but of course it was from some unlikely and altogether unpredictable quarter that the puff of ill wind blew, bringing no good at all to her week's labors.

She'd done fine in Lancaster, Pennsylvania, hanging out in diners and country-and-western bars and asking of those who worked in the plant how things were going. People gossip in a perfectly friendly way, and they talk about those fellow workers who have hit a streak of good luck, those who have made a down payment on a new car or bought some new furniture, or a new shotgun, or just made good on some old and by now rather wilted IOUs from card games that otherwise would have been long forgotten. And they talk about those who have been unlucky too, those who have been laid off for showing up drunk once too often, those who have been divorced and thrown out the houses they had worked for years to pay for and furnish and heat.

It was to the less fortunate that Susan went with her packet of photographs and a few crisp hundred-dollar bills as well to enlist their aid in identifying some of these people who might have been in town within the past six weeks or so. It wasn't actually getting the unfortunates to spy on their luckier friends; it was more a way of getting them to share in the windfall, to enjoy a piece of good luck themselves. Because, after all, she wasn't the law, and she wasn't going to turn this over to any lawyers or police. It was part of a story she was working on for the television program, just background, nothing that would ever be traced back . . .

She found two people who had seen the other out-of-towners, and could pick out from her sheaf of photographs the likenesses of Henry Snelling, managing editor of *Vista,* and the fat guy too—Leonard Castle. They'd been here together.

Susan had even figured out that the likely place for them to have stayed would be the Lancastrian Red Rose Inn, where she was staying herself, and she showed the pictures around to some of the waitresses on the breakfast shift, friendly girls eager to be helpful to the nice lady who tipped so generously, and, yes, one of them remembered having served those two at her table in the corner.

So far, so good. And the next step had been to take up Georgina McKittrick's offer and go to talk with ex-President Farnsworth, for no more than fifteen minutes and off the record, with no cameras and no tape recorders, and only on the subject of the stolen manuscript.

That was all perfectly agreeable to Susan Flowers, at least at this stage. The man she was really interested in was Castle, after all. And this was the next logical step in preparing the ground for that assault.

But Farnsworth stopped her dead, not by being clever or tricky, but by the exercise of raw power. He'd denied to Susan that he'd known about Castle going down to Lancaster. He wasn't sure he believed Susan's informants. "In the law, a man is entitled to confront witnesses, to cross-examine them, to find out what they're really saying or why they may be saying it. And those are important safeguards. In the law we have them and on television programs we don't," he said, sounding like a civics lecture—him, of all people, taking the high road and standing up for morality and the Constitution.

He'd been unflappable. He'd denied and stonewalled, which was not altogether surprising. What Susan had hoped to do was stir up the still waters with this stick she'd found and then see what happened. She hadn't expected Farnsworth to go to the phone, call the president of the network, and ask him to call his dogs off.

She got the word from Ditson. "Farnsworth got the story killed. From upstairs. Sorry."

She went in to ask if that killed the part about Castle too.

"I don't see what we can do with Castle unless we've got Farnsworth in it too. There's nothing left, is there?"

"Maybe not right now."

"Well, in the future, who knows what evil lurks in the hearts of men, right?"

"It's a good story. He's an interesting guy," she protested.

"I'm sure he is," Ditson said, "but not now, or at least not to us. Look, why don't you take the rest of the day off? You've been knocking yourself out, and this is frustrating. Part of the job, but not a nice part. Go get your hair done or something."

"Thanks," she said, knowing he meant well.

She didn't go to get her hair done. She went home, put on a pair of jeans and an old tee shirt, took the blinds down from the dining-room windows, and put them into the bathtub for their annual wash. Then she polished all her pretty copper pots and got them to shine like new. Then she cleaned the grouting in the shower. Those were the nasty jobs she had been saving up for such an occasion, knowing that every few months she was glad to have something arduous and physical to do, taking her mind off other problems by switching it off entirely. When she was finished with the grouting, she cleaned the tub, showered, and went out to the neighborhood Chinese restaurant for a double order of spare ribs. Then she went home, got into bed, and tried to pick up the thread of Braudel's history of commerce and industry from where she'd let it drop on her last attempt.

And she was asleep in twenty minutes.

In the morning, she felt better, but not all better. She knew she was wasting her time, but it seemed even more of a waste not to type up the notes of her conversation with Stu Rosenthal from that quick trip she'd made to Los Angeles. After all, Ditson hadn't closed the door forever. There might be a time when this could pan out after all. Hurriedly but accurately, she put what was important down on paper:

Rosenthal thinks Castle is a smart operator because he knows his limitations. Castle was representing Bart Blackpool on some other project, presumably some autobiographical book, and there were difficulties. Rosenthal had been working on a screenplay for Blackpool's production company (Rorschach), and that hadn't been going well either. According to Rosenthal (not for attribution) he and Castle flew out to Blackpool's ranch with some vet from UC Davis whom Blackpool had hired to treat an eagle that had got shot. Castle saw how deeply Blackpool was concerned with the eagle and figured that the actor would be willing to lend his name and something of his personality to a pro-conservation coffee-table book. Rosenthal gets a quarter, the photographer gets a quarter, and Blackpool's half gets turned over to the Sierra Club.

Rosenthal is friendly to Castle and obviously grateful. He says that Castle's talent is to see what people want and then try to work out a reasonable way of giving it to them. It isn't tricky or clever or in any way dishonest. He just listens better than a lot of other operators in the business.

As far as Rosenthal remembers, he was the one to make the pitch to Blackpool about the conservation book. Castle had talked about the idea to him and let him sell it to Blackpool. "I did what Castle did, which was next to nothing. The trick was to let Blackpool think of it himself, just as I'd done. But I realized, later on, that Castle had laid it all out for me, an hour or so before, when we'd been down at the pool."

Blackpool is evidently a difficult guy. Rosenthal was very careful about what he'd say. I had the feeling that he was holding back a lot. It seems to have been quite a coup on Castle's part, particularly if Rosenthal is right about there having been some autobiographical project that was going or had gone sour. Castle must have had a hell of a weekend out there, and he came out of it smelling like a rose.

First printing of *Wyoming Wilderness* is now 130,000 copies. Main selection of Literary Guild. Rosenthal's 25% share is apparently more money than the writer has seen in quite a while. Odometer of his white Porsche shows only 1480 miles.

She pulled the last sheet out of the typewriter, stapled the pages together, and stuck them into the Castle folder.

*

He looked through the rear window. He saw nothing familiar, nothing recognizable or in any way menacing. He really doubted that he was being followed. Some nut had been waiting for him, which was bad enough. But it was hardly likely to be a whole army of assassins with walkie-talkies and three or four cars, which was what they'd need to mount the kind of operation Castle had begun to imagine. No, no, that was impossible. A single crazy with a handgun, that was all there was.

That was, of course, enough.

4

Castle sat there and watched the man foam at the mouth. It was something he got to see only rarely and he found it more interesting than disgusting. It wasn't just a phrase: the man was actually foaming like a rabid dog, little bubbles of spit boiling up on his lips and hanging there. The veins in his forehead were throbbing too. Castle wondered if Farnsworth might not drop dead right there in the living room of his apartment. Just keel over and drop dead.

He listened as the ex-President yelled at him about loyalty and ethics and honor and decency.

Every now and then, he tried to interrupt, to bring Farnsworth back to this solar system, if not actually to earth. "It wasn't a betrayal," Castle interjected for perhaps the twentieth time. "You made out better than you would have otherwise. You made more money and you got a lot more attention."

Farnsworth was having none of that. Farnsworth was furious that something had been done behind his back, no matter that it had worked out well. To think that this man had been the President of the United States! It was scary. The Republic had been lucky that Farnsworth hadn't started a world war out of personal pique. If there were a red button on the desk beside Farnsworth with which to destroy Castle, there was no question but that the man would push it. Even if a couple of hundred thousand others would be incinerated or dissolved along with him, Castle was sure Farnsworth would push the damned button down through the inlaid Florentine leather top of the expensive desk.

Castle smiled, not from geniality, but out of perversity, because it annoyed Farnsworth. It drove the old guy nuts. After a while, it was perfectly spontaneous, almost irresistible for Castle to smile, as he thought about what a fruitcake this man was. The trouble was that his pride was hurt. His dignity had been offended. This wasn't a betrayal but lèse-majesté . . . And in other, slightly more savage times, Farnsworth would have sent Castle off to the Bastille or the Château d'If. Or St. Paul's Fortress or Lubyanka or whatever it was they had in Moscow. Democracy just didn't sit well with Farnsworth. His temperament was simply not suited to it.

That was why he'd made such a shambles of his administration.

Not even these observations, interesting as they were, could sustain themselves under the weight and duration of Farnsworth's tirade. Farnsworth's range was limited. He kept calling Castle a "stupid little fuck," and once the slight shock value had worn off, Castle began to see it as the worst word Farnsworth knew. Farnsworth seemed to shrink down to some enraged six-grader in a playground.

Castle also found himself wondering how long it had been since Farnsworth's last fuck, stupid or smart, little or big. Evidently, he got off in other ways, and his effusions of bodily fluids were from the mouth in those little viscid bubbles.

It was the woman who had done it, this Flowers person. Castle was curious about her. She had actually gone all the way down to Lancaster and shown people pictures of him and Hank Snelling. And Farnsworth had seen them too.

Why had she tipped her hand that way?

Castle watched and listened, as if he were hardly even involved, as if he were a potted plant that just happened to be here in the room. Of course, this demonstration must have been what she had come to see —proof that Farnsworth hadn't been playing games.

But had Farnsworth blown up this way for Ms. Flowers?

"Excuse me," he said, breaking in with what seemed to be a much more interesting subject. "Did you let Ms. Flowers know how upset you were?"

It was very odd. Farnsworth broke off from his ranting, answered Castle's question with a nearly normal, conversational "No, of course not," and then returned to the pitch and volume of his preceding routine, picking up pretty much where he'd left off. It was as if Farnsworth were two people—or as if Castle were two people, only one of whom the former chief executive was occupied in dressing down.

"Then there's no harm done, is there?" Castle protested as Farnsworth paused for breath. "Any piece they do on you or on the book will help us."

"There won't be any piece. I had it killed," Farnsworth said, and then he resumed his ranting: ". . . the arrogance, the impertinence, the impossible gall of it! Who in the hell do you suppose you are? Well, I'll tell you who you are. You're nothing, absolutely nothing, a stupid little fuck who thinks he's somebody but isn't anything at all. Nothing. Something I'd wipe off my shoe . . ."

Castle got up and started toward the door. The Secret Service operatives could prevent people from approaching the ex-President, but they didn't hold on to them and keep them from leaving. Castle wasn't a prisoner. He could just walk out of the room and out of the building . . .

"My lawyers will be on your ass," Farnsworth shouted.

"You haven't been hurt. You've been helped. There's nothing for them to do."

"They can break our contract. You won't get a dime, not a dime, you stupid fuck!"

"The publishers pay me; I pay you. There isn't a lot you can do about it, Mr. President."

"Come back here, Castle."

"I wish I could stay," Castle said, "but I have another appointment and, as much as I'm enjoying this . . ."

"I'll just bet you are. You're a Democrat. I should have known from the beginning. A fucking Democrat! All you wanted to do from the beginning was humiliate me, to get some crazy kind of revenge . . ."

"I haven't voted in years," Castle said, and he closed the door behind him.

He could still hear Farnsworth raging: "Come back here, you dumb fuck. You prick! You little shit! You come back here! I'll tell you when you can leave . . ."

The elevator door closed behind him. The last thing Castle saw was the face of the Secret Service man in the hallway, trying not to let his grin show.

He hurried back to his office, where there really were people waiting for him. He hadn't been looking forward to their visit, but one could never tell. If an ex-President behaved like a scuzz-ball, there was no reason why a porno queen and her manager shouldn't turn out to be models of decent behavior, ladylike and gentlemanly in every way.

Besides, there might be money in it.

*

For all the notoriety of Wanda Lathem's professional accomplishments, it was Dan Lucid who operated as the mouth. The talker, anyway. He sat there playing with an unlit cigar—trying to cut down on smoking? threatening to light it?—and talking about spin-off deals and packaging ideas, promotion and publicity for a book that existed only as a gleam in his greedy eye. Ms. Lathem, listless and indifferent, seemed almost sleepy. Just tired, Castle wondered, or was she drugged?

"You like that?" Lucid wanted to know.

"Like what?"

"The title. *Coming into My Own.* You like it?"

"It's too early to worry about titles. Let's have a book first. The title will come out of the book."

"Still, it's a thought, isn't it?" Lucid insisted.

Castle agreed that it was a thought.

Lucid was more or less what Castle would have predicted, a flashy little man, heavily laden with gold chains and a watch like a huge gold cookie. He wore shoes of some reptile, probably endangered. He had monograms on the cuffs of his pastel shirt and collar points that were rather longer than necessary. But the man was no fool. He'd been able to parlay an investment of a few thousand dollars into an impressive figure. His films were "classics," if such a word could be used in connection with that kind of picture. At any rate, they seemed to play perpetually, not only in the sleazy grind houses of inner-city tenderloins but also on VCRs in respectable upper-middle-class bedrooms and dens all over the country. Wanda Lathem was a household name, even if it wasn't a particularly nice name.

Or, in Lucid's inelegant formulation, she'd become "a fucking celebrity, just like any other fucking celebrity in the country."

Not surprisingly, Castle found himself thinking back to President Farnsworth. There wasn't all that much difference after all. Maybe Lucid was a little less hypocritical, a little less devious.

"What clinched it for me is the offer on the perfume. Just like what Sophia Loren has. Better, because hers just has her first name on it, and ours will have both names. They're going to call it 'Decadence—Wanda Lathem's perfume.' I tried to get them just to go with Wanda's name, but they know what they're doing, I guess. But it'll be her picture, and her name, and what will look like her signature, on every bottle of cologne, every jar of body lotion, and every lipstick. The whole schmear, right down to the nail polish."

"Congratulations," Castle said.

"The party announcing it is tomorrow. You gotta come. You'll see. They're really going to do it right. First class, all the goddamn way! It's at the Hampshire House, on Central Park South."

"I know where the Hampshire House is," Castle said. "Is she all right?"

"She's just a little beat," Lucid said with a leer. "She'll be fine."

"I hope so," Castle said.

She managed a small smile. "Oh, yeah," she said. "I'm just a little . . . beat." The hesitation could have been because she was trying to remember the word Lucid had used or because it was part of a routine, the same joke they'd used before.

She wasn't gorgeous. Not bad-looking, but not gorgeous. In fact, what was difficult, Castle thought, was connecting this perfectly normal-looking person sitting in the chair in his office with the erotic excesses of her films. It was crazy, but she looked like anyone in a typists' pool or at a receptionist's desk. Maybe that was part of her success, that non-glamorous quality of hers, the way she managed to imply that these weren't special or rare attributes but available to anyone. She had auburn hair that was a little lighter on top where the sun had bleached it. She had green eyes with attractive yellow glints in them, although, now that her lids were drooping in a half-doze, Castle couldn't actually see them. She had a figure more pert than voluptuous, with a smallish but high bosom and a narrow waist. Her long legs were probably her best feature.

What she'd learned to do was to repress her gag reflex, so that she could perform impressively in the oral sex scenes of Lucid's porno epics. It was a weak joke, like the joke of her name—Want-to Laythem. But the timing of the films had been fortunate, as Lucid, at least, seemed to understand.

"What really made her was a combination of two things," Lucid was saying, and Castle had the impression that he'd said these things before, that they were a part of his pitch. "To begin with, there was the rating system the movie producers put in. As soon as you had X-rated films, there was an acknowledgment that these things existed and that adults had a right to look at them if they wanted to. And then there was the growth of the home videotape market, which is where the so-called decent people watch our product. That made it respectable and wholesome. It wasn't something just for freaks and perverts. It was for the normal American family after they've finished with the turkey and have gone upstairs to their bedrooms."

Castle nodded. "Product," for God's sake. It wasn't Wanda who'd been turned into a whore by this, but Lucid. They weren't even movies any more, but "product."

". . . And with these endorsements, we've got it really going. We've turned the corner. It's time for the book."

"I suppose it is," Castle said. He was thinking of Farnsworth. He was thinking that it probably was time for a book about Wanda Lathem, but that it wasn't necessarily a wonderful time. Ms. Lathem didn't seem to be having such a good time herself.

"And you'll represent us!" Lucid insisted. "You're the best, and that's what Wanda ought to have. First class, all the way!"

"You're very kind to say so," Castle said.

"You will represent us. We've got a deal, right?"

"Why not?"

"And you'll come to the party tomorrow? Bring someone along with you, someone fun."

"I might do that. I might bring my sister," Castle said.

Lucid brayed as if Castle had made an extremely good joke, brayed and then held his hand to his chest and all those gold chains.

"Anything wrong with that?" Castle asked, staring at him and leaning slightly forward.

"No, nothing. Nothing at all. Bring your mother, if you like. Whatever you do is fine with us. Right, Wanda?"

"Right, Dan."

"That's what I like about this girl. Nothing fazes her. Nothing at all. She just sits there, taking it all in . . . Hey, how about that for a title? You like it? *Taking It All In?*"

"It's been used," Castle told him. "Pauline Kael's last collection of film criticism was called that."

"You're putting me on."

Castle shook his head no.

"Maybe I ought to start reading her."

"She doesn't review your kind of film," Castle warned.

"You mean skin flicks? You can say it. We've heard the word before. It's okay. But maybe she should. It sounds like she'd be good at it."

"Quite possibly," Castle admitted.

"Your name will be at the door," Lucid promised. Then he roused Ms. Lathem, who yawned—an interesting shot for the dust jacket,

Castle supposed—and managed to find the energy to come to a standing position.

*

Castle really did take his sister to Wanda Lathem's party. For one thing, he thought it might amuse her. For another, it was possible that she might get something funny out of it for one of her columns. And finally, he wanted to give her the opportunity to warn him away from this project if her instincts told her that it was going to be more nuisance than it was worth. He didn't think he was unshrewd himself, but he knew he didn't have her spooky ability to sense trouble. He realized he half hoped she'd tell him to drop it, to walk away from them and let someone else pick up the commission on what promised to be a relatively simple sale.

Lisa was only two years Leonard Castle's junior but she looked a decade younger, probably because she took care of herself better, as women often do, exercising and watching her diet. Sometimes in the early mornings, through the wall that divided what had once been their parents' huge apartment into the two separate flats they now lived in, Leonard could hear the sounds of her daily workout. Because of her career as a newspaperwoman, she could sometimes be helpful to her brother, just as he could often be useful to her. This was one of those occasions when it was not clear who was doing the favor for whom, but with all the champagne and curried shrimp and the stone crabs and the caviar, neither of them was complaining.

The party was a standard industrial wallow with members of the press and various other tastemakers and celebrities in attendance, most of them because they were willing to be bribed by good food and drink and the prospect of their own glamorous company. For these they suffered to stand around, eat, drink, listen to a trio playing new-age jazz arrangements of show tunes, and bless the introduction of some book or film or product—in this case, Depravity, the daring new line of Contessa Cosmetics, with Miss Wanda Lathem as its spokesperson.

"Listen to this," Castle said, and he read from a press release they had picked up on their way in. " 'Everything about this campaign will be handled in good taste, with the dignity and style for which Contessa Cosmetics is well known. There will be glamorous clothes and the best high-fashion photographers so that Wanda always comes off as a lady.' In boldface caps, no less. You love it?"

"You think they meant it?" Lisa asked.

"These people aren't fools, and with this kind of investment, they aren't letting maniacs and morons write copy for them," he answered. "I told you it might be amusing, in a sociological way."

"And did I doubt you? Did I argue? I think it's perfectly delicious," Lisa said. "Let's circulate."

He handed her a glass of champagne from one of the waiters' trays, took one for himself, and made his way toward Lucid and Wanda to congratulate them and let them know that he'd made his promised appearance.

"Nice to see you," Lucid said, and grinned, remembering their exchange of the previous afternoon. "And did you bring your sister?"

"Oh, yes," Castle assured him. "She's over there, talking to Kurt Vonnegut."

"You're kidding," Wanda said.

"Why not?" Castle asked. "People have sisters."

"I'm still getting used to this ladylike business," she said. "I guess. I keep forgetting I'm respectable now."

She giggled. Castle looked at her. She seemed altogether different from the day before, up and wired rather than down and lethargic. Pills of a different color, perhaps?

"My sister is a columnist," he explained. "This is right up her alley."

Lucid took Castle's elbow and steered him toward a short, sleek man in a nubby silk suit to introduce them. "Leonard Castle, this is Wally Kempf. You two ought to get to know each other."

Kempf was marketing director for Contessa, the host of the party and the moving spirit behind Decadence—Wanda Lathem's perfume. "You're agenting the book, I understand?"

"That's right," Castle said.

"I'm delighted. It's quite something. What Andy Warhol predicted just a few years back—throwaway celebrities."

"Are you planning to throw her away?"

Wally Kempf grinned. "No, no. I'm not planning anything. But one must be prepared for all eventualities. I'd say, judging from the young lady's condition this afternoon, that she may dispose of herself one day without anyone else having to raise a finger."

"And then you change the signature line on Decadence, is that it?" Castle asked.

"It's an option we've kept open," Kempf admitted. "And meanwhile, whatever she does with herself that gets sympathy or attention of any kind . . . can only help us."

Castle wasn't altogether delighted to be in the same boat with Mr. Kempf, but that was what he'd agreed to. "And what do you think of Mr. Lucid?" he asked. He was playing a game, trying to see how candid the marketing director would allow himself to be. It seemed to be part of the man's routine not just to admit unpleasant truths but to assert them defiantly and pre-emptively.

"I think he's got his hands full. He's worked hard to create all this, and now that he's got it going, he finds that it's all riding on her. So he's got to put up with her, which is an awful lot."

"From her?" Castle asked.

"It can't be easy."

"That's interesting," Castle observed. "My sympathies run rather the other way—I mean, as much as they run at all. She's the one I'd be inclined to worry about. He looks as though he's doing okay, relatively speaking."

"Hang around. We'll see. Maybe we're both right," Kempf said. And then he excused himself and allowed one of his assistants to introduce a writer for *Women's Wear Daily*. Castle turned toward the food, but was stopped by an attractive young woman who asked him, "Aren't you Leonard Castle?"

"Yes, that's right."

"I'm Susan Flowers. How do you do?"

She extended her hand. Almost without thinking, Castle took it. And then the penny dropped. "Oh, I see. Susan Flowers from *Periscope?*"

"That's right," she said. "I'd been hoping to meet you."

"You might have called," he said dryly. "My number is in the book. It would have been a lot simpler than snooping around the way you've been doing."

"You're right," she said. "And now that the story has been killed, I'm sorry. Sometimes we have to do unattractive things."

He wasn't sure whether her "we" referred to people in television or was more general, extending even perhaps to himself. She knew, he assumed, about his connection with Wanda Lathem. She was criticizing him—or, worse, refraining from doing so—on account of the way he and Lucid were both making money from peddling Ms. Lathem's flesh.

"Is that an apology?" he asked.

"Close to," she said. She was petite and energetic, and she gave the impression of being always on the verge of laughter. Castle attributed some of that to her discomfort in an awkward situation, but he also supposed that she knew how becoming it was.

"You were even down in Pennsylvania, I hear."

"Yes. I admire what you did for Farnsworth. He didn't seem to appreciate it . . ."

"Oh?"

"Either that, or he was putting on one hell of an act. But the story is dead. He pulled some strings upstairs and had it killed. He and his book are off limits. But you're not."

"As they used to say on playgrounds, 'Is that a promise or a threat?' "

"Which way would you rather take it? I meant it as a compliment. I think you're an interesting man."

"You say that to all the fellows."

"Actually, I don't. What you do and how you work . . . from what I've seen, I think it's terrific. If you were interested, if you felt like cooperating with us, I could see a wonderful segment in it. Good for us and good for you too, I'd think."

"I'd have to consider it. A lot of what I do is private. Confidential. There are some things I'd be willing to expose to the camera. But some are nobody's business but mine and my clients'."

"Think about it," she said. "It would be a different arrangement in a friendly piece. We wouldn't be out to get you."

"So you say. But what happens in the editing rooms isn't always up to you, is it?"

"There are risks in everything," she admitted.

"I'll give it some thought," he said. "Meanwhile, let me ask you something. I can't understand why you went to Farnsworth, or why, having gone to him, you told him about Pennsylvania and showed him the pictures. Why did you tip your hand that way?"

She took a sip of champagne, obviously stalling, using the seconds to decide how to answer. And then she said, "You were the one we were after. You were the one we were going to confront, on camera the way they like to do."

"Me? Whatever for? Farnsworth wasn't big enough for you?" Castle asked.

"He was too big. As we found out anyway. And everybody knows what a son of a bitch he is. You were the one I thought was . . . intriguing."

"You mean, not everyone knows what a son of a bitch I am?"

"Are you?" she asked. "Why don't you let me take you to lunch one day? We can explore that question. I owe you that much at least."

"Oh, at least," he said. He liked her brazenness, which was more amusing than offensive. And he was tempted—as of course she meant him to be—by the ways in which he could put such an opportunity to use. It was millions of dollars' worth of publicity if it could be harnessed properly. Who could say when an appropriate occasion might present itself?

"Is it so terrible a prospect?" she asked.

"No, no. Lunch will be fine. Call me and we'll set a time for it."

"Oh, my God!" she said.

He was mystified and couldn't understand the reason for the sudden change in the woman's expression, but then the musical fanfare registered and he realized that she was looking past him. He turned around to see Wanda doing her sword-swallowing trick, using a celery stalk rather than her usual prop, while the combo played stripper music and she did little bumps and grinds. The suggestion, however, was clear enough even without the music and dance, and clearly obscene. She withdrew the celery stalk from her gullet, caressing it as she did so, and then dropped a formal curtsy and blew kisses to the crowd, which responded with a round of applause.

"As I say," Susan repeated, "we all have to do unattractive things sometimes. Do you have to hang around here, or are you free to leave?" She put her glass down on a passing waiter's tray.

"I'm free to leave," he told her, "but I'm here with my sister."

"Lisa Barr?"

"You know her?"

"No, but I'd like to."

"Let me introduce you," he offered.

He led the way through the throng to his sister's side and made the introduction. The two women exchanged appropriately friendly greetings, but then Lisa asked pointedly the question that Leonard Castle had been wondering about and had thought of putting to Ms. Flowers himself. "Are you here because of your interest in Contessa? Or Wanda Lathem? Or to meet Leonard?"

"To meet Leonard," she admitted candidly.

"To catch him at an awkward moment?" Lisa asked.

"Not at all," Susan said. "There aren't any cameras here, none of ours anyway. It was just the first chance that presented itself. I really came to apologize," she said.

Castle broke in and said, "Lisa, it's okay. She's been very nice."

"Well, in that case," Lisa said, "I really am happy to meet you—even here."

"Thanks," Susan said, and then to Castle, "I'll call you tomorrow and we'll talk some more."

After she'd gone, Lisa allowed an arched eyebrow to ascend a quarter of an inch, interrogatively.

"She says she's interested in a segment about me," Castle explained.

The other eyebrow was raised now too.

"I know. It's risky, but it's also tempting."

"You're a big boy. You know what you're doing. But be careful, won't you?"

"Of the program or of her?"

"As long as you ask, both, brother. Both."

"A last glass of bubbly?" he offered.

"No, let's split," she joked.

"I'll get your coat," he said.

On the way to the hatcheck room, he passed Wally Kempf, who said, "Not leaving already, are you?"

"Have to," Castle answered.

"That's a shame. But it went well, don't you think?"

"Fine, fine."

"We've got to get together to talk one of these days," Kempf said.

"Fine. Give me a call."

"Will do. A hell of a performance, wasn't it?" Kempf said, and then, with a wink, he added, "But then, she always gives great performance, doesn't she?"

It wasn't until they were in the cab on the way uptown that Castle allowed himself to process some of that exchange with Kempf. Had the wink been just a piece of meaningless locker-room naughtiness? Or had there been some suggestion that Kempf knew Wanda's talents rather more intimately—or an assumption on Kempf's part that Castle too had enjoyed the same attentions?

For that matter, when Castle had said he was leaving, there had been an edge to his comment about how that was a shame. It was possible to interpret that as the regret a host is supposed to express when a guest leaves, but there were other readings too—suggestions of an after-hours orgy, perhaps, for some select group.

He was imagining things—or he hoped so, anyway. "What do you think?" he asked his sister, knowing that he wasn't letting her have all the information but trusting her to react correctly nonetheless.

"What's to think?"

"Should I drop it?"

She shrugged.

A shrug was hardly an expression of violent disapproval. He was almost disappointed. After all, she'd enunciated just a few minutes before the governing principle—that he was a big boy now.

"Well, we'll see how it goes," he said.

She nodded.

The cab had slowed. It pulled up at the front gate of their building. Castle paid the cabbie and they walked together to their entrance, rode up the elevator, and then, without speaking, parted in the hallway as each of them went into a separated half of what had once been their home.

*

It seemed unlikely to Castle that Lucid could be the one who had been trying to kill him. Lucid had reason, maybe, but that had been so long ago. Who carries a grudge around for that length of time? If people in publishing did that, there would be bodies stacked up on Park and Madison and Fifth and the Avenue of the Americas every garbage pickup day. In any business where large amounts of money and work and time were wagered in a game in which the results were determined by subjective opinion, there had to be strong feelings. But professionals picked themselves up, brushed themselves off, and turned their attention to the next project and a new roll of the dice.

They had been heading south on Park Avenue. Castle told the driver to go up the ramp, make the loop around Grand Central, and head back north. He kept looking behind him. After this maneuver, he'd feel confident enough to risk going to ground. It was a risk that he would have to share. If he was wrong about having shaken his pursuer, then he'd be bringing his trouble with him—which wasn't something he wanted to do. This was his problem. He didn't want to inflict it on anyone else.

5

Transcription of cassette of Mr. Dan Lucid:

Everybody fucks everybody.

No, no, I don't mean it like it's some kind of orgy, although I never turned down an invitation to an orgy either, come to think of it. It's just how it is, how things are in the world. People take advantage of other people any goddamn way they can. That's what it all boils down to, what Marx said and Darwin too, for that matter.

The difference is that it bothered the hell out of Marx and he wanted to change it. Darwin just described how it worked in nature.

Any jerk from the streets will tell you the same thing, because that's what he sees from the time he wakes up in the morning until his eyes close at night, or glaze over in the afternoon from booze or drugs. He knows he's being fucked. The thing about the middle class is that they spend a lot of time and energy denying that, kidding themselves, pretending that the world is a lot nicer place than it is, which is certainly okay by me, except that they get to believe it, begin to think that their fairy stories are true—and then they look at somebody like me and they get all upset and call me a criminal and a monster.

Well, it just isn't so. I mean, where do you suppose I found Wanda in the first place? You think she was walking on a college campus like June Allyson in *Good News*, wondering whether Peter Lawford would carry her books or not? She was a little street whore from Providence, Rhode Island, just peddling her ass like any other street whore. Fuck or starve, you know? She knew what the score was, and she was out there doing what she had to do. She was a runaway, of course. A kid from a broken home. You could do the whole sad song, tell the story about how a nice girl got into such a terrible fix—only she was never such a nice girl, wasn't really all that smart, didn't have a whole lot of ambition, wasn't any different from any other hooker from the beginning of time. She could have been a waitress, I guess, or a typist—if she'd ever been able to learn how to type. But she was also a little bit lazy, and she was a little bit greedy. Waitresses don't get paid as well as whores and have to stay on their feet for long periods of time. A whore gets to lie down, and except for the very best whores, the john does most of the work, pumping away at the broad, who doesn't have to do a whole lot.

And like all those other hookers, at least at the beginning, she was kidding herself, pretending that this was only a temporary thing, something she had to do to tide herself over—which is one way of describing what life is, something you do on a temporary basis to tide yourself over until you die. She thought she could make it as a singer or a dancer, because she had two feet and could croak along to the records on a phonograph. So, along with those other sterling qualities, she was unrealistic, which is, as far as I'm concerned, the original sin, the one and only. All the rest is bullshit.

So, anyway, there she was, turning tricks in the evening and occasionally hauling her ass to auditions up in Boston, and she wasn't getting a whole lot of offers or parts, or not parts in plays anyway. Not even in the chorus of a road company or dinner theater. She could strip, of course, or be a go-go dancer, stand behind a bar and shake her tits at the customers, but as the guy in the joke says who's cleaning up after the elephants in the circus parade, "At least it's show business."

You don't have to be any kind of a prophet to figure out what would have happened to her in five years—drugs, almost certainly, and if she wasn't lucky enough to OD, she'd wind up as a bag lady, mumbling to herself and freezing to death some winter night, looking like she was a hundred years old and maybe in her early forties. I mean, this isn't an original scenario, it goes back to Emile Zola, the French writer, and it's just the same as when he wrote about it, only a little uglier now, maybe.

So with Wanda, when I made her the offer of a role in a film, I wasn't out there looking to corrupt the young and the innocent. I was doing her a favor. I mean, not because I'm a nice guy or anything. I'm not claiming that. But it was a legitimate business deal, a chance for her to get screwed only three or four times a week instead of ten or fifteen times a night, and with a camera rolling. And with a little of the glamour and fun of show business thrown in.

I mean, you think she wanted to be a singer or dancer because she had talent? Because she had this urge to express herself? Look, when this girl cops a joint or takes it up the ass from some gonzo who's hung like a horse, she's expressing herself more honestly and accurately than she could do in any other medium. What makes these movies work isn't just the fucking and the cum shots. They've all got that stuff. No, it's her. There's something about her expression, her character, her being that is up there on the screen and communicates itself to people who watch the films. She's fuckable. In both senses. I mean, she's sexy but she also invites people to take advantage of her. There's that waiflike thing she's got, and it's funny how that works. Some people have it and you feel sorry for them, and other people have something almost identical, and you don't feel sorry at all but you want to pile it on, you want to see them really get it. It's like chickens that gang up on a wounded bird and peck it to death.

So when she's getting it up the cunt and up the ass from two guys, and sucking a third guy, and giving hand jobs to a couple of others all at once, there's something right about that, something appropriate, like she could be fucked to death and it'd be the right way for her to go.

I don't take credit for seeing all that at the beginning, but there may have been something there, some subconscious recognition of that . . . that vulnerability of hers that I picked up on, even then. I mean, she hasn't got huge tits, right? And her face is okay but not classic or anything spectacular. She's got okay legs. But there's something that comes across, to coin a phrase. And I guess I must have reacted to that without even knowing what it was.

I give myself too much credit? Maybe so. Maybe it was just luck, but in that case it was her luck as well as mine. In that case, there isn't any such thing as personal responsibility. You do what you can, and others do what they can, and what happens is the result, which you can call luck or fate or whatever. I always wanted to be in movies, to make films. I applied to the film school at UCLA, as a matter of fact. Not a whole lot of people know that, but it's true. I was like a whole lot of other kids, I guess, and I liked to read and I just loved movies. I figured that the greatest life in the world would be making movies, because the work would be great and the perks would be pretty terrific too. I mean, what other industry has starlets hanging around all the time hoping for the chance to give you a blow job in exchange not for a part or even an audition but just an introduction to the next guy whose brother-in-law might know an accountant at one of the studios.

It's pathetic. But there it is, and those broads can be so stupid when they leave Keokuk to come out to the Coast that they don't know what to expect. And if they are, if they're shocked and offended, there are buses they can catch that go the other way, but you don't see them lining up for tickets, do you? No, they're getting their hair done and scrimping for new clothes so that they can look terrific at the next party they go to and maybe catch somebody's eye.

Cooze and coke and terrific cars. You think I'm crass and awful? What the fuck else is American culture touting? What else is American life about? The good life! The gusto! All those people driving on all those freeways in southern California, what do you think they're hurrying after? They want their share, and if they've already got their share, they want more.

So I figured movies would be a good way to get myself some of those goodies, and I'm not ashamed to say so. But there are a couple of hundred thousand other bright guys who have had the same thought and the competition is tough out there. My break came when I got an introduction to a semi-gangster who bankrolled fuck films and he made a phone call to one of his people and I got a job. Nothing spectacular, but it was a start. I would go to real estate offices and look through their listings to see what was available. We wanted locations to shoot at, nice outdoorsy places, maybe with a pool or a hot tub, and preferably with a view of something nice to look at. And I'd try to find a house that was up for sale but still furnished—usually that was because somebody was going through a divorce. And I'd see if I could make a deal with the owner, not for money but for some kind of trade. He'd let us use his place for a weekend for the exterior shots, and we'd let him fuck the star. We'd paid her anyway, and it was part of her job to fuck whoever the director and producer told her to fuck. So the girl would do a guy without a camera turning, and we'd get these great production values for that opening scene.

It was a job. It was a foot in the door, I told myself, thinking that it could lead to other things in a more respectable part of the industry maybe. Of course, I was a dumb schmuck then and I didn't realize that there isn't all that much difference, that the rest of the industry isn't a whole lot different. But I hustled and I produced, and there would be all these terrific houses that turned out always to have the same bedroom, which was actually a set in a soundstage they'd put up in what had once been some kind of factory in Santa Monica.

Finding Wanda was mostly a matter of coincidence, I guess. For one thing, there was the given in skin flicks, which is that fucking just isn't terrific to film, nothing visual, nothing as good as cocksucking for instance, where you get to see a face on the screen. So that was part of it. And the other part was what I was trying to get at a moment ago about Wanda's looking like some poor bedraggled waif. It was actually some Greek, not a shipping tycoon, but a nephew of one, or a cousin twice removed. He did okay, though, and he had this spread up near Chatsworth somewhere with a barn for horses and a little pond with trees around it. It must have been worth half a million, which was big bucks back then. Anyway, it was terrific, and we were all set to shoot up there on the usual arrangement—quim. But he didn't want to prong the star. No, he wanted this other girl, this nothing of a girl who was just there in the big orgy scene at the end as an extra piece of ass. He pointed to her and said that that was the one he wanted.

Well, I agreed to that, sure, but it was tough finding out who this bimbo was. He'd been watching a film we'd made a month or so before, and it's tough to keep track of these broads from day to day, let alone from month to month. But that was the one he wanted, and even though I had to knock myself out finding her, I realized that there was something about her that was special, that the Greek guy was absolutely right. I mean, you wanted to do something to her, really to stick to her, and the more I thought about it, the more I realized that this was a quality that had come across on the screen from a bit part in a fuck film, and that this was gold, pure gold, just waiting to be picked up and put on the market.

Still, what was missing was the opportunity, but there was some kind of fuck-up somewhere, in every sense, and the producer wound up in the hospital. I think he'd put the wrong broad in a movie—somebody's girlfriend. I mean, that's the difference, maybe, between fuck films and the other kind. The other kind, people ask you to put their girlfriends into the picture, and in ours, they're not so eager for you to do that. So the wrong broad showed up with some beefcake's dick in her mouth and then cum all over her face, and somebody got angry as hell about it, and our producer wound up in the hospital with a few cracked ribs and a broken leg, having been worked over by a couple of the wide boys.

Which meant that I was asked to take over and finish this picture that they were in the middle of shooting. And I talked to the director and the cameraman—a nice old souse who had once been a real cameraman—and we gave Wanda a featured scene to herself in the picture. *Riding High*, I think it was called, because there were horses in it and the gimmick was that we had a lot of girls wearing chaps and nothing else. So Wanda had a ride for herself. And as in anything else, all she needed was a break and a chance to show what she could do.

I think we did a couple of films that way, with Wanda as one of the featured players and with me getting the producer's credit, but then our backer had a stroke. Some of these guys really do just die in their beds, you know. It isn't fair. You want them to go down in a Bonnie and Clyde blaze of gunfire, which is what they deserve maybe, but it doesn't work that way. The life of crime doesn't make you immune to all the ordinary perils. And some blood vessel in the guy's head gave out and he fell down and that was it. Which meant that there was an opening in the dirty movie business, and as any casual observer could probably guess, openings in that business tend to get filled.

Now that I think about it, I guess I figured I was out on my ass and I had mixed feelings. I'd earned a few dollars and I'd had a couple of funny evenings now and then, but I had always assumed that this was a little detour, that I was still going to go ahead someday and rejoin the mainstream on the right side of the tracks. All it took was a little push, and here it was. I was scared that this was the moment, and that I was going to succeed or fail now. It was like walking into a casino and you wonder how your luck is and how you're going to feel in about an hour. I was keyed up that way. But I was also relieved. I'd never really identified with the porno producer bit, never thought that this was the real me.

A dumb story, right? Like the one every hooker will tell you, about how she's only doing this for a while, and that when she has her shit together she's going to get her ass back where it belongs. What you've got to realize, though, is that most of them really believe it. That this is what keeps them going. And that when they stop believing that story they've been telling themselves, they get into lots worse trouble and start hitting the bottle or the needle or both.

But I got a call from some guy in San Francisco who wanted me to fly up and talk to him. I think I told him that I wasn't interested, but he wasn't having any of that. He told me that I ought to come up and talk to him, that he'd make it worth my while. And while he didn't exactly threaten me, he wasn't the kind of guy people say no to very often. It's just not a very smart or healthy thing to do.

What I thought would happen was that I'd go up and listen to the guy's pitch and then tell him that I wanted to get out of the business. I figured that he might force me to do another picture or even a couple of them, but if he saw that I wasn't interested and wanted to get out, he'd probably be able to find other guys to do what I'd been doing. He just didn't want to be left in the lurch, which was reasonable. But that wasn't how it worked at all.

What actually happened was a hell of a lot smoother and more sophisticated—which I guess I ought to have expected. This man— let's give him a name and call him Mr. Sid, which is close enough but won't get me killed—wasn't just some goon. He hired goons when he needed them, but he was way past that kind of thing himself. He also hired guys from the Harvard B. School and the Harvard Law School too. And he was a hell of a lot more polished and smooth than a lot of guys in what you'd call the straight world.

To begin with, there was a suite at the Mark Hopkins with a great view of the bay and a little bar stocked with Chivas Regal and Boodles gin and Stolichnaya vodka. And the assistant that Mr. Sid sends over to welcome me to San Francisco and thank me for coming to town for this interview is a guy with one of those thin dispatch cases that maybe holds three pieces of paper, and he never even looks at them because he's got all the stuff in his head anyway.

And there's no horsing around. I mean, the guy comes out with it up front, as if they already knew what I was going to say, which they probably did because I'd been working for them, indirectly anyway, for a long time and they pay attention, just the way the big corporations are supposed to do and don't always manage to bring off. But he's very up-front, and he knows that this is a distasteful business, and that I'm only in it for the experience and for the money. They're in it because they can declare profits on these pictures and launder money that they've made in other ways, as for instance bookmaking, which he mentions, and hookers and drugs, which he doesn't. But it's a tax thing, primarily. Or that's what makes it particularly attractive for them. They've got the girls to start with, and they've got the distribution at the other end, so it's all "rational," which is the word the guy used, but it's the tax advantages that make it irresistible. And what's in it for me is a piece of the declared profit, which is frequently higher than the real profit, and I can do this for as long as I want and I can get out any time. Or I can save up the money and then use it to back some other kind of picture if I want to take that kind of gamble and make the transition to what the guy called "general theatrical outlets," and keep this open as an option to return to in the event that my first venture isn't the kind of success I'd been counting on.

And then we go out to dinner at Trader Vic's and I get to meet Mr. Sid and his wife, and this lawyer-manager type and his wife, and it's the Bongo Bongo soup and the Diamond Head salad and Christ knows what else, and there's not a hell of a lot for me to say except thank you very much, and I really appreciate it—because there aren't any strings and it's just like a real business deal except for what I'm actually going to have to do for the guy.

So what happens is that I'm suckered in, and Wanda is along for the ride because I know that Wanda has exactly the right quality for this kind of thing. And she's willing to do whatever I want her to do because she knows that I'm only in this for the time being, and she's got this faith in me that one day I'm going to jump across those tracks —and I'm going to take her with me, of course. She's going to be another blonde bombshell in slightly naughty comedies that are perfectly clean and wholesome except maybe for a shot or two in a wet tee shirt that shows off her tits.

At first, it was flattering. It was just what I wanted to believe myself, and here she was agreeing with me and betting her ass that I was going to make it. But after a while, I knew better, and I knew that her belief in me was ridiculous and pathetic. I was stringing her along with the story of how someday I'd make the move to legitimate films. But it was a long time before I realized that what I was doing with Wanda was exactly what Mr. Sid and his smooth Ivy League types had been doing with me. I mean, that time I went up to San Francisco, they could have set me up with a broad. Half a dozen of them. A redhead, a blonde, a brunette, and a prune Danish, like in the joke, you know? But they didn't. There was a suite, with me all alone, and you're about twenty times as alone in a suite as you are in a single room. All that fucking space, and nobody to share it with. I could pour myself a Stoli and walk around in the dark looking out the windows at the lights of the city and the ships in the bay, and . . . and imagine what I was going to do someday, when I'd made my pile and was ready to make my move.

It was crazy, but they were playing me exactly the way I was playing Wanda. That dinner with Mr. Sid and his wife, and the other guy and his wife. And no question about it, these weren't casual bimbos they'd picked up for the evening. These were the authentic spouses, and nobody alluded in any way whatsoever to the kind of movie they were financing and I was making. Nobody made so much as an off-color joke. It was all civilized and refined, and art and theater and books and ballet—which was just what I wanted to hear. It was a glimpse into the dream world I wanted to live in anyway. And I could go back to my suite and keep up the pretense all by my lonesome. I could get laid back in L.A. if I wanted to. Or I guess I could have gone outside or just down to the bar and picked up some dame. But Mr. Sid and his people knew what would get me, and they left me alone to get myself, walking around with the glass in my hand and the ice tinkling, and the lights twinkling down below me.

Everybody fucks everybody, but most of the time we fuck ourselves. Because most of us are just dumb enough to sucker ourselves. Which is exactly what happened. Wanda fucked herself, just the way I fucked myself. And presumably the guy who worked for Mr. Sid fucked himself too. I sure as hell hope so, anyway. And Mr. Sid? Him too, in spades.

Along with the transcription of the cassette, there was a note from the typist:

> Dear Mr. Castle, I promised to have this back to you by Thursday and I have delivered as promised. I find the enclosed material distasteful and objectionable, and I should be very grateful if you could find someone else to continue with the typing of Mr. Lucid's reminiscences. I appreciate the work you've given me over the past years, and I hope to be of service in the future—but not with this man or this deplorable project. Sincerely, Mildrid M. Conklin.

Leonard Castle read the note, very nearly crumpled it up to throw away, but then thought better of it. He kept it with the other pages. Let the writer see that this was lively material and that there might be some interesting reactions to it.

For his own part, he thought that maybe he'd misjudged Lucid and that perhaps he wasn't such a bad fellow after all.

*

The picking of a writer was always a matter of some delicacy. It had to be a person the publisher trusted, someone who could deliver a publishable manuscript more or less on time. It had to be somebody the star would talk to, not just answering questions but opening up to so that the book would have as much personal flavor as possible. And in this particular case, it had to be someone Wanda Lathem's manager was comfortable with too, which was why Castle had left the note of protest from the typist in with the packet of manuscript pages. His expectation was that Lucid would tend to like people who liked him— and this was a way of helping that along, enlisting from the prospective writer a certain amount of understanding for the producer.

The short list Castle sent to the editor in chief of Barbizon Press had three names on it, and next to each of them there were a couple of phrases. Beside Pete McCracken's name, Castle had noted: "Recently divorced—might find this an appealing kind of subject."

McCracken was Barbizon's first choice, and there was a lunch at the Côte Basque at which everybody got to take a look at everybody else, the idea being that if people couldn't get on for a couple of hours, they might not do well in a fairly intensive association that was going to extend over six months. McCracken showed up at eleven-thirty at Castle's office, read some of the material Castle had assembled for him, and listened while Castle told him about Lathem and Lucid. "Frankly, Lucid may be the more interesting of the two, but it's Wanda's face up there, not to mention other portions of her anatomy. It's Wanda's name on the cosmetics and perfumes. It will be Wanda's book. So you have to be able to stand her."

"Yeah, I'd guess so."

"She's not easy to like."

"That's what my ex-wife says about me," McCracken answered, and he laughed. "And maybe she's right. But this is just too good to be true."

"What is?"

"The anti-feminism of it. The exploitation. All those things that Marissa kept talking about, they're right here. It's what you'd expect. Marissa had her consciousness raised, and there was no place left for a lowlife like me. Sexist pig that I am, I'm looking forward to meeting Wanda. I think there are a lot of people with my kind of bruises. So maybe this book could go. So I'll get on with Wanda."

"I hope so," Castle said. "Oliver Barrett is an old pro. He'll be the editor."

"He's okay. I've heard good things about him."

"It ought to fly," Castle said. "Let's walk on over. It's not very cold out, and walking to lunch is the only exercise I get these days."

McCracken looked drawn and haggard. The trauma of his recent divorce might have been part of it, but there was a likelier and simpler explanation—he was still making the adjustment to self-sufficiency, finding his own meals and dealing with his own laundry. He was wearing khaki pants in need of pressing, a good tweed jacket that might have benefited from a cleaning as well as a pressing, and desert boots with the laces spliced together where they had broken. There were circles under his eyes. He'd been staying out late, either eager for company or just because he'd been dreading the empty apartment, a messy kitchen with dishes in the sink, a pigpen of a living room with papers all over the floor from the previous Sunday, and a bedroom cavernous and empty, the worst room of all.

Enough of Castle's friends had been there so that he could supply the details. Castle had therefore predicted that McCracken would be vulnerable to a proposal like this, its very seediness being an important part of its attraction. McCracken was at that dangerous place where he felt that he deserved to be punished. And for a journalist of his reputation, three or four months with Wanda Lathem and Dan Lucid would be cruel and unusual enough to satisfy whatever masochistic needs his personal problems might have aroused.

The other possibility, of course, was that this would be exactly the wrong thing, that he'd be unable to cope with it. But if that were the case, they'd all know soon enough. There would be no pages forthcoming, or the pages would be terrible. In that case, there were always the other names on the list with which he and Barbizon could bail out, if it came to that. Still, Castle's hunch was that this might be just the right fit.

The lunch went well enough. At any rate, McCracken kept nodding, either in agreement with what the others were saying or maybe just to confirm that this was all happening, that it wasn't a scene from some private nightmare but actually was taking place in what people refer to as the real world. Castle heard Wanda make her first intimate revelation to her amanuensis—that her real name was Margaret and that her parents had called her Peggy but at school she'd been called Knobby because she'd matured early. Not exactly earthshaking, Castle thought, but it was a start.

She looked to be in better shape than on previous occasions, however, neither too high nor too low. Of course, it was always possible that she had arrived either by accident or by design at a pharmacological equilibrium. On her own or with Lucid's advice and cooperation? Castle saw that Wanda's nose was bothering her a little—the aftereffects of Bolivian marching powder, no doubt. But she seemed to be paying attention to the conversation, and even to be taking occasional bites of her veal.

The quiet one was Oliver Barrett. At first, Castle assumed that he was just sitting there and soaking it all up, amused or even appalled, but calculating as to how to convert his reaction into a profitable commodity. That was the object of the game, after all, as Barrett had been around long enough to understand. It was only over coffee that Castle began to wonder whether the editor was okay. It wasn't his silence so much as the way the man seemed to be following the course of the talk, apparently listening to Wanda tell how she'd tried out for the baton-twirling team in her junior high school but had dropped her baton and had been so humiliated that she'd run off the field and had hidden in her room for two days.

"I was such a dumb kid I thought that the thing you had to do to make the twirling team was to be able to twirl. What I didn't know was that all you really needed was big tits." She laughed, but not too loudly.

McCracken looked as though he were listening to Albert Schweitzer expounding on the rich yield of his life and thought. And Barrett too seemed totally absorbed, almost hypnotized. Castle tried to catch his eye, to look at Barrett and have him look back, just to acknowledge that they were both at the same table. But it couldn't be done.

The dessert cart had been admired and resisted, and the five of them sat over their coffees, accepting refills from the attentive waiter's silver pot. Abruptly, Barrett called for the check, apologized to everyone about another meeting he had to hurry back for, and took off.

After he'd gone, Castle said something reassuring about how Barrett often scheduled himself too tightly, but he couldn't actually remember whether that was true or not. He had an uneasy feeling about the editor, which it would have been altogether pointless to share with Lucid or McCracken. It was Castle's business, after all, to smooth out these kinds of wrinkles. When he got back to the office, he called Barbizon, asked for Oliver Barrett, and was told that Mr. Barrett was in a meeting. He left word for Barrett to return the call.

He sat at his desk, playing with his silver letter opener, balancing it on the ball of his index finger. He was thinking that Barrett ought to be pleased, ought to be damned grateful that things had worked out so well and that a writer of McCracken's talents and credentials and reliability was willing to be involved in a project like this. It would only make Barrett's life easier. When the manuscript finally appeared, it would be more or less on time and in decent professional shape. There would be nothing to do but argue about a sentence here and a paragraph there and then send it off to the printer.

What the hell was Barrett doing, putting on this nice Nelly act?

Castle put the letter opener back on his blotter and turned his attention to the details of an offer on the South American Spanish rights to another book. He read through a letter from a corresponding agent in Mexico City and scrawled a note at the bottom to ask whether it wouldn't be possible to get a few pesos more if the European Spanish rights were thrown in as well.

Effie buzzed. Barrett was on the line. Castle picked up and said, "Hello? Oliver? You seemed troubled at lunch. Was it my imagination or your stomach? Or do we have a problem?"

"Ah, shit, I don't know, Len. It's okay, I guess. I just don't feel happy about it. I kept thinking that this wasn't what we went into this business for, you know?"

"It's not a perfect world, Oliver. We're old enough to have figured that out a long time ago."

"I know, I know. But we're still responsible for what we do in it, aren't we? Or are we old enough to have figured a way out of that too?"

"What's so terrible? What's bothering you? The girl?"

"Not really. I kept thinking about McCracken. He shouldn't have to do this. He kept nodding and agreeing with everything, and acting as though he were with it and for it, but it just made me sick. He's too good for this kind of shit. And I'm responsible."

"Not really. I'm a better candidate for blame than you are. If there is going to be blame. I think it'll be good for him, frankly. I think it'll be like Zola palling around with whores to write *Nana*. It'll take his mind off his problems. It could even be an interesting book."

"You're kidding yourself, Len. You know that, don't you?"

"I don't think so. Not really. I don't think I'm kidding at all about who's responsible. If you want out, I can take the package to another editor. Another house, for that matter. So it'd still happen. And if it's going to happen anyway, there's no reason for you to worry too much about your contribution to the corruption of a writer—if such a thing is possible. Mostly, they do it to themselves. You know that, don't you?"

"It's just a feeling I had there at lunch. I'm sorry. It was good of you to call. I shouldn't need to have my hand held like this."

"We all have our good days and our less good days, Oliver. It comes with the territory. But this'll be okay, I think. This book will be all right. McCracken's a pro, and the girl is cooperative. And even Lucid isn't so bad as I thought he'd be. I really think it'll work out."

"All right. No more fidgets, I promise. No vapors or maidenly sighs . . ."

"It'd be worse never to have them, wouldn't it?"

"I guess. I'll be in touch," Barrett said.

So the deal was still on track and moving.

Funny about a man like Barrett having that kind of reaction, though. Castle hoped his assurances had been appropriate and that Barrett hadn't, in some spooky way, been right.

What the hell! We're all grown-ups, he thought. Except maybe for Wanda. Or Peggy. Knobby.

Unless she was the most grown-up of them all.

*

It was only three weeks later that Castle thought back to Oliver Barrett's moment of hesitation. The contracts had been signed and the checks had cleared. Work on the book had begun. Castle had all but closed the file on Wanda Lathem, for whom there was little further that he'd have to do. Now it would be McCracken's job and then Barrett's and then the publicity people at Barbizon, and of course Lucid. Unless something went wrong somewhere, some absurd personality conflict or misunderstanding . . .

"Dan Lucid on two," Effie announced. "And he doesn't sound happy."

"The end of the world?"

"At least," Effie said.

It was a routine they had established to remind themselves that nothing was quite so serious and final as it appeared to some of their volatile and nervous clients.

"Good morning," Castle said, cheery and affable. It was a disarming technique that sometimes did a little good and could certainly do no harm.

"I'm going to kill you," Lucid said. He wasn't shouting, which made it sound almost serious. "I'm going to blow your fucking head off with a cannon."

"And what have I done to deserve such ire?"

"It's this writer you found. This guy you recommended."

"McCracken? What's the problem?"

"They've disappeared. They've run off together."

"He and Wanda?"

"Right. Him and the cunt. They've vanished."

"Are you sure? Maybe they've gone out for a hamburger?"

"For three days?"

"Maybe they've gone away for a weekend, then. Is that so terrible?"

"I'm telling you, they've run off. He's stolen her. And you better do something about it. You know where he is. You tell him. You wise him up about what's going to happen if he isn't back here in twenty-four hours. You got that? It's not going to be pretty. Him first and then you."

"I haven't the vaguest idea where he is," Castle protested. "I haven't heard from him in two weeks."

"Then you'd better start looking. While you can still see."

The sound of the phone being slammed down into its cradle rang in Castle's ear.

"Problems?" Effie asked.

"You might say so, yes. We've got to find McCracken."

*

He gave the cabbie Susan's address.

The quirks of love, Castle thought, may be expressions of our personalities but they are also luxuries. Back in the old days, a man's choices would have been pretty much limited to one or two possible mates. And once the choice was made, a man—or a woman—would be stuck, the way they were stuck with the same plot of land, the same mule, the same cow, and the same flock of chickens. All this fine-tuning of two sensibilities was . . . an indulgence. And unnatural.

Now that a little reality had come blowing in through an open window, he realized this. He needed Susan. He needed someone, and she was there. And he was grateful.

Nervous, maybe, but grateful.

6

There were gulls that soared and hovered in the icy winds over the river. Through the window of the boathouse, Pete McCracken could watch them slice through the salt air, scanning for signs of food below. Every now and then, one would swoop down to hunt and feed. It was cruel, maybe, but clean.

McCracken worked at an old oak desk on which the varnish had yellowed and darkened. His electronic typewriter made quiet clicking noises he could barely hear over the sounds of Wanda's voice in the earpiece of his tape recorder. Wanda was still asleep, but as the cassette turned, her words came babbling off the tape, into his ears, and out onto the page. He could get five or six pages done in these early-morning stints, not just transcribing but shaping and editing so that he was actually turning her rambling narrative into a draft of what he now saw as an exciting manuscript. It had a primitive eloquence to it that Marissa's more sophisticated tirades had never approached.

In fairness, McCracken had to admit that the injustices of which Marissa had complained had been mostly theoretical. The disadvantages against which she and her enlightened sisters were struggling might have been real enough, but they were less dramatic than those of poor Wanda, whose consciousness had never been raised, who had never read Gloria Steinem, let alone Simone de Beauvoir, and who had been forced to liberate herself with whatever intellectual tools she could find at hand. For Wanda, it had been no mere matter of principle but a life-and-death struggle.

The irony was that Marissa's two-year campaign of feminist argument and protest had been invaluable in preparing McCracken to listen to Wanda with a better ear and to understand the implications of what she was saying. He couldn't possibly have done it if Marissa's complaints hadn't educated him and brought him along to a place where he could fill in the gaps and make the right connections. The fact that Wanda had been sexually exploited in so spectacular a way made her a possible feminist heroine, because her experience was emblematic of what other women feared, an extension or extrapolation of their own worst moments.

The rules of their collaboration were complicated too. McCracken knew that other people would assume that he too would take advantage of Wanda's availability. There would be sniggering references in print and knowing looks and winks from the interviewers on television programs. He knew he couldn't prevent that kind of thing, and he understood that Wanda wouldn't mind, having developed an admirable toughness about such matters. He even realized that it might be useful for the promotion of the book. But he was sufficiently self-aware to realize that it would be risky, to say the least. In a way that Marissa had never suspected, it turned out that she'd been right about his need for a little consciousness raising and liberation.

At the beginning, he'd decided that it would be better to keep the relationship with Wanda strictly business. He had promised himself that he would not go to bed with her. There was a kind of quixotic appeal to the idea of not taking advantage of someone who, in the parlance of the fifties, was so spectacularly "easy." It would also be a way of meeting those sniggers and winks. But his unilateral resolution had not taken into account the fact that Wanda might be uneasy about his failure to make the inevitable moves. She had been so conditioned by her experience with Lucid—and before that too—that she took it as an insult if men didn't try to fuck her.

"You're not queer, are you?" she asked, the second or third time they got together to work. This was when they were still in New York.

No, he told her, he wasn't.

"Then what is it? I don't do anything for you? I don't turn you on? You like fatties or something? Kids?"

"No, no. It isn't that. You're just fine. You're an attractive woman, as I'm sure you know. It's just that I don't want to let anything get in the way of the book . . ."

She nodded but didn't believe it. The question was still hanging and it loomed larger and larger with the passage of time. McCracken tried to see it from her side and imagined how it would appear to someone who'd gone through what she had. That powerlessness Marissa had

spoken about was inescapable and basic with Wanda. It wasn't just a
speaking point to say that she had been robbed of authority even over
her own body.

It was, he had no doubt, a tough thing to have to adjust to, but he
was sophisticated enough to understand that there are ways a mind
can escape from almost any predicament. Was it too much to suppose
that she was identifying with her tormentors and exploiters? Was she
perhaps converting the situation to some contrary and more bearable
version in which she was the powerful figure and the men were her
slaves, her toys and playthings, not only craving her favors but depen-
dent upon her for their very livings?

If something like that were true, then his own disinclination to
complicate their partnership wouldn't mean much to her. She would
see it only as a lack of interest that would be a threat—because if she
couldn't arouse his lust, then she couldn't control him. Obviously, a
woman like Wanda would feel the need to tame and control those men
who were using her and penetrating her in every possible way and
through every available orifice.

In other and shorter words, if he wouldn't fuck her, then what
might he do to her that would be even worse?

A tough and terrible question. Still, he hoped there might be some
way they might find out of their predicament. What had failed in his
relationship with Marissa might be just the right thing for Wanda.

And maybe it would have worked if they'd had a chance. Who
could say what might have happened if they'd met every day for a
couple of hours, much the way a therapist and his patient meet every
day to explore together the old injuries and complaints that have af-
fected at least one of them and more likely than not, both. The quality
of attention, the eager listening of an alert intelligence, is a part of the
cure, and even though McCracken was no therapist he didn't think he
was flattering himself to claim a quality of humane attention that
might do her some good. To have a man interested in her brain more
than in a few of her nerve endings would be a novel situation.

But they never had that chance. They'd been working together for
only a week or so when Wanda showed up one morning looking like
death warmed over. Pete had asked her whether she felt up to working. She nodded but he wasn't convinced. He asked her what had
happened.

"Oh, Dan had a little party last night. A business thing for some of
those people from the cosmetics company, you know?"

"No, I don't know, actually. Tell me."

"Some of the distributors. I don't understand it. They've got these regional outfits the main company sells to, and then these regional guys go around and put the stuff in the actual stores."

"And?"

"And it was important that those regional operations guys be enthusiastic about the new line."

"I still don't get it," he said. "What happened?" But by now the question was no longer a request for information. It had become a delaying stratagem. He'd had a flash, a dismaying leap to what seemed to him a likely but nonetheless unacceptable surmise.

"What do you think happened? I fucked them. Or went down on them. Or both. Who remembers? It was a gang bang, you know?"

"I see," he said, not knowing what else to say.

"Do you?" she asked. "Do you see?"

"I don't know," he admitted. "Probably not. What do you want me to say?"

"I want you to tell me the truth," she said. "I mean, does it get you hot? Or angry? Or make you want to laugh? Or disgust you? You just sit there asking questions and writing things down, but I never know that anybody's home."

"I don't know what I feel about it," he said. "Not disgusted. Maybe a little hot. I've never been part of a gang bang and I guess I'm curious. But not all that curious. I think I'd feel bad afterwards, which is more important than how I'd feel before it. Or during. How did you feel afterwards? How do you feel now?"

"It's what I do. Like it's my job. So I'm not even really there."

"But you are there."

"Part of me is. But I can be doing it and thinking of something I saw in a movie or something that happened ten years ago or even a dress I saw in a magazine ad. Anything. So the real me isn't actually there, not unless I want it to be. It's tough work, though. I mean, like shoveling snow or washing floors. It's fucking hard work." She laughed at her proto-joke.

He still didn't know what to say.

"The thing that bothered me most was what I was going to say to you today, which is kind of dumb. I mean, nothing gets you hard, hunh? That's scary for somebody in my line of work. Makes me think I'm over the hill and losing it. Makes me wonder if I shouldn't maybe pack it in one of these days. And what is there for me to do then except shovel snow and wash floors for real?"

"Is that your idea or Dan's?" he asked.

"What idea?"

"That the only alternatives are fucking a whole roomful of business-men or washing floors."

"Oh, no. That's the truth. Or if you really want to know, the truth is probably worse. Girls like me wind up dead of an overdose. Or they turn into bag ladies and wander around mumbling to themselves and rummaging in trash cans."

"There are other possibilities in life, though, aren't there?"

"Oh, sure. I could go and clean myself up. Learn how to type, maybe, and get a job in Omaha or Kansas City or one of those clean places in the Midwest where the wind blows all the dirt away."

"You could. Or it could even be better than that, you know? You wouldn't have to be a typist."

"What the hell else am I going to do? I never graduated high school, for God's sake. You think there are a lot of want ads for ex-porno stars with no education?"

"There's going to be a lot of money coming out of this book. There's money coming out of the cosmetics deal. Don't you get to keep any of it? All you have to do is invest your share of it and live off the in-come."

"Dan handles all that for me. He takes care of me that way."

"I hope so."

They were in the living room of Pete McCracken's apartment. Or, actually, it was the apartment of a friend of Pete's, out of town for a couple of months to do research for a magazine series. He'd sublet his apartment to Pete as a favor when Marissa had thrown Pete out. If you leaned out of the window, you could look down the street and get a thin slice of a view of the Hudson. They were in Pete's friend's study, a pleasant book-lined room.

"Have you read all those books?"

"It's not my apartment," he explained. "I'm only subletting it."

"You think the guy whose apartment it is read all those books?"

"I'd guess he's read most of them, sure. I've read a lot of them. Why?"

"It's something I like to do. But who has the time? I'm a slow reader, you know?"

"You can speed up if you work at it."

"No, I like to read and then stop and think about it. It's a way of getting away."

"Is that what you want to do? Get away?"

"No, not really. I mean, sure, I'd like that but I don't believe in it any more. I'd never make it. And even if I did, it would only be with some other guy taking me over, with the same setup as I've got now but with somebody different than Dan and maybe worse for all I know."

"You could be on your own?"

"Nah, I don't have the guts for it. Or the brains. Dan says my brain is in my twat."

"But that's not true, is it?"

"Sure, it's true. What else am I doing?"

"You're working on a book?"

"No, no. You're the one who's working on a book. I'm just doing what I do and letting you watch, just like in the movies. And the readers will be jerking off, just the way they do in the theaters. Dan says it's a great swimming pool full of cum, and it's money in the bank."

"What about women reading the book?"

"I guess a few women might read the book," she said. "But just to imagine what it's like to be me. To scare themselves. Or to get off on it. The way they like to imagine getting raped or being a hooker but just for a couple of hours."

"You don't think there could be anything more in it? You don't think it could say something about relationships between men and women, and what we do to each other, and how we could change things?"

"You're a nice guy," Wanda said, "but you're full of shit, you know?"

"Why?"

"I think you get off on not fucking me, and how noble it makes you feel."

"No, I think that if I fucked you—or if we fucked each other—it would change things between us. It'd have to be better or worse. Because either I'd be using you, just the way those men did, and maybe just the way Dan does, or else we'd become friends, and I'd want to help you, and it wouldn't work because you wouldn't let me. Dan certainly wouldn't. And either way, I'd feel bad. Which is what I want to avoid. If it feels good, do it. You must have heard that one. But the other side of that is if it feels bad, don't do it. And my guess is that this'd feel bad, one way or another."

"I don't know. It's scary. I keep having the feeling that if you don't fuck me one way, you're going to fuck me another."

"Does everybody fuck you?"

"They mostly want to. And they mostly try."

"And you aren't bothered by that?"

"Shit, no. I let them. I lie back and let them, and it makes them crazy. It's as if they didn't count, and some of them know that, they figure that out and it makes them really angry. And then the fucking turns into a kind of a war and I like that because I know I'm going to win. They all think they've got such big guns, you know, but after they shoot off once or twice, they're left with these poor shriveled little weenies they try to hide. Like I've never seen one before. In a way, it's really a funny kind of business."

"I guess it is," McCracken said.

"Oh, come on! What are you trying to do, get me to ask you for it? Is that the game? You want me to invite you? Okay! Let's do it. How about tearing off a quick piece?"

"Just to prove how little it matters? Just to see my big gun shrivel up? Is that it?"

"No. Yes. Maybe partly. I don't know. It just makes me feel spooked. I don't know what the game is here, and I keep thinking that it's dangerous not to know."

"I scare you?"

"Yeah, a little."

"What scares you about me? I don't think of myself as a scary person, particularly."

"The way you come on as a nice guy. It's a setup. Got to be! And one way or another, there's going to be the old catch. I'm going to get it, with that typewriter and tape recorder, and every one of those books on the shelf all shoved up my twat."

"You really think that that's all there is? No other possibilities? No other choices?"

"None that I've seen, mister."

"I don't know what to say. I think you're wrong, but I don't know that I can prove it."

"It's a power trip, that's what it is. That's what it's got to be," she said. "You're just showing off, figuring that if you don't fuck me, then I'll think about it, the way a kid thinks about whatever she can't have. It's a mind-fuck, but that's just another kind of fucking. It all depends on your tastes, I guess."

"You think?"

"I know. Look, let's cool it for today, okay? You've got enough to keep yourself busy there with your machines. I'll see you tomorrow."

And she walked out, a touchy tough kid, trying to keep him from seeing that her pride had been hurt.

He spent the afternoon typing up their conversation, leaving out most of what he said but putting down her words verbatim, along with descriptions of what she'd been wearing, how she looked, what her gestures had been. Sometimes she made a fist and looked as though she was going to take a bite out of the knuckles when she was thinking. Sometimes, when she was trying to twist the truth, she acted it out, twisting a strand of hair above her ear. What he wanted to convey was the impression she'd left with him that she really wasn't such a hard case, that she was still a kid in a lot of ways. That she was hurting was not necessarily an invitation for someone else to hurt her more.

He felt the temptation. He knew what it was that Lucid had found and had been able to market so well. But as if he were proving something to Marissa and showing her that he wasn't anywhere near the monster she'd called him, he wanted to be decent to Wanda. Or maybe he wanted to prove it to himself.

In the late afternoon, he walked over to Broadway, took a subway down to Times Square, and wandered around the dreadful porno houses on Forty-second Street and Eighth Avenue until he found one that was showing a Wanda Lathem film. *Tickled Pink* was the name of this one. He went inside and watched the film for a while, and saw Wanda's performance in a complicated series of athletic positions in an oddly chosen series of locations. The finale was with Wanda and three men with whom she managed simultaneous intercourse on a merry-go-round (admittedly, they weren't up on a horse but in one of the carts). By the time the film had reached that point, the erection Pete had experienced in the first few scenes had faded. It just wasn't sexy any more. It wasn't exciting or even very interesting. He looked around at some of the other men in the not very crowded theater. Most of them were staring at the screen, but there were two or three who were asleep. One was snoring. A dangerous thing to do in this neighborhood, McCracken thought.

He walked back uptown, feeling mostly lousy. He wondered whether he ought to be doing this book. Was he up to it? Was it the wrong kind of thing for him to be doing now? If he quit, whom would Castle and Lucid get that would be better? Some younger, tougher gunslinger, who'd not only fuck her but maybe write a chapter describing what it was like . . .

He knew he was being a sap. He knew it was a silly and sentimental idea, but on that walk uptown it occurred to him for the first time to take her away somewhere, to hide out for a while and help her get her head straight. He even thought of his brother's place up in Maine.

A dumb idea.

But it kept coming back.

*

Within the next few days, they both realized that their collaboration on the book was only an excuse, an occasion for another, much more important transaction that was going on. They were struggling with each other, engaged in a debate about their fundamental beliefs, a moral and intellectual struggle that felt like mortal combat. Heart and soul and body too, they fought about what life was like. McCracken remembered a detached phrase from one of his teachers at St. John's, an old philosopher who drank more than was good for him and wrote better and clearer prose than most of his colleagues liked. In an ethics course, Professor Haverton had begun one of his lectures by announcing, "There are different ideas of excellence, of what men should do, and what they deserve . . ."

In that shabby classroom with the glare of morning light dazzling in from the tall windows, McCracken had been struck by how much of the world's experience, both its triumphs and its disasters, that phrase invoked. What else did people fight about except their differing ideas of excellence?

It was Wanda's conviction that the best and safest course was indestructibility, to be endlessly fuckable but unaffected by it, to be attractive enough to confine all men within her narrowed vision of what the dangers were of the social and natural world. McCracken's scrupulous disinclination to use Wanda was just what she couldn't tolerate. Her suspicion of his motives and her inability even to admit exceptions to her dismal view of men offended McCracken because it tended to confirm Marissa's unfair appraisal of his character and their failed marriage.

And of course the terms in which he and Wanda struggled were ridiculous and inelegant. She wore more and more provocative clothing, outrageous miniskirts and sheer blouses with nothing underneath so he could see the dark circles of her areolas. She described in juicy detail the fuckings she'd endured, which was great for the book but also served as a challenge to him, an invitation but a taunting one. He saw it as daring him to try his best on her. Or his worst. And see if she even noticed.

In one sense, that was exactly the difficulty, that she could make no distinctions while he was convinced that there was more to a man than lust and aggression. Life was more than an unlovely struggle in which we try to assert ourselves in an awful void.

Not that anybody who lived and worked with Dan Lucid would have much occasion to celebrate the refinements of life. McCracken kept asking Wanda about Lucid, what he was like, what he had made Wanda do, and how she felt about him. She was delighted to recount the indignities she had suffered and the humiliations. She was proud of herself for the oddest things.

"I remember once he was raising money for one of the movies. There was a party for some people in Miami, where there's a lot of funny money, from drugs, I guess. Anyway, we were down there to see some investors for a film. And Dan decided that it would be fun for me to be the door prize. Nothing special about that, I guess, but that's what bothered him. He wanted it to be interesting and have a little class. So he figured out that I'd be blindfolded, and that whoever won could come and fuck me before dinner, and that after dinner I'd have to guess who it was. That way, none of the guys would feel that they'd really lost out. And the thing of it was, I sat there at dinner at this guy's house in Coconut Grove, and I felt as if they'd all fucked me, even though it had been just one guy who came almost right away. I mean, I blushed a lot and felt like a big fucking cow. But it was a great success, that party, and Dan raised his quarter of a million or whatever it was. We got the movie made."

"Isn't that more than most of the movies cost to make?"

"Oh, yeah. Usually they're pretty cheap. But Dan wanted some outdoor stuff, some production values. I think this one had a scene on a merry-go-round, and we had to rent a whole amusement park."

"Did you get paid any more?" McCracken asked.

"In a way. It got plowed back into the business, so I had the benefit of it. It was a stepping-stone . . ."

"Was it worth it?"

"It wasn't such a big deal. I mean, to you, every little hard-on is a big deal, and you probably take cold showers or run off to church and confess or something. I could show you what a big deal it isn't. Like that," she said, and snapped her fingers. "Or maybe not quite that fast." She laughed.

"But what if I'm right?" he asked. "What if we do something like that and we find out that we like each other? Or that we like each other more, because we already like each other. You'd just go back to

Dan and put on a blindfold and fuck anybody he told you to fuck who'd won you as a party favor? How would I feel about that?"

"You want to take me away from all this?" she asked. "That old chestnut? That's almost as old as 'How did a nice girl like you get into a business like this?' "

"That's what's going to sell the book, though. Some of those old lines are true, which is why they last so long."

"So then what? You take me off to some gorgeous place in the mountains or down at the shore, and you fuck me a couple of dozen times, and then you're bored. I mean, you're no different from anybody else. You've climbed Mount Everest. But you sure as shit don't want to live there. So you climb back down and go on with your life, whatever that is, and Mount Everest is still out there in the cold. That's another old chestnut, and that one's true too."

"But Lucid is different," he said. "Lucid is the pits, and it's safe there because when you're at the bottom, there's no place left to fall. All you have to do is convince yourself that you like it there."

"I do like it."

"Without the drugs?"

"Come on, don't be such a jerk," she said. "Everybody uses drugs."

"Not like Dog Yummies. Not to keep their friends and lovers in line. Not the way he does."

"You watch it, mister. You fuck around with him and he's not going to like it. You paint him as some kind of monster in this book, and it'll be your ass, I'm telling you. And he's nasty when he's crossed."

"I have no doubt."

"He could fire you off this project, you know. Any time. Any fucking time."

"That's true. And if I weren't satisfied that I had a free hand to do it the best way I knew how, I could quit just like that. Any fucking time."

"And are you? Going to quit?" she asked.

"I don't know. Not yet," he said.

She got up, grabbed her coat, and went to the door. "You really can be a boring little man, you know that? I mean, talk about self-righteous and all that? You don't fool me, not a bit. You're just like everybody else. No better. Not a damn bit better."

"Not a bit better than Dan Lucid? I'd be sorry if that were true."

"I'll see you tomorrow," she said. "If I feel like it. If I think I can stand it."

"If I can stand it, you can stand it," he said. "You just don't know how to deal with not getting fucked over. It's not so tough. Try it."

She looked back at him, and then left, slamming the door behind her.

He figured the odds were about even. She'd either get to the point where she trusted him a little and began to like herself or she'd be unable to do that and would set up some situation where Lucid could rescue her and pull her back down to where it was awful and safe.

But unless she did something like that to interfere with the process, McCracken had a growing conviction that they'd make a break for it. What she'd asked about what would happen after they took off together was a tough and important question, though. What the hell was he going to do with her after that first couple of weeks? Was he prepared for that kind of responsibility, not just to her but to anyone?

But especially to her. She was right in a lot of ways about some of those dark impulses. There was an awful fascination she had, a kind of challenge to men that he felt just as other men did. Even Dan Lucid. The issue, though, was how he behaved, given that feeling.

Some men were better than Daniel Lucid. And McCracken sure as hell hoped he was one of them.

What happened was close to what McCracken had expected, if not exactly on target, which wasn't surprising. If one could figure exactly what was going to happen, it'd hardly be worthwhile getting out of bed and going through the motions of living. One could just lie there, stare at the ceiling, and imagine the experience. In any case, the one thing he couldn't have predicted, not having quite the vision or the arrogance to allow for it, was that Wanda would translate her insecurity about a man who didn't immediately jump into the sack with her first into a challenge, then into something like a child's curiosity, and finally into actual desire. She began to dress more demurely, and to please him her talk was less liberally peppered with four-letter words. There was a different tone altogether to her recollections about her career in pornographic films. At one point, she broke off and shook her head, saying, "I don't know. It's just not going to work, this business. I'm hung up on you. It's like a sappy schoolgirl's crush. It's nuts!"

"That's very flattering."

"No, not really. I'm not exactly your average schoolgirl, am I?"

"Who says I go for schoolgirls?"

"The thing is, I think about you all the time, even when I'm balling Dan or one of his friends. And I have these crazy thoughts that I'm betraying you. What's really betraying you is that I don't want to talk about this stuff any more, which means it's impossible to do the book, which means that there's no reason for these goddamn meetings any more."

"What can we do to make it better."

"Fuck me, for Christ's sake!"

"And then what?"

"Whatever you want."

"It's not that easy."

"I didn't think it would be," she said.

"You like your life? You like what you're doing? You like the way Lucid treats you?"

"The God's truth?"

"The truth," he said.

"No," she said. "No, no, no. I don't like it. I do it, and I tell myself how great I am to be able to stand it, but I don't like it."

"You want to leave it? Leave him?"

"He'll come after us!"

"You're a free human being. This is America. There aren't slaves here. You can do whatever you want. If you were married to him, you could divorce him. And if you work for someone, you can always quit."

"He'll still come after us."

"He's got to find us. And there are police. There are private body-guards. There are ways of surviving. We're not helpless."

"If you say so."

"Then we'll take off," he said. "Today. Now."

"Not yet," she said. "Give me five minutes first."

"Sure," he said. "What for?"

"Take off your clothes," she told him.

*

The doorbell kept on ringing.

"Get dressed," he said. "I'll go see who it is, but it could be trouble. If you don't hear me call up to you, then you go down the back stairs and out the kitchen door. You hear me?"

"You don't think it could be some kid selling Girl Scout cookies?"

"Not at nine o'clock at night. I wouldn't count on it."

There was another long wavering peal from the old electric bell.

"Yeah, I'm coming," McCracken called down. He had an aluminum tennis racket that he could use as a weapon. He guessed it was better than nothing. "Don't try to go anywhere," he told Wanda. "Just hide out there in the woodshed."

"You've got to be kidding," she said.

"You can't climb the hill, and if you go around to the front, he'll see you."

"Or they will," she said.

"Jesus!" He hadn't even thought of that, but it figured. Assuming the worst—that it was Lucid—there was no reason to think he'd be alone. "You ready?" he asked.

"Oh, sure."

"Then go," he said, and he went down the front stairs, jiggling the tennis racket in his right hand. From the front hall, he tried to peer out through the little windows that surrounded the big Georgian door.

It wasn't Lucid, though. It was Leonard Castle, sporting a jaunty houndstooth cap and a stadium coat with a mouton collar.

"What are *you* doing here?" McCracken asked.

"I could ask you that very question," Castle said. "Are you going to invite me in? Are we perhaps going to play tennis?"

"Oh, sure. Come on in," McCracken said, and he called out to Wanda that it was okay. "Welcome to Maine," he said. "What's going on?"

"You have any hot coffee?" Castle asked. "You have any rum or brandy to put in it?"

They went back to the kitchen to get something to warm Castle up. "You aren't just passing through, are you?" McCracken asked.

"Not exactly. I flew up to Portland and rented a car and drove on up here. It only took five hours. A mere nothing."

"A problem?"

"The problem is that you're a fool. You think you're safe and sound up here? You think it's hard to find you? It only took me four telephone calls and a little thinking. And if I can do it, it's not exactly impossible for Lucid."

"He's mad, hunh?" Wanda asked.

"He's talking about shooting people with cannons. I'm on the list, but I don't think I'm at the top. I think that honor probably belongs to one of you. And the other is a close second."

"I was afraid of that," Wanda said.

"I guess I should have called you," McCracken conceded.

"That would have been nice, yeah," Castle said.

"I only figured that if I kept you out of it, I'd be protecting you. I didn't want to get you involved."

"I'm only protected if he thinks I don't know where you've gone. It doesn't do me a whole lot of good if he's sure I'm lying when I tell him I haven't the foggiest idea where to find you. That I don't even know how to get in touch with you, for Christ's sake! The truth is irrelevant."

"I'm sorry."

"Is there a telephone up here?"

"No. I thought it'd be safer not to have one."

"No, no, no. You're not better off if you can't hear warnings. If people can't call you, that doesn't mean you're safe. What's going on with you two, anyway?"

"It's a long story," McCracken said.

"Maybe not so long," Wanda said. "The short version is that I don't want to go back to Dan. I don't want to do those movies any more. I want to have a life . . ."

Castle looked at her, looked at McCracken, then looked back at Wanda. "Good for you," he said. "I'm not surprised. I'd kind of thought that might happen."

"You did?" Wanda asked. "Why didn't you give one of us the hint?"

"I didn't want to spoil it. If it was going to happen, it had to be your idea. You two had to come up with it on your own."

McCracken nodded.

"He's pissed off, though, right?" Wanda asked.

"What do you think?" Castle asked.

"And what do we do?" McCracken asked.

"For one thing, you leave here. You go someplace where nobody would think of looking for you. Your brother's summer house isn't exactly obscure and remote. Go someplace nobody goes. Someplace neither of you has ever been. And let me know where you are!"

The kettle began to whistle. Wanda poured the boiling water through the coffee and then poured the coffee into mugs. "There's brandy," she said.

"Here," McCracken said. He passed the bottle to Castle along with the coffee mug.

"Have you ever been to Biloxi?" Castle asked.

Neither of them had.

"Someplace down there on the Gulf coast might do. It's far away. The weather is nice. And nobody goes there. Anywhere from Pensacola over to Biloxi. You find yourself a quiet spot that looks pretty and work on the book down there. This is nuts."

"And then what?" McCracken asked. "We've got to come up for air sooner or later."

"Sure, but later is better than sooner. Give him a month or two, and he'll find himself another girl. And with his piece of this book, he'll be in a better mood than he is just at the moment."

"A piece of this book? What for?" McCracken asked.

"Because we have a deal. He's a son of a bitch, but he's the one who made this happen. She's her own boss and she can do whatever she wants. He's got no claim on her. But he does have a claim on the book."

"I don't know . . ."

"I do. And I'm telling you, Pete, that the deal has got to stay the way it is. When you're screwing somebody, you don't ever want to go too far with it, because after a point your patsy's going to turn on you. Leave him a little room, a little something."

"He's right," Wanda said.

"All right," McCracken agreed.

"Good. Now, as long as I've dragged my ass up here, you got something for me to see?"

"Oh, sure. Have you eaten?"

"I stopped at a place on the road. I had a two-pound lobster. It was terrific. You have a place for me to sleep?"

"Oh, yeah. There are all kinds of rooms up here. It's like a boardinghouse," Wanda said.

"That's what my brother says every summer," McCracken told them.

"All right, you get me the manuscript and I'll take it to bed with me, and you two go and pack. In the morning, we'll take off at seven o'clock so we can catch the ten o'clock plane out of Portland. You'll go straight on down to Pensacola. And then you'll call me. I only hope this goddamn book is worth all this trouble."

"She is," McCracken insisted.

"I never doubted that," Castle said.

And in the morning, having read the 160-odd pages McCracken had given him the evening before, he was able to tell them that everything would be all right. "It's just a matter of time and a little diplomacy. But the book is fine. It will do fine. And if the pie is big enough, it won't be so terrible a thing for Mr. Lucid if he has to share it a little more fairly than he'd intended to do. It's going to be okay."

In the car, on the way down to Portland, McCracken mentioned that a lot of the credit had to go to Marissa and the women's lib stuff she'd been reading and thinking and talking about for the past few years. To her and her damned consciousness-raising group, and to their divorce.

Castle nodded as though that were a fascinating piece of news and had never occurred to him before. He managed to let it appear that his smile was not one of self-congratulation but of approval for the terrific job Pete McCracken had done.

It was a terrific job. But they'd both done it.

*

He had the cab slow down but he told the driver not to stop at Susan's apartment house. He passed it and then had the cabbie pull up fifty yards down the block and on the other side of the street. Castle was being foxy. Literally. He had figured out that the safe way to do this was to go into the vestibule of some other building and stand there for a while, watching to see what the traffic was like and noting what other vehicles stopped and what pedestrians seemed to be loitering inexplicably.

Speed wasn't the object now, but safety. His own and Susan's.

7

"Well," he said, "you know how it ended up. McCracken wrote the book and it was terrific, every bit as good as Leonard thought it would be. And it turned Wanda Lathem into a legitimate celebrity, which is no mean trick, and it turned her life around, which is maybe more interesting but not the kind of thing that it's easy to talk about. Certainly not on television."

Susan Flowers nodded, took another tiny sip of her very good Graves, and prompted him by admitting that there were limitations to all media.

"Sure, sure," Barrett said. "That's easy to say, and then you think it lets you off the hook. But it doesn't. This idea you've got of doing a segment on Leonard Castle, for instance, is going to be troublesome because you can't really show what he does. You can talk about it, but that's death on television. And you can't show people thinking."

"You think he put a lot of thought into this?" she asked.

"It's chemistry. Human chemistry. And he came up with the formula. If it were a blend of tea or a perfume, he'd be a millionaire. But it's tougher than that. He knew that McCracken was exactly ready for Wanda Lathem and all the issues that she was dragging along with her, like those clanking chains on Dickens' Ghost of Christmas Past. It was a brilliant stroke!"

"And what happened to Lucid?"

"Fundamentally, Castle bribed him. But even there, he was clever about it. He had to figure, first of all, that the guy was motivated more by greed than by lust, which is true but wasn't obvious to everyone.

And then he had to figure out a way of bribing him that wasn't going to wreck the deal for everyone else."

"And how did that work?"

"Well, I can tell you, but that part of it has to be off the record. Okay?"

"Okay. Off the record."

"He reworked the contract to cut the pie in three pieces, a third to Wanda, a third to Lucid, and a third to McCracken. And then he offered to buy Lucid out for a hundred thousand dollars, out of his own money. That convinced Lucid that his third was worth more than that, which it was, but only if Lucid butted out and let Wanda do the publicity tour and make the appearances on all those interview shows, and do all the press interviews . . . All that bit. It put the book over. That and the timing, the fact that we were just about ready to have a porn star talking to us over our second cups of coffee or whatever. So Lucid came out okay."

"Wasn't there anything in the book that had to be toned down or cut out?"

"Here and there, we had to soften it up a little, but if you read it hard and hold it up to the light, you can see it pretty clearly. He's not a nice man. And he's kind of proud of that, in a way, so he let us get a lot of him down on paper. McCracken wasn't unhappy."

"And all that was Castle's doing?"

Barrett nodded. "All I had to do was run through the manuscript and change *which* and *that* every now and then. It was a piece of cake."

"Then why did you leave Barbizon?"

"I'd been thinking about it for a while. I'd been hitting the bottle pretty hard, and I knew I had to change the way I live or stop living." He smiled, raised his Perrier and lime in a kind of toast, and took a sip. "Terrible stuff. Tastes just like water, you know? Anyway, I'd been thinking about how the grass might be just a little greener on the other side of the fence. And Castle helped me out."

"You mean you're going to do McCracken's job?"

"More or less. A different kind of project, but, yes, I'm the writer this time. Or editor, really, because there's a whole lot of manuscript."

"Another biography?"

"An autobiography."

"I don't suppose you can tell me who it is?"

He shook his head. "Not yet. Maybe in a couple of months."

"Off the record? I promise, we're not out to get you. Or anyone. It's just that I'm fascinated by Leonard Castle and I think there's going to be a terrific story there sooner or later, one way or another."

"Oh, yes. If you can get it on film or tape or whatever you use. If you could get the sense of what he does and how he does it, sure, it could be a good story."

"Who is it, then? Who's your subject?"

"Off the record, now!"

She held up her hand like a witness, swearing.

"Helen Burke."

"Terrific!"

"I fly out to see her on Tuesday. That's why I couldn't make it next week."

"Well, good luck. I'm sure it will be exciting."

"Hollywood in the good old days. The Glory That Was Tinseltown!"

"And he just had this lying around?"

"I don't know. He said he'd been looking for the right person for some time. I took that as a compliment."

"I'm sure it was meant that way," Susan said. "Look, when you get back, let's keep in touch. Maybe this will be the right way to get Castle on the screen and show how he operates."

"I'll be glad to keep in touch, but I don't think you're going to get anywhere. Unless you want to have a truck follow him around when he walks. He says he does his best thinking when he walks around on the city streets. Not that it's terrific television to show a guy walking . . ."

"It might make a good fifteen seconds."

" 'Like a long-legged fly upon the water,' " Barrett said.

Susan finished the Yeats line, " 'His mind moves upon silence.' "

"Very good," he said. "Not that it was a test. I just think out loud sometimes."

He didn't look like a happy man. Susan had the impression from the way he held his glass, and from the way he held himself, that he might shatter at any moment, or even explode into thousands of tiny bits. He had an air of refinement which was neither required nor even permitted by the career he'd made for himself.

As if he'd intuited her thought and were commenting on it, he said, out of the blue, "Publishing has changed from what it used to be. I went into it for the simple reason that I loved books, loved well-made sentences, and wanted a life where I could surround myself with what I admired and keep company with people who shared my . . . my respect. But there's no respect any more. Not for sentences or for books. Not even for people. That's what I like about Leonard Castle. He finds ways to admit a little decency here and there, even on a project like Wanda Lathem's book, where you wouldn't expect anything but the air of an outhouse. Or some other kind of house."

A smallish man whose hair had receded to leave a monk's tonsure, he wore immaculate tweeds and a suede vest with brass buttons. When he stretched his legs, Susan had noticed his oxblood cordovan shoes as highly polished as if he'd picked them out of a shop window and put them on five minutes before. He wore these clothes as a proclamation of those standards he was unable to consult in the course of business.

Susan understood what he was saying. Why he was saying these things now and to her was another question. As likely as not it was the momentary feeling of complicity and understanding that resulted from her lucky recognition of the line from Yeats.

"How long has it been since you've worked on a book you liked?" she asked.

"I can hardly remember. But years ago, I published poetry and decent fiction. Back then, every house had a couple of poets on their list, as a matter of social responsibility. As a matter of honor! Not any more. They don't even bother with first novels, most of them. They're all run like fast-food chains with Whoppers packed in plastic—except that ours are literary."

"And you've left all that?"

"For a while. We'll see what happens. My half of what this Helen Burke book does could be enough for me to retire on. Or if the book does less well but my part of it looks okay, I can find another assignment like this one. Sooner or later one of them will hit. It's a way out. A better way out than a lot of people ever find."

"And there was nothing you had to do for Leonard to set this up for you?"

"Nothing to speak of," Barrett insisted. "I've got to run," he said. He signaled for the waiter.

"No, no," Susan said. "I had this nice wine and you just had water. Besides, I'm still on an expense account."

"Thank you," he said, remembering his freedom and smiling.

*

Helen Burke had been working on her autobiography for twenty years. There were two Louis Vuitton trunks filled with the spiral-bound notebooks in which she had set down her recollections in a spidery but legible hand in various colors of ink; there were also brown manila envelopes into which she had packed away old letters from friends, enemies, lovers, and strangers, as well as occasional press clippings and even theater programs and menus from restaurants or the dining salons of ocean liners. There was no shortage of material.

The trouble was that Miss Burke was aware that her name was legendary. Along with Bette Davis and Joan Crawford, she had been one of the undisputed queens of the silver screen. Her films still played, not so much on late-night television as on PBS and at film festivals in art houses and in courses in universities. Miss Burke felt a certain obligation, a responsibility to what her public had made of her and what it seemed to require of her in exchange, but she was not quite certain how to discharge this duty. Tell the unvarnished truth? Let them see what their adoration had done to her? Or give them yet another of her performances, which was what they expected and what she had learned to trust?

Between revelation and concealment, or candor and dissimulation, she vacillated, knowing perfectly well that it was her own indecision that kept postponing the publication of what would obviously be one of the great Hollywood stories. She owed it to her public and to herself to have that story written and published properly. She didn't need the money, but she accepted large advances from publishers as her proper due—and then returned them when they failed to show her the respect to which she thought herself entitled, hounding her to meet deadlines, or slavering for intimate revelations of the bad behavior of some of the troubled men and women of great talent and great soul with whom she had lived and worked over the years. It was quite within her power to look some editor straight in the eye, tell him he was a vulgar little man, and write him a check for half a million dollars, returning the advance payment in a gesture that she was to describe in the next spiral-bound notebook as one of characteristic grandeur.

She could always sell the book to another publisher the next week, and for even more money than she had returned. In any event, she hadn't spent their filthy lucre but merely put it into certificates of deposit where they had been generating interest—that she of course retained.

In her way, then, she had become a legend of publishing as well as of the halcyon days of the movie business. A legend, or even, in certain circles, a joke. Her book had been gestating for the better part of two decades, after all, and no fewer than nine different houses had signed

contracts for it. What was different now was that her doctor had
suggested that she ought to put her affairs in order.

It had a chilling sort of sound. "You mean I'm going to die?" she'd
demanded.

"Yes," he'd said, unflinching. "We're all going to die. We're all terminal, as some wise man has suggested. But some of us are more
terminal than others."

"A year?"

"About that. A lot depends on you, how you take it and how you
take care of yourself. And what you have to live for."

"Will there be much pain?" she had asked, not sniveling. That
wouldn't have been any way for a Helen Burke character to read the
line.

"No, I'll see to that."

"Thank you. And thank you for your honesty."

"I owe you that. I wish I could do more."

Miss Gargan had helped her outside to the limousine that was waiting for them on Bay State Road, and they had been driven out to
Logan and flown back to Nantucket. She had felt like a sack of goods
being handled and hauled. The bleak winter day hardly registered
except as what was right and appropriate to set the mood of the action. Or like background music that was supposed to indicate feeling
but not be obtrusive or distracting. A gray, dank day with an ominous
bite to it that made one look up for snowflakes. Miss Gargan, her
companion and—almost—her friend, had responded to her employer's
mood and kept quiet, letting the older woman gaze out of the windows
and gather her thoughts.

There were no other houses visible from her house, only rolling
meadow and the little bluff that fell away to the beach below. To the
east, there was nothing then but water and then Portugal, which was
why the house was called Estoril West. Only Helen Burke's more
literate and intelligent friends got the joke, realizing that Estoril was
the place where deposed royalty went to live out their last days in
comfortable exile.

She could see the water from her bedroom window. She found it
soothing to look out and watch the endless motion and the infinite
variation of color and mood of the sea. Into that water she had
dumped rages, grudges, regrets, and, yes, triumphs and successes too.
Nothing mattered, nothing could stand up to the challenge of that
inhuman perspective. She had thought often of following along with
those daydreams and recollections, and having at last jettisoned all

that cargo of caring, walking down the weather-beaten wooden staircase to the water's edge, to keep on going into a last fade-out. Now that the appropriate moment had arrived, she knew she lacked the courage. It would be heart failure or Dr. Matthews' needle, but not that floating watery end she had imagined and almost longed for.

She went to her closet, an entire room that had been refitted with racks and hangers, and she found her gown from *The Grand Duchess*. It still fit, which was a silly thing to feel proud about, but then it was too late to think about revising the habits and foibles of a lifetime. She put on the elaborate gown, got the ruby-and-diamond necklace out of the wall safe, and fastened it around her neck. Then she lay down on the fauteuil and stared at herself in the full-length mirror, a frail old lady in ridiculous finery. Those terrible and heartless stones would continue to sparkle when the neck upon which they hung had rotted away.

Do it now? Walk out like this, wearing the gown and the necklace, and march down into the surf?

No, the insured value of the necklace was $450,000. She didn't have the nerve for that. Or the heartlessness. Think of all one could do with that kind of money.

She studied her image in the mirror, a little birdlike creature whose looks were gone. Not just her beauty but her looks. She could hardly recognize in that wizened oval of a face the visage that had once adorned the lobbies of those theaters in the huge posters and the two-sheets. Nothing was claimable as her own—except for the nose. That little button nose was still sending out its message of endearing fragility, of impish wit, of independence of spirit. She had regretted her nose back then, thought it an imperfection in an otherwise regular and classic face. But it was what had made her, what had marked those otherwise ideal and therefore unremarkable features with character and individuality. There had been any number of girls with perfect faces, but they had done nothing and gone nowhere. They were like those man-made sapphires that jewelers could spot only because they had no imperfections in them and were flawless—which just doesn't occur in nature. Her mark of naturalness, her touch of mortality, was that little button nose.

She wrinkled it. She laughed. She lay down on her four-poster bed and might have dozed off. Miss Gargan came looking for her, found her, made her take off the necklace and put it back into the safe. Obediently, she took off the gown too, let Miss Gargan hang it up in the closet, and accepted instead a pair of jeans and a ragg sweater with a cowl neck, which she put on. And she went downstairs for an omelette and a cup of decaffeinated coffee. After lunch, she instructed Miss Gargan to call Leonard Castle in New York to tell him that she wanted to see him.

Mr. Castle insisted on speaking with Miss Burke. Miss Burke sighed, but she accepted the telephone from her companion and listened to the agent's questions. This time, she told him, she was serious. She assured him that this time she was going to do it. He may or may not have believed her, but it didn't really matter. He wasn't going to risk losing her as a client. Miss Burke might admit to moments of some vagueness and confusion in recent months, but she hadn't lost all her marbles and she knew that having her name on his client list was worth a plane trip up to Nantucket every now and then for someone like Leonard Castle.

She might not be able to choose which dress she was going to wear, but she could still make certain people jump, even important people. So she wasn't altogether unimportant herself. Not just yet, anyway.

*

The car was easy to spot. Barrett supposed that there might be half a dozen Rolls-Royce station wagons in the country, but on Nantucket the odds were that this was Helen Burke's. As he approached the automobile, the driver asked, "Mr. Barrett?"

Barrett nodded. The driver took his overnight bag and held the door open as he climbed up and into the huge car. The seats were upholstered in soft pigskin. The back of the driver's compartment was done in burled walnut and there was a panel that probably contained a bar.

Barrett leaned back and enjoyed the ride, deliberately letting his mind go blank so that he'd be relaxed at his meeting with the great woman. The first few minutes were terribly important, and he wanted to establish a relationship in which there was something approaching equality of respect. He looked out at scrub pine and beach plum that wasn't all that different from the familiar vegetation of the Hamptons. A little more bleak and windblown, maybe. And the occasional cars they passed on the two-lane blacktop road all had Massachusetts plates. Other than that, it was a perfectly ordinary countryside. And for all of Helen Burke's celebrity, there was an ordinariness that she shared too—as Castle had explained.

"She's not well," Castle had told him. "And she wants that book now, as a kind of monument to herself. It's her last grasp at immortality. You're important to her, and she knows that you're not just another writer. The fact that you've never done this before is a plus, an actual advantage. You're not really a writer but an editor and a literary adviser. She likes that because it means that she's still the author, but it's good for you because you aren't like the other collaborators she's had. She may not treat you like a mere employee or a servant. The first half hour will decide how it's going to go."

It was important that he not screw it up. If he worried about it and let himself get tight and nervous, he'd only be decreasing his chances of projecting that confident authority that she'd be looking for. What he had to do was not think about it, let it happen, react naturally to whatever note she sounded.

They turned in at an impressive stone gate and drove up to a large, rather squat house, the center of which was an old Cape Codder to which wings had been added at various times. There were plantings of bayberry bushes on either side of the large front door.

"Mistah Barrett!" she trumpeted theatrically, welcoming him and, at the same time, announcing herself by that unmistakable diction.

"Miss Burke," he said, much more quietly. "What a great pleasure."

"Come on in," she said. "We'll get you something to drink, and then we'll get to work, if that's agreeable."

"That will be fine," he said, grateful that there was to be no preliminary audition. He much preferred to be judged on the quality of his work—and to judge her on her willingness to cooperate reasonably with a collaborator.

There was a large parlor with a grand piano at one end and a couple of leather sofas drawn up to a fireplace at the other. Miss Burke introduced Miss Gargan, her companion, a woman in her fifties with her hair drawn back into a bun. She offered him a seat near the fire that was blazing in the hearth. A uniformed maid brought in a tea cart and Miss Gargan thanked her and seated herself to serve.

"We have whiskey if you'd prefer," Miss Burke offered. "Or brandy. But tea is what we drink."

"Tea will be fine."

"It's Keemun and very good," she said.

"Milk or lemon?" Miss Gargan asked. "Sugar?"

"Just a little sugar, please."

She passed him a delicate cup of excellent tea, poured a cup for Miss Burke and one for herself. Her employer stared into her cup and stirred her tea. Miss Gargan told the editor, "I've set you up in the study with everything you'll need."

"Thank you," he said.

"It will take him a long time to dig through all that old stuff," Miss Burke said, and she laughed. "Weeks, maybe. Maybe even longer!" It was almost a cackle.

"I hope I can get some idea of what you've got sooner than that," Barrett said.

"It took long enough to live through it, Mr. Barrett."

"I'm sure it did. But I ought to be able to tell from a few samples what you've got here, and whether we can work together."

"Good," the actress said. "A quick study. I was a quick study once. I could learn lines just reading them once. Did Mr. Castle mention that I'm dying?"

"He said you haven't been well. I was sorry to hear it."

"You should be glad. It has made me a most reasonable person. Hasn't it, Miss Gargan?"

Miss Gargan didn't answer.

"Mr. Castle tells me you're very good," Miss Burke said.

"I appreciate that," he said.

"He's no flatterer," Helen Burke said. "But we'll find out quite quickly enough whether we can work together."

"My hopes are high," he said.

She nodded. He wondered where the catch was. It appeared to be perfectly straightforward.

When they'd finished their tea, Miss Gargan led him into a small room that she said was originally a dying room. "These staircases are very narrow, the ones in the original part of the house. There was no way they could get coffins up and down the stairwells. So there was always a small bedroom on the first floor."

"Not inappropriate, I think!" Miss Burke called from the doorway. She still had the most wonderful fricatives and dentals and plosives, so that English, when she spoke it, crackled and popped like a breakfast cereal.

There was a pretty campaign desk in dark mahogany with brass fittings. Arranged on top of it there were yellow legal evidence pads, pencils and a pencil sharpener, a large magnifying glass with a jade handle, and a high-tech chrome desk lamp that could be adjusted on its complicated series of arms and springs to any position one liked.

"Anything you want copied," Miss Gargan said, "Soames can take into town and have Xeroxed for you. He was your driver and he does whatever needs doing."

"It looks fine," he said.

"There's a tape deck over there on top of the bookcase. The tapes are in the closet, if you like music while you're working. And if you're hungry or thirsty, just ring. Hilda will try to get you whatever you want. The bell pull works. Miss Burke will be taking her afternoon lie-down."

"Just put it together to make it the book we both want," Miss Burke said grandly.

It was, he decided, a line she'd rehearsed.

Which meant that she'd been as nervous about their meeting as he'd been. Maybe even more.

He sat down in the comfortable chair behind the campaign desk, opened the first of the notebooks, and began to read.

*

The trouble was in the notebooks.

Barrett's first reaction was that she was crazy. And he never entirely ruled that out. What complicated the issue was her ambition, her sense of what preposterously lofty level she ought to reach in her recollections of a life of epochal significance. What she owed herself or her public was literary, in the worst way. High-flown, highfalutin claptrap with a generous dash of oriental spiritualism and as little as possible in the way of mundane information. Facts, figures, names, dates, and addresses were beneath her dignity to mention. Indeed, as she said explicitly in one of the diaries, in lilac ink:

> Our souls operate not only in this world but in other, alternate worlds, some better, some worse, but all of them intricately combining to include the vast number of possibilities from which we think we are selecting in this life. Thus, the lover from whom we separate here, with regret or relief, behaving well or badly, may in some other universe, some alternate existence, be the lifelong companion, the soulmate, the true spiritual complement. And the sharpness of the encounter in this life and on this plane may be an expression of the richness of that alternative existence which has found only this imperfect and temporary expression.

He read a number of such passages in various notebooks, from different periods and in an assortment of hues, and he didn't pay much attention to them until he realized that the practical effect was an excuse for the memoirs to invent, embroider, embellish upon or entirely ignore the circumstances of this particular and arbitrary plane of existence.

There were contradictions that didn't trouble her at all, renditions of marriages that had failed that were, by turns, friendly, bitter, noble, silly, sordid, or grand. Or not failures. She still talked to these husbands, long divorced and long dead, as if they were in the next room and might, at any moment, reappear, wearing some 1935 set decorator's idea of grand threads, smoking jacket, or riding outfit, or white tie and tails, or maybe one of those World War I aviator's suits with the leather helmet with the goggles and one of those swell silk scarves.

Children she'd never had not only spoke to her but wrote her letters from Groton or Emma Willard. Abortions, perhaps? Or just fantasies, not even embodied to the blastula stage?

What she lacked in hard facts she made up for in adjectives and adverbs, of which she had acquired a very peculiar set. "Numinous" was one of her favorites, and "significantly" was another: "In that numinous pause, he returned my gaze significantly . . ."

Back at his editor's desk, he'd have scrawled over such pages with a blue pencil, or bundled them up to be returned as quickly as possible to their source. But these weren't the ravings of any gushing fool. This was what he had to work from, make a book of, and whip into some decent and minimally intelligible form.

He had been working for only a couple of hours, starting with the early notebooks and then skipping ahead, sampling here and there, getting more and more anxious as he realized how serious the problem was. Was she crazy? Or was she shrewd too, using this absurd loftiness as a way of protecting herself from the confessions that she feared might hurt her, losing for her the admiration that the public had lavished upon her for half a century?

On the top sheet of the yellow pad she had so thoughtfully provided, he'd written down five different birth years. There were also two different birthdays in four different cities. Her father was always named Calvin DeGroot Burke, but her mother's name wavered a little, sometimes Mary Bridge, sometimes Marie DuPont, sometimes Martha da Ponte, and in one notebook, Mary Wildflower, a Seneca Indian who was the daughter of an Italian engineer who worked as a bridge builder in the Tri-City area in the 1880s.

The specificity was tempting, but Barrett realized that Helen Burke had starred in *Cayuga Princess,* and might have been claiming for herself some Native American heritage, in either this or some alternate world.

He pulled the embroidered bell pull and, when Hilda appeared, asked for a bourbon and ice.

The next hour or so was a little more encouraging. In the manila envelopes, there were newspaper clippings of pieces written by reporters who lived entirely on this plane and in this world and who wrote for editors and readers with some curiosity about who, what, when, where, and maybe even why. There were two marriages. And there was a divorce from a third husband, so there must have been three marriages. There was a daughter who did in fact go to Emma Willard but was killed in an automobile accident in Florida.

It was weird. If she'd been trying to conceal these things, why would she have saved the clippings? Why would she have turned them over to him along with those ethereal and absurd ravings in the spiral notebooks?

More to the point, there was the basic question of how to handle her, how to get her back to this world, this plane of existence, where if a thing happens one way, most people take that to mean an exclusion of alternative renderings. He had to be firm, but not so heavy-handed as to make her rebel. She could fire him if she chose. She needed him, but there might be other things she needed more—like the ability to live with herself and with her past. He drained the last of the drink and jiggled the ice cubes so as to get a small one that he could fish out and suck on, the way he'd done when he'd been a young boy at a soda fountain in Salem, Massachusetts.

It took him a while, and he still wasn't sure of himself, but he came up with a kind of a plan, a strategy that had at least a chance of success. If he could get her to take the first couple of steps, he could go the rest of the way himself. And in time, there'd be a book.

From what Leonard Castle had led him to believe and what she had confirmed herself, time, in a way, was on his side. Significantly, he chewed on another numinous ice cube and then went to find the great Miss Burke to see whether his stratagem would work.

She was refreshed by her nap, and there was a quality of attention he hadn't felt before. She was curious, waiting to see how he'd reacted to his hours with the material she'd set before him. Miss Gargan was curious too. Almost immediately, he reassured them both, telling them that it was "just wonderful. It is of enormous spiritual value for its insights and its philosophy. It will be a great book!"

Miss Burke was pleased but still wary.

"The only question I have in my mind," he told her, easing back onto one of the leather sofas, "is how to take the reader by the hand

and lead him up the slopes, through the foothills and into the mountains. Too sudden, and we're going to lose people for whom your
vision could be very important in their lives."

"Yes," she said, "I see what you mean."

He was on firmer ground now, recognizing in her answer the old
Hollywood bullshit, which was very like the current product that was
shoveled out on publishers' row in New York. She meant, of course,
that she hadn't the vaguest idea of what he was talking about.

"We must think of your life as a pilgrimage," he said, "and your
readers are pilgrims too, but they're just starting out at the beginning,
while you've reached this high plateau. It's important that you make
allowances for their inexperience and their deficiencies of insight. If we
start out with the simple version of your life story, set down what
actually happened in this world, we can begin to admit some of those
alternative worlds and happenings in the same way that they began to
disclose themselves to you. Wouldn't that be a generous and tactful
way to hold out your hand to them? They're willing, but they're likely
to be afraid to make the great leap . . ."

"I see," she said. "You want the truth first . . ."

"The literal truth. The other truths, the more abstract and figurative
truths, can come in as we go along."

"Yes," she said. "That's a good idea. I'd like that."

"Good," he said. "Then we're going to have a fine book, I'm sure of
it."

"There's only one problem," she said, smiling but avoiding his eyes.
He realized that she was looking just above his head, staring at the
wall behind him as she spoke. "I'm not going to be as much help to
you as I'd like. There's a lot I just don't remember."

"And there's a lot she doesn't want to remember," Miss Gargan
volunteered. "She doesn't like to talk about some parts of her life or
think too much about some of the things that have happened."

He was undeterred. This was what he had more or less expected.
"How would it be if I were to put together that simple narrative at the
beginning, doing it on my own, just the way anyone else would if they
were doing your biography. That's what would happen anyway,
sooner or later, with someone like yourself. I'd show you what I'd
found, and you could tell me what you remember. Things I've got
wrong I can correct that way. And it could jog your memory about
some of what happened. But once the reader has that as a kind of map,
he can begin the climb up the mountain."

She looked up at the ceiling. There were tears welling up in her eyes.

Barrett was impressed but not intimidated. That was one of the tricks she'd always been able to do, crying on cue. "Yes," she said, the tears trickling down her cheeks now, "yes, that will be wonderful."

"Yes," he said. "Wonderful indeed."

Miss Gargan led her away, obviously displeased that her mistress had been upset this way. Barrett waited but the companion did not return. There was no argument from her. Miss Burke, whatever her frailties, was still in charge. He poured himself another bourbon in celebration. He could write whatever he wanted, use anything of hers that was halfway sane and coherent, and publish it after she was dead.

There'd be a book after all, and maybe even a good book.

*

It had been okay in the cab. Taxis were a familiar part of his life, after all. But this business of standing in a doorway, skulking there like some derelict trying to stay warm, that was upsetting. It was the novelty as much as anything else that disturbed Castle. He felt strange and strangely vulnerable.

Outrageous that a competent, valuable, respectable man should be thrust out this way through the invisible boundary of real life and into this nightmare existence. It was not only frightening but humiliating, and the humiliation was worse than the fear.

He checked his watch. Another ten minutes, and then he'd be satisfied.

But Jesus! Ten minutes?

An eternity!

8

Effie brought in the messages. "The one on the top is interesting," she said. She put them down on his desk.

Castle looked at the top slip: "Amy Breckenridge. Please call." And a number.

"The senator's wife, I assume?"

"That's what I assume too," Effie said. "But I didn't ask her."

"I'll see what she wants," Castle said.

"This isn't a delicatessen," Effie said. It was another of their old lines they traded back and forth.

"Sometimes I wish it were," he said.

There was money in it, but there were going to be headaches too. He knew that much even as he punched up the numbers from the slip.

And yes, it was the senator's wife, or now almost ex-wife, as anyone who read the tabloids knew perfectly well. And yes, she wanted to meet with Leonard Castle, but she couldn't come to his office, and they couldn't meet anywhere in public, and she didn't want him to come to her apartment.

"That cuts down on the options," he said dryly.

"Be on the corner of Fifty-seventh and Fifth at three o'clock. I'll come by in a cab. We can drive around and talk."

"Which corner?"

"The Tiffany corner."

He jotted that down on the pink message slip, thinking as he did so that it would make a good title for something someday. Maybe even for this.

He was there at the appointed time, and a big old Checker pulled up and stopped. A door opened. Inside, a small woman in a dark ankle-length mink, dark glasses, and a kind of turban on her head beckoned. Castle got into the cab beside her and closed the door.

"The park," she said to the driver. "Just drive around." And to Castle she said, "How do you do? And thank you for meeting me this way. It's extraordinary, I know, but these are extraordinary circumstances."

"It's no big deal," Castle said. "If it makes you feel comfortable . . ."

"Comfort isn't the issue, Mr. Castle. It's safety. It's my personal safety. There is a lot of Breckenridge money, as I'm sure you know. I married him for it, and I've suffered for it, and now I'm fleeing from it, because it buys a hell of a lot."

"I'm sure it does. But what can I do for you?"

"I want to write a book about my life. About my life before and during and after Jonas Breckenridge. And yes, all the things you've heard about me are true. I am an alcoholic, and I've been convicted of possession of prohibited substances, and I've been committed to mental hospitals . . . That's all true. The question is how I got that way, and what I have to do to save the little bit of life I've got left."

"And you want me to represent you, and to find you a publisher?"

"That's right."

"I guess I can do that."

"He'll try to buy you off, you know. And the publisher too."

"Maybe."

"There may even be physical threats. I mean it."

"You have a right to write your story. And within certain limits, you have a right to publish whatever you write. I don't like intimidation. I'm not sure I believe that the senator would actually do such a thing . . ."

She smiled, just managing not to laugh.

". . . but if it happened, I think I'd resent it, and it would be counterproductive."

"Fine," she said. "What do we do now? Are there contracts? Do you send me papers or what?"

"I don't think we need them. My fee is ten percent of whatever I can get for you. Which means that you don't pay me anything. What happens is that I pay you your ninety percent out of what comes from the publisher."

"Fine."

"Do you have anything on paper? An outline? A sample chapter?

That makes it easier for me to sell the book. It isn't essential, but it's helpful."

"I'll get that to you."

"You'll be writing the book yourself? Some people need editorial assistance," he told her.

"I don't know. I'll try it myself. Then you or the publisher can decide. The important thing is to get the book done."

"Do you mind if I ask you to go into a little more detail about why you are doing this?"

"I don't mind," she said, but she didn't answer immediately. She looked out at the trees that blurred by as the cab cruised the uptown drive of the park. "Part of it is revenge, and part of it is for my self-respect. But I think a lot of it is for the children, so they'll know, so they will understand I'm not the terrible creature they think I am. Or that, if I am, it's because of what he did to me. I thought about it for a long time, and it's something I've got to do."

"All right. Then you should do it."

"You have a card or something?"

He gave her one.

"I'll send the sample chapter as soon as I can. A couple of weeks maybe."

"And where can I reach you?"

"You can't," she said. "I guess you can call the number I left this morning. And leave a message. That'll get to me. I'll call you from time to time."

"Whatever you say," he told her.

"Out onto Fifth Avenue," she told the driver. "I'll get out at the corner." She held out a twenty to Castle for the cab fare.

"That's all right. I'll just take the cab back to my office."

"Thank you," she said. "Thanks for everything." And she jumped out, slammed the door, and crossed the street, trudging along with her hands in her pockets and her eyes downward. Castle watched her. Every few steps, she'd look around and then trudge on again.

The light turned and the cab headed south on Fifth.

*

Barrett got out of the cab in front of a modest bungalow in Culver City. There was a palm tree that took up most of the front yard, which was one way to tell that this was an older house. Barrett was uncomfortable in Los Angeles or, indeed, anywhere in the Sunbelt. He had the feeling that everything he saw had been put there within the past fifteen minutes and that, therefore, it might all be taken away within the next fifteen. Back East, in New York and Boston and Philadelphia, there were other centuries. Here, there was only the jumble of styles, mission or Tudor or aggressive high-tech.

This somewhat seedy bungalow was, in its way, reassuring to him, however, mostly because it looked dejected. There is an authenticity to disappointment, an unimpeachability. It isn't fake anything else. Barrett didn't even mind the absurd concrete turret into which the front door had been set. He rang the bell. A woman in her mid-forties answered the door. "Yes?"

"Miss Stephens? I'm Oliver Barrett."

"Come on in," she said. "I got some coffee I just heated up. You want some?"

"If it's no trouble."

"No, no trouble." She was wearing blue jeans and a light cotton version of a lumberjack shirt. "I'm still waking up. I work at night and I go to school in the afternoons. It's rough."

"What are you studying?" Barrett asked.

"Psych. At UCLA. And at night I do word processing for a law firm downtown."

They were in the kitchen. He watched while she rinsed out one of the mugs and poured him a cup of coffee from the percolator on the stove. "Thank you. I appreciate your seeing me this way."

"I wouldn't have missed it," Miss Stephens said, topping up her own mug. "I don't know whether it will do any good or not or what kind of book you're working on. A puff piece, probably. Fan magazine stuff . . ."

"No, no. I'm really trying to find out the truth," he told her.

"That's what you said on the phone. Well, I've hated that woman all my life. And her story is my story. So, if you're interested, I'll be happy to tell you."

"You mind if I tape you, so that I get it all accurately?"

"Go right ahead."

She led him back into the living room, a small rather dark room, with a spool rocker by the big stone hearth and a couch that had a bedspread thrown over it as an impromptu slipcover. She took the rocker. Barrett sat down on the couch and took a Sony micro-recorder out of his coat pocket. He set it on the arm of the couch and switched it on.

She took a sip of her coffee, cleared her throat, and started to talk. "As you know, my father was Sidney Stephens, the director. My mother was Zelda Foxcroft, and she'd been a novelist back in New York and was a playwright, or anyway she'd written one play that got put on. So she came out here the way they used to do in those days, for a six-month assignment that stretched out to a lifetime. And she met my father and they got married. And about three years later, I was born.

"So far, nothing special. And the fact that my father then ran off with Helen Burke wasn't anything special either. Happens in Hollywood all the time, right? Well, I guess it does. It did then, and it still does. But then six months later, he killed himself, which makes it a little different. Anyway, it happened to my parents, and I grew up feeling that there was something wrong with my mother and with me, and that if we'd only been prettier or more lovable or somehow better than we were, it wouldn't have happened.

"But that's wrong. It wasn't my fault and it wasn't my mother's fault, either. The thing was that Helen Burke planned it all from the very beginning. She'd been assigned to this picture she didn't like, and she couldn't quit because she would have been suspended. That was the way the studios worked in those days when everybody was on contract. But the convention was that if you could get fired, you would just be reassigned to another picture. And she wanted my father to fire her, which he didn't want to do. I don't even think she had any objection to the picture, as a matter of fact. She just didn't like the leading man—Edgar Oldfield. I think she tried to get him replaced, and she couldn't. And then she tried to get herself fired or released, or whatever, and my father didn't want to do that. And she set out to ruin him, in the most cold-blooded and deliberate way to destroy him.

"In the first place, she did the picture and she let him know how sorry she was and that she'd been wrong, and so on and so forth. And she was a beautiful woman, which I'll grant her. But she was also glamorous, which is a different thing, a convention really, especially out here. There are people whom we all just grant that to, as if it were one of the perks of the job. She was a movie queen and she acted like one, and she had a white Rolls that brought her to the studio every day, and she was glamorous.

"Well, first of all, she believed it, which is a part of how this all happened. She had no idea of what the limitations were on how people should behave. Or on how she should behave. There wasn't anything she couldn't have. There just weren't any restraints. That happens out here. And other people accepted that too, and went along with her. Which is how she was able to think up such a thing in the first place."

"What happened exactly?" Barrett prompted.

"Well, for one thing, there was an affair, which I'm pretty sure she initiated. My father probably wouldn't have had the nerve. I mean, she was on the A list and he wasn't. She outclassed him by a lot. It was just a series of accidents that had got her loaned to the studio where my father worked for this one picture and that got him assigned to direct it. But she was out of his league. So I think she was the one who made the first moves. And he was willing to play. He was flattered, as she'd expected he'd be. And he left my mother and me . . . ."

She took a sip of her coffee.

Barrett had the impression that she not only had told this story before but had worked on it, or worked through it, with professional help. A psychology major? Of course, of course. And a veteran of some analyst's couch too, he was pretty sure.

"So, anyway, they went off to her place in Palm Springs, and they lived there for a couple of months. Which is a part of it, because if I'm right in the way I've worked this out, and I'm pretty sure I am, the question is how she felt every morning and every night. It was as if she were killing him. I mean, she didn't just shoot him. She left that messy part of it to him to do to himself, which he did eventually. Because they were out there together just long enough for him to give up his contract and for my mother to file for divorce, and then Helen Burke threw him out. Just like that! She told him he'd been an ass, and that when people crossed her she was entitled to destroy them. And now that he was out of a job and was getting divorced, he could get out of her house and go back and pick up the pieces of his miserable little life any way he pleased."

"There were witnesses to this?" Barrett asked.

"I've talked to her chauffeur. Or the man who used to be her chauffeur. He was in a VA hospital. He's dead now. But I can play you the tape of what he said. I got it on tape just like you're doing now. The thing is, though, that if he'd been a little tougher, he could have come back. I don't know whether my mother would have taken him back right away or ever. But I would have. I mean, he still would have been my father. And he could have got some kind of job sooner or later, one way or another. But she'd figured him right. She wasn't an intellectual, but she was shrewd, as a lot of these people are, which is how they got where they are. She knew he was proud. And that she'd set him up in exactly the right way to make him most uncomfortable. He wasn't the kind of man who could admit he'd been a fool and beg people's pardon. Even in that phrase, we use the word 'beg,' and that's not accidental. He didn't want to beg. As we say in another phrase, 'I'd just die.' That's what he saw as the choice. And so he went and got himself a gun and went back to her house and sat down on her front doorstep and blew his brains out, leaving a mess for the chauffeur to clean up, and the police, and in another way my mother and me."

"What mess was that?"

"The rest of our lives."

"It was terrible, but surely, you had your own life to live . . ."

"Yes, you'd think so, wouldn't you? But there were problems. I mean, aside from the psychological problems that you'd expect. My mother took it very hard and she became what I guess you'd call withdrawn. Not quite a recluse, but pushing toward that. She never left the house. And then she had a stroke and was an invalid for a long time. You must have wondered what someone my age was doing going to school and taking courses. It's only two years ago that she died. And until then, I'd been taking care of her."

"I see."

"And you know what she wanted? What kept her alive all those years? She was hoping to hear about the death of Helen Burke, see it on television or read it in the paper. Just to know that she'd outlived the old bitch. But she didn't. Some people are lucky and others aren't."

"That's the truth," Barrett agreed.

"So tell me, are you going to use this? Are you going to put down what happened, what that woman did?"

"I'll check into it some, but, yes, assuming that it's all true and that it happened just as you've said, I'll use it."

"There won't be much in the papers. The studio covered it up a lot. They've got press agents, or they used to have them, who got stuff into the papers, which was easy. But they had others, who got paid a lot more and had much more important jobs, which was keeping unattractive and unpleasant stuff out of the papers. And there was just too much money tied up in Helen Burke. She was too valuable a piece of property to let something like this come anywhere near her. So if you're telling me the truth and you really want to check, the only way to do that is to go through the old records out in Palm Springs, the police blotter from back when my father killed himself. You'll see that it's true, just as I've told you."

"I'm afraid I will," Barrett said. "And I'm sorry."

"Oh, I've got used to it by now. That's the amazing thing. You can get used to damned near anything."

"Well, I appreciate your taking the time . . ."

"I appreciate your listening to me."

"I'll be in touch," he promised. He turned off the machine that was still running, and shook the hand that she'd extended. He wasn't sure how far he meant to go with this, and he had the idea that she knew that. But he couldn't not shake her hand.

*

Castle was on the phone. Effie came in, closed the door behind her, and took a sheet of paper from his scratch pad to write out her message: "Barrett outside, upset."

Castle nodded his acknowledgment and held up his right hand with the fingers splayed, meaning that he'd be free in five minutes. Effie nodded and went out to relay that, leaving Castle to deal with the editor at the other end of the line.

". . . a real gold mine of a book. There's no question of that. And we made a fight for it here, but management is concerned about the politics of it."

"That's bullshit," Castle said. He could blow off a little steam, because in the first place the sale was off, at least to this house, and in the second, if he goaded Watkins just a bit there might be some response, some inadvertent revelation of truth that could be useful in the next round of negotiation. "Politics is no reason to pass up a million-dollar property. The Robinsons are rich but they aren't crazy."

"No, no, I'm serious. If we do this, the chances are that it will hurt Jonas Breckenridge next fall, and whatever kind of a son of a bitch he may be in his personal life, he's a decent liberal senator. Think of who's going to get his seat if he goes down. Some right-wing crazy! The Robinsons don't want to be part of that."

"Very public-spirited of them, I'm sure," Castle said.

"Well, it is, in a way," Watkins said, not quite whining.

"Look, if they don't do it, somebody else will. So where's the logic?"

"By that logic, you could make a case for publishing *Mein Kampf,*" Watkins said.

"I could and I would," Castle said. "That's what a free press is about. Even a Hitler has a right to be published. But that isn't the question."

"There isn't any question. It's out of my hands, Len. That's what I'm trying to tell you. It's a decision from upstairs. You don't have to convince me. Even if you did, it wouldn't do you any good. The Robinsons have spoken."

"And it's just politics and public spirit and all that? Or did somebody get to them?" Castle asked.

"Your guess on that is as good as mine," Watkins said.

"Well, it's possible, isn't it? I mean, it's still a family-owned firm. Do you think I should go to a house that's owned by some conglomerate? Would I be better off?"

"I'd think about it," Watkins said. "In your position, I might very well go that route."

"I appreciate your frankness," Castle said.

"I didn't say anything," Watkins said, managing not to sound scared.

"I know," Castle said. "I was making a little joke."

"It's not a very nice joke," Watkins complained.

"It's not a very nice piece of business, is it?" Castle countered. "I'll be talking to you."

"Good luck," Watkins managed to say before they hung up.

Castle ran his fingers through his hair, buzzed Effie on the intercom, and told her to send Barrett in.

He came in talking, spewing words from the doorway.

"Take it easy," Castle told him. "Sit down. Catch your breath. Relax a little."

"I'm sorry," Barrett said. "I just flew in this afternoon. I stopped at my apartment to drop my luggage and I came straight here."

"What's the trouble?"

"I'm not sure I can do this book. That woman is a monster."

"Hard to work with, you mean?"

"No, no. It's much worse than that," Barrett said, and he explained that his subject was wonderfully cooperative although very vague. He told Castle how he'd formed a plan of writing what would be, in effect, a biography of the movie star, and had gone out to California to talk to people who had known her. And he'd discovered that she was, in a number of ways, a monster, a selfish, arrogant, cruel, tyrannical woman who had wrecked the lives of relatively innocent people around her. "Any book I'd do about her would destroy her. It wouldn't be an autobiography or even a biography but an exposé."

"So? What's the matter with that?"

"I don't feel good about it. I'm torn, frankly. It's not what I had expected."

"Life is often like that."

"And as you told me, she's not well. Dying, in fact."

"That could make your position easier."

"I know that, and I don't feel very good about it. It's like cheering for the vultures. It's worse than that. It's joining the vultures! And the minute she goes, I go into action and destroy her memory. It's a hell of a thing to look forward to."

"Are you sure it's as bad as you're painting it?"

Barrett told Castle about Sidney Stephens and Zelda, and their daughter, the woman he'd talked to in Culver City. And he told Castle about his trip out to Palm Springs to verify her story, which checked out as well as anyone could expect, after the studio press agents had done their work all those years ago. "And that's not the only story, either. The thing is that this is characteristic, absolutely typical. This is the way she was."

"So write it that way."

"And feel like a bastard?"

"You want to feel good? You take all the money you're going to make on this and go on a nice cruise. It will do you good."

"I keep telling myself things like that. It's not enough. I'm telling you, Len, I feel serious discomfort about this project."

"If you didn't, you'd be less of a human being and less of a writer. I think you ought to hang in there. Figure that it will clarify itself one way or another. It probably will. Life has a way of tidying up some of its own messes. Believe me. Give it a little while longer. I'm asking you, as an old friend, to do that. Not just for the book's sake but for yours too. Trust me!"

It was an old bullshit line, but it worked sometimes. Mostly it worked if the people to whom one said it wanted to hear it, wanted an excuse to do what a part of them had already decided to do anyway. It was a temporary expedient, but it was the best Castle could come up with on the instant. He watched while Barrett sat there scowling. Thirty seconds passed. Forty-five. Castle watched the sweep hand of his Tiffany desk clock climb toward the vertical.

"Okay, I'll go with it for a while. But I'm uncomfortable about it."

"You've made that clear, Oliver, and I appreciate it. We'll stay in touch, I promise," Castle assured him.

Barrett got up and shook hands across the desk.

*

Finally, finally, finally, they'd managed to get together. It had been one of those evenings that began to loom, acquiring through its many delays and reschedulings an odd significance that was not entirely arbitrary. She was working on him, after all, and she knew he knew that. She'd been talking to various editors and clients about him. And she'd been perfectly straightforward on the telephone, letting him know that she thought he was interesting.

And on her side, she knew that she was a threat to him, that her connection with *Periscope* was both attractive and dangerous, and that these postponements might be interpreted by Freudians as signs of that ambivalence on his part.

It was when she called him to congratulate him on what he'd done with Wanda Lathem, with her and for her, and repeated her suggestion that they should make another attempt at that dinner engagement, that he laughed and told her to pick a night. "I'll get free, I swear. I don't care what it is. We've got to do this."

"Tomorrow?"

"You're on," he said. "What kind of food do you like?"

"Almost anything," she said.

"That's not terrifically helpful, but I'll figure something out."

"I'm sure anything you like will be fine with me," she told him, which sounded nice but still made it into a challenge, as they both perfectly well knew.

"Shall I pick you up?"

"Sure," she said, and she gave him her address.

It was fun to be the one for whom schedules were rearranged. It was also fun to play that wonderful old role from romantic novels and be the dangerous woman of whom the man is a little bit afraid. Susan Flowers was no fool and understood that it was her connection with the television program that gave her this power and even made her dangerous to someone like Castle. But just as she was willing to wear perfumes from a bottle or dresses that she'd bought in stores if they made her attractive and gave her a good feeling, she was likewise willing to take advantage of her job and exploit its cosmetic benefits. A woman who doesn't take advantage of such things is . . . crazy!

"About eight?"

"Perfect," she said. "I'll see you then."

It was not only pleasant to know that she was important to him, it also gave her a little flutter. She wasn't supposed to react this way to the prospect of dinner with a man, not at her age and condition of life. This was schoolgirl stuff. It was also delicious.

She told herself that it was unfair to get her hopes up, that almost inevitably there'd be something that would go wrong, some difference of taste or opinion, some incompatibility. That was certainly how the odds were. On the other hand, what if the evening went well, as she had a sneaky notion that it might?

Easy there! Down, girl! she told herself.

It was only by an old instinct that she hadn't set their date for the same day. She'd been right of course, and now she had twenty-four hours to look forward to their evening together. No matter how the actual evening went, the anticipation of it would be pleasant. And then, either as a coincidence or as an omen, Mike called to ask her, with an arrogance for which she could hardly fault him, whether she wouldn't like to spend a nice filthy evening with him. "Like, how about tomorrow night?"

"Sorry, darling, I've got other plans."

"Change them."

"I could," she said, "but I don't want to."

"You're kidding. You're doing a number on me!"

"Am I? It's inadvertent, I assure you. I'm telling you the simple truth. Just as you've always told me you were doing to me, among other things."

"Well, excuse me!" he said, giving the line an exaggerated reading the way Steve Martin used to deliver it.

"No, no," she said, quite cheerfully, "I'm the one who ought to offer some sort of apology. It's just that I have this other thing to do."

"Well, enjoy your thing, there," he said. "I'll call you."

"Bye-bye," she said, and felt fine, and realized that it wasn't anything that she owed to Leonard Castle particularly. It had just worked out this way.

Of course, if Castle was anywhere near the negotiator and manipulator he was reputed to be, he'd be able to sniff out this little edge and use it, turning it to his advantage.

It would be interesting to watch him. And if he performed well, she'd enjoy the prize as much as he.

She went to the powder room to splash water on her face and freshen her makeup so that she could get back to work.

The next evening, he was prompt, appearing at exactly two minutes after eight. Susan had taken a long luxurious bath and had dressed with careful negligence in a good white silk blouse and a black skirt that had mockingly girlish flounces. The outfit seemed right for her mood, which she was rather enjoying. She didn't ask him in for a preliminary drink. There would be drinks later, if all went well. Or maybe not, if they went very well.

"Where are we going?" she asked.

"I found a place a couple of blocks from here that looks okay. For people like us, most of the fun of eating out is the gamble of it, the risk taking. It's almost as if good food isn't enough any more."

"I don't object to it," she said. "But I know what you mean." She wondered whether he was talking just about food or meant to generalize to other appetites as well. And if so, what would that mean about his view of their prospects? "What place did you find?"

"Aubrey's," he said.

"Oh, I adore it. It's wonderful. A little French bistro that got picked up in a big storm and dropped down on Second Avenue."

"Well, for me it's an adventure. I have all those places on Amsterdam and Columbus to work through, and there must be three new ones a week. If I ever get out of this business, I may go into plants and ferns for new restaurants. The market is limitless."

It was a fine evening and they walked the three blocks. She noticed his energy, his long strong stride that he had to adjust to her slower pace. He was a big man but not flabby, she realized. Shamelessly, she wondered what it would be like to have all that muscular weight on top of her.

Aubrey's was crowded as usual, but the maître d'hôtel welcomed Susan and Leonard with even more cordiality than was customary and seated them immediately at a corner table. She was pleased, not only with the maître but with Castle, who had really taken pains to walk up and down the streets of her neighborhood, find a promising place, and go in to explore, have a drink, look at the menu, perhaps take a peek at the food on people's plates, and then tip the headwaiter to be certain that a decent table would be immediately available for them when they arrived.

He was showing off a little, but she didn't object to that. On the contrary, it was interesting to see, even in this relatively unimportant matter, the kind of thought he put into the transactions of life. She wondered what she could do to hold up her end and properly compensate such exertions—and she realized that that was exactly what she was supposed to wonder.

They ordered kirs, which were brought right away.

"I talked to Oliver Barrett," she told him. It was business, but then the sparkle of their exchanges had been based in business, the risk and the tantalization. At least for a while, that was the place to begin.

"When was that?" he asked.

"Two or three weeks ago," she said. "I guess three by now. He was very excited about the Helen Burke project."

"Since then, he's been having second thoughts," Castle told her.

"Oh?"

"There's something wonderfully innocent about Oliver. He's really a nice fellow. And he takes it as a personal insult if people don't measure up to his expectations. A good quality, in a way, but it's also a pain in the ass. He expected Helen Burke to be that wonderful woman he'd seen on the screen. It bothers him that she's done some less than admirable things in her time."

"Aren't you taking chances talking to me this frankly?"

"No, not really. For one thing, there's no camera crew. For another, unless you've got a toy in your purse recording all this, I'm not saying any of this. And then, frankly, the ace up my sleeve is that Helen Burke is very ill. She could die at any time. And *Periscope* has its limits. Good taste will protect me. You're not going to attack the memory of one of the great stars of motion picture history, or not until the corpse is cold. So I'm safe on this one, wouldn't you say?"

"You're safe on a lot of them. I went to see Barrett because I'd been thinking there might be something we could do with Wanda Lathem."

"There might be. That's sort of fun."

"It's very touchy, though. And we can't show any of her films . . ."

"Not if you want to keep your license, you can't."

"It was the negotiations that interested me and the way the book came about, with McCracken and you on one side and Lucid on the other."

"You found out all about that?"

"Mostly. But it's dead. Lucid and his lawyers would be all over us. It just isn't worth it. You turn over a rock and find crawly creatures—it isn't exactly surprising."

"No, but it's interesting sometimes."

"That's what I thought. Can I ask you a question?"

"Sure."

"Did you bribe Oliver Barrett somehow? Was this Helen Burke assignment a payoff for something?"

"Not really, no. There was a little fooling around, but nothing I'd call a bribe."

"Can you tell me about it?"

"Why not?" he asked, letting the question hang in the air. He was taking chances and he was making sure she realized it. This was showing off too. And flattering.

"What I asked him to do was to get me some Barbizon stationery.

Just blank letterhead. It was no big deal. And if I'd wanted to, I could have taken any letter I'd received from the firm and gone out to some not quite scrupulous printer and ordered myself some of it. But the point was to make him feel like a conspirator, which wasn't tough to do."

"But why?"

"For a couple of reasons. Mostly, the way to make a friend is to get someone to do you a favor. People hate obligations they've incurred, but they like to feel generous and magnanimous. He felt as though he was my blood brother, which was nice when we were working Lucid."

"What did you do with the letterhead?"

"I wrote a letter to myself estimating what the first printing would be and what the proceeds would be from the book. Lucid wouldn't just take my word for it. He wanted to see something on paper. So I gave him a paper. But I was telling the truth, was underestimating, as it turned out. And with this little trick, I got him to believe me. Then we could work out a deal where we fundamentally bought Wanda Lathem's share of the book back. And her freedom. Her whole life, in fact. And Oliver wanted to cooperate with that."

"That's very clever," she said.

"Oh, well. That's the fun of the job. It's those little pieces of business that keep me interested."

"Not the books?"

"Not really. Some of them are okay. Some are pretty good, actually. But some aren't. And I don't have a whole lot of control over that part of it. A little maybe but not as much as you'd think. I look at them as a series of deals. It's just like real estate deals or corporate mergers, putting pieces together and finding out what people want and what they're willing to settle for. That's always fascinating. And it keeps changing."

The waiter approached to ask whether they'd made their choices, which prompted them to take a look at their menus. Susan picked the seafood crêpe and Castle chose the bouillabaisse. "Some wine?" he offered.

"Sure, lets."

He picked a *fumé blanc* from a good Sonoma Valley vineyard.

"Now," he said, "in the name of fairness and to satisfy my curiosity, tell me a little about yourself."

"What would you like to know?"

"Whatever you'd like to tell me."

She started with what was on her résumé, her education and career experience, but he made a little drawing-forth motion with his hand. "Sure, sure," he said, "I can see all that. I mean, you're wearing it. Tell me something I can't see."

"Like what?"

"I don't know. Answer the hard questions. Are you happy?"

"God, I don't know."

"Then, what would it take to make you happy? A man, or a better job? Both? Or all the money in the world, so you wouldn't need either one?"

"I'll take all three, if I can have them. Then I'll let you know what I'm willing to give up."

"You never married?"

"Nope. I've been asked."

"I have no doubt. But you wanted something better?"

"I guess I wanted to find out who I was first. Something dumb like that."

"Why is that dumb?"

"Because you find out who you are by living. Whatever you do, whatever you decide, that's just drawing cards. How you play is what makes the difference."

"I'll drink to that," he said, "as soon as he opens the bottle."

The waiter did the bit with the wine, pouring some for Castle, who approved, then pouring Susan's and finally filling Castle's glass.

"It's good," she said.

"Oh, sure, a 'nice unpretentious little wine,' as they say. I almost bought the vineyard once. I was thinking of chucking the business and moving out West to do something 'real.'"

"You wish you had?"

"As you say, it's how you play your cards. It doesn't make a lot of difference, probably. Do you ever think about something like that, getting out of New York and doing some semi-cornball thing?"

"You mean like running a country inn up in Connecticut?"

"Exactly."

"It's crossed my mind," she said, smiling.

"Well, it's always there, in that crossing in the mind, a place to run to for twenty seconds now and then," he said.

"But it's so uncomplicated. And we like complication and subtlety and . . . all that," she said. "I do, anyway."

"You can't not take it with you. You always go home again. There are a whole lot of titles that are a hundred and eighty degrees off that way. And the simple things in life are generally boring."

"What about an evening like this, with the two of us having dinner?" she asked. "Is that boring?"

"No, but it sure as hell isn't simple," he said. "Unless we're playing that game too, which would make it one I hadn't noticed so far."

She nodded, both agreeing and conceding. It was close to a declaration that he knew how they were reversing roles, how the mere possibility of the television segment on him or on one of his clients made her the pursuer and him the quarry. And how they had different rights this way, or anyway a different selection of possible moves and responses.

For one thing, it would be easy now for her to invite him up for that drink, a part of the game, almost an expected move. In a strange way, that took a lot of the pressure off. It wasn't real but a charade, a play version of the evening they were enacting as they went along.

To insist on the role reversal and its playfulness, she insisted, when the check was presented, on paying it with her Amex card and putting it on her expense sheet.

From there, it was only a step or two—three blocks, actually—to her invitation that he come up for a nightcap.

"I'd be delighted," he said. "But will you respect me in the morning?"

"Well, that all depends, doesn't it?"

"I'm sure you'll let me know."

"Probably," she said, laughing, as she opened the vestibule door.

*

The telephone was ringing when Castle opened his apartment door. Ordinarily, he'd have let the machine answer it, but at five in the morning he knew it had to be Susan calling to say good night. Who else would be calling at such an hour?

He picked up the phone. "Yes?"

"Leonard, Helen Burke is dead."

It took him a couple of seconds to shift gears.

"Are you there?"

"Yes, Lisa, I'm here."

"Well, I just heard it on the news. I was up, reading. And I turned on the radio. I assumed you'd want to know. You've got a book in the works, after all."

"Yes, that's true," he said. "But I don't know what I can do about a death. Those things happen."

"You can do something about Barrett. He needs propping up. You know that."

"I guess so."

"Well, now you have something else to think about as your sleepy little head hits the pillow. I won't even ask where you've been, although I could probably make a good guess."

"That's tactful of you, Lisa."

"You're welcome, dear brother."

"Thank you," he said.

"Sleep well," she said.

"You too."

"Oh, no. I'm already up for a bright new day."

He was about to say something like "Good for you," but she'd already hung up.

She'd been looking out of the window, watching for him. That was how she'd timed the phone call of course. It was irksome. But there wasn't any way for him to complain. She was probably right about Barrett, after all, so she'd done him a favor.

How to prop Barrett up?

Sleep on it, he told himself, and he got undressed and climbed into bed for a few hours of sleep. He closed his eyes for what seemed like a few seconds at most and then opened them to see that there was light coming in through the windows. He got up, dressed again, and set out for what he hoped would be an undemanding day. He was only a little late getting into the office. There was still coffee in the pot and Effie brought him some with the messages that had been accumulating. "This one's interesting," she told him.

He glanced at her impressively regular copperplate handwriting and saw the name. "Who is Roger Livesy?"

"Administrative assistant to Senator Breckenridge," Effie told him. "That number is the senator's office."

"They've got their ears to the ground, don't they?" Castle observed, and he took a sip of the hot coffee. He'd only made the deal on Amy Breckenridge's book three days before, with Ralph Gordon of Plantagenet Books. Gordon hadn't been his first choice, but he owned Plantagenet and he was exactly the right kind of curmudgeon who wouldn't be intimidated by threats or susceptible to blandishments from someone like Breckenridge. And when he got his act together, he could publish a book as well as the bigger houses—or maybe even better because he had his own money riding on the bets he made. If he cared enough about a book, he could give it a kind of personal attention and care that it just wouldn't get from the employees of the larger houses.

Castle called Gordon and told Gordon's secretary that it was important enough to interrupt him in his meeting.

In a moment, Gordon was on the line. "Yah?"

"Ralph, this is Leonard Castle. I've had a phone call from Senator Breckenridge's office. Before I call them back I thought I ought to check with you. Have you announced anything, either in a general way or to them in particular?"

"Christ, no."

"Well, I sure as hell haven't."

"You think she would have?" Gordon asked.

"I don't know. It's possible. I'll try to get hold of her, but that's not easy."

"Why don't you just call Breckenridge and find out what he wants?"

"I never like to be unprepared."

"Those personal-hygiene flicks from the army must have really got to you, hunh?"

"They sure did," Castle said. "I'll let you know if it's anything worrisome."

"I'd appreciate that."

He tried to reach Amy Breckenridge but couldn't. He called the senator's office and asked for Roger Livesy. It took only a moment or two before he was put through.

"Mr. Livesy? This is Leonard Castle. I'm returning your call. What can I do for you?"

"The senator would like to see you," the voice at the other end informed him.

"I'm here from nine to five, pretty much every day."

"Well, you understand, Senator Breckenridge is a busy man. We were hoping we could persuade you to come down here to Washington. We'd send the senator's plane for you, of course."

"I'm sorry," Castle said. "I can't spare the time. Could you tell me what this is about?"

"I think you know what it's about," Livesy said. "Let's not play games, shall we?"

"No, no. No games. Just tell me, why don't you?"

"This book by the senator's ex-wife that you're representing has got to be stopped," Livesy said.

Castle thought for only an instant. He was pretty sure he was being recorded. "I can understand that that would be the way the senator might feel about it, but that isn't my view of it at all. As I say, I'm here from nine or a little after until about five. If you'd like to see me, or if the senator would, it's not difficult to arrange. You have the number, I believe."

And with a smile of cautious satisfaction, he hung up the telephone.

For five minutes or so, he sat there staring at the ceiling and taking occasional sips of his cooling coffee. Then he went out to tell Effie to get a message through to Amy Breckenridge that it was important for them to talk.

"Shall I tell her what it's about?"

"I think she'll know. I'm going out for a walk," he said. "I've got to clear my head and think a little."

"Enjoy!"

He was down in nether Chelsea by the time he'd figured out what his next moves ought to be in each of the games he was playing. He looked around him, mildly surprised, and he flagged a cab to take him back to the office.

*

Amanda Barnes was not at all the kind of person with whom Oliver Barrett felt comfortable. For one thing, she dressed outrageously, in that high-style peasant mode in many layers of incongruous prints and textures. On her head, she wore a recycled cloche from some thrift store. And her language was similarly high-style guttersnipe in tone. "Let's face it," she said, sprawling across the love seat of Barrett's living room with her legs splayed apart as if someone had just snatched away her cello, "my stepmother was a fag hag. The fruits just went bananas for her. They were right, of course. She had that streak of cruelty they adore. But there's a limit to what they'll stand for, don't you think? And if they're turned off, she'll just fade away. There's still money to be made from the old girl, as you've discovered yourself. And I don't mind your making a buck out of her poor dear memory. But there's no need to piss in the well. Have you got anything to drink? My mouth is a sewer."

He very nearly bit his lip trying not to agree with her. "Yes, of course. Fruit juice? Beer? Soda water?"

"Fruit juice would be lovely. Or even lovelier if you had a little vodka to lace it with."

"I think I can lace it for you."

"Blessings," she said, and rearranged her legs. Barrett supposed there was some headmistress at an old-line prep school whom the girl was still determinedly defying. He went off to his small but efficient kitchenette to find some grapefruit juice and vodka for Helen Burke's stepdaughter. It was important to keep an open mind, he told himself. It was important to find something about her to like. If he could like her, then she'd like him, and from mutual toleration there might come some mutual benefit. He had no clear idea what her errand was, but she had announced herself as the stepdaughter of the late Helen Burke and he'd checked her out. She was legitimate. She was a potential ally or, for that matter, a potential enemy. It was obviously better to have an ally.

He poured a generous slug of vodka into the juice, dropped in three ice cubes, and put it on a little silver tray with a paper napkin. He brought it out to her. "You said you had a proposition for me?" he prompted.

She took the drink from the proffered tray, gulped down a couple of swallows, and smiled. "Yes, I do," she said. "Now that she's scattered out over Nantucket Sound, there isn't any Helen Burke any more. I mean, she's whatever we all agree that she was. And that means that you've got a lot of influence, putting this book of hers together. Whatever you put down will be what a lot of people think."

"Yes?" he prompted, wishing she'd get to the point.

"Well, some of what she did was . . . unattractive is the mild word for it. You could also call it fucking outrageous, or just plain shitty. Any of the above. But what's the point? I mean, those industry moguls were right, you know? The reality doesn't matter; it's the image that counts. And if she has the image that all those fans out there can adore, why disappoint them? Why ruin it for them and for us too?"

"Whom do you mean by 'us'?" Barrett asked.

"The family. Me and my brother, and Sarah Nutall, who is also a stepdaughter by another marriage. We weren't very close, but we've gotten to be friendly in the last few years. We were all victims of the same tornado. She's not a bad person. Not my kind, maybe. She's a microbiologist in Oregon."

"And what is it that you're protecting?" Barrett asked.

"Her last four pictures, she had a piece of the producer's gross. And she had a half interest in the two television specials she did. Those get replayed every now and then, and checks show up in our mailboxes. Not for huge amounts, but then we don't have to do anything. We want to keep that alive. We want to keep the business going. You can put in little blemishes here and there, do it with the warts and all, as somebody said. But if you could leave out some of the festering sores and the boils, that'd be a favor to us."

"You're asking me to lie, then, is that it?"

"Not necessarily lie but leave out some of the less attractive parts of the truth. We'd make it worth your while."

He raised his eyebrows.

"Are you interested?" she asked. She drained her drink and set it down on the end table beside her. He picked it up and slid a coaster under it so it wouldn't ruin the finish on his table.

"What is it that you're offering? And in exchange for what, exactly?"

"I thought that for five thousand dollars you'd let us take a look at the manuscript before you turn it over to the publisher. And you'd promise to consider our objections if we have any to make to what you've got there. Is that fair?"

"I'd have to think about it," he said after a moment.

"Okay. I can understand that. All we're looking to do is to keep the thing within certain limits. We're not trying to be absolutely misleading. You'll still be able to imply that there might have been certain flaws in that polished surface that people saw. We had more reason to hate her than you ever could, right? I mean, you saw her . . . Once? Twice?"

"Just once," he admitted.

"For a couple of hours, she could seem to be quite human, if there was something to be gained by it. But you think about what you want to do. I'll call you in a few days, okay?"

"That'd be fine," he said, and he showed her out, relieved to be rid of her.

From the telephone booth on the corner, Amanda Barnes called the number on the business card in the pocket of her fringed cape. She identified herself and asked to be put through to Leonard Castle.

"How did it go?"

"Just the way you said it would. He hated me. And he hated the proposition. He'd have thrown me out in another five minutes, I swear. It was terribly funny!"

"You didn't laugh, I hope."

"Oh, no. I was just as earnest as I could be."

"Good."

"He'll do his worst, I'm certain, just to spite me," she said. "Or to show how he can't be bribed."

"What did he say when you offered him the money?"

"Oh, it was too wonderful. He didn't say anything for about half a minute. And then he managed to unclench his teeth enough to tell me he'd have to think about it. The way he'd have to think about leaping off the roof of his building."

"I appreciate your cooperation," Castle said.

"Look, I'm happy to do it. I hated that old bitch and so did my brother. So did Sarah Nutall, for that matter. If he comes out where we all want, I'll be the one who's grateful to you for giving me the chance to get back at the old bag. Warts and all, I think is the phrase, but she was all warts. She had warts on her heart."

"Is there anything else I can do for you?" Castle asked. "When are you flying back to Los Angeles?"

"You've done more than enough. I'm going to get out of these ridiculous clothes, see some friends, catch a play this evening, and fly back tomorrow."

"Have a good trip," Castle said. "And call me after you've had your next talk with him."

"I told him I'd call him in a week. So I'll have word for you then."

"And I'll let you know when I've seen the first draft and we know where we are," Castle promised. "I'm pretty sure we'll both get what we want."

*

Amy Breckenridge lit a cigarette and pulled the sheet of paper from the old Underwood on the trestle table she was using as a desk in Deedee's gatehouse in western Connecticut. Deedee and Bob Waterford were in Europe, on the Costa Smeralda actually, but they had been willing to offer their gatehouse as a kind of sanctuary. Amy and Deedee had been roommates in their senior year at Vassar, and Deedee was one of the few people to whom Amy had been able to turn for protection.

No hesitation, no reservations, no second thoughts. Which was terrific, considering what a thug Joe could be if he was crossed.

The main house was closed up, the water shut off, the toilets filled with antifreeze, and the refrigerators and freezers emptied. The elaborate alarm system was working, though, and Deedee had warned her old roommate not even to approach the main house because there were sensors that would call the security people and alert the sheriff's office. The gatehouse, which Deedee and Bob used as a guesthouse when they were in residence, was well stocked. It had food, liquor, blankets, linens—everything but a telephone, the absence of which was a kind of blessing. It suited Amy to sit in solitary splendor and wrestle with her life on these pages that she inserted into the typewriter at which she pounded for hours at a time.

She hadn't wanted the editorial help that Leonard Castle had offered. Not to begin with, at least. She preferred to come to terms with her life in her own way and at her own pace, facing unpleasant parts of it that she would not want to explore even in sympathetic company. She'd been over some of these things with one shrink or another and knew well enough in what caves her monsters lurked. But she also knew she had to fight them alone, on her own.

Her self-esteem was at stake. There were times when she was heartily sick of what she'd done, what she'd allowed to happen, and what she'd closed her eyes to. There were also times when she was proud of herself for what she'd suffered. She was a pretty tough character if she could feel equal to the indignities Joe Breckenridge had heaped upon her—from the time she'd been a college girl and he'd come down from Yale Law School to Poughkeepsie in that big red convertible of his. He'd been wearing khakis and an out-at-the-elbows cashmere sweater and he looked over the crop like a bull gazing at the new heifers. It wasn't just that he was the spoiled son of a millionaire, which was true enough. It was his cynical certainty of how the girls would react to his slightest show of interest, how they would put up with his rudeness and crudeness, how far they would go—or let him go—rather than risk losing him.

There were times when she could remember how she'd thought she was being original, making excuses for him, even feeling sorry for him because of the way most girls behaved, whoring after his money and his family's power. She'd told herself that his cynicism was an inevitable consequence of the gold-digging he'd found at every turn and on every date. But that was probably what every girl told herself, making the same excuses for him—and therefore for herself as well. Amy's first impression of him was in a gesture that seemed to epitomize all of their lives: he was sprawled in an easy chair in one of the lounges in Main, surrounded by Vassar girls, and she saw him snap his fingers and wait as the girls raced one another to light the cigarette that dangled from his sneering lips.

She'd been disgusted by that little scene, but more by the behavior of the girls than by Joe's willingness to test them and see how far they would go to undercut each other and demean themselves. The fact that none of them behaved this way with any other young men hardly excused them in Amy's eyes. She thought, on the contrary, that Joe

Breckenridge had managed to see through them, had brought out their worst and truest natures. It followed that he needed to be rescued from such predatory creatures as those awful girls who had flocked around him for all the wrong reasons.

She'd walked away and had tried to put the tableau out of her thoughts. It remained, though, and held her attention, so that, when she was invited a couple of weeks later to come along with a group of girls he was treating to pizza in one of the crummy bars not far from campus, she accepted, as eager as a naturalist who has an opportunity to make further observations of the behavior of his chosen beasts. There hadn't seemed any risk in going along with such a crowd. It was just an absurd and interesting thing to do, piling into his big red Olds convertible that way with eight or nine other girls. There was safety in numbers, wasn't there?

Well, there might have been, but Amy's attitude had been wrong, critical, amused, close to hostile. She'd said something or reacted, laughing or failing to laugh, in a way that had caught his attention. They'd been at a big round table and Amy had been as far away from Joe Breckenridge as she could get, which meant that she was directly opposite him. He noticed her, responded to what he took to be her challenge or maybe just tested the authenticity of her indifference. It was convincing enough to intrigue him. He invited her to switch places with the girl beside him. Amy refused, so he came around to her side of the table. And she hadn't known whether to feel triumphant or defeated, proud or humiliated. There were limits to how rude she could let herself be. After all, she was drinking his beer and eating his pizza, and she had come along on this "gang date" more out of curiosity than friendliness. She was there on false pretenses, then, and felt she owed him a minimal show of civility. So, tempted as she was to get up and leave, she couldn't quite bring herself to do that. She looked, instead, at the girl whom he had displaced, Carole something, with huge tits and a vacant face, who was now sitting where he'd been sitting before, utterly forlorn and obviously envious . . . And it was just too damned silly!

Her mood changed a little, the outrage transforming itself into an odd kind of dispassionate amusement. She was, for those few minutes, the wry observer, the wittily rueful non-participant, exactly the kind of girl Joe Breckenridge had been looking for and only seldom found. Amy saw through layer upon layer, understanding immediately that it wasn't just Joe Breckenridge's arrogant assumption that he was entitled to the good things of the world, but beyond that a dejected conviction that the good things of the world weren't what they were cracked up to be, that mostly they were worthless fakes. He'd proved to himself that these girls weren't any different from anyone else, that they weren't at all unattainable or distant. He had a kind of Midas touch in reverse, by which everything he touched or looked at or spoke to turned from gold to pot metal.

It would have been dishonest to deny that she was pleased to have captured his attention. She felt good about his having come all the way around the table to be next to her and talk to her. And she hadn't had a lighter or a book of matches at the ready to light his cigarettes with either. In fact, she'd told him to cut it out and stop being such a show-off when he'd done that bit at the pizza joint.

"I can't help it," he said. "I guess I just bring out the worst in people." And he rolled his eyes to let her know that it was a sexual boast.

"That must make life very drab for you," she said, evading the innuendo and taking him seriously. "Perhaps you should consider changes you might make. For your own sake, first of all, but for everyone else's too."

"I can stand it," he said, raising his beer mug.

"Can you?" she asked, teasing him, challenging him to be better.

And the answer, she now knew, after twenty years of study, was that he could stand it, that he could stand it better than most of the people around him. Better than she could, at any rate.

She remembered another evening—she thought it was another evening—in a setting someplace just off campus with the air alive with a light rain or a heavy mist that made showy halations around the streetlights. It had been coolish and dank, and she'd been drinking some. They'd all been drinking. There'd been a group of them again, but smaller this time, and it had diminished further as the girls gave up and went back to their rooms to study or wash their hair. Amy and Peg were the only ones left, and Joe of course. Peg was Joe's ostensible date. Anyway, she was the one girl who was always included and next to whom Joe generally sat. The three of them were walking along streets that were mostly dark, the foliage of the trees having begun to turn color but not yet having fallen to make piles of debris. Joe had taken Amy's hand and put it into his pocket, which had struck her as an uncharacteristically thoughtful thing to do, because it was chilly, and even though she wasn't uncomfortable her hands were cold. He had Peg's hand in his other pocket.

But then Amy had realized that her hand wasn't in his pocket at all.

He was wearing a raincoat that had a vent so that one could reach in through the pocket for keys or change or whatever in the trouser pocket inside the coat. And he had guided her hand through that vent and onto his penis.

He'd opened his fly and had pulled his penis out. It wasn't visible because the front of his raincoat was buttoned. But there it was, unmistakable and erect. And then she realized that Peg's hand was also there, that the two of them were holding each other's hands on Joe Breckenridge's penis.

It was such a crazy thing to be doing. Funny, of course, but outrageous too. Everything was funny then, either because of the alcohol or because Joe turned everything into a joke anyway. Amy had the impression that he was just turning his cock over to them, as if to say, leave me out of it and settle this between yourselves. After the joke had run its course, she pulled her hand away, but Peg hung on doggedly.

Maybe he was testing them to see what kind of good sports they were. Or what whores they were. Or what he could get away with.

More likely than not, it was just a thought that had crossed his mind at that instant, and there was hardly ever any reason for him not to act out some idea he'd had, not to pursue some momentary fancy.

Certainly this was the first time he'd tried it with Peg. She decided later that she had been grossed out. And while she might have expressed her reluctance right at that moment, there was no way for her to go along with it at first and then complain about it later, which was exactly what she did. It made her into a bad sport, which was unattractive. Worse, it was unshrewd. Nobody ever got anywhere taking a high moral tone with Jonas Breckenridge. He'd heard all that blather before from a series of authority figures and prep school masters, and he'd tuned it out permanently.

The next time he came back to Vassar, it had been to see her, Amy.

Peg was suddenly ancient history. Peg was, Amy now realized, lucky to be well out of it. But that was impossible to see back then.

Amy put out her cigarette, stretched, and put another sheet of paper into the Underwood. This was crazy. She wasn't going to publish this, was she? She wasn't going to let her children see this. Did she have that much nerve? Or that much anger? Would they see it as honesty or as a betrayal of their father and of the family's secrets?

But all such questions had to be postponed. The thing was first to get it down, get it onto the page. What these weeks of effort had taught her was that she was tougher than she'd supposed. She'd been able to stand Jonas and his escapades the first time around, and she'd even been able to stand her own cowlike passivity as she'd gone over the events of those years. She could laugh or cry now or sometimes waver between the two, but she could stand to think about it. Sometimes she could even understand what had happened in ways that surprised her.

Some of those therapists had done some good, after all.

Surely, what he'd seen on that fateful walk was her willingness to put up with his whims, whatever their cost might be, as long as there was a covering of respectability. The raincoat—a London Fog trench coat, she remembered—was emblematic of that external cloak of propriety they conspired to maintain for the rest of their time together. And with every passing moment and every succeeding day, it was more and more difficult to complain about what he was doing, and how, and with whom.

She got up, stretched again, poured herself a cup of beef bouillon from the thermos, and resumed her typing. It sounded like some sniper's rapid fire from the cover of some high perch.

She only wished it were as safe as that.

She knocked off at dusk and walked the two miles to the garage where there was a phone booth on the outside of the cinder-block building. She called her number in New York and punched in a code that cued her machine to spit back its messages. One of these was from Leonard Castle, asking her to call him as soon as possible.

*

Castle left the vestibule of the building in which he had been standing. He walked around the block, all but inviting his assailant to make another attempt. It was hardly a pleasant walk, but at least he had the feeling of freedom of action and of movement to counterbalance his fear. He wasn't so abjectly reduced this way.

He rounded the block a second time, stopping every now and then, looking behind him, scanning the opposite sidewalk. It did seem safe enough.

In fact, it was hard to believe that the events of the earlier part of the evening had actually taken place.

That someone should be so enraged at him, and so vindictive . . .

But he hadn't imagined it. Not at all.

Once more, then, to be triple sure.

Maybe he'd just wear the bastard out, leading him around and around the block this way.

9

LIVESY: Well, here we are. Just the way you wanted. Senator Breckenridge, this is Leonard Castle.

BRECKENRIDGE: Well, we all know who we are.

CASTLE: I appreciate your coming. On a matter of this kind of impor-
tance, I thought it'd be better all around if we dealt in person,
face to face . . .

LIVESY: If you'll remember, I invited you to come to the senator's
office in Washington . . .

CASTLE: Yes, you did. And if you'll remember, I said that was incon-
venient. I knew Senator Breckenridge had a speaking engagement
here in New York. So he had to be up here. I had no plans to be in
Washington. And I have no particular need to see him. You're the
ones who wanted to see me.

BRECKENRIDGE: I think we can forget about all that now. I think we
might move on to more substantive matters. You're representing
my wife's book, is that right?

CASTLE: That's correct. Your ex-wife's book.

BRECKENRIDGE: She's not altogether stable, you know. She's been
hospitalized a number of times for psychiatric evaluation and for
episodes of depression and paranoia.

CASTLE: Yes, she was quite candid about her history. She seems perfectly reasonable now, though, I must say.

BRECKENRIDGE: Still, it's a precarious balance. Don't you feel any
concern for a woman like that? Don't you feel some obligation to
protect your own client?

CASTLE: You mean, to protect her from an attack you might make on her to discredit her book? That can't be what you mean!

BRECKENRIDGE: No, not at all. I would never do such a thing. But there are all kinds of players in any high-stakes game. There are enemies of my enemies who aren't necessarily my friends. There are people who might think they'd be doing me a favor and would use whatever ammunition they had at hand in order to defend me . . . I can't always control all that. What Political Action Committees do is up to them.

LIVESY: The senator feels an obligation to his ex-wife, and for her own good is trying to protect her from some of the consequences of an unwise course of action.

CASTLE: Well, that's a much more interesting opening than what we've been talking about on the telephone, where I was more or less an accessory to blackmail.

BRECKENRIDGE: I think Mr. Livesy here owes you an apology for an excess in zeal in his efforts to protect me.

LIVESY: I do apologize.

CASTLE: That's quite all right. I'm afraid I didn't take the remark very seriously. But I don't take this particular tactic very seriously either. You're not worried about attacks on your ex-wife. You're worried about what she's going to say in this book about you and about her life with you. And you want the book stopped. Isn't that right?

BRECKENRIDGE: Motives aside, that's the bottom line, yes.

CASTLE: And you've been breaking deals with publishing houses and threatening people all over town for a month or so, to make sure that her book never sees the light of day.

LIVESY: You'd have a very hard time proving that.

CASTLE: This isn't a courtroom, Mr. Livesy. Until we start talking honestly to one another, there's not a whole lot we're going to get accomplished. I was willing to meet with you, but as I told you, I'm a busy man. This isn't the Senate, and I don't have time for tactics and games and bullshit.

BRECKENRIDGE: There's no need to be offensive, Mr. Castle.

CASTLE: Isn't there, Senator? You're trying to muzzle my client. You're throwing your weight around, your power and money, to prevent her book from getting published. It's a violation of her constitutional rights and it's restraint of trade too, as Mr. Livesy can tell you. You're a lawyer, by the way, aren't you? You sure as hell sound like a lawyer.

LIVESY: That's right, I'm an attorney, yes . . .

CASTLE: Well, then you know damned well that what you're doing is wrong . . .

LIVESY: My conscience is clear. I'm trying to protect the senator. I'm trying to make sure that his chances for re-election aren't ruined by the venomous outpourings of an embittered woman. I believe in the senator and in what he's trying to do for the country. And I'll do anything I have to do . . .

CASTLE: Sure, sure, sure. Who was it who said that patriotism is the last refuge of a scoundrel?

BRECKENRIDGE: I think that was Dr. Johnson. Look, why don't we start over on this? Let's see if there's a way of getting together on this.

CASTLE: You want the book not to happen.

BRECKENRIDGE: That's right.

CASTLE: Well, that's a matter for you to take up with your ex-wife, I'd think. It's her decision, not mine. And then, my interest is in having the book happen. I get ten percent of its earnings. No book, no earnings. It's as simple as that.

BRECKENRIDGE: I think we can figure out ways of compensating you. For your good offices here in these negotiations. Amy and I have had our difficulties, which we don't need to go into here.

CASTLE: I suppose I could relay an offer. But I'm not sure she'll be interested.

LIVESY: Why not?

CASTLE: She's got enough money from the separation agreement. Money isn't the issue here. I think she's trying to make a declaration here, to the world, or to your children, or maybe just to herself, that what's happened to her was terrible, and that a lot of her problems have been caused by what she'd been made to live with.

LIVESY: That's ridiculous on its face. That's bullshit.

CASTLE: Is it? Then we've got nothing to talk about.

LIVESY: That may be the only sensible thing you've said this morning.

BRECKENRIDGE: Let's take it easy here. I'm not sure I understand what you're getting at. You want me to admit to everything she'd have written in the book? Then she doesn't have to write the book!

CASTLE: More or less, that's it. But I don't think you'd have to admit it to the general public. There are other parties here. I mentioned the children. The issue here is Amy's self-respect. She's got to

have that. If you're serious about this, you've got to leave her a
little better off than she was at the beginning of this business.
Better off with the kids and better off with herself too. Otherwise,
she's going to go ahead with the book because she sees it as the
only way she can live with herself.

BRECKENRIDGE: She's told you this?

CASTLE: Some of it. Some of it I've guessed at. But I'd certainly give it
some thought if I were you. You come at her the way you were,
with threats and so on, and you don't leave her a lot of choices
except to fight. You make some sort of offer to talk to the children
about how your lives together have been, and rework the arrangement on visitation so that she gets to see them . . . Well, you
might get somewhere. She doesn't seem crazy to me, I'll tell you.

LIVESY: And you don't think that's blackmail?

CASTLE: She claims that you've been blackmailing her for years and
that she's been living with extortion and threats for as long as she
can remember.

LIVESY: That's absurd.

CASTLE: You were the attorney when she was committed to McClean's
in '78, weren't you?

LIVESY: That's correct.

CASTLE: And you arranged for her release when she agreed not to file
for separation, even though the senator was living apart from her
and was sharing an apartment with Elvira Scoville? Was that just
a coincidence? And was it also just a coincidence that the senator
was running for re-election that year?

BRECKENRIDGE: Let's suppose that's all true. You can understand that
these are family matters, laundry I'd just as soon not have washed
in public. If I were to admit to you that that was what happened,
would she be likely to give up the idea of writing and publishing
this book?

CASTLE: I'd certainly be willing to discuss that possibility with
her . . .

*

Castle switched off the tape player. "The rest of it is saying goodbye
and who's going to call whom and that business. But that was the
meeting. That was what happened. He pretty much admits what
they'd been doing. And if they try to deny it, you've got my word and
the tape, together."

"This wasn't what I expected. I've been writing. I honestly expected that there'd be a book."

"I know that. If you don't mind a word of advice, I'd put the manuscript away in some safe place. I mean in a safe-deposit box somewhere in a bank you don't ordinarily use. And I'd leave it there. Who knows what's going to happen in a year or in five? You might want to come back to it someday. You might want to work on it again. There are circumstances in which you might want to publish it, or to circulate it privately."

"You're right, of course."

"So, you made out all right," he said. "It's not so bad that there isn't a book right now."

"You've gone to a lot of trouble. And you haven't been paid. There ought to be some way . . ."

He put his hand up in the traffic-cop gesture. "No, no, I'm satisfied. I had fun, actually. It's nice to stand up to the big guys every now and then, and it's even nicer to win. I've got no kick."

"I was afraid you'd say that," she said. "And I brought this along, just in case."

She handed him a small box.

"Well, okay. I don't want to be rude about it. And I love presents," he said. "Can I open it?"

"Please do."

He took off the silver paper and opened the box. It was a Mont Blanc pen, but not the ordinary kind in the black plastic. This one was in solid gold.

"You didn't have to do this, you know."

"I know that. I wanted to. As a small token of my appreciation."

"Well, okay," he said. "And if you ever do go back to the book, give me a call. I'm still your agent."

"I promise."

He popped open the cassette player and handed her the tape. She took it.

"Put that in the safe-deposit box too."

She nodded. He thought she was about to say something else but then he saw that she was too choked up. She blew him a kiss and all but ran out of the office.

*

Perhaps thirty seconds later, Susan Flowers came in. Amy Breckenridge had left the door to Castle's inner office open and Susan just
appeared, wanting to know, "How long has that been going on?"

"What are you talking about?"

"That was Amy Breckenridge."

"And?"

"And you didn't think I'd be interested? I am in the news business,
you'll recall."

"Yes, that's true. But this wasn't something I wanted to communi-
cate to the media."

"Which is another way of saying you don't trust me to keep a
secret."

"Not at all," he said. "Why don't you sit down? You're upset. Calm
down a little. It's no big deal, really."

"I'm perfectly calm. It's just that I'd thought we'd got to a different
place, and apparently I was wrong."

"That's ridiculous," Castle said. "I don't tell you every little thing
that goes on in the office. And you never led me to believe you expected me to."

"Amy Breckenridge is hardly a little thing. She's doing a book,
right? And you're representing her. That's a fairly big thing, for my
money."

"Well, it would be if it were true, but it isn't. She's not doing a
book."

"She's become an Avon lady? What else would she be doing here?"

"We'd been talking about a book, but she's decided not to do it. I'll
be happy to talk to you about this, really, but not this way. This is
hostile and unpleasant."

"I'm sorry," Susan said. "I was passing by and I thought I'd come
up and find out if you were free for lunch. Just on a whim. I wasn't
spying, I promise. But when I saw her out in the hall, I couldn't help
wondering what you'd been keeping from me, and why."

"It isn't that I don't trust you. On the contrary, I'd be glad to tell
you anything you want to know. But this was a particularly delicate
piece of business. Not very attractive, and maybe even dangerous. I
wanted to protect you."

"I see."

"Good," he said. But he saw that she didn't see at all. She'd closed
down and switched off. It had been the wrong thing to say, and all
kinds of feminist alarms had gone off. Her lips were set. Her stare was

level and icy. "Helpless little Susie is so grateful to the big man for protecting his poor and adoring bit of fluff—is that it?"

"Not at all," he protested.

But it was too late. She'd turned away and was already sweeping out through the outer office and into the hall.

How dumb!

What he should have said was that Amy Breckenridge must have been in the office next door, the Icelandic Mission to the United Nations. Or across the hall, at the National Association of Pet Cemeteries.

He thought of going after her, but decided it would be better to let her cool down a little. Maybe even a couple of days.

Shit!

*

McCracken hadn't wanted any part of it. He had already done his share and more, and the book had done well enough. The writing of the manuscript and then the publicity tour for the hardback edition had taken up the better part of a year of his life. And his involvement with Wanda had been as much her responsibility as his. They had both been consenting adults. In a way, their affair had been necessary for her as a stepping-stone on the way to her liberation from Lucid, just as it had been a useful and pleasant interlude for him during his recovery from the wounds of his divorce.

But to meet again a year later and try to go back to that precariously balanced relationship, part friendship and part mutual exploitation . . . Well, he had not been enthusiastic. He hadn't believed that there was much anyone could do to promote paperbacks anyway. They either moved or didn't, riding on the success of the hardback edition and governed by mysterious forces that seemed beyond the manipulations of publishers, let alone mere authors. In any case, it was Wanda whom the interviewers wanted to talk to, not Pete McCracken. Wanda, or, as she was now calling herself, Margaret Iannacone.

But despite all his objections to the publishers and to Castle too, objections McCracken thought were logical and reasonable, he had been unable to persuade Wanda when she'd called to plead with him. She asked him, in the name of their friendship, to come along with her, at least for the first couple of weeks of the tour, just the northeast corridor from Boston to Atlanta. She conceded that there wasn't a lot for him to do, but it was important to her. As far as he was able to tell, she wanted him along for luck, for the confidence he gave her and the feeling of being somebody.

"But of course you're somebody. They wouldn't be talking to you on these television programs if they didn't think you were somebody!" he'd tried to tell her.

But she still thought of herself as a freak, a moral monster whom they had on their programs only to stare at. She could stand it, though, if he were there, at least at the beginning. "Please, Pete?"

In the end, he'd given in and had agreed to come along, knowing that it was silly and that he was wasting his time but figuring that he owed her this relatively small effort. He could go on to other books and other subjects while she was stuck with this one role, this one life. He wasn't happy about how she had been picked up and turned into an emblem of a certain group of mad-eyed radical harpies who wanted to ban pornography on the ground that it was an assault against women, but he understood that Wanda—or Margaret now—hadn't been the source of this idea. It was just out there for her to use or be used by, a gimmick for talk-show hosts who wanted a more serious pretext for having her on their shows than the mere gawking. (Oh, yes, no question but Wanda was right about that: people watched her and listened to her, thinking to themselves what a marvel it was that she'd fucked so many different guys so many different ways and survived!)

It had also become clear that there was a little acting out now and then, not so much from the talk-show hosts as from their assistants, their talent coordinators and associate producers, all those people who wander around studios looking officious and carrying clipboards and stopwatches. And if she thought it might do her some real good, Margaret might excuse herself while Wanda showed up, just for old times' sake, to boff another rube. After all, it wasn't at Lucid's orders any more but on her own whim now, and she was a free woman and could do anything she wanted to. There was no point in proclaiming one's freedom and then not using it, not doing anything with it.

Well, that was okay with McCracken, or almost. It wasn't, as the saying goes, his ass. Last time around, on the tour for the hardback, he'd been able to pick up on what was going on—and he'd felt relieved, actually, that there wasn't going to be any exclusive lifetime contract between himself and Wanda, that he had an honorable excuse now to go his separate way. He didn't have to feel responsible for her any more. (And yet, somehow, a part of him suspected, then and still, that she'd set it up that way, that she'd worked it deliberately to let him catch her that time in the motel room with the kid who played the bass guitar in the group that was to appear on the same show the next morning. The Kansas Coastline, the group had been called, or some such name.)

So, yes, he'd agreed, and he'd met her in New York and they had renewed their acquaintance as he'd expected they would, eating, drinking, and sleeping together once again. And why the hell not?

Now that they were into the second week of it, though, McCracken's enthusiasm, modest even at the start, had begun to wane. She was getting on his nerves in little ways that were unimportant and that she couldn't do much about. Stupid things, some of them, to object to. It bothered him how she'd pepper her conversations with "like" and "you know," instead of just shutting her mouth and allowing herself a moment's pause in which to think. And he tried to explain to her about prepositions and the cases of pronouns, but he couldn't get her to see that there was anything wrong with "between you and I," no matter how simple and clear he tried to be.

"Look, doll," she said, "if I could handle that preposition stuff as well as I handled the proposition stuff, I wouldn't have needed you in the first place, would I? I could have just sat down and done the book myself. I can talk body English and make my points clear."

"I'm sure you can, dear."

By the time they got to Baltimore, he'd pretty much decided to excuse himself, claim to have some emergency back in New York, and take off. She was doing fine and didn't need him any more. The Baltimore schedule was a full one with a newspaperwoman for breakfast, a morning television show, and then a radio talk show in the afternoon. McCracken's plan was to tell her on the way to Washington that he'd been called home and see how she took it. With any kind of luck, he'd be back in his apartment by midnight.

But nothing works out the way people plan. As it happened, the morning television show was organized around the general topic of degradation, which was general enough to admit a fairly wide variety of suffering guests. There was a representative from a shelter for battered women, and there was an old bag who had once been in movies and actually turned into a bag lady before she'd found God and been saved by some monks, and there was a mud-wrestling team that was supposed to appear at some hospital benefit that had been canceled because of the protests from a number of women's groups. And then there was Margaret Iannacone, better known to the audience as Wanda Lathem, former star of hard-core pornographic films.

In the green room, McCracken did a double take when he was

introduced to the other guests on the show for that day. The old bag
who had found God was Jill Morgan, who really had been up there in
the musicals of the forties, singing and dancing her way into the hearts
of all Americans. And she was doing some dopey dinner-theater gig,
not even in Baltimore but out in the country somewhere. If you caught
her at the right angle in the right light, you could see that it was the
same face all right. But she'd really given it some hard wear along the
way.

Naturally, Jill and Margaret hit it off at once, not only commiserat-
ing with each other but admiring each other for courage and resilience
and toughness or maybe just being too stupid to know when to quit.
They took over the show, not quite condescending to their host, a
runty little guy who was trying to imitate Phil Donahue and be cute
and boyish. They won the audience over and were generous in their
support of the mud wrestlers, who did what they had to do and made
the best of their options. Pity the poor working girl!

After the show, they exchanged addresses and phone numbers and
were about to go their separate ways when Jill thought to ask Margaret what her next appointment was.

"*Chesapeake Speaks,*" Margaret told her. "Some radio talk show, I
think."

"Me too!" Jill said.

It was a not quite amazing coincidence, but they decided to make
the most of it. Of course Jill would come along in the limo the paperback publishers had laid on and join Pete and Margaret for lunch . . .

So he found himself spending the most of the day with Jill Morgan,
and yes, it was a dumb story, the collapse of the studio system and the
loss of the security of being on contract, and she'd reacted in the worst
possible way by trying to hide in a bottle. She'd lost her house and
money and credit, and damned near her life. She'd fled California,
come back East, and had worked strip joints and had even turned a
few tricks on the way down toward her bad days as a bag lady. And
then the Pauline Brothers had helped her dry out and given her a job
at the monastery in the kitchen preparing vegetables and washing
dishes. A dumb story, but Pete McCracken was enough of a stylist to
be alert to the honesty and the simplicity with which she told it. She
wasn't out to score points. She was generous with her praise for the
Pauline Brothers and what they did, not just for her or for former
movie stars but for the hopeless and the lost, whoever they were and
however they presented themselves.

"Have you ever thought of doing a book?" he asked.

"Really! What a terrific idea!" Margaret had managed to see the possibilities, had leapt ahead to a further sharing, not just of lunch and a limo but of her great success. It was decent of her. She could have reacted the other way and been jealous and possessive. But no, whatever her sins, jealousy and possessiveness weren't among them. "Pete could write it with you," she suggested. "And Leonard Castle—he's our agent—could get you a terrific deal. It'd be just what you need for your comeback."

"I don't think I'm making any comeback. I'm just doing this bit for the dinner theater to get some money together for the brothers. Their organ is in terrible shape and needs an overhaul."

"Their organ?" Margaret asked.

"The pipe organ," McCracken explained. "Like in a church."

"Oh, yeah, right. But why stop at that? Why not get yourself a little something out of it, a nest egg . . ."

"It's something to think about," McCracken said. He saw it as a definite maybe, but it was a way of extricating himself from Margaret and returning to New York.

"You think?" Jill asked.

"Why not? It worked for Margaret here."

"Well, that's different. She was exotic. I was just a bum, you know. There's nothing interesting in that."

"There wouldn't be if you were still a bum, but you aren't. You've come back, you've taken hold of yourself. The brothers are a terrific story in themselves."

"Oh, yes, they're wonderful. They've been marvelous. I could do it for them. And . . ."

"And?" he prompted.

"I had a kid once. I had to give it up for adoption. That's what the studio made me do. If I had a book like yours, and went around to all the cities, maybe I could find him. Or he'd find me."

That was what did it. It was more than a maybe now. It was mouthwatering. "Let me go and make a phone call, will you?" he asked.

"Who are you going to call?" Margaret asked.

"The man you suggested. Leonard, of course. I think he might be interested in this."

"See? Just like I told you! Between you and I, it's already happened," Margaret said.

"It's scary. I'm not used to good things happening. I can hardly believe it," Jill said, but Pete McCracken was already out in the lobby, digging for change to make the call to New York.

*

Castle hadn't exactly drooled with excitement but he'd been willing enough to meet with McCracken and listen for ten or fifteen minutes to the pitch the writer wanted to make. Castle had looked first to McCracken's own interest in the Jill Morgan story—which was minimal. McCracken had done well on his piece of Wanda Lathem's book, and now he wanted to take off some time and work on the novel he'd been toying with off and on for years. He could afford a little self-indulgence now. A year or two, or even more if he was thrifty.

So McCracken wasn't looking for work. He was doing a good deed, then? As delicately as possible, Castle asked him if that was his purpose.

"I guess so. I think she's an impressive lady. And I think this is going to be dynamite. Really. It isn't everybody's cup of tea, maybe, but the basic drama is there, just begging to be turned into somebody's gold. And you've done okay by me. I figured the least I could do was let you know about her. The degradation and redemption is all there, but that's just the basic recipe. The icing on the cake is that lost kid. She had to give up her child back in the forties, and it's mother love and sacrifice, *Lassie, Come Home,* and apple pie, and Christmas Eve all rolled into one. You could vomit, except that she's modest and reasonable. And even halfway intelligent to talk to."

"You couldn't be persuaded, if everything you're telling me is true, to have anything to do with this?"

"I don't know. If she wants somebody to go over what she's written, and if the money's right, I guess I could find a couple of months somewhere. But I'd prefer it if you could find another guy. Or maybe a woman. I'm not an important part of this."

"And you say she's living in a monastery?"

"That's it, on that card," McCracken said, pointing to the index card he'd already flipped across the agent's desk. "Believe me, it's worth a trip."

"I appreciate your coming by," Castle had said. And he'd telephoned the woman, half hoping that she'd be ridiculous and absurd, one way or another unacceptable. But she was pretty much the way McCracken had described her, sober and direct, not at all self-pitying, and almost amused by what had happened to her. And not too eager, either, which was often a warning signal. She was willing to talk, willing to consider the possibility of a book, but only because she wanted to repay the kindnesses of the Pauline Brothers, and because there was the chance that this was a way of finding her long-lost child.

Hemingway once said that a writer's most important piece of equipment was a portable, foolproof shit detector. It was vital for an agent too, and Castle's hadn't gone off. There had been no whistles or bells, or any ominous whirrings or rumblings. "Next Tuesday, then?" he'd said, flipping the pages of his desk calendar.

"Any time. I'll be here," she'd said. And she'd given him directions for getting there, to hell and gone, somewhere out in the middle of Prince Georges County.

When the appointed day arrived, Castle was tempted to call and cancel. He wasn't sick but neither was he quite well. Instead, he was tired, slightly achy, and somewhat depressed. At best, he was fighting off a virus. More likely than not, he'd be undone in a day or so and would have to stay in bed for a while. But because it would have been so easy to plead illness and forget about Jill Morgan, he'd been unwilling to do so. Feeling like a fool, he put in a few hours at the office, then caught a cab for Pennsylvania Station and took a train down to New Carrollton, the stop after Baltimore. He took a couple of aspirin on the train, which helped the muscle aches, but he still felt generally punk. He found a cab that would take him to the monastery, and on the way wondered what it would be like to be nursed by monks. If he didn't get any worse, it might be interesting to lie on rough sheets in a white-washed cubicle and eat barley soup from a pottery bowl that was brought in by some tonsured fellow with a distant and yet kindly expression. The peace and quiet of a monastery would be a pleasant change.

He was surprised by this kind of daydreaming. Ordinarily, he supposed monks to be mostly misfits and nuts about whom the best one could claim was that they were harmless. If they'd been decent to Jill Morgan, that didn't mean they were necessarily sane or tolerable. They probably got up in the middle of the night to pray. A socially acceptable kind of insanity was all it was.

The building looked to be institutional but comfortable, like some small college or, more likely, an executive conference center. There were beautifully kept lawns and gardens and, off to one side, a group of fruit trees in a small orchard. Castle dismissed the cab and rang the bell at the front door, a real brass bell, brightly polished, which one sounded by tugging on the rope attached to the clapper. It was peculiarly operatic. A monk opened the door.

"I'm Leonard Castle," he said. "I'm here to see Jill Morgan, if that's possible."

"Certainly. Do come in. I'm Brother Timothy. Won't you sit down?"

The entrance hall had a couple of leather sofas flanking a large stone hearth in which there were logs on enormous cast-iron andirons. On the opposite wall was a refectory table with a pair of Spanish lamps. Castle sat down on one of the sofas, or actually he perched lightly on the edge of one of the cushions. He was like a cat, relaxed but alert and ready to pounce. Or flee. His fatigue was gone and the achiness forgotten.

She appeared and said, "Mr. Castle, it was good of you to come all this way."

"It's a pleasure," he said, taking in a lot from the first instant. The brassy blonde was now dulled down to light brown with streaks of gray. The face was like a model of itself in dough. There was something broad and flattened about her body to make him think of Eastern Europe, Poland or maybe Czechoslovakia. What had her name been before the studio came up with Morgan? He couldn't remember.

"There's a parlor where we can talk. Would you care for coffee or tea?"

"Nothing, thank you," he said, and he followed her into a smaller room in which there were a couple of Windsor chairs on either side of a drum table. There was an opening high up on the wall that was covered by a piece of grillwork—where some superior could listen in? Or to suggest that to the guests as a possibility? Or was it just a heating duct?

"Pete McCracken is a very generous man," she began.

"He can be. He was interested in what you had to say."

"He's done wonderful things for Margaret. Or Wanda. She told me how he'd helped her."

"Actually, I think they helped each other," Castle said.

"It often works out that way," Jill Morgan said. "Bread upon the waters coming back ninefold."

"But often soggy, I find," Castle said. "Tell me about the child."

"It was 1947, and I'd made the move from second lead up to leading lady. I'd done a couple of musicals, and I'd been offered *London Bridge,* which I was very excited about because Lenny Peterkin was going to be the leading man and he was such a wonderful dancer. Anyway, I was pregnant and I was Catholic. I didn't want to have an abortion. And marriage was impossible because the man was already married and he was Catholic too. And his wife was ill, which made it worse. I mean, even now, I can't blame anyone. It just seems terribly sad. Then, I thought it was the end of the world, and I went to the head of the studio—I was twenty-four years old, you have to remember—to tell him I was going to have this baby. It was a way of ending the suspense, I guess. It was like being on a high ledge and being afraid of heights, so that eventually you just leap as a way of getting down. I was doing that. A desperate leap or a leap of faith. Certainly, I was handing over my destiny."

Castle was listening, but he was also looking at the way she had her hands in her lap, loosely held, like two sleeping puppies. She didn't gesture much or show any agitation. There was, as McCracken had reported, a directness and a serenity that was appealing and convincing.

". . . and what Mr. Feingold said was that they'd be willing to hold off on the film for a few months. I was to go ahead and have the child, and they'd arrange for it to be adopted. He was very understanding and fatherly. It was only when I asked whether there might be some other choice besides adoption that I realized there was an iron fist inside his velvet glove. There used to be a morals clause in all the contracts, and Mr. Feingold said that he didn't like that clause any more than I did and didn't want to have to invoke it, and that as long as there was no public scandal he wouldn't. The implication was that I might be able to go through a pregnancy in secret, but there was no way I could bring up a child without word getting out, and then the morals clause would kick in, and I'd be fired. Automatically."

"So you did what he said."

"I did. I had the child. It was a little boy. And I signed the papers the studio lawyers had prepared for me. And they took the baby away and I never saw him again after those first couple of days in the hospital."

"Yes, I see," Castle said. "That must have been very hard for you. But if you were to do this book and if someone were to come forward and claim to be your son, how could you possibly tell whether he was really your child or just some fortune hunter . . ."

"There's not much of a fortune, I'm afraid," she said.

"Still, people have been mugged and killed for a few dollars. There will be the appearance of prosperity at least, and maybe some of the substance too, from the book itself. Let's just assume that there may be people who'd like to claim you as a parent. How would you be able to tell the authentic one from any of the others?"

"There was a rattle," she said.

His heart sank. Was that what she'd been counting on all those years?

". . . and it looked like it was silver, but it wasn't. It was made out of platinum. And instead of beans or pebbles or whatever they put in rattles, this had rubies."

"I don't understand," Castle said.

"Well, I wanted to give the child something, and it had to be . . . something worth holding on to, maybe, but nothing so precious that people would steal it. I thought a little silver rattle from the birth mother might be something a child would hold on to. And if there was ever a need, if he or his family was ever so much in want that they had to pawn a baby's silver rattle, then—assuming they went to somebody honest—they'd get some real help. And that'd be something they'd remember."

"Unless it was just lost."

"Oh, yes. The rattle could be lost. Or the baby could have died. All kinds of terrible things could have happened. One must hope for the best and endure the rest. That's what they tell me around here, anyway. And it's true."

"I admire your attitude," Castle said.

"I'm not so serene as I sound," she admitted. "Faith isn't something you wake up with and just have, from then on. I have my doubts too and times when I'm close to despair. But that's what prayer is for. Not to make something happen but to prepare ourselves to accept whatever comes. To accept the good things is sometimes just as hard as to accept the bad. I sound awful, don't I, smug and insufferable. But it isn't like that. When it's right, the way it is a lot with the monks here, with Brother Timothy for instance, it's absolutely the opposite of that. Not smug and pious but meek and simple, like . . . like a kitten in your hand, feeling the warmth of your hand and purring. Does that make sense?"

"I think so," Castle said. "You mean that you'll do the book in order to see what it brings, and you won't be too disappointed if it doesn't work out."

"I'm not sure I won't be disappointed, but I'll try to accept my disappointment somehow."

"You won't say anything in the book about the rattle? Or will you?"

"I don't know. It wasn't the greatest idea in the world, but then I was only a kid and I didn't have a whole lot of time. It seems very melodramatic now, but I'd been in the movies ever since I was fifteen and I didn't know very much about life off-screen. It's just like what some studio screenwriter might have dreamed up, isn't it?"

"A little, maybe, but that's part of its charm. That, and your admission, your recognition of how it was."

"That's not so bad, then, is it?" she said, and smiled. "After all, charm will get us sales, and sales will get us readers, and if there are enough readers, maybe my dream will come true and there will be some word of what became of my little boy."

"Exactly," Castle said. "I couldn't have put it better."

"You'll represent the book, then?"

"I'd be delighted. I really would. I'm sure it will do well. Maybe it will even do what you hope."

"Our prayers are answered, but sometimes it's hard to understand what the answers are or what they mean. That's what the brothers tell me."

"You work in the kitchen here?"

She nodded. "I did that dinner-theater thing, but that was for some money for the chapel organ. And for my nerve, to see if I could face the public again. I was the old countess in *Royal Scandal*. It's not a big part. I just had the one song. But people were kind . . ."

"I'm sure you did well."

"It did well for me. It was enough to get me together with Margaret Iannacone. And with Pete McCracken, and now with you. Who could have predicted any of that? It couldn't have happened if I'd been peeling vegetables all that time for the refectory here."

"No, probably not," Castle conceded.

"Are you sure you wouldn't like some tea?"

"All right, thank you. Yes, I'll take a cup of tea. And then I have to get going. There's a train I can catch in an hour and ten minutes that will get me back to New York not too late." He didn't tell her about the cold he was fighting off or how he had almost called to cancel their meeting. He knew that she'd take his reluctant appearance as another sign. "Can I telephone for a taxi?"

"Brother Thomas will drive you back. He's another of my particular friends. You're our guest, after all."

"There's no need."

"Oh, they wouldn't have it any other way. China tea or Indian?"

"Either one," he said.

"I'll get it. And I'll bring you a small packet that may be useful for you. Sample pages, you might say. I've been working on this for months."

"Really!"

"It began as a spiritual exercise," she told him. "But I knew that there'd be a moment when it wanted to turn into something else. And you see, it has!"

*

Jack Ditson's memo was centered on the blotter of Susan Flowers' desk: "Castle still backburnered? Let's talk."

The preposterous jargon of penny-pinching cablese was a nostalgic kind of gesture these days, almost like the lapeled vests Ditson wore when he was feeling dandyish. Now that copy got bounced off satellites by high-speed computers with their agile modems, it was no longer an economy to dream up portmanteau words like "backburnered" to keep costs down. But he'd learned those words and that habit, which was now a signature, almost a private joke.

What she was avoiding, of course, was the first word of the memorandum. She had been right to object to Castle's condescension, and yet she supposed there were other ways to have handled it. She had acted without thinking, which was unusual for her, and she was sorry —not for him but for herself. Or for the relationship, which she had begun to enjoy and therefore had tried too soon to test, almost hoping it would fail. As of course it had.

She might have called him, might have expressed her regrets in any number of ways—a small silly gift, liquor, or, even better, flowers, or maybe a hookah, as a peace pipe, with a small nosegay in the bowl. But she had done none of these things, choosing instead to wait for him to make some move in the direction of mollification. And he was every bit as proud as she, and hadn't called or written, or sent some token, as he perfectly well could have.

She'd decided to let fate and happenstance take over. Either they'd be thrown together somehow or they wouldn't be, and one way or another external events could nudge them in the direction that they were likely to go anyway. It was a small town, really, the New York of communications and publishing and image-mongering that they both lived and worked in. There are times when the best thing to do is nothing at all.

But that was nonsense. She'd been wrong. The proof of it was that his name on Ditson's memo was enough to set her pulse rate a little higher, make her breathing a little faster and a little shallower. She folded the memo and went down to see Ditson.

"Did you ever see Jill Morgan?" Ditson asked.

"Sure, I must have. As a kid, I guess. And now and then on television. She disappeared."

"That's right. And she's back. She was a drunk and a bag lady, and she found God. And Castle's peddling her book. Which makes me wonder whether we shouldn't be keeping closer track of him."

"You think this is hot?"

"He thinks so. And he's no dummy. Or is he?"

"No, he's no dummy," she agreed.

"You two have got together? For dinner and like that?"

She nodded.

"Maybe you'll ask him what the deal is with Morgan. If he's interested, we might be too. We might even be interested in him and what he's doing with her."

"I'll look into it," she promised.

"How's it been, so far?"

She told Ditson how Castle was understandably private. There were impressions she'd picked up, most of them favorable, from her observation of his dealings with President Farnsworth and Bart Blackpool. Castle was the man who had put Pete McCracken together with Wanda Lathem, and that had turned out well, and of course also profitably. But there were parts of his business life he didn't want to share—as, for instance, his possible representation of Amy Breckenridge's memoirs, which Susan now thought unlikely to appear.

Ditson's eyebrows shot up, but all he said was "I can understand his not wanting us to know about some of that. But this is different. This looks like the full-court press, and my guess is that he'll welcome publicity. I want to be at the head of the line when he decides who is going to get the first shot at Jill Morgan."

"You really think there's anything about Jill Morgan that could be so wonderful?"

"I don't know. But at the steam room of the club, there were three guys that asked me about it. Three different guys, at three different times. Now, if there's nothing there, then your friend Castle is a goddamn genius. And if there is something, I want us to have a piece of it."

"I'll see what I can find out."

"Appreciate it."

She went back to her desk and had a cup of coffee. Should she just call and pretend that nothing had happened, that no unusual length of time had elapsed? Or should she be breezy and make a joke of it?

Mostly because she'd thought of it, she decided to send the hookah with the flowers. She had to go out and buy the hookah at a tobacco shop and take it to her florist. She left the accompanying card that said, "Peace, Flowers." And she called him late that afternoon.

"Len, I'm sorry."

"I got your hubble-bubble. That was a funny kind of tobacco they put in it, though. It looked like flowers. The worst smoke I ever had," he said.

"All right, I'm sorry for that too. It was corny, I admit."

"To what do I owe this sudden outpouring of regrets?" he asked.

"My boss asked me to find out about Jill Morgan," she said. "I could have ducked it. I was glad to have an excuse. I really was a little hasty."

"That's okay. We all have our sore spots."

"Decent of you to say so. Dinner? A *grande bouffe?*"

"Sure," Castle said. "I'd love to. When?"

"Are you free tonight?"

"I can get free."

"Good," she said. "I'll see if I can get us into Lutèce. I'll get back to you."

She hung up, and stared at the telephone. Feeling . . . ? Mostly okay, she thought. What she'd said was mostly true. In a perfect world, it would have been absolutely true. But even in this world, there was nothing to prevent her from hoping that it might grow into the truth. Maybe the fact that she wanted it to be true was enough.

*

Barrett? Senator Breckenridge? McCracken?

No, it just didn't figure. Castle might not have been perfect, answering the prayers of each of them like some benevolent and omnipotent god, but he'd done decently by each and all of them. He didn't think he'd driven any of them around the bend with the kind of rage that prompts someone to pick up a gun . . .

He was standing in the vestibule of Susan's building now, and longing for his former position across the street. Now he was as much afraid of the reception he might get as he was of this not quite imaginary but not quite believable assailant.

And he recognized this spiritual shabbiness and hated himself for it.

He raised his finger to the button beside her nameplate, hesitated, and lowered it again.

A moment more. Just for safety's sake.

10

A snowfall in New York is a reprieve from dirt and sharp edges. As if by magic, the city gleams, its contours smoothed and rounded so that homely objects become elegant abstractions of themselves. Fire hydrants and street signs seem to be modeled in marble by an Arp or Brancusi or perhaps by some divine hand at play with a toy city. To step outside is exhilarating. One's breath catches and eyes dazzle. It is astonishing that such a possibility was there all along. What everyone took for granted as the gritty reality was just another temporary appearance, for this is real too. This is the cold actuality crunching underfoot. One stoops down and grabs a handful of the stuff to feel it, mold it, toss it up into the air, and demonstrate yet once more that the senses aren't lying.

Travel, even for a few blocks, turns into a childhood adventure. The automobiles disappear. A few taxis with chains on their wheels come clanking through, but mostly the streets are wonderful pedestrian malls that soon become playgrounds as the plows leave obstacles—or barricades—piled along the curbs. One must contrive some passage over and around them. Even serious men and women of business are transformed and feel themselves to be on the verge of laughter.

It doesn't last. The particulate matter of furnaces and motors turns the amazing whiteness gray and the cleanliness grimy again, as tires and variations of temperature reduce the crystalline treasure to slush. One's hopes have been raised only to be dashed again, and midwinter's gloom returns, darker, deeper, even more unbearable for its momentary remission.

An experienced New Yorker, Leonard Castle had tried to keep himself from being seduced by the allure of that first snowfall, knowing full well the disappointment that would follow. But his caution hadn't turned out to be of benefit. He'd missed the lift of the first day or so of snow and was no less severely stricken by the aftermath of grime and slush. He'd also caught a cold and was sneezing, which is a boring thing to do. Every so often, for no good reason, he had to stop whatever he was doing and devote fifteen or twenty seconds to a tickle in the nose, helplessness, a distressing reduction to primitive physical organism, a helpless spasm, and then the blowing and dabbing that never do much good.

What made it all the more difficult to bear was his general feeling of uselessness. He found himself, in late February, asking himself what the point was of fighting his way downtown and into the office. What good was he doing? Where was the benefit? The books on the shelf behind his desk were supposed to be accomplishments and achievements but they felt like indictments. Who would read any of them in five years? Who would care? Sure, some of them had made a few dollars, but they were gimmicks, literary versions of the Hula-Hoop or the propeller beany, dumb and ephemeral productions. Or they were celebrations of personality for which democratic societies were such suckers. That was the point of having kings and queens who could ride around in their golden coaches and wave and smile, and pose for postage stamps and money, and let the rest of the country go about its business. In a democracy, we have to invent our nobility and then, boring quickly, we depose them and find another set. Every damn week, in *People* magazine!

Oliver Barrett's book about Helen Burke had done well enough, because it catered to the mob's Jacobin impulse, that passion to tear down the idols, show up the heroes as fakes and frauds, and assert equality—not by claiming the talents and virtues of the illustrious but by seizing on their frailties and defects. Those characters are no better than anybody else!

Helen Burke was dead and didn't care, but Leonard Castle, who had engineered the book by setting Oliver Barrett up to react as he did, felt an occasional twinge of regret. Or, no, it wasn't a twinge but something more bearable if also more distasteful—not the pain of a sick tooth but that taste and odor of decay that the dentist sometimes opens up when he gets in there with his drill. Not even the Novocain can protect us against that sickening wafting.

When Barrett had behaved exactly as Castle had planned, Castle had taken no satisfaction in the fulfillment of his predictions. In fact, it only depressed him. He'd have preferred for Barrett to have done the surprising, quixotic, but splendid thing, turning down Amanda Barnes's offered bribe and still protecting Helen Burke's memory. Let some other muckraker come along to stir up those old yellowing newspaper clippings and make of them a profitably fetid soup. But no, Barrett had been so outraged, so deeply offended by Amanda Barnes's offer that he'd proved his virtue and gone after Helen Burke as if the dead actress had tried to buy him off herself.

Castle had avoided Barrett ever since. Their only connection now was the occasional signing of a check to Barrett's order in which Castle took a grim satisfaction.

Jill Morgan's book was more uplifting and optimistic, full of talk about second chances and second acts, redemption and renewal, but it was all the more dismal in its results. There had been a month's madness, much of it engineered by Castle and the publicity department of her publisher, but no less impressive for its having been managed, about Jill Morgan's lost child. The cruelty of the old movie studios! The poor little rich girl, forced that way to give up her baby! The degradation and suffering—oh, how they love degradation and suffering!—of the drunken and forlorn woman, an ex-movie star, stripping in sleazy little theaters over adult bookstores in the tenderloins of Wilmington and Philadelphia and Baltimore! And worse, worse! And then the intervention of the Pauline Brothers, and the book, and the television interviews, and lo and behold, the restoration of the long-lost son!

Drew Fontaine was almost certainly the child Jill Morgan had been forced to give up for adoption. He was the right age and had been adopted in Los Angeles County at the right time. He hadn't kept the rattle she'd given him but he claimed to have had one that he'd sold and had turned out to be platinum.

Castle had been suspicious, nevertheless. He had figured that some enterprising hustler might have somehow discovered the story of the rattle—perhaps from someone who worked for Hanratty, Wilde, and O'Neal, the publishers of *Riches to Rags . . . and Back!* But *Periscope*'s staff reporters had confirmed every one of Drew Fontaine's not very impressive claims and had declared him to be authentic.

Jill Morgan had surprised Castle too. She had not been relying exclusively on that platinum rattle as a mark of her child's identity. There was another test, about which she had spoken to no one—not even to him—and which Fontaine had passed. He had been able to show her a small strawberry birthmark at the base of his spine, nothing important or disfiguring, nothing anyone would ever bother to have removed, but something rare enough to be trustworthy. The man was her son, she had no doubt, and he had been restored to her by a beneficent providence. Castle, the people at Hanratty, Wilde, and O'Neal, and the staff of *Periscope,* which aired a segment about Jill Morgan and her search for her lost child, were mere instruments of destiny.

Ms. Morgan was grateful enough, but her serenity was oddly annoying. Castle felt apprehensive, realizing that even if Drew Fontaine was the biological child to which she'd given birth, that didn't actually guarantee his decency or his loyalty. Lots of people had given birth to children who turned out to be disappointments.

Fontaine had claimed to have been the tambourine player in a country-and-western band. It was exactly the kind of thing some hustler would have done in order to cash in on a connection with a celebrity. *Periscope's* reporters had confirmed that there was indeed a group called Calhoun T. Jones and his Amarillo Armadillos, and that they had been playing in bars and roadhouses in Arkansas and Texas for a year or so, but it was not a connection that went back very far. Three years before, he'd been leading exercise classes in a shopping-center fitness studio in Albuquerque. He'd also sold used cars in Waco, Texas, and had worked as a bartender in a Best Western Motel and Restaurant in Brunswick, Georgia. There was no record of arrests or criminal convictions, and no civil judgments against him, at least under the name of Drew Fontaine. On the other hand, he didn't have much of a line of credit established anywhere.

But then, as Susan Flowers commented, who wants to lend a traveling tambourine player large sums of money?

The worst Castle could say was that this lightweight, this drone, had seen a way of cashing in on his mother's fame and had joined up with Cal Jones in a minor role—it's tough to screw up on the tambourine—so that the group might get a few bookings and move a couple of classes up in the places they played. Fontaine was able to carry a tune, just barely, and he could sing sentimental songs like "My Bonnie Lies over the Ocean." It was a way of parlaying himself and the group onto some local television appearances. And even this wasn't so very heinous—or so much more tasteless than the show *Periscope* had put on, bringing this Fontaine fellow to New York in secret and then springing him on Jill Morgan while their cameras were focused in on her face and the tape machines were whirring to record how the glistening tears spilled down over her cheeks. It was Ralph Edwards and *This Is Your Life* all over again.

Say that the guy was only protecting himself, was giving himself a way to put the connection with Jill Morgan to some use for himself, in case it should turn out that she was not so welcoming or generous as he thought she ought to be. He'd learned fairly late in life who his mother was and he wanted to cash in on that any way he could. What was so terrible?

Probably nothing, but neither was there anything selfless and noble and disinterested. There was about that fellow an air of sour resentment, a quiet inward-turning quality that was off-putting. He may have had a few tough breaks in life, but he'd let them turn him bitter and angry, which was unattractive and, worse, untrustworthy.

It wasn't just an aesthetic or abstract question now either, but a hard practical problem. Castle had taken off his slush-covered boots and had left them to dry in the corner on yesterday's *Wall Street Journal.* In stocking feet, with his shoes still in his hands, he went to his desk to see what messages had accumulated. It was still early in the morning, but there were emergencies and even, on occasion, pieces of good news that could break through the leisureliness of the publishers' day, which usually started a little after ten.

Among Effie's pink square slips, one caught his eye. He sat down, dropped his shoes on the carpet beside him, and read it again: "Ina Sinclair of HW&O—Morgan check will be delivered today."

It was the check for Jill's share of the paperback rights to *Riches to Rags . . . and Back!* and Castle would have to turn over to his client $220,000. One way or another, sooner or later, he'd have to give her the money, there was no question of that. His fears about what she'd do with it didn't apply, or more particularly his worry that that son of hers would cajole or extort or swindle most of it away from her and then flee. He could see it, though, could predict the events as clearly as if they were moves on a chessboard. It wasn't even the money that was key but the fact that Fontaine would then take off, leaving Jill Morgan alone again and more desolate than she'd been that day when Castle had first met her in the Pauline monastery. That was a dismal prospect.

He got up and went to the door to the outer office. "Bobo? Can you do something for me?"

"Under your desk."

"What?"

"They're under your desk. Your shoes!"

"Oh, yes, so they are. But I want you to run a little errand for me."

"Today? With the streets like this?"

"The streets aren't like this in Brunswick, Georgia."

"Georgia?"

"I want you to do a little detective work for me," Castle said. The chances of Bobo's finding out anything important in a matter of a few days were slim. All those expensive hotshot journalists from *Periscope* had gone over the ground already. But to do nothing was . . . unimaginable. "Come on in," he said, and in his inner office he explained to Bobo what he wanted him to do.

*

Three weeks later, the weather had relented and there was one of those odd days, utterly false in its promise but no less delightful for that, with real warmth and almost a scent of grass and flowers. One had the sense that life might yet be endurable until the real change in the season came along.

Castle had walked to work, allowing himself an extended period of anticipation. The meeting he had arranged was melodramatic, or maybe even silly, but that seemed to him allowable. Indeed, what had made Jill Morgan's appearance on the *Periscope* show less offensive than it otherwise might have been was her childlike belief in these abrupt shifts and reversals, the way she saw life in bold black-and-white contrasts of . . . good and evil, or right and wrong, or maybe just faith and despair. There was a sincerity and a simplicity to her that had had a Midas touch and could turn the brass of the program's intention into pure gold.

Well, if that was her talent and her nature, it seemed right to Castle, her agent and would-be protector, to go with that, use it and exploit it if need be for what he was convinced would be her benefit. He got to the office a little before nine, was in fact the first one there that morning, and he put up the coffee himself, so that when Effie appeared he could offer her a cup.

"You're in a good mood this morning," she said.

"Oh, yes. It happens sometimes," he answered. "Cheers!" And he went over with her, one more time, what the procedure was for each of the players in the little drama he'd arranged for the morning. Mrs. Hudgins was due to arrive at nine forty-five and was to be put in the conference room. Jill Morgan was supposed to show up at ten-fifteen and she would be accompanied by her son, Drew Fontaine. They were to be shown into Castle's inner office right away. Then Effie was to call the coffee shop across the street and ask for Bobo, and he'd bring Mrs. Keane up and take her into the conference room with Mrs. Hudgins. That would be Effie's cue to buzz twice on the intercom in the inner office. And then? Then they'd all see how good and evil would sort themselves out.

To pass the time, Castle occupied himself with his correspondence, dictating a series of short notes or sometimes just instructions for notes that would explain why he was unable to represent such and such a client at this time but sent his best wishes for what would be a well-deserved success, et cetera, sincerely. There were three like that, and two more to corresponding agencies in other countries that had to be reminded that promptness in payment was a necessary precondition to future dealings with some publishing houses. Some of those people seemed to be as much interested in arbitrage as in publishing and were waiting for the dollar to sag a little before making payments that were long overdue. And there were a couple of notes to editors requesting the return of the material specified hereinunder. These were deliberately impersonal so that they could be taken—or ignored—as form letters. Castle wasn't trying to break possible deals but merely to nudge these lazy bastards along a bit.

On his desk, to the right of the blotter, there was the large checkbook for his authors' account. In his pocket, the gold Mont Blanc he liked to use to make out large checks. From time to time, he glanced at the clock on his desk, but he forced himself to continue, dictating doggedly into the cassette recorder and actually getting a fair amount of work done in the hour. When the door opened, and Effie came in to ask if he'd like a second cup of coffee, it was five of ten. "Yes, thanks," he said, and he didn't ask who had arrived.

She told him anyway. "Mrs. Hudgins is here. She's in the conference room. I gave her some coffee."

"Thank you," he said.

"And I've put up a fresh pot."

"A good idea," he said. It had begun. It was happening. Jill Morgan arrived on schedule, with Drew in tow. Effie showed them into Castle's office and Castle welcomed them and seated them.

"It was kind of you to ask that Drew be here," she said. "He's been such a help these past months."

"I'm sure," Castle said.

Drew said nothing. Castle did not feel called upon to draw him out. He noted details of the young man's appearance that tended to substantiate the suppositions that had guided Castle's actions of the previous weeks. Even aside from the Rolex Oyster on Drew's wrist, there was the suit, tapered and European and too trendy but obviously expensive, and the shirt that looked to be custom-made. The tambourine player posed himself and stared out of the window, managing somehow to preen and sulk at the same time.

"Now, this check," Jill Morgan said, "is for the paperback edition?"

"It's your share of the advance. You and the publisher of the hardback edition share that money, fifty-fifty. What I have for you this morning is your part of the advance payment. If the paperback edition sells well, as I expect it should, there may well be some more money in a year or two. Not a great deal, but a few thousand. And that too would be shared equally between you and the hardback publisher."

"I understand," she said.

"There is one other matter that I'd like to discuss with you, though," he said. "And that's why I asked particularly that you have Drew come here with you this morning."

Drew looked from his mother to Castle and back to his mother, alert and even apprehensive. Castle was relieved to discover that he felt no remorse at all, no compunctions about what he was about to do.

"This is a great deal of money. You've already had a sizable sum from the hardback edition of this book, and now there is more. Your way of living, your investment plans, your future . . . that's all your business. But as a friend, or as an associate who wishes you well, I thought I owed it to you to let you know something about Drew's past so that you could make the important decisions you'll be facing prudently and intelligently."

The intercom buzzer sounded twice with Effie's signal.

"Excuse me," Castle said, and then, into the phone, "Would you bring them in, please?"

The door opened and Bobo brought in Mrs. Hudgins and Mrs. Keane. Mrs. Keane was carrying an infant in her arms.

"Well, there you are, you son of a bitch!" Mrs. Hudgins said.

Mrs. Keane just stood there, holding her baby, weeping wordlessly, and staring at Drew.

"What is this?" Drew asked.

"I thought you might be able to explain it to us, actually," Castle said to him. And then, to Jill Morgan, Castle explained, "These are women Drew married and abandoned. Two of them, anyway. There may even be more, but we only had a brief time in which to work."

"Is this true?" Jill Morgan asked.

"Hell, no," Drew said.

"Are you denying that you married me?" the first woman asked. She was perhaps thirty, but it had been a hard thirty years. She had a bouffant hairdo of the kind that had been popular in the late fifties and she wore too much makeup, but her anger was pure and without artifice. "He did! He married me because my daddy owned a shopping center and he could open up an exercise studio without paying any rent and get credit to buy all of those damned machines."

Angry and disjointed as she was, she nonetheless made it clear that she'd been a young divorcée and that he'd come along one day and picked her out as the easiest mark in Albuquerque. He had married her and then taken all the money out of the business and disappeared.

"At first I was so dumb that I worried that he was dead. Now I'm sorry he isn't."

"Is that true?" Jill Morgan asked.

He nodded.

The other one, the weeper with the baby, was from Brunswick, Georgia, and Drew had moved in with her too and had fathered a child. He had promised to marry her but then he'd taken off, driving away in her almost brand-new Subaru and also stealing Willard's camera and his shotgun.

"Who is Willard?" Castle broke in to ask.

"He was Willard Keane, my late husband. He was a firefighter and he died in a fire. This one was after me because of the insurance, just like my brother Yancy warned me."

"And that's Drew's baby?" Jill Morgan asked.

"Yes, ma'am," the woman replied.

"My God, my grandchild!"

"I never married her," Drew insisted.

"I never married your father, but you're still my child, aren't you? And this is my grandchild. Grandson? Granddaughter?"

"Grandson," Mrs. Keane informed her. "His name's Clyde."

"Have you anything to say for yourself?" Jill Morgan asked her son.

"He's got a hell of a nerve," Fontaine said. "I don't see what right he had . . ."

"That will do," his mother said. Turning to Castle, she said, "I'm grateful to you for making clear to me what I think I saw. It's very hard. I've felt guilty about what I did to Drew. It never crossed my mind that in his anger at me, he'd behave badly to other women and try to get even with them for what I did to him. In a way, I'm responsible for them too, these women and that little boy. It isn't easy."

"All I wanted," Castle said, "was to protect you from what I was afraid he might try to do. I was worried that he'd take whatever money he could get from you and then desert you just the way he deserted them."

"Yes, I see that. And I see what it is that I have to do. It's all so wonderfully clear now."

"You can't believe this man," Drew protested.

"Oh, but what I believe has nothing to do with it. It hardly makes any difference."

"Don't listen to him!" Drew pleaded.

"How much did my son steal from you and your father?" Ms. Morgan asked Mrs. Hudgins.

"Eleven thousand dollars and change," she answered.

Jill Morgan asked Castle how much money she was to receive.

Castle didn't want everyone in the room to know. He opened his checkbook, wrote her his check for $220,000, and handed it over. She looked at it, tucked it into her wallet, and then took out her own checkbook. She wrote a check for twenty thousand dollars. "If you'll accept this, with my regrets, I'd be very grateful to you," she said to Mrs. Hudgins.

"Yes, of course," the woman answered.

"You don't have to do this, Mother," Drew protested, but it was clear that he didn't expect her to listen to him.

"And for you," Jill Morgan said to Mrs. Keane, "there is the car and the gun and the camera, and support for the child. Is that right?"

Mrs. Keane nodded.

"Let's call it a hundred thousand dollars," Ms. Morgan said, and she wrote the check. "Go on, dear. Take it, please. For the child's sake!"

Mrs. Keane took the check.

"And for you, my poor, dear, angry, hurt son, the rest. You see, you have nothing to fear from Mr. Castle. It's up to you to decide now whether you will abandon me or not, whether you will remain the good and dutiful son you claim to be, or just an operator and a hustler, as he fears you may be. Either way, I shall be content. It's up to the Lord to decide how I am to be punished or rewarded. And it's up to you. I'd rather have it that way."

"You've got to keep some of it for your income tax," Castle prompted. It was all he could think of to stop her from wiping herself

out. This was not what he'd expected. This was what he'd tried so
hard to prevent.

"How much will that be, do you think?" she asked.

"I don't know. Your accountant would be able to tell you that. But
in a rough way, you've got to figure forty percent."

"Well, ten percent would be twenty-two thousand, and so forty percent would be eighty-eight thousand. I'm afraid that leaves you only
twelve thousand dollars. But whatever there is is yours."

"But . . . that's all there is," Castle said. "You're leaving yourself
with nothing."

"Not at all," she said. "I've given a sizable sum from the first check
to the Pauline Brothers. I can always go back there. I'm even inclined
to think that it might be better all around if I were to do that. Drew
wouldn't feel that I was a burden to him. And the brothers were my
real family. They were the ones who took me in when I had no place
else to go. And that's what home is, isn't it? I can work and pray
there, and be happier than I was before they found me. Or after I left."

"It's not what I'd do, but I think I can understand it," Castle said.

"It's lousy," Drew said. "The whole idea is just to make me feel
bad."

"That's not my idea at all," his mother said. "And how you feel
must depend on what you do, which is up to you, isn't it?"

"Is it? Is that what you think?" he asked, his face contorted with
hurt and anger.

"It's what I believe, my dear."

He looked as if he were about to make some reply, but he didn't.
Instead, he got up and marched out of the room.

"My guess is that he's on the way to the bank," Castle said. "You
can stop payment on the check."

She shook her head. "No, no. I meant what I said. I owe him that
much at least. Let him have the money. And then we'll see how he
behaves. Toward me, and toward them and other women too, perhaps."

"You think he'll change?" Castle asked.

"I shall pray that he may. And now, Mrs. Hudgins, Mrs. Keane, if
you'd indulge a foolish woman, let me take you back to my apartment
and we can have lunch together and get to know one another just a
little bit. Mr. Castle, if you'd care to join us?"

"I wish I could. I have a busy day still."

"I understand," she said. "But I want you to know that I'm grateful
for your kindness."

"You'd better make the deposit," Castle reminded her, "if you want your checks to clear."

"Yes, I'll do that directly. Thank you again. And God bless you."

"God bless you," Castle said.

"He has, indeed," Jill Morgan said, and she led the other two women out of the office.

*

"I think it's awful," Susan said. "If you hadn't sprung them on her that way, she might have had more time to think, and she might have acted differently."

"Sure, she'd have acted differently," Castle protested. "She'd have given it all to him. I'm positive that that's what she was planning to do."

"Did she say so?"

"No, but I had that feeling. She's no fool, you know, and she was wise to him. The only trouble is that normal people would protect themselves against someone like that, and she wanted to give him everything so there wouldn't be any selfish motive left to confuse things. He'd have nothing more to gain from her."

"Still, she might have kept back some . . ."

"She could have done that. If I hadn't reminded her about income taxes, she'd have given out the whole two hundred and twenty thousand."

Susan didn't say anything. She was putting together another taco from the pan full of meat and the little bowls of shredded lettuce, grated cheese, chopped tomatoes, and chopped onion that she'd set out on the kitchen table. Tacos and champagne, she had explained, was what she'd wanted on her sixteenth birthday party. And it was still something she liked to have, late at night, on intimate occasions.

"I guess the only question is how you feel about it. Are you proud of yourself?"

"Not especially. But I'm not ashamed of myself either. I did more than a lot of agents would have done."

"Maybe too much?"

"What's eating you anyway?" he asked. "Do you really disapprove?"

"I don't know. I feel . . . involved. If I hadn't shown you those reports, you wouldn't have found those women. It isn't something you did all by yourself. We did it together."

"And do you disapprove?"

"I'm not happy about it."

Castle took a bite of taco. Impossibly awkward food! Good, but messy. He drank a little champagne, thinking that Dos Equis would go better with tacos. "I don't think I'm the problem here. I think you're unhappy, maybe, but not so much with me as with the show. *Periscope* was just as hokey as I was, and they had the cameras rolling. They were turning a mother's tears into money and I think that's as troublesome as anything I did. But it's more comfortable to blame me."

"That's not true."

"Okay," he said.

"It's not!"

"I said, okay."

"Besides, the cameras were our excuse. Our reason, anyway. What was yours?"

"A quarter of a million dollars, nearly. As I keep telling you, I was trying to let her know what kind of a creep he was so she wouldn't give him the money. I didn't think for a minute that she'd sit there and write all those checks and hand them out like that . . ."

"So you're not responsible."

"Sure, I'm responsible—in part. And she's responsible in part. And you are, if you want to think so. It's that kind of world. Nothing is clear-cut and simple. I think what she did is dumb. She thinks it's pious and Christian . . ."

"I don't think it makes any difference which it is. I feel sorry for her and sorry that it happened this way."

"She's well rid of him."

"She'd be rid of him if she hadn't given him the money."

"She only gave him twelve thousand," Castle protested.

"As she said, she gave it all to him."

"She felt she owed it to him. Maybe now her conscience is clear."

"Hers may be, but what about yours and mine?"

Castle took another sip of champagne. Susan wasn't stupid. She knew she was goading him. But why? And how should he respond?

"You know what I think?" he began. "I think we need a vacation. I think we need to get away. New York is a funny place. This is where people buy and sell things, and you get the feeling sometimes that everybody is going around with that squinty look you see in bargain basements where they're all looking at price tags and trying to find good buys. It gets to you after a while. I think we should get away for a couple of weeks. What do you say?"

"Away from New York or away from each other?"

"Oh, come on, now. Away from New York is what I meant. To-gether is what I meant. Are you trying to pick a fight?"

"You're not taking me seriously. This is an ethical question, nothing emotional, just rational and logical!"

"Sure it is, but our attitudes aren't always rational and logical. Mine sure as hell aren't. Think about it. The trip, I mean. The Caribbean or the Aegean? Doesn't it sound good?"

"I'll think about it," she said, but her expression was hardly enthu-siastic.

Castle drained the last of his champagne. There was a bit of taco still on his plate, but he left it there as a monument to his self-restraint. "It's late," he said. "I've got an early day tomorrow."

She didn't protest or try to coax him to stay. She didn't even accom-pany him when he went to her bedroom to get dressed to make the trip across town.

Just as he was about to leave, she came in. "I'm sorry," she said. "I didn't mean for it to end like this."

He assumed that she was only talking about their evening together. In the cab, on the way through the park, it crossed his mind that there was another, larger antecedent and that she might have been talking about their relationship.

It was three in the morning. He hesitated, but he decided that she was probably up anyway and he called his sister. They weren't twenty feet apart, on opposite sides of the wall that divided their apartments. Sitting in the dark, Castle told her what had happened, what he'd said and what she'd said. And then, at the end, he asked her, "So, what do you think?"

"I think it's a terrific idea."

"What is?"

"The trip. You ought to go."

"Alone?"

"You're a big boy. Why not?"

"I'll think about it," he said.

"It's cheap, in the long run," Lisa told him. "Cheaper than a shrink."

"That's true enough," he said.

"Good night, brother."

"Good night, sister."

*

From the writings of Mihail Szabo:

In *Humoresque*, there is a nice piece of dialogue in which Joan Crawford, playing the usual rich socialite, says to John Garfield, the upward-mobile violinist, something condescending about his not liking martinis. I think the line is "Oh, well, they're a cultivated taste—like Ravel."

One could do a fascinating study about the politics of such lines, the level of culture of the filmmaker and what he assumes his audience's level to be. The Soviet cinema is a people's cinema, but Hollywood's is even more rigid in its prejudices about caste and class.

In either case, though, one can manipulate. Think of Nikita Mikhalkov and what he did in *Slave of Love* or *Oblomov.* And then pair him with somebody like Blake Edwards, who took Ravel, perhaps wrenching the name from Joan Crawford's sneering lips, and turned his "Bolero" into a pop hit in *Ten.* Was this an intentional joke? Dare one hope?

*

This island is noisier at night than Beverly Hills. I sleep badly anyway, even in the well-policed silence of those Angeleno streets, and I have no objection to the nighttime noises here, the braying of the donkeys or the clop of shod horse hooves as Spiros' big roan stallion wanders about on its regular rounds. And then, sometime after four in the morning, apprehensive cocks start crowing to signal the sun that it may as well rouse itself.

But one ought to be tough-minded. The cocks are signaling no such thing. There was a moon last night, and the stupid chickens had no idea whether it was moonlight or dawn; they were reacting automatically to the sky's brightness.

One could in fact construct an alarm clock in the shape of a rooster and equip it with a tape recording of crowing noises. Either it could be set to go off at a given time or, for purists, it could have a photoelectric cell so that it would respond to light and crow exactly as a real rooster does.

This might be a joke in a film, a bit of business for an elegant aristocrat (whom I already rather like) who wants to keep with him some memento of château life in his pied-à-terre. Or, should the worst come to pass, so that I never again get to make another film, I might try to sell this device to some mail-order house catering to silliness deluxe like Horchow or Neiman-Marcus.

*

There was a storm last night, quite a violent one, and from somewhere a broken branch was driven against the wall of the house. I spent much of the morning replacing a broken windowpane, and the satisfaction I have derived from that domestic chore is altogether disproportionate to the magnitude of the task. (Or parvitude?)

Anybody can fix a windowpane, after all. Still, the measuring of the opening must be accurate. The preparation of the mullions, the scraping away of the old putty and the digging out of the old glazing points, is slow and rather soothing labor. And then the fitting in of the cut glass to the prepared opening is extraordinarily satisfying. But what most pleased me, I think, was the insinuation of the new glazing points into the wood. It is very like the graceful inclusion of plot points in a scene in a film script—the same neatness, the same craftsmanliness.

For a time, I was depressed, feeling anew my isolation here and my inability to make films. That absurd girl and her harpy of a mother who have exiled me here are scarcely the mythic creatures one expects to influence one's destiny. They are suited, rather, for low comedy, slapsticks and pratfalls. I seethed in resentment and chagrin for a time, walked to the *agora* for a cup of coffee, and then settled down as the quiet rhythms of the village brought me back to a better sense of things. If the pleasure of fixing a windowpane was so acute, was this not an occasion for celebration rather than regret? Did I need the abstract satisfaction of plot points if I could work actual glazing points into the old wood of a window frame?

I am looking at that window now. It would be impossible for anyone to say which was the pane I installed, to pick out the new piece of glass from the older ones. That too is an interesting alternative to the great value we put on our individuality, on our signing of our work one way or another. This is mine, my film, my life, my world, Hitchcock says as he crosses the street with a poodle in some street scene of a film, and in the audience, we accept that as his right, almost his duty. But is there not a higher ambition—to make a piece of work of such classical perfection that it has no idiosyncratic taint to it at all, that it has the clarity of, say, a pane of glass? Is there an individuality that arises from self-discipline and self-denial?

Is there, perhaps, a benefit in this enforced silence of mine? It would be a great joke if Lila Love and her mother had been the midwives to my rebirth as an artist.

*

The rhythms of the village are such that even an eccentric like myself learns to respond to its cues. The natural and artificial events of the day repeat themselves, and one responds. I listen for the announcement of the mail on the loudspeaker and note which of the villagers have received letters. (Do the young girls with fiancés working in Athens or Germany or South Africa or America write to themselves so the other villagers will not think they have been forgotten? Or do they have an arrangement with the postmistress so that she will call out their names whether there is a letter or not?)

Late at night, when the villagers have gone to bed, I find my hand longing for a fountain pen. It is the time to turn to this journal, to unburden myself of all I have been unable to express during the day— because my Greek is not that good and because there is no one here to whom I could speak comfortably, even if I were a better linguist. And it has nothing to do with my career as a film director, or my notoriety as a—child molester? statutory rapist? (Pederasty is the crime that dare not speak its name; mine isn't actually sure what its right name is. Pedophilia, I suppose, but that's not accurate either.)

My isolation, though, has nothing to do with any of that nonsense but comes only from the fact that I am a foreigner, a *xenos*, someone from outside the village.

*

A letter this morning from a magazine editor invites me to set down my side of the story and offers a significant sum—$3,500, which translates into an astronomical number of drachmas. It is a tempting proposition, but my instinct is to keep silent, at least for the time being. When I do make my public confession or apologia, it will probably be longer than the five thousand words the enterprising editor suggests and will not be confined to my relationship with Lila Love—an encounter of little significance save only in its aftereffects. That I was stupid, insufficiently suspicious of the motives of people in a notoriously corrupt town, I admit at once. But for me to make my case in a reasonable way, it has to be in the context of the rest of my life, my childhood, my education and apprenticeship, my flight from Hungary, my films both in Paris and in Los Angeles, and, in short, my whole being. I am not a monstrous European preying upon American innocence. I am not even an innocent Humbert Humbert, entrapped by Lila Love's scheming *Lolita*.

The girl looked to be in her late teens. If I'd thought about it, I'd have supposed she was nineteen or so. Surely, no younger than seventeen. What is hilarious and grotesque is that her mother's obvious acquiescence—or, no, more than that, approbation and delight—mooted the question of her age. I simply never gave it a thought. If her mother had no protest to make about Lila's being too young, it was hardly my obligation to act *in loco parentis.* But that Darlene might be pimping for Lila, and, worse than that, using her as bait for a blackmail scheme . . . that never occurred to me. Neither one of them seemed intelligent enough to be able to think that far ahead.

If they'd been just a little smarter, they might have succeeded. I could have found some small part for her in some film or other, could have arranged a way for the studio to pay them off for the time and effort they'd invested in me. I'd have been disagreeable about it, but I'd have come around. It's what one does out there in La-la Land. Budgets have padding in them for the coke snorters and pill gobblers, for the time wasted as these actors and technicians return from their pharmacological vacations. A little green nookie? Tuck it in somewhere, above the line, in all those wonderfully miscellaneous items that seem to testify to thoroughness and honesty in the balance sheets but are actually cupboards for hiding fifty-seven varieties of peculation.

But they wouldn't wait. They wouldn't accept my promise to find something for Lila sooner or later. Instead, they threatened me and gave me a deadline—I was to pay up by such and such a date or they'd go to the police—so that when the deadline passed, they had to choose between going to the authorities or losing all their credibility as blackmailers. Terrorists too fall into that same trap, paint themselves into a corner where they are forced to shoot a hostage or two just to maintain the level of threat they need to continue their negotiations.

What Darlene couldn't understand is that when they turned the matter over to the police they would lose control of it. It was now a case in which they might be witnesses but were no longer the principals. The issue now lay between the People of the State of California and Mihail Szabo. It was not, in other words, a civil case. (Actually, it was a very uncivil case.)

A criminal case.

In the Eastern countries, this is the point at which politics intervenes too. A party member, a man with influential friends, can, at this stage, get the charges dropped. In the United States, I suspect the same possibilities govern, but there is no functionary, no party official or government bureaucrat to whom one can turn. It is, instead, a more abstract and whimsical process by which the democracy consults itself, deciding whether to feel vindictive or compassionate. The newspapers do not dictate these moods but they reflect them accurately enough. And they are relatively sensitive barometers to the erratic emotional weather. The journalists cry out for vengeance, run stories of the families of the bereaved victims of some brutal killer, and then, the moment the trial is over, run almost identical stories of the sufferings of the family of the condemned murderer, the tide of sentiment already having begun to run the other way.

I was the foreigner who had come to the welcoming shores of the land of the free. But I was also the spoiled brat of Hollywood, the depraved *cinéaste* whose pictures offended the middle-class pieties of the heartland (perhaps by appealing to emotions they had so severely repressed?). And I had fucked their innocent little girl!

Off with my head. To the guillotine!

More realistically, I was told I could almost certainly expect to serve a short prison term and undergo a regimen of psychotherapy.

The prison term was not an attractive prospect. The psychotherapy, though, was what terrified me. That was all too familiar, being exactly what political prisoners in the East are subjected to if they are not lucky enough to be beaten to death. I chose, therefore, to jump bond and flee, which is admittedly unsporting and ungentlemanly. But if one already has a reputation as a cradle snatcher, there is no danger of further difficulty in terms of reputation. It didn't seem unbearable also to be called unsportsmanly.

I hauled ass. My friend Maurice lent me this little house on the island of Lesbos. He uses it only in the summer and fall. Winter is not the season for island life. Those who can afford to do so return then to the great cities.

I was broke and grateful. And I have even come to see my sojourn here as thematically necessary and correct.

On the beach, not far from where I now sit, there is a cove where Orpheus' head is said to have washed ashore after the Harpies tore him apart. That severed head continued for a time to sing.

I had not known this when I accepted Maurice's kind offer. I do not think he knew it either. I am, nonetheless, delighted by the story and its celebration of this place. It is a connection. It carries authority and makes this exactly the right refuge for me to have chosen.

In a way, this is my home, then, as much as it is the home of any of those villagers—for I am Orpheus' child.

*

Ari is the village idiot.

The phrase is an old one, but it requires nonetheless an explanation. Those of us who do not live in villages can have no idea how comfortable a role there is for the afflicted, how secure they can be, even serving certain modest requirements of the village and therefore earning not only their keep but their self-respect as well.

Ari looks after the chickens who wander about at the east end of the village. There is a footpath from his post that meanders up the mountainside toward the shrine of St. Zaccharius, a chapel not much larger than a breakfront way up at the peak of our mountain. Once a year the women make the climb along with the priest and they celebrate a mass up there. It's a strenuous climb, but then these women are hardy.

Aristotle—this may have been his name, but more likely it was given to him in jest when he was a boy; and then, as with so many of the village jokes, it lost its cruelty and turned intimate and affectionate —warns the chickens when he hears the sound of a motor, truck or car or motorcycle. And he shouts when he sees a hawk circling over his flock. He mostly sits there on the broken wall, looking out at the chickens, smiling, and occasionally drumming on the thigh of his heavy twill pants in a slow rhythmic thud.

He is unremarkable, not unlike any other retardate in such a setting. But I am struck with how much better off he is here, in this little Lesbosian village, than he would be in Paris or London or New York, not to mention Budapest or Moscow. All those government workers, all that social bureaucracy, and they cannot begin to approximate the reality of a social structure that is still alive and functional here in these tiny island villages and towns.

What the society here accepts is interesting. The range is different from what is acceptable in New York or Los Angeles. An idiot like Aristotle would almost certainly be confined there in an institution, unless his parents were wealthy and fairly determined. Even then, he'd be kept at home, shut away indoors for his own safety but also because it would be, to a degree, shameful to have such a child. Here, there is hardly any shame to Ari's existence. He is the village idiot, which is to say, ours.

The sexual limits, however, are narrower. A girl who violated the strict code of acceptable behavior, in speech and dress and attitude, might be married off it it weren't too late for that. Or she might—if she had any spirit and fought for her right to self-expression—be shipped off to Athens, where the odds might be about even as to her future. She'd either get a job and find her place in that more cosmopolitan society or fail, and turn to prostitution.

That, of course, would be a sad thing and a family disgrace, but not the end of the world. I have the impression that in such families the mother finds excuses to get to Athens every so often to visit the wayward daughter. Or perhaps they meet in Mitilini, which is the biggest town here on the island. There is an acceptance of how things are, of what happens in the world to make our plans provisional and our expectations flexible, both for ourselves and for others.

In that kind of way, I shouldn't at all mind being the town's pedophile, if that, indeed, is what I am.

Except, of course, that I have only the most theoretical idea of what it must be to make love to a very young girl. Unripe fruit is not my dish. Lila was young, I admit, but already overblown, like a forced plant. (It was her mother who had forced her.)

It's her mother who would not be accepted here. The wisdom and toleration of village life ends at that kind of cynical exploitation of another human being. If someone were to take advantage of an Ari— or of a Lila, or of someone like me—the village would rise up and drive that person off with rocks and shepherd's crooks and dog whips. Over the mountain and out of sight . . .

I am dreaming, wishing, projecting. I have confided in no one. They know I am a filmmaker and a writer. They know I am a friend of Maurice and that I am more or less looking after his place during the winter. If they were to find out what I am accused of, that I am a fugitive from prosecution on the charge of statutory rape, they might behave to me quite differently from what I am imagining here.

In which case, I suppose I envy Aristotle. He is their idiot. Whose idiot am I?

*

I have been listening to some of Maurice's tapes. There is a small collection but the music is good and bears repeated hearings. This evening, I have been listening to *Don Giovanni* and thinking about it from a new perspective—that of the Commendatore, Donna Elvira's father, who turns into a statue. How had I failed to notice him before, or to pay proper attention to him? He is the fulcrum on which the entire machinery of the plot turns! I suppose he is hidden in plain sight, which is to say that the wonderful theatrical effects of the graveyard scene and then of his final visit are so satisfying that one doesn't feel impelled to question beyond the surface. But that is the artifice that conceals artifice.

The terrible thing that has happened—it hardly matters what terrible thing—has transformed him from a growing, evolving, flesh-and-blood creature into a monomaniac, a stone figure, a statue of himself, incapable of any further growth or adaptation.

Which is, more or less, what has happened to me.

Understanding this, I wept—not for myself but for the Commendatore. Which is the blessed dispensation of art.

The only bitterness was later, when I realized it was quite pointless even to daydream about a film version in which this idea could be fleshed and communicated. The statue cannot create either, but is limited to those perceptions and responses and impulses of his life before that *coup de foudre* . . .

*

Drew Fontaine, maybe? He might have reason enough, Castle supposed, but he didn't have the character for it. He didn't have the fixity of purpose. Or, putting it another way, Castle didn't think Drew cared enough about anything in the world to do something like this. An indolent and sour resentment was more his style. And he could be dangerous at close quarters, picking up a knife or gun or skillet, whatever was at hand . . .

But to acquire a gun and lay in wait for Castle? Too much effort for that kind of lazy bastard.

Darlene Love perhaps? She too had her reasons, but she was too practical. She would be intent on the only kind of revenge that ever made any sense—trying to recoup and to live well. Oddly, she was too self-centered to waste her time and accept the risks of a project such as shooting Castle.

Still, the thought that there were possible candidates was sobering. As it was sobering to realize how much of his professional life had flashed before him, as if he were a drowning man . . .

He had to get hold of himself. He forced himself to leave her building and walk over to Third Avenue. There was a bar there where he could have a quick brandy and make a telephone call.

Like a sane, normal person.

11

Castle had been exploring the island in a rented automobile. He was staying at Mithimna, a picturesque if rather touristy town on the north shore of the island, but he had already inspected the sweaters and shawls, explored the beaches, and climbed up to the Genoese fortress to admire the view across the strait to Turkey. He was not quite bored but restless, at some transitional phase between the pressures of work and life at home and the relaxation of a holiday. The first few days had been easier, with the disorientation of jet lag and a mild bout of traveler's tummy. Now that he was in reasonable physical shape, however, he felt dissatisfied, at loose ends, and wanting . . . he had no idea what.

People, maybe? Not a good idea, he told himself. He spent all his time at home with people, trying to figure out what they wanted, what they would settle for, what they could be persuaded to. This restlessness was probably a good thing, all the better for its mildly distressing quality—like medicine. He needed to find himself, to get back some sense of his own preferences and capacities. All the small decisions of life were now his own—when to eat, what to eat, when to go to sleep, when to get up, what to do with himself for the morning, the afternoon, the evening.

He had decided to explore the island, not out of scholarly interest or any feeling of obligation, but in the hope that it might speak to him, prompting him to some curiosity or even appetite. At the very least, there would be the likelihood of some modestly attractive scenery, a prospect of the hills and the sea or perhaps something more modest, maybe just a very old, gnarled olive tree, lit the right way, with a goat

grazing beneath it. Such things, sometimes, can seem to speak sooth-
ingly to one willing to attend to them.

But he got lost. He had gone through Kaloni on the way out, and he
wanted to try a different route coming back. He either misread the
map, or the map misrepresented the way the roads turned. He wasn't
worried, for on a small island it is impossible to go too far astray. He
wasn't even particularly annoyed, inasmuch as he had had no fixed
goal in mind, and one hill, or one village or beach, was every bit as
good as another. He could always stop and ask how to get back to
Mithimna. Or stop when he felt hungry or thirsty, and ask then.

Come to think of it, he was thirsty. It had been some hours since his
late breakfast. He could do with a coffee or a *gazoza*, which was a kind
of weak fizzy lemonade. He saw a village off to his left, took the
turnoff, and drove until he reached the central square. There, exactly
as he had anticipated, there were a couple of cafés. Almost certainly
one of them was the socialist café and the other the Communist, but
Castle had no way of distinguishing between them. One had some of
its tables disposed about a large tree that dominated the square, an old
oak probably. Castle parked, got out of the car, and took a seat at a
table beneath that big tree.

After a time, a waiter came out to ask Castle what he wanted. Castle
told him in pidgin Greek that he wanted coffee and a *gazoza*, which
was hardly exotic but nonetheless puzzling to the waiter. Only one
person? Which did he want, then, the coffee or the *gazoza*?

"Coffee, *neh. Gazoza, neh,* " he said, meaning coffee, yes, *gazoza*, yes.
He didn't know the word for *both*.

A man at a nearby table said something in Greek, explaining to the
waiter that the man wanted both. And then, in English, he asked,
"That's what you meant, isn't it? That you want both?"

"Yes, that's right. Thank you," Castle said. "Will you join me?" He
looked at the man, then looked harder. "Mr. Szabo, isn't it?"

He'd said the wrong thing. The man was evidently pained at having
been identified. But he put the best face on it that he could. "Sure,
thanks."

"I'm Leonard Castle," Castle said. "What a pleasant surprise!"

"Have we met?"

"I don't think so. But I've heard of you, of course. I'm a literary
agent in New York."

"And you're here to sign me up?" Szabo asked him.

"Not at all. I'm on vacation. I'm here for a *gazoza* and a coffee—as
you know. I was just driving around the island and I got lost."

"Really!"

"You don't believe me? Well, I don't suppose I can do much to convince you until I leave—which I'll do as soon as I've had my coffee."

"And *gazoza.*"

"And *gazoza,*" Castle acknowledged.

They sat in silence for a few moments. The waiter brought out two coffees and the lemon soda.

"I ordered yours medium," Szabo said. "I hope that's okay."

"I'm sure it will be fine. How do they come?"

"Sweet, medium, and bitter. The bitter's all right, once you develop a taste for it."

"Are you talking about coffee?" Castle asked. "Or is that a remark of more general application?"

"Take it any way you like," Szabo said. And then, after a pause, he added, "I'm sorry. I haven't been very welcoming. But you can understand my suspicions."

"Oh, yes."

"The villagers don't know about my troubles back in the States."

"I see. Well, I certainly shan't be the one to tell them. I can't even order for myself."

Szabo smiled and almost chuckled. It was like a car with a weak battery that coughs but can't quite turn over.

"I've admired your films," Castle said. "And I assume that your troubles, as you call them, are the result of a setup."

"Thank you."

"Tell me, is there anything to see around here? I was looking for the road back to Mithimna, the one that doesn't go through Kaloni. But if there's something to see . . ."

"It's not very spectacular, but there is a famous site. The cove down that way, maybe three miles, is where Orpheus' head is supposed to have washed ashore."

"Ah, yes?"

"You know the story?"

"Orpheus and Eurydice! He looked back, which is always a dangerous thing to do."

"Yes," Szabo said. "I'll show you the cove, if you like. If you'll let me retrieve my bad-mannered welcome."

"I'd be grateful," Castle said, thinking that this man had been badly used, was lonely, was eager for company and the chance to speak English.

It was just what he'd been looking for! To be piqued to curiosity and perhaps even to action. To be diverted by someone or something outside himself.

Castle tried to pay for the *gazoza* and the coffees, but Szabo insisted. "This is my village, at least for the moment. Zeus Xenos has already been offended. Please!"

Together, they drove off toward the beach, passing Aristotle, who waved, and then the town abattoir—which was used once a week, on Thursdays—and the bone house, where corpses were left for a year for the flesh to fall from the bones, which could then be interred in a small plot. Szabo explained these things to his guest.

Castle was interested in what Szabo had to say. He was also interested in Szabo—how to draw him out, how to get him to talk about himself, and then how to restore the man's fortunes somehow, as if he were the good fairy waving some magic wand over the poor man's head. It would be a hell of an accomplishment.

The cove was perhaps a half mile across. There was a steep hill on one side, with sparse grass and outcroppings of gray rock. A man named Nikos owned it and grazed sheep there. The neck of land on the other side was lower, a small peninsula on which there were several houses, some still under construction. "That one," Szabo said, pointing to the closest, "belongs to an eccentric German. He used to be a concert pianist but he had a nervous collapse and doesn't play any more. Fortunately, his wife has money. They come in the summer. I think there are two or three grand pianos in that house."

"And the others, the ones that are still being worked on?"

Szabo explained how people built on Lesbos, putting what they could into a building and then leaving it to go off to jobs in other parts of Greece or other parts of the world, to earn money to bring back the next year and do another room or two.

It was a bright, clear April day, but a little cool.

"Do you want to go out?" Szabo asked.

"Into the water?" Castle asked, surprised. "It's a bit chilly, isn't it?"

"To swim in, perhaps. But there's a pedallo. I know the man who owns it. He wouldn't mind our borrowing it."

"Why not?"

They took off their shoes and socks, rolled up their trouser legs, and pushed the pedallo into the water. Then, side by side, they pedaled out into the water of the cove, not speaking, feeling the gentle rocking of the water, the slap-slap of the pedal-driven paddle wheel, and the delicate warmth of the sun at their backs.

"Agreeable," Castle said.

"Yes, for a week or two. I've been here five months."

"Surely you could travel about, go anywhere you like in Europe."

He shook his head no, but didn't explain. They had reached the end of the sheltering promontory and the motion of the waves changed, becoming slower but more forceful.

"Perhaps we should go back," Szabo suggested. They turned the boat around and headed for shore. The return trip was less agreeable, because the sun was in their faces now, and the sport of the excursion had begun to feel like work. The Greeks were small people and the pedallo had been built to accommodate them. Castle had to scrunch down as much as he could, so that pedaling wasn't natural and easy.

Still, they made it back, tugged the boat up onto the sand, and tethered it to the tree to which it had been tied when they'd found it.

"I have no money at all," Szabo explained. "I am living here mostly on the charity of a friend of mine from twenty years ago who owns a house here and allows me to live in it. I jumped bail, which cost a great deal, and I can't work."

"I see," Castle said.

"I say this not for sympathy but so that you will understand how it is with me. I can't travel around Europe. I haven't even been to Mitilini in more than a month. I have no car. The bus is dreadful."

"We will go this evening," Castle said. "You will be my guest. I insist! It would give me great pleasure."

Szabo hesitated but only for a few seconds. "All right, I accept. With pleasure just as great."

*

They had eaten squid and had drunk a surprisingly good bottle of white Cambas at one of the restaurants in the port overlooking the harbor. The yachts and sailboats of the season had not yet appeared, and there were only working vessels, some of them rather in need of paint, tied up along the quay.

Szabo had been talking ever since they'd set out in Castle's rented car, not about his troubles with Lila Love and the law enforcement agencies of the state of California, but about his earlier life in Paris and in Budapest, his boyhood—he could remember the Nazis—and his young manhood under the Communists.

What Castle noticed was the wry, Mittel-European wit, the detachment, as if the stories Szabo was recounting were merely odd anecdotes demonstrating the quirkiness and unpredictability of life rather than chunks of his personal history. He thought it was bizarre to have survived the Germans and the Russians only to fall victim to American puritanism and democracy. "The soldiers are right, you know. The safety or the danger of a particular position has nothing to do with one's survival. It is a question only of whether the bullet has your name on it. And you never hear the shot that kills you."

"You're exaggerating, I hope. You're not dead, after all."

"No? Physically, I'm in excellent shape. But artistically? I cannot work alone. Film is a collaborative enterprise, like the building of cathedrals. I have had several offers from Arabs who have more money than they know what to do with. You think they want me to make an art film? 'Go, take these two million dollars we'd otherwise feed our camels or wipe our asses with and make a good film.' No such thing, effendi. They want me to do porno so they can make even more money. I told them to eat pork—and at the same time I wished I had some pork to eat."

"Still, you could make films for other producers, for legitimate ones."

"It's possible. Anything is possible. But my need is known. And these people are superstitious, which is understandable. Nobody knows what's good and what isn't, or what will make money and what won't. So they're all very nervous and crazy. And superstitious. And one of their superstitions is that they don't like to hire people they think might need the work. I need the work, and that's generally known. So I'm unlucky and untouchable."

"What would it take to restore you?"

"You're going to snap your fingers? Fix it all?"

"I've been thinking about it."

"You're wasting your time," Szabo said.

"Not at all. I'm on vacation, remember."

"Some vacation!"

"Would a hundred thousand help?"

"Drachmas?"

"Dollars."

"Oh, yes," Szabo said. "It would be enough to sprinkle in their eyes and dazzle them a little. But that's a great deal of money."

"I may be able to work out something. Tell me, have you ever written anything?"

"That's what I've been doing for the long days and nights I've spent here on this island. I have filled dozens of notebooks."

"Would you mind if I took a look?"

"Not at all. Even without the blandishment of large sums of money."

They drove back to Skalahori, the village where Szabo was house-sitting, and Castle spent half an hour skimming through Szabo's journals. At length, he looked up and said, "Fine! I think I can do something for you. It remains to be seen how much, but I believe I can help you. You accept?"

"But of course, with deep thanks."

"We'll have a brandy on it," Castle said. It was late but the cafés in the square were still open. The men of the village used them as living rooms more or less, drinking, talking, or just watching television. Castle asked Szabo to order the best brandy they had.

The waiter brought the bottle, a Metaxa VSOP. Szabo approved. The waiter poured them their drinks.

"I'll be in touch," Castle promised.

"I'll be here, waiting," Szabo promised.

*

The next day, Castle flew from Mitilini to Athens, where he caught a plane for Iraklion. He'd wanted to see Crete, to visit the place at Knossos and to see the less fancifully restored Minoan ruins at Phaestos. And he did go out to Knossos, where he dutifully followed the guide around the ruins, admiring the primitive energy of the murals and trying to get some feeling for the brutal and yet elegant civilization that had flourished here so long ago.

But it was only with difficulty that he could focus his attention. His mind kept wandering—not just to Mihail Szabo and his problems, but to Jill Morgan and Helen Burke and, with depressing frequency, to Susan Flowers. The Swedish bimbos he saw lounging around the pool back at the hotel in Iraklion made him uneasy. They were not only topless but also, somehow, sexless, like caryatids in rococo concert halls. Real breasts could not be so perfect as those they flaunted.

Unless, of course, his libido had extinguished itself? No, that couldn't be the case. He didn't believe it. It was the way those Swedish girls were ageless—really, it was impossible to say whether they were seventeen or twenty-seven. They had that leathery look of people who spend a great deal of their time outdoors, either skiing or sunning themselves. Like Lila Love?

Of course, she'd be fading a little. Szabo had alluded to the overblown quality of the girl, the early ripeness that warns of impending rottenness. Of course, now she'd be older and a bit shopworn . . .

Of course! That was the solution to the problem. Szabo had been too close to see it, but Castle could stand back and appreciate that there might be a way to solve the man's difficulties, not just one or another but all together, by the same brilliant stroke. If it worked right, or could be made to, it would be a beautiful thing, an aesthetically satisfying thing to see.

And to boast to Susan Flowers about?

Well, maybe not that, but still worth doing. And more fun than anything he could see on the bulletin board of the hotel lobby with its offerings of excursions to Agios Nikolaos, or the great Samaria Gorge, or the caves of Matala on the south coast. To hell with all that!

Castle walked over to the Olympic Airways office and spent half an hour negotiating and cajoling until he was able to get himself onto a flight that would allow a connection on to New York. And yes, he could stop over in New York but fly on to Los Angeles on the same ticket.

"Fine, that's what I'd like to do," he said, feeling more energetic and cheerful than at any time since he'd begun his vacation.

*

From the writings of Mihail Szabo:

I have had what the French call *une nuit blanche:* not just a sleepless night, but a blank screen on which one projects all kinds of disconnected and unedited rushes.

From the lateness of my evening with Castle, I'd have expected to fall at once into unconsciousness, but no, the opportunity for talk, the stimulation of a good dinner and good prospects, the brief interval of hope and the inevitable return to earth . . . it was all too much for me. I was like an overwound clock, unable to tick or to strike.

In Hollywood or London or Paris, there would be three occasions like this in a normal month, vistas opening up and then not so much closing as merely fading, melting shut. One can get used to that.

If there was anything just or apposite in my troubles with Lila Love (what a gorgeously vile name!), it was as a kind of punishment for that L.A. steadiness that is unimpressed by anything. Ninety-nine times out of a hundred, that is the correct and necessary reaction. Mr. X wants you to direct his thirty-million-dollar epic? Mr. Y wants to give you a three-picture deal? Ms. Z is willing to commit to your next project? We learn at first never to show our feelings, and soon thereafter, from bitter experience, not even to have them. And the same possibilities and offers, after hours, we meet with the same display of blasé indifference—a little coke? a pair of twins to help you get to sleep? a mother offering you her daughter as she might offer a canapé? Why not?

Even while it's happening, we don't quite believe it. And then, later on, it's all beyond recall, like yesterday's promises from agents and producers, or last week's commitments from actors and actresses.

But I am out of practice. Castle's style is New York rather than Angeleno, and I found myself believing in him. I can't think why I should.

Perhaps it was the earnestness of those tramp freighters with their patina of rust, moored just across from the restaurant where we ate. They looked to be real, although it doesn't require any sophisticated economist to point out that the take from the frivolous yachts, the sloops and ketches and motorboats that use those slips in season, is vastly larger. Those are the real boats; these illusory ones.

Still, I liked the man. And it was nice to join him on a kind of holiday from depression. I trust his vacation is as much a treat as mine was.

It is getting light. The roosters have been making their usual racket. Now I will perhaps be able to sleep for a few hours.

*

The only thing that makes information difficult to find is that there's so much of it, a sea of data through which one must try to navigate. The telephone directory established the fact that Darlene and Lila Love lived out in the valley. Castle drove out there and saw that it was a little tract house, but even one of those tract houses in southern California represents a fair amount of money. Did they own it or just rent?

That took forty-five minutes or so in the county clerk's office. With the large ledgers containing the records of title, Castle was able to determine that Darlene Love owned the house, subject, of course, to a first mortgage with Sunset Savings and Loan Corp. Where had she been able to get together the kind of money she'd have needed for a down payment?

The date of the transfer was on the title. With that, all Castle had to do was go to the library and read through back issues of the L.A. *Times* for the month or so preceding the sale, combing through the real estate ads until he found the offering of Darlene Love's house. From Jack England, Realtor. The logo at the top of the ad showed a turret that looked like a piece of Windsor Castle, underneath which, in

Olde English lettering, there was the motto: "Stately Homes of England."

Terrific!

Castle cruised by the storefront office in a small shopping mall. Actually, it wasn't a mall so much as a few satellite stores flanking a supermarket. England's operation didn't exactly knock him over. He parked his car and walked up and down a couple of times, pausing as he passed Jack England's little enterprise to adjust his necktie, using the plate glass as a mirror. He could see England inside and, at a smaller desk closer to the front door, a young woman, some kind of assistant.

Castle went into the Tower of Pizza on the other side of the dry cleaner next door to Jack England, Realtor. He ordered a cup of coffee and dawdled there, drinking the coffee and pretending to read a newspaper until he saw England stroll out and get into a well-maintained blue Datsun that was maybe three years old. England drove off. Castle left a decent tip and walked over to the realty office to see what he could learn from the girl.

"Hi, there!" he said cheerfully. "Jack in?"

"You just missed him, I'm afraid," the young woman said. She was perhaps twenty-five and had a nice face on which she'd put more makeup than she needed. She was wearing a navy-blue sweater set. Castle couldn't see her shoes.

"And what's your name?" he asked.

"Sheila. Sheila Rafferty."

"Hi, I'm Leonard Castle. You sold a house four years ago to a Darlene Love. At this address," he said, handing her a blank envelope with an address and a date written on the front.

"Before my time, I'm afraid."

"Still, you could help me out, maybe. You've got records you keep. Or Jack does."

"Surely," she said.

"Closing statements?"

"Of course."

"Maybe you'd let me take a look at that one? The date's there on the envelope, if you file them that way."

"I'm afraid you'd have to wait for Mr. England to get back."

"Look, Sheila, I'm in kind of a hurry. It's no big deal, but I have to get all the way back to Anaheim this afternoon."

"What's this about?"

"Just a credit check," he assured her.

"I don't know . . ."

"Look inside the envelope," he said. "That's for helping a guy out, okay?" He winked at her.

It was a long shot, but it worked. People with too much makeup like that kind of thing. She also liked the contents of the envelope—an engraving of Ulysses S. Grant in an attractive shade of green.

"Nobody will know but us chickens," he said, looking as boyish and harmless as he could.

"Gee, I don't know."

He held his hand out for her to give him back the envelope, but she didn't know about that either. She shook her head at her own naughtiness and then got up and went to the filing cabinet. It took her only a moment to lay her hands on the right folder.

"You can look at it, I guess."

"That's all I need. Half a minute's look."

He ran his eyes down the legal-sized sheets. The binder was entered there, with the notation: "Certified check from Lawrence B. Golding, DDS."

"You're an angel," Castle said, handing back the file.

"You won't say anything about this, will you?"

He put his finger to his lips. Then he blew her a kiss. She blushed and grinned. He winked one last time and left.

He had what he needed.

*

The most impressive object in Darlene Love's small living room was a large free-form coffee table in polished redwood into one end of which there had been worked a giant cribbage board with brass pegs almost the size of railway spikes that were disposed apparently at random.

Mrs. Love's tube top in Day-Glo orange not only showed off her figure but positively proclaimed it. In comparison, her black velvet slacks were almost conservative.

Her daughter was wearing crimson short-shorts over what was either a bathing suit or a leotard in electric blue.

To be fair, Castle conceded that they were at home and could wear whatever they liked. Or hated.

"I'm grateful to you for finding the time to see me at such short notice," he said. "But I think I can make it worth your while."

"That's what you said on the phone," Darlene Love prompted him.

"Would you like a lemonade or something? Lila, be a love, would you, and go get Mr. Castle and me a couple of lemonades."

"Thank you, no. I just had lunch a short time ago," Castle said.

"Just the one for me, then, dear," Darlene said. Her daughter skulked off toward the kitchen to fetch the drink. She did look older than what had to be her true age. Her mother, for all the brassiness of her bleached blonde hair and that bizarre tube top, could have passed for an elder sister. No doubt, that was her intention. "Now, let's talk a little straight talk here, Mr. Castle," she said. "What are you selling?"

"Fame and fortune, madam. Exactly what you've been after for years. I'm a literary agent." He handed her his card. "I want to propose a book contract to you, from which will come not only substantial amounts of money but also the possibility of film or television sales. It doesn't take a genius to figure out that Lila Love could probably play the part of Lila Love fairly convincingly. This is that golden ring you've been trying to grab hold of. And I admire that. I admire ambition, however unorthodox your methods may have been."

"Just like that?"

"Just like that."

"Things like this don't just happen, mister. When something falls out of the sky, it's usually pigeon shit."

"I like your directness," Castle said.

"What's the catch?" she asked. "There's got to be one."

"No catch. It's just that I think there's money to be made here. Your previous system of shaking the money tree doesn't work any more. The young lady is of the age of consent. She's legal now. Unless you put her out on the street, you need some new scam, or let us call it a method of accumulation of assets. If you and she are willing to consider a candid autobiography—my tentative title would be *Jail Bait*—I think I can get you a decent advance and a real chance at some other very attractive opportunities. Your daughter is an idea whose time may very well have come."

"I think you're crazy," she said, scrunching down onto the sofa and looking at him through half-closed eyes. "I haven't the vaguest idea what you're talking about."

"Of course not. But Mihail Szabo had the impression that he was not the first to enjoy your daughter's friendship. He didn't know about Dr. Golding, for instance. But I do."

She sat up straighter.

"This is the kind of project that is going to get itself done, one way or another, but it seems to me that the fair and decent thing would be for you to participate in the proceeds."

"You mean, someone could steal her life? Put it in a book?"

"Or on the screen," Castle said. "And all you could do would be to sue on the grounds that it was true and that you and she had actually done all those terrible things. It would be pretty tough for you to enlist the sympathies of a jury that way. On the other hand, if you and she were to step forward and bare your breasts, so to speak, expressing your remorse at what you'd done, what you'd been forced by cruel circumstance to do to keep body and soul together . . ."

He didn't need to continue. She was already nodding her comprehension and her eagerness.

Lila returned with a tall glass of pink lemonade into which she'd stuck a paper umbrella. "Am I supposed to have not heard any of that?" she asked.

"Did I say that?" her mother asked.

"How do you know about Dr. Golding?" Lila asked Castle.

"In this town, information is not only a raw material but the basic industry. It's not hard to find out anything you set your mind to learning. The kind of book we had in mind . . . well, it made certain assumptions about you and your mother here. If you hadn't been the kind of people you are, the book wouldn't have its quality, its shock value and its appeal."

"It's got to be shocking? Is that what you're saying?"

"It's got to be true, but I don't see any problem there. If you keep on with the business about the poor innocent girl who was taken advantage of by the wicked film director, that's not interesting. A lot less interesting than the real story. And now that there's a different kind of moviemaking, movies for cable and so forth, there's a market for adult material with greater freedom in its moral assumptions. You see that, don't you?"

"And what do you get out of this?"

"The agent's fee is ten percent of what you get. If you get nothing, the agent gets nothing. If you get a lot, then the agent gets ten percent of a lot, but in that case you can afford it."

"And who writes this?"

"A writer, I'm sure, can be found. They're not exactly in short supply out here."

"I don't know," Darlene said. "I just don't know!"

"Have you got something better lined up? Or something as good?" Castle asked.

She didn't answer.

"You've got anything at all?"

"You've got a pen?" Darlene asked.

"I'll have the papers drawn up. And Mr. Al Hobart will be your actual agent. He's an associate of mine, but he's out here while I'm usually in New York. He'll see you tomorrow and you can work out the details. But you have my card. If you have any questions or problems, you call me any time. Collect. I'm eager for this to go forward, believe me. I think you've made the intelligent decision."

"I'm really going to be in the movies?" Lila asked.

"Why on earth not, my dear?" Castle replied. "If Flipper can do it, you can do it. All you need is a little luck and push and shrewdness. And you've got your mother in your corner."

"You're full of shit, Mr. Castle, you know that?" Darlene said. But then, allowing herself a smile, she added, "But I like that in a man."

"You'll hear from Mr. Hobart tomorrow," Castle promised.

He said goodbye and drove back to his hotel for a bath and a stiff drink. The worst of it was over, he told himself. When he was out of the tub, he called Al Hobart, an agent he knew in Los Angeles and with whom he'd done some business now and then, to offer him the Love book, *Jail Bait*.

Hobart was eager but worried. "Gee, I don't know, Len. You really think a thing like that'll go?"

"Believe me, it'll go. I'll talk it up in New York and help you out."

"Then what do you need me for?" Hobart asked.

"This is only a small piece of a bigger project. I want to keep it at arm's length to avoid conflict of interest."

"You want to explain any of that?"

"Sure," Castle said, "I'd be happy to. What it means is that my client is Mihail Szabo."

"Oh, I see. Well, okay, then. Sure, I'm happy to help out. Anything I can do."

Castle gave him a concise summary of his conversation with Darlene and Lila Love. What he wanted was for Hobart to draw up an agreement and get out there the next day to sign them up, or better yet, have them come to his office.

"And for this, you get what kind of piece?"

"I'll take half of the commission on the book. Anything you can work out here for movies or television is your doing and you ought to have the full benefit of that."

"That's decent of you," Hobart said.

"I want to be fair," Castle said. "You'll let me know when they've signed?"

"I'll call you the minute they leave."

Castle depressed the little button on the phone and then made the next call, to Harry Gitlitz of Gitlitz, Schine, Monk, and Lapidus. Gitlitz was Szabo's lawyer.

He wasn't exactly overjoyed to hear the mention of Mihail Szabo's name, but as Castle spoke, explaining what he'd done, what he planned to do next, and what he hoped in the end to accomplish, Gitlitz warmed up quickly.

*

It was short notice, but Gitlitz managed to get an appointment for himself and Leonard Castle with Charlotte Parsons, the assistant district attorney in charge of the Szabo case, the next afternoon. The two men went upstairs together and waited in the reception room, watching police detectives and civilian witnesses parade in and out. Occasionally, defendants' lawyers, the ones with the briefcases and the vests, announced themselves to the receptionist and were either shown on back or invited to find their own way.

Gitlitz tried to reassure Castle, reminding him that they'd been lucky to get an appointment at all, and suggesting that Ms. Parsons was probably tied up with other cases. "They're all overworked," he said.

"Oh, sure," Castle agreed. "But if I were she, I'd file my nails for a while, even if I had nothing better to do, and let us stew out here a little."

"Don't let it get to you," Gitlitz told him.

"It doesn't, if you expect it," Castle said. "It's just part of the game. You and I both know that, but she doesn't know whether we do or not."

"I think you're making too much of it, but maybe," Gitlitz said, grinning. Gitlitz was a litigator and negotiator of considerable reputation. He was short, a little on the pudgy side, and he had red hair and freckles, so that he looked unintimidating, but then he knew that and used it. Castle could see how he was terrific with juries, getting them to feel sorry for him.

Eventually, the receptionist announced that they could go on back to see Ms. Parsons, whose office was the fourth door on the left.

Ms. Parsons, a woman in her early forties, was talking on the phone, which she had cradled on her shoulder. She was saying,

"Right, right," and every now and then making notes on a yellow pad. With her left hand extended palm upward, she indicated that they were to take the chairs that faced her desk. They sat down and waited another couple of minutes until she hung up, greeted them, apologized, and asked what she could do for them.

"It's about Mike Szabo," Gitlitz said. "Mr. Castle has just seen him in Greece."

"Yes?" she asked, with an audible sigh.

"He's in terrible shape," Castle said. "I felt sorry for him."

"Well, I've got other candidates for sympathy who are lots higher on my list this week. He's a fugitive from justice, you remember."

"He's mindful of that," Castle said. "That's what we wanted to discuss with you. He'd like to come home."

"I think that's an excellent idea."

"There is one other piece of information I've had from Mr. Castle, however, which I think bears on the case," Gitlitz said.

"Other than Mr. Szabo's homesickness?" she asked.

"I understand that Mrs. Darlene Love and her daughter have signed with an agent here in Los Angeles to represent them in their efforts to market an autobiography Lila Love intends to write. The working title is *Jail Bait,* and it is to be a candid confession of their operation with Szabo and others before him, whom those two shook down and blackmailed. Szabo was actually an honest man who wouldn't pay off."

"Is this true?" she asked. "There was never any suggestion of blackmail in the original investigation."

"Until Szabo, they'd all paid off," Gitlitz explained. "She was shrewd enough to keep her demands within reasonable limits. Szabo was just stubborn or maybe foolish and he wouldn't play. You can call Al Hobart, who is the agent for the book, and he'll confirm what they will admit in print. He's in the phone book. You can call him right now if you like. But what Mr. Castle says is absolutely true."

"I see," she said, and leaned back in her swivel chair. She twiddled with a lead pencil and thought for a moment.

"He'll accept a conviction," Gitlitz said. "In fact, he'd be happy to do so if he could be assured of lenient treatment—no jail time and no shrink."

Her eyebrows ascended at this demand.

"He's Hungarian," Castle said. "The Communists use psychiatry for political prisoners. Understandably, he's afraid of it."

"I'll talk to the district attorney," she said. "I can't promise anything but I'll see how he's disposed."

"That's fair. That's very decent," Gitlitz said.

"The only trouble is that there's been so much publicity on this one. We can't have the impression that these movie people can get away with murder," she said, putting the pencil back in the marmalade crock on her desk.

"But the publicity that's coming, when Lila Love's confession hits the newspapers and magazines, isn't going to make you look any better," Castle said.

"As I say, I'll speak to the district attorney."

"He'd be willing to be arrested when he lands in New York. That'd look even-handed enough."

Her eyebrows shot up again. "You wouldn't be planning to use this some way or other yourself?"

"Of course I am," Castle said. "I'm Mr. Szabo's agent. I believe he's a talented man, a valuable artist, and a decent fellow. I want to do whatever I can for him. But who wouldn't?"

"I'll recommend the deal," she said, smiling at the effrontery of the man before her.

"Terrific," Gitlitz said. "Thanks. We won't keep you."

"I add my thanks to his," Castle said. "It's been a pleasure."

*

From the writings of Mihail Szabo:
Adjusting to catastrophe is not, after all, so difficult, as I now begin to discover. The accommodation to good fortune tests us much more severely. Can I believe not only in my good fortune but in my worth and its justice? Gift horses are the only ones we look in the mouth, for we know pretty well those we've owned or, after long and careful consideration, have haggled over and bought. The meaning of the proverb has nothing to do with the common sense of the situation. It addresses rather this physical feeling in the pit of the stomach, the apprehension, or, no, the certainty that we are only being set up for some crushing blow. This is what makes it impossible to enjoy the return of prosperity and sunny skies, the restoration of our powers, the return of what we used to think was rightfully ours (but have learned better). Adversity is such a good teacher that its lessons are difficult to ignore, even in good times.

Mr. Castle has come through handsomely, as if to demonstrate how trivial were my grounds for despair. It isn't that Leonard Castle is trivial. On the contrary, he is a fellow of considerable power and, just as important, ingenuity. But he was here, after all, on vacation, and our meeting—he insists, and I believe him—was altogether an accident. His decision to pluck me out of the dark oubliette in which I languished was, I'm quite convinced, rather whimsical, or at least made for more complicated reasons than the usual motives. It wasn't for the money, or even to do me a good turn, but to show the fates that they could be managed, that their work could be redone and considerably improved upon if only a man like Castle deigned to involve himself.

It is also possible, I suppose, that he was as much a creature of the fates as I was, but that way lies madness. In that case we are all automata, bumping about in random ways for the amusement of some idiotic deity no civilization has been cruel enough to imagine.

Certainly, I am grateful to Castle. He has managed to get the charges against me reduced to some new formulation I don't pretend to understand—lascivious carriage, I think, which sounds like the name of a sports car. There is to be a reprimand and a small fine, but no jail term and no compulsory psychotherapy. I am, moreover, to fly back to JFK next week, where I shall be met by police and a crowd of photographers and reporters, so that I can formally surrender myself into custody and, as Castle points out, get several million dollars' worth of publicity in the bargain. The first magazine appearance of a section of these journals will appear the following week.

Instead of that $3,500 I was once offered, I am now getting $35,000 for the same thing, on top of the sum from the publisher that can only be described as absurd. If I can make more films, fine; and if not, I can live for years on the proceeds of these literary efforts. If I were to remain here, I'd be the richest man in the village.

But the money is almost beside the point. My dignity, my honor are largely retrieved. And all because of a little detail that I knew about but hadn't seized upon, or hadn't tried to manipulate. The fact that Lila had passed her eighteenth birthday and that she and her mother would no longer be able to play their old game was the great key. They would now need some new way to make a living, some new racket or con, or even some legitimate kind of work. Castle had seen that this was the key and he'd turned it—to show off, I think.

Even more than gratitude, I feel admiration, for the conception in the first place, and for the style with which he managed it.

*

A last entry. Also less joyous than it ought to be. I am beginning to realize that the journal is coming to an end. I cannot write with the same innocence as I had when I began, because I know that there will be editorial eyes scanning this for the good bits, the publishable parts, and I am trying to please them, others, more than express my own spontaneous thoughts and feelings. That's less satisfactory than the conditions that obtained when I began, not only for myself but for the journal. The air of deliberation, the sense of artifice and performance, will be perceptible to the reader I have in mind, that friendly but critical intelligence I am trying to speak to now that I am no longer merely muttering to myself.

*

My knowledge that I am about to leave the island has turned me into a tourist, attracted or repelled on frivolous grounds of personal preference. The necessity that roots most people to a landscape—and that until very recently connected me with Lesbos—no longer applies and I am aware of a weightlessness that is not altogether pleasant. It is what most people desire, the freedom to come and go as they please, to pick an attractive place and light, but all they can do is light. There is no substance, unless they have more faith in their caprice than I do in mine. To have the courage of one's whims!

I have been traveling about, saying goodbye not only to villagers but to vistas, trees, buildings, tonalities of light. The likelihood of my returning here in the foreseeable future is not great.

Ari waved at me today, which brought tears to my eyes. He recognizes me. I have been here long enough to register upon his limited consciousness. And when I am gone, he may wonder for a brief time what has become of me, but life will go on and he will sit on his broken wall, minding the chickens and pounding on his trouser leg, grinning like the idiot he is . . .

But he is at home here, as I am not anywhere.

The Russians did this, driving me out of Hungary, making of Hungary a place where it was impossible for a person like me to stay. After the first dislocation, there is no other.

*

Al Hobart had been in the building before, but never this way, by invitation, with the receptionist expecting him and a private secretary welcoming him and offering him coffee. Usually, he tagged along with a client he'd managed to arrange an interview for, having fast-talked

some talent coordinator, and while there was always the possibility
that his client might actually be booked onto a real show, there was
the more realistic interpretation that people were just doing their jobs
—he in having arranged the interview and the talent coordinator in
seeing the talent, tap dancer or magician or baritone with singing dog,
just in case every other member of Actors Equity and the American
Guild of Variety Artists should be out of town for the show's tape
date.

But this time, it was quite different. In the first place, they'd called
Hobart, inviting him over. Not with the client, or "at least not for this
first meeting," but you didn't have to be a card-carrying genius to
figure out that there was interest, and not just in some talk-show spot
for six minutes either. What they were talking about was at the very
least a segment of *Periscope,* and maybe even a whole hour-long special—on Lila Love as an example of the new Hollywood!

He had a copy of the galleys of *Jail Bait* in his hand. It was almost
certain that they had a set of galleys too, or lots of them, but it was
nice for Hobart to have something to put into his attaché case, an
actual object he could touch and, more important, show as evidence
that there was real interest. Lila Love wasn't just some passing phenomenon, but a piece of history, and this book was a monument that
would endure in libraries and so forth. Forever!

Not that Hobart would actually say that kind of thing, but it was
impressive, to the television executives whose work was broadcast out
onto the airwaves to disappear at once. Or to himself, for that matter.
It wasn't the greatest book in the world, maybe, but it was an honest
to Christ book. He could hold it up. He could open it. There were lines
of print, just like in the Bible or the encyclo-fucking-pedia!

He accepted the coffee from the gorgeous blonde secretary. She gave
great coffee, not just in a cardboard container but in a china cup with a
saucer. At these salaries, she could probably type too. Hobart hardly
had a chance for more than a sip, though, before he was shown into
Granville Haggerty's office, which wasn't quite big enough for a circus, maybe, but it could have held an exercise class easily enough, and
without anybody bumping into the baby grand piano that was tucked
away in one corner.

No desk, of course. At that altitude, executives didn't have to do
things that required a desk. This was the realm of the purely cerebral,
with attendants standing by with note pads and word processors and
Xerox machines and whatever else was needed. On the big executive
sofa, one of those high-tech jobs with chrome and black leather, there

was a woman from *Periscope.* But Haggerty was the main man, the decision maker.

"It's good to see you," he said, which was one of those suave remarks that covered all bases, applying just as easily to people he'd met before as to those he hadn't. And, most important, it worked with those people he wasn't sure about, might have met but couldn't remember.

"It's good to meet you," Hobart said, confident enough to let him off the hook.

"This is still in the thinking stage, which is why we didn't want to have Miss Love here. No point in getting her hopes up too early. But there's a real chance that she might be just the right peg for the story we're working on. If there's a fit, then we're golden."

"I understand," Hobart said, understanding perfectly well that when they were encouraging it meant that they had doubts or wanted something. Did it follow that these honest expressions of iffiness meant that this was a sure thing? He had a good feeling down there in the guts. He nodded and said, "I appreciate your consideration."

"Did you ever hear from the district attorney? I mean, directly?" the woman asked.

"Only once," Hobart said. "You have to understand that this wasn't exclusively my deal, Miss . . ."

"Flowers."

"Yes, forgive me, Miss Flowers. It was a joint thing I had with Leonard Castle, who is quite a well-known agent in New York. He was representing Mike Szabo. And he and Harry Gitlitz, who was Szabo's lawyer, went to the district attorney's office to work out a deal that would allow Szabo to come back to the States. And at that time, there was a call I had from their office, from the district attorney's office that is, to verify that I had a deal with Lila and Darlene Love. The DA's people wanted to make sure that the Loves were planning a book, as of course they were. But that's the only call I ever had. I'm sure there's no intention on the part of the district attorney or anyone else I know about to prosecute the Loves."

"No, no. Of course not," the woman said. "Had Mr. Castle brought you the Love book or was that something you went out and found on your own?"

He hesitated. What did any of this have to do with the price of cheese? But not knowing what they were trying to get at, he figured he'd better stick to the truth. "As a matter of fact, Castle had been in touch with Darlene Love and he turned them over to me. I guess, mostly, because we're old friends, but he didn't want to have the appearance of a conflict of interest, representing both Mike Szabo and Lila Love. You can understand that."

"Oh, yes, I understand," the woman said. "He set up a deal with the Loves that he turned over to you, and then he went to the DA to say that there would be a book from Lila Love and used that to change their attitude about Mike Szabo. Is that about it?"

"That's about it," Hobart said. "But I don't see the point . . ."

"Miss Flowers is also interested in Leonard Castle," Haggerty said to Al Hobart, "but that's *very* speculative. If I could ask you not to say anything at all about that, especially to Mr. Castle . . . ? I'd be grateful."

"I understand," Hobart said.

"Now, about Lila Love," Haggerty said, "what's she up to? How have you been able to get this book of hers to work for her, either in movies or television or anything else that you've been able to put together?"

Hobart did his number. They gave him about fifteen minutes, and he put on what he decided, later, was a pretty good show. For a week or so, he was confident, and then for another week, he was hopeful, but nothing happened. And when Haggerty didn't return his calls, he began to ratchet his hopes downward. He hadn't screwed up. It was just the way they worked, getting a bee in their bonnets one day and then, just as suddenly, having the bee fly away. Go figure it.

What he hadn't seen or heard and couldn't imagine was Susan Flowers thanking Haggerty for wasting twenty minutes with this nonsense so that she could probe for information about Castle. "It's what I'd guessed, but I wanted to hear it from Hobart."

"No problem. Happy to help out. It's the least I can do. You don't get out here all that often."

"No, I don't. I should. Maybe I will. You never know," she said.

"I keep trying."

"You're sweet," she said.

"I'm a dirty old lecher, and you know it."

"No, you're a sweet old lecher."

"This Castle sounds like an interesting fellow," Haggerty said.

"I've been playing with this for a year now. I think there could be an interesting piece, if only we can get him on camera and show what it is that he does. I'll be making my pitch for it in a couple of weeks.

And as long as I was out here on this other thing, I thought I'd pull this string to see what happened."

"The office is yours, any time," Haggerty said. "So am I."

*

Back in New York, she decided that the only decent thing was to call him. It was business, after all. She really was proposing the segment about Castle. It had been a pretext at one time but not any longer. If anything, the relationship—friendship, or love affair, or whatever she decided to call it—was now *pro forma* while the business uses to which each could put the other were the reality. Still, one can be friendly and honest in business dealings. She called him and they met for lunch, which was nicely neutral. Dinner had a way of stretching on into the night, and she didn't want that, or not now anyway.

They decided on Chinese food, and over the winter melon soup she told him that she'd talked to Al Hobart.

"Oh?" Castle said. His spoon, midway from bowl to mouth, didn't even waver.

"He came clean. We tricked him a little, I'll admit, but the point is that I know what you did—with Lila Love and Al Hobart, and with Gitlitz and the district attorney. It was a nice piece of work."

"Thanks," Castle said.

"I'm going to propose the piece, the one we've been talking about all this time."

"You don't really have to do that, you know."

"I know. I want to."

"In fact, I'd prefer it if you didn't."

"I was afraid of that. But I really want to go ahead. I think it's terrific. It's what our viewers want to know—or what they'd want to know if they knew enough to ask the right questions. It's not so much about you, although you're the star, as it is about how the world works, how all the different games fit together."

"What if I refuse to cooperate?"

"I hope you won't do that."

"I don't know. I'll have to think about it."

"Why? For spite?"

"No, it's just that what I do is better done quietly. There's a point at which self-promotion gets in the way of what I do."

"You could have told me this six months ago, you know."

"I know. I didn't take it seriously then. Or a better way to put it is that I didn't think it through then. I'd figured that we could use each other. Or that mostly I could use you—as I did with Jill Morgan's kid and his background. I never thought this would get to the point where I'd have to decide."

"That's where we are."

"So I see. Well, give me a couple of days, would you?"

"That's fair. I'll be bringing it up next Tuesday. So you can have the weekend, if you like."

"Okay."

"I may bring it up, either way."

"That's up to you," he said.

She nodded. "A little more soup?" she offered.

He allowed her to ladle some more soup into his bowl.

"You know, I just stumbled into this thing with Szabo," he told her. "I went on that trip that was supposed to be our trip. I needed to get away, even if you didn't. And I went to Greece, figuring I'd have it mostly to myself in early April, which was how it worked out. And I got lost on Lesbos and stopped at a little café for coffee and to ask directions. Szabo was at the next table. It just happened to be the town where he was staying."

She nodded. The waiter took away the empty tureen and brought them their mu-shu pork and the little pancakes that go with it.

"The gallant thing would be to say that I'd have rather gone with you than picked up Szabo and had him write his book. But I don't know. It's a good book."

"It is," she agreed.

"I have a lot of successful books I've represented. But not so many good ones. I'm proud of this."

"You ought to be," she said. "We'd get that in. I promise you that."

"No, no. I'm not worried about what you'll do to me. It's a question of whether the segment on me is a good thing for me to have, even assuming that it's friendly and upbeat and complimentary."

She poured him a little tea.

"I wonder, though, what it would have been like if you'd decided the other way. If you'd come with me. One of those big ifs." He paused for a moment, took a sip of tea, and asked, "What happened to us? We were doing fine, I thought."

"We were," she said. "Maybe that's what was wrong."

"I don't get it," he said.

"That was what scared me a little. It was too good, too serious. I was liking it too much."

"What's the matter with that?"

"Nothing," she said, staring at her plate. "But when I've got a lot invested in a relationship, then I start to worry about what's going to happen. Usually, I get hurt. And I guess a part of me thought that if I stopped it there, then I'd be in control. Sad, but in control."

"Jesus! I don't remember any of that."

"It's what we were talking about, though. I'd been sniping at you about Jill Morgan and the money, and what you'd done . . . That was a question of control. Of manipulation. I was worried that pretty soon you were going to start controlling and manipulating me."

"Ah, I see."

"I'm sorry."

"Me too. But it's not terminal, is it?"

"I don't know."

"What does that mean, that we've still got this program to get through, one way or another? Another test?"

"Not a test, really. But I'm in control, aren't I?"

"I guess so," he said. "Have a pancake. They're the best part. Anybody can do the pork part of these things right, but the pancake takes talent."

"You're not angry."

"I'm not angry," he said. "Sad, maybe, but that's just another word for grown-up, isn't it?"

A couple of minutes went by in which they ate without talking. It was Susan who broke the silence, announcing, "If you don't want this segment, I won't propose it."

"That's fair of you. What does it do on the personal side of the ledger?"

"I don't know. I wish we could keep these things separate."

"Do you?" he asked.

"What do you mean by that?" she asked him, not sure whether he'd been insulting.

"We enjoy what we do. And part of that is the personal side of these business relationships. They really do involve us. Our daytime lives are more real than anything else. That's all I meant."

"Oh, I see."

The rest of the lunch was uneventful. They parted at the door of the restaurant and he promised to let her know his decision as soon as possible.

He didn't call. Instead, he sent her a ridiculously expensive bracelet from Buccellati.

At the office.

She was, for the first thirty seconds, delighted.

Then she realized that she couldn't accept a present like this if *Periscope* was going to do that feature on him. This was his way of letting her know he'd decided he didn't want the segment.

And as a personal present? This was too much to accept unless she planned to resume the relationship seriously.

That was a flattering thought, and it pleased her.

But after a little more thought, she realized that it was trickier than that. It was up to her about the relationship. This was a serious enough present to be a farewell gift too.

She was tempted to send it back.

And then she realized that it didn't matter. He had figured all this out. And the bottom line was that she was supposed to keep the damned thing, and that it would be a reproach to her every time she wore it.

*

He'd had the brandy, which he'd taken like a shot of whiskey. And then he'd made the call. He listened to the ringing of Susan's telephone.

"Hello?"

"Susan? It's Leonard."

"Are you all right?" she asked.

"I'm not sure," he said.

"Have you heard?"

"Heard what?"

"About Byrd?"

"No. What about him?"

"Where are you?"

"I'm in a bar, actually. A couple of blocks from your place."

"Come on over," she said. "Now. We'll talk when you get here."

"Okay," he said.

He'd wanted to ask her what she'd been talking about. Why, for that matter, had she begun the conversation by asking him if he was all right?

But she'd hung up.

But she was all right. And he'd find out quickly enough. In a matter of only a few minutes.

12

Castle had been going through his files, checking over the projects that were presently in the works, considering their progress and the relationships in each instance. There was nothing where a substitution would be appropriate—or even possible. It had to be a new subject, a new client. McCracken needed a new celebrity to play with. Weeks had gone by, and McCracken had kept calling, desperate for work, by turns angry or depressed, but either way in need of the quick infusion of cash that a new book would bring him. He'd pleaded with Castle to find him something in a hurry.

"What in hell happened to all the money you made on the Morgan book?" Castle had asked. "You gamble it away?"

"I gave it away," McCracken had said.

It was one of those terrible situations McCracken's sister had found herself in. One of her children had leukemia and needed a bone-marrow transplant, which wasn't covered by medical insurance because it was still considered experimental. And the hospital that did the procedure insisted on a cash deposit of $50,000. McCracken explained all that, and then asked Castle, "What else could I have done? What would you do? I sent her the check. I mean, time is a factor in this. It's got to be right away or the odds get worse. And after taxes and buying this place up here in Maine, that was pretty much all I had. You've got to help me out."

"I will, I promise," Castle had replied, and now he felt the pressure himself. It was his problem as much as McCracken's. And he'd been looking for a suitable subject. In a hurry. He hadn't felt this eagerness, this actual need for a client, since the days when he'd first taken over the agency. It was ridiculous, almost demeaning, but also a challenge, and it made him feel as though he'd been reduced in rank and age and were back in his early twenties again. Could he still hustle that way if he had to? Could he browse through a magazine or spend a morning watching television and then pick up the phone, make a few calls, and create something out of thin air and then sell it to someone? It was his métier, after all, and here was his chance to show his stuff.

The right kind of client and in the right time frame! It was a hell of an order. Castle wasn't sure he could bring it off, but he was aware of an agreeable charge of energy from the uncertainty. It was a bizarre kind of fun to be on the spot that way. He kept the tiny Sony in his office turned on, although with the volume way down, and he glanced at it from time to time. He had a list on the back page of a pocket notebook, and every now and again he'd jot a name down, but never with much conviction. This one was a drunk and could hardly remember his own name, let alone the details of his early days in swashbuckling movies. That one was a moron and couldn't say "Welcome back" after a commercial unless there was a cue card underneath the camera.

No musicians. McCracken had said he was tone deaf.

A politician? Some kind of industrial wheeler-dealer? Iacocca had been a big hit, but how many Iacoccas are there? Frank Perdue, then?

What a dumb-cluck idea!

He asked Effie and Bobo to write down their suggestions. Names. Any names they could think of. Or even categories. Famous transsexuals. Famous chefs. Famous surgeons. Famous athletes?

He called McCracken to ask how he felt about sports.

"Nope, ideally that's not it," McCracken told him. "But thanks for checking."

"That's okay. I'll get back to you."

He turned up the volume and started listening to the audio part of the talk shows. He was desperate.

So were the talk-show hosts, apparently. A program of marital rapists? A program of female impersonators? Sex and diets were the two things American women seemed to be interested in, and inasmuch as they weren't unconnected, it left the field pretty damned narrow.

Famous whorehouse owners? Maybe McCracken might want to go out to Nevada and spend six months or so with his tape recorder and other equipment going and then come back and make a book out of that?

Not such a terrible idea!

But it wasn't exciting. Not after the book about Wanda Lathem. McCracken wouldn't want to get typecast as a dirty young man.

Castle looked up from his doodling on the yellow pad on his desk. The television set showed three couples with young men and older women, which was the hot subject of this morning's show. That or the audience's attitude toward this new phenomenon. It wasn't actually so very new, and there wasn't a whole lot to say about it, but Dickie Byrd was playing it for all it was worth, getting members of the audience to express their shock or their distaste, or, on occasion, the envy that underlay the disapproval of the others. The women were "in their prime sexually," and so were their younger partners. The clear implication was that these people were world-class sex champions, doing it all the time and having more fun at it than "this puritanical society of ours feels comfortable with."

What nonsense. Let them fuck goats if that's what they want to do!

That Byrd was ridiculous. His capacity to be boyish and prurient at the same time, with those blue eyes of his opening wide as if he'd just this minute figured out about the birds and the bees and couldn't quite believe it . . .

But the audiences ate him up.

And suddenly it was clear as crystal. Byrd and McCracken! They'd hit it off wonderfully well. They were two professionals. Get them together and the odds were that they'd produce something.

He buzzed Effie. "Get me Dickie Byrd, would you?"

The only question was why there hadn't already been a book by Byrd. Or about him. Such an obvious idea, it must have occurred to half a dozen people.

There had to be some difficulty somewhere. But that was only a challenge, something to make life interesting. There'd be a way to talk him around. There had to be. It felt right. It felt better than right. It was terrific. Impossible to miss with this!

Effie buzzed and announced, "I have Mr. Byrd for you."

"Hello? Mr. Byrd? Leonard Castle here. How would you like half a million dollars for almost no work?"

"What is this, some kind of joke?"

"No, no. I'm absolutely serious. I can get you half a million dollars. Are you interested?"

"I've heard about some of your miracle deals, Mr. Castle. You must be thinking about a book."

"That's correct."

"No, it won't work. It's been tried before . . . ."

"I'm sure it has. But this time, it will work. Let's have lunch and discuss it."

"You're wasting your time, Mr. Castle."

"I don't think so. It's half a million dollars we're talking about. And you have to eat lunch anyway, don't you?"

"Your time and mine too," Byrd said.

"I wouldn't want to do that. I'll tell you what. You come to lunch with me, and if you think your time has been wasted, you let me know. I'll make it up to you. Call it a side bet of . . . five hundred bucks?"

Byrd laughed. "You're a persistent fellow!"

"Of course I am. I'd get ten percent of that half million."

"Okay. I'll have lunch."

"The Four Seasons? Tomorrow at one?"

"Fine!" Byrd said, the laughter rippling below his speech. "I'll see you there."

*

The lunch was pleasant enough. Castle had booked a table in the room with the fountain. At a table across the water, he and Byrd could see a man having lunch with a six-year-old. It was obviously a divorced father and his daughter, who was probably celebrating her birthday. She'd be a terror in a few years. What could any poor teen-aged male do to please her after this kind of childhood.

"All she needs now is for the captain to bring her a telephone," Castle suggested.

"What for?" Byrd wanted to know.

"Oh, to let Mommy know what a good time we're having."

And sure enough, by the end of the meal the phone appeared. "You called it," Byrd said.

"Yes, but that doesn't make me feel any better about it."

Deliberately, Castle had kept away from the subject of the book, but now that they were having coffee, he asked bluntly, "What's the big problem? There has to have been one. Why haven't you jumped at any of the other offers you've had?"

"No time," Byrd said.

"Come on," Castle said. "I promised I wouldn't be wasting your time and I'm not. But if you're going to give me that kind of bullshit, you're wasting mine. What's the real answer?"

"It's just not my bag," Byrd said.

"There's an awful lot of money the world would put into that bag if you were willing to claim it."

"What would I do with more money?"

"Even Rockefellers want more money. Maybe they want more money more than the rest of us because they know how nice it is in large quantities. A real answer!"

"That's the real answer," Byrd insisted. "On camera, I work. There's something about my eyes and my cheekbones, or my tone of voice . . . It's something physical. But if you read transcripts of the shows, I sound like a moron. So I just keep away from print. It doesn't do good things for me."

"There's a way around that. All you need is the right writer."

"Believe me, I appreciate your interest. It's very flattering and all that. But it won't work. I've tried it before and it just didn't feel right."

"With a writer?"

Byrd nodded.

"And you didn't hit it off?"

Byrd nodded again.

"Just the one time?"

"This was a pro," Byrd explained. "And . . . and I think it was my fault more than his. It's a question of control. On the tube, I know what I'm doing and can feel my way. On the page, it's all imaginary."

"Most people would put it exactly the other way. The tube is imaginary, with those microwaves floating out on the ether. The book is the real thing. That's what people want. It's a souvenir as much as anything else. It'll have your face on the cover. It'll be like a little shrine to St. Dickie Byrd in homes all over the country."

"Very funny," Byrd said.

"It's true. That's what these books are. But the thing is that I've got a writer. He's a pro too, but he's a lively and decent fellow. A friend of mine. He's looking to do something, and I think the two of you would make a good match."

"Who?"

"You've met him, I'm pretty sure," Castle said. "When you had Wanda Lathem on your show, I think he was there. Pete Mc-Cracken?"

"I don't recall," Byrd said, smiling, because he didn't like to be rude.

"And then again, on the Jill Morgan book. He was there for that too. You can see how versatile he is."

The waiter topped up their coffees. Byrd was thinking about it.

"I'm still skeptical," he said. "But I hate to take that five hundred from you. It doesn't feel sporting, you know? So, okay, I'll meet him."

"That's all I ask. Give him a couple of hours. Or a couple of days. See how it feels. And then, if you're still dead set against it, we'll let it drop. Fair?"

Byrd nodded. "Fair enough," he agreed.

*

The next day, with McCracken in his office, Castle had to begin all over again, working from the other end.

"Byrd? He's a lightweight!" was what McCracken said up front.

"You're desperate for money? Byrd is money. Believe me. If you can swing this, it'll be bigger than both the other books put together. And it could be interesting. It isn't a question of what Byrd knows but what he embodies, and that can be quite complicated. Think of yourself as a naturalist describing some animal life. The animal doesn't have to understand what's going on."

McCracken said, "I just never liked him. On television or when I met him in the studio."

"Maybe that's good. Just don't tell him, right off, how you feel about him. Let it happen however it happens. You go take a look, and in the meantime, I'll keep thinking," Castle promised. "Fair?"

McCracken nodded.

"He's not sure about the project and it will be your job to sell him," Castle cautioned.

"I sell *him?*" McCracken asked. "That's clever. The salesman has to sell himself first, right?"

"That's true, but irrelevant. I've been thinking about my conversation with Byrd yesterday, and my hunch is that there's some secret there he's not happy about, something that would be troublesome if it were to appear in print."

"Such as?"

"I haven't the slightest idea. But I've got the feeling that something's bothering him. He must have turned down exactly this proposition maybe a dozen times in the last year. He'd have turned this down too, except that I'm such a hell of a salesman. So, you go and do your part, okay?"

"That's the most interesting thing about him, so far."

"It may not be anything . . . juicy. There may not be anything at all. But from the way it went, I'd make a small bet there's some kind of skeleton in the closet."

"To which I do not, of course, refer."

Castle shook his head.

"I'll do my best," McCracken promised. "It could even be fun. It could be a lot better than I thought at first blush."

"If it doesn't go, it's not the end of the world. There are other possible subjects. We'll find something," Castle promised.

"No, this may be it," McCracken said. "It sounds okay, now that I think about it. And thanks."

"That's all right," Castle said.

But was it?

That night, talking on the phone with his sister, Castle said, "I've got a funny feeling about it. And what it is, I think, is the same feeling that both of them probably have too. Each of them. I look back and I don't see what the hell else I could have done at any particular point, but the whole thing seems arbitrary. Rigged. And I keep thinking that if it falls apart somewhere, I can't even imagine where the damage is going to be or what's going to happen."

"What's new about that? When is it ever any different?" she asked.

"I don't know. No different, maybe, but more extreme. These are both very hyper people."

"You did your job."

"I know. But every now and then, I ask myself what the hell that is and I don't know any more. I just don't know."

"I'd tell you you need another vacation, but the last time you took one you just used it to recruit a new client."

"That's not true."

"True enough," Lisa said. "Meanwhile, what's new with that Flowers woman? You patch that up?"

"No. That's dead, I'm afraid."

"Oh?"

He didn't feel like talking about it.

There was a long silence in which each of them was waiting for the other to say something. But neither of them did.

"I guess I'll say good night, then," he said.

"Good night, brother."

"Good night, sister."

*

At the beginning, McCracken managed pretty well. Byrd was what social scientists would have called "well defended," but McCracken had a couple of things going for him that he didn't hesitate to use. For starters, there was Castle's offer of the large sum of money and the weight that gave to his recommendation of the writer as an able fellow. Just as important as Castle's endorsement, however, was McCracken's old Harvard diploma, a seal of approval in which Byrd was poignantly eager to believe. It was a brand name, like the J. Press label in his suits or the Mercedes emblem on his key chain. For all his money and influence, and for all the recognition his program had earned him, Byrd was still upwardly aspiring and had a devout belief in recognizable names that were supposed to be hallmarks of quality.

On the other hand, McCracken approved of Byrd's lack of a Harvard diploma—or at least of the fact that he was self-taught and self-made. So far as McCracken had been able to discover, Byrd had never gone to any college. He'd begun work early, selling advertising time for a local radio station in Fort Myers, Florida, and occasionally filling in when one of the announcers telephoned to claim car trouble or admit to his hangover. Byrd had performed well enough on these six-hour stints of *Platters and Patter* to make a plausible case for himself as deserving of a chance at his own show. And not just as a disc jockey either. Byrd had ambition, even then. He wanted a call-in show, just like the ones in Miami and Chicago and New York. Talk radio, or two-way radio, was the hot new thing in those days, and Byrd had a flair for it, mostly because he was able to see that it had nothing to do with the subjects under discussion but was really a platform for the demonstration of personality. It was like a pop singer doing a song. Getting the music and lyrics right was only the beginning. After that the singer was performing the real business of selling himself, his unique personal timbre and rhythm. And on these discussions of the flat tax or the death penalty or the right-to-work laws or the Vietnam War, the thing that made the program go so well was Byrd's boyishness, his idealism, his willingness to be wised up but, at the same time, his assumptions of the goodness and decency of mankind at large, his listening audience in particular, and, most especially, the caller, for whom he had more hope than most people might think was warranted.

He'd done well at Fort Myers and better yet on a larger station in St. Augustine. And then the big idea hit him, that this would do even better on television than on radio. That was the astonishingly simple key to his success—just like the advice that the inventor of Coca-Cola is supposed to have had from someone, to bottle the product.

That was what McCracken had been able to discover, having combed the periodical room of the New York Public Library for information about Byrd. His parents? His private life? Was he married? Divorced? His education—even if it was just through high school— had to have been undertaken somewhere. It was interesting for a man as much in the public eye as Byrd to have so little on the public record. The information, if he ever volunteered it, would hardly be stale.

The first few days were interesting ones for McCracken. It was like trying to tame some wild animal. Or trying to get a child with a learning disability to accomplish some task that to anyone else would be painfully simple. McCracken had mixed feelings about Byrd, but he had been pleased by Byrd's decision to go ahead with him and do the book—and then that delight had turned to frustration as the first week passed and Byrd showed himself not so much unwilling as simply incapable of opening up. McCracken didn't take it personally. It was a problem Byrd would have had with anyone. But inasmuch as Mc-Cracken was the one who happened to be there, he was the one who felt the exclusion and the responsibility for finding a solution to the problem.

Byrd's producer and senior associate producers met on a daily basis, but there were weekly meetings in which the whole staff participated —apparently as much for the benefit of morale as for the program itself. It was Byrd's view that the cutthroat atmosphere of some other production organizations hurt the performance of the staff and the quality of the shows. On Byrd's program, every assistant talent coordinator felt that he or she had access to the top man and could propose an idea and get a reaction. They all worked harder because they wasted less energy in grousing or worrying. Byrdsong Productions was a happy shop.

McCracken had few opportunities to talk with Byrd, but on the other hand, he had carte blanche to hang around. "Come and go as you please," Byrd had suggested, and he'd given McCracken an office in which to work. "Marge Piersall is the office manager. She'll set you up with whatever you need. And we'll see what kind of routine we can work out together, you and I. Okay?"

McCracken had eagerly agreed and he had been coming in every day, arriving early in the morning and staying on until quite late in the evenings. Byrd treated him with cordiality but then he treated everyone that way. It was as if McCracken had been hired on as a production assistant with no definite duties. The subject of the book they were supposed to be doing together just never came up—not even in Byrd's introductions to other people on the program. "This is Pete Mc-

Cracken. He's going to be hanging around for a while," was the most specific description McCracken had heard of his own function—or of Byrd's plans.

McCracken decided to push just a little and he found a moment in which to ask Byrd when there would be a good time for them to start work.

"Oh, we'll get to it. There's no hurry, is there?"

"Can you let me know what's been written about you, or what you think is the best or most informative piece?"

"There hasn't been anything really informative. And nothing I'd call best. Some is just less bad than the rest, but mostly it's junk. That's why our book is going to do so well, right?"

"I guess so," McCracken said. They were in Byrd's office. Byrd was lying on a couch with a hot towel on his face. It was his version of an hour's nap and it only took ten minutes. "I'll tell you what, though. Why don't we have dinner together one of these nights? Another setting, a bottle of wine, a little relaxation . . . just what we need, right?"

"That sounds fine," McCracken said.

"Set it up with Pammy," he said. Pammy was his scheduling secretary. She looked in his book and gave McCracken the first available dinner, which turned out to be eleven days away.

McCracken smiled and thanked her, but he went back to his cubicle and collapsed into his chair, putting his head down on the desk top. Eleven more days? By then, he'd have wasted nearly a month on this crazy son of a bitch!

He discussed the situation with Leonard Castle, meeting in the agent's office early on a Tuesday evening. Castle advised patience.

"But for how long?" McCracken asked.

"For as long as it takes."

"I don't even know where he was born. Or when. The stuff that's usually in the first line of a canned bio!"

"That's understandable."

"Is it?" McCracken asked.

"Sure. If you knew that, you could go check it out, and you'd find out who his mother and father were."

"You think his real name is Byrd?"

"I have no idea. You think it isn't?"

"I haven't the slightest idea," McCracken said. "If I had to guess, I'd go with Fogel or Vogel, or Fogelman, or Vogelsang, or . . . something in that line. If he were a real Byrd, a Virginia Byrd, he'd have proclaimed that five times a day from the rooftops from the time he'd learned to talk."

"Maybe you ought to ask him what his real name is."

"I might. But I'll want to be careful about picking my moment. If I ask him before he's ready to give me an answer—never mind the true answer, but any answer at all—that could scare him off. That could wreck the whole deal. So it's dicey."

"Still, nobody has ever got this far with him before," Castle said. "Remember that. Every time you get discouraged, think of that. For whatever reason, the man has made a deal. At least part of him wants to work with you. A part of him is your ally. You have to find out what part of him is holding back, and why. And when you do that, you'll have won. Right?"

"I just wish it were that simple."

"I didn't say it was simple," Castle said. "He's a complicated fellow, and it's up to you to unravel the complications before you can make an intelligent guess about what he's hiding. It may just make itself clear one day, but you need to be there when that happens, which involves patience and persistence. Just hanging around."

"I'll keep after him," McCracken promised. It wasn't clear whether he was promising Castle or himself. Castle hoped it was the latter.

And the next day McCracken went back to Byrd's offices—or Fogelman's or Vogelsang's?—to listen in as Byrd and his staff kicked around the programs that were scheduled for the coming two-week period.

There had to be other ways to skin this particular cat. Some employee or, better, some ex-employee who was willing to talk might supply the information that McCracken needed for the first probing question that would allow all the rest of the information to come gushing out. This was dumb! He had been patient, just as Castle had suggested, but Byrd was playing games. The message was huge and inescapable—hang around until you can't stand it any more and then leave, but it will be your fault, not mine.

McCracken was convinced by it and it was consistent with Castle's guess that Byrd was ambivalent about the book.

But how could he find some ex-employee? That wasn't so easy a trick to perform. He couldn't just walk into the office manager's office and ask. Mrs. Piersall would report back to Byrd, who would be offended that McCracken had gone behind his back.

He thought about it for a good while. He got up, closed the door of his cubicle, and sat quietly, reading a magazine and waiting for the minute hand of the clock to complete another circuit around the dial. And then one more, to be safe. He had formulated a plan now, and although it was rather a melodramatic one, it seemed justified by Byrd's complicated attitude. The worst that could happen was that Byrd would back out of the deal, in which case McCracken would have his life back. This nine-thirty-to-six routine was ridiculous. He might just as well have a job as do this.

He sat in that damned little box until eight o'clock in the evening, allowing the last and most eager of the beavers to call it a night and take off. He turned off the light in his cubicle, opened the door, and stood there looking and listening. Nothing. Nobody.

He walked down the corridor toward Byrd's office. Byrd's was the corner office, of course. Next to him was Jim Pennybaker, the producer of *Byrd Calls.* And next to his office was Marge Piersall's, with the filing cabinets with all the employment data McCracken wanted to examine.

The cabinets were locked, as McCracken had expected. He tried Mrs. Piersall's desk, but that was locked too, as he'd assumed it would be. But he'd also supposed that there'd be a key tucked away somewhere. He looked around the office. The coat closet? The water cooler? The plants! There was a table with pots of ivy and African violets that Mrs. Piersall watered twice a week. She called them her babies. He lifted each of the plant pots out of its larger pottery holder until he found one with the desk key. With that, he was able to get into the center drawer and find the key to the filing cabinets. From there on it was just a matter of that patience Leonard Castle had recommended, patience and calm. McCracken flipped through drawer after drawer until he found the personnel folders. It took him only a few minutes to learn his way around the system.

Terminations. Yes, there they were. And not a lot of them either. But just as he was about to congratulate himself, there was a noise. His first thought was to hide behind one of the desks. Or in the coat closet. But that was no good. No, no. The smarter way was to tough it out. He closed the filing cabinet, sat down at one of the desks, took a yellow evidence pad, and started writing. The thing was to look as though he belonged, as though what he was doing was perfectly legitimate.

A cleaning man in a blue uniform came in with a big rubbish basket that he pulled along on rollers and he emptied the wastebaskets.

"Evening," McCracken said.

"Evening," the porter answered, and he pulled his trash basket after him and down the corridor.

McCracken ripped the page off the yellow pad and put it into his pocket. He went back to the filing cabinet and resumed his search. Jill Byrne, Alexander Millwood, and Leslie Conover. He wrote down the names, addresses, and phone numbers. Then he put the file back, locked the cabinet, put the key back in the desk drawer, and locked the desk.

Getting out of the building was easy. He just took the elevator down and signed out. He was legitimately entitled to be there, after all. The security man simply assumed that he'd been working late, which was correct.

At home, he called the numbers of the three former Byrdsong employees, ready with a plausible story about an adjustment in a profit-sharing plan that needed a signature. Jill Byrne's mother didn't even wait for his explanation but told him right away that her daughter was married now and had moved out to Tacoma, Washington, where she was now Mrs. Arthur McCann. She told McCracken he could call her there and gave him the number, for which he thanked her. Alexander Millwood was tougher. For one thing, he answered the phone himself. For another, he wanted to know how McCracken had found him.

"Jill Byrne gave me your name," he said.

"Jill did?"

"That's right."

"And you want to know what?"

"Anything you can tell me about Dickie Byrd."

"Why me?"

"You used to work for him. Former employees are often good people to talk to."

"Is there money in this? For me, I mean?"

"There might be. It depends on what you have to tell me."

"It's worth a drink, I guess. Or two."

"Name the place. I'll meet you any time you say."

Millwood named a bar down in the Village.

"Is this evening convenient?" McCracken asked. It sounded good, and he didn't want Millwood to have second thoughts.

"Why not? Say in an hour?"

"Fine, I'll be there," McCracken promised. "I'll ask at the bar for you, okay?"

Millwood said that would be okay.

There had to be something. A man who'd been fired for simple incompetence wouldn't have asked that kind of question—was there something in it for him? McCracken felt certain that Millwood had some clue to that secret Byrd had been so careful to conceal.

He'd find out soon enough. He took a cab down to Sheridan Square and walked over to the address on Christopher Street. He looked in through the window. Jesus!

All men. A gay bar. He hesitated. Was Millwood putting him on? Or testing him? Was Millwood gay? Had Byrd fired him because of that?

McCracken swallowed hard and opened the door. He went up to the bar and asked the bartender if there was an Alexander Millwood around.

"I don't know anybody's name," the bartender answered.

"I'm supposed to meet this guy . . ."

"Well, sure, that's what life is all about, isn't it, sport?" the bartender asked. "Can I get you something?"

"Buy you a drink, good-looking?"

A tough in leather with a big gold hoop in his ear appeared out of the gloom. McCracken managed a friendly smile and said, "No, thanks, I'm meeting somebody."

"Won't I do, dear?"

"It's business."

The tough shook his head reproachfully. "And you looked like such a nice boy," he said.

"Another time, maybe," McCracken said, neutral but negative. It worked, at least for the moment. The tough went away.

"I'll have a beer," McCracken said to the bartender.

He nursed the beer for a few minutes, checking his watch several times. He'd finish the beer and then clear out—that was the bargain he made with himself. He kept looking at the door but there was no sign of Millwood. No singles came in at all. McCracken was close enough to the bartender so that he'd have heard anyone announce himself as Millwood and asked whether anybody had been looking for him. Nothing. It was a setup, a gag. It had to be . . .

He drained the last of the beer, put the mug down, and was about to leave when a young man in blue jeans and a UCSD sweatshirt spoke up. "I'm Millwood. You're looking for me, I think."

"That's right."

"I'll take that drink you offered."

McCracken signaled the bartender. "Another beer for me, and . . ."

"Bourbon and branch," Millwood said.

McCracken paid for the drinks. Millwood led the way to a table.

"It's okay," he said. "Nobody's going to rape you. You're as nervous as a shit-house rat."

"Why is a shit-house rat more nervous than any other kind?" McCracken asked.

"Well, he's got the problems they all have, plus all the shit to contend with," Millwood said. He giggled and brushed back a lank hank of blonde hair that had fallen over his left eye.

"I see," McCracken said. He took a sip of beer. "Is this why you got fired?" he asked, looking around the bar. "Because you're gay?"

"Nope."

"Then why?"

"For fifty bucks?"

"I'm listening," McCracken said.

Millwood grinned. "Okay, I'll trust you. Because *he* is. He came on to me one night. So then I knew. And the old guy couldn't stand that. So I was out."

McCracken reached into his trousers pocket for the fifty-dollar bill he'd folded in quarters and stored there and handed it over. "A bad deal," he said.

"I thought so," Millwood said, taking the money.

"You think it had ever happened before?"

"Maybe. I don't know. I was still in the closet then. He didn't know when he hired me that I was gay. Maybe he guessed it. Or maybe he didn't know whether I was or not and didn't much care. Maybe he just liked me. Or was hot for my bod, you know? I figured if I said no, I'd be out on my ass. So I didn't say that, but I was out on my ass anyway. That's how it goes, sometimes."

"I appreciate your telling me."

"I need the dough, you know? That's one of the consequences of unemployment."

"So I hear," McCracken said. He finished his beer, set his mug down, and said good night. Looking neither left nor right, he walked back to Sheridan Square, where he was able to catch a cab and get back uptown.

*

"Does it make sense?" Castle asked.

He had come into the office early to meet with McCracken and had listened as the writer recounted the events of the previous evening.

"You're the one who decided he had some secret he was trying to protect. I guess this would qualify, wouldn't it?"

"It might," Castle agreed.

"Then what do I do?"

"That comes later. What we have to figure out first is what got him to go along with us, even this far."

"I'm afraid to think about that!"

Castle looked at McCracken and then smiled. "Well, sure, that's one possibility. It could be just that he thinks you're attractive. Which isn't necessarily a disadvantage. Women use attractiveness all the time, don't they?"

"If that's what it is," McCracken protested, "I'll wind up just like Millwood. If I say yes, I'm out. And if I say no, I'd guess I'm also out. It's a no-win situation."

"Maybe. Unless he's thinking of something else."

"What else could it be?"

"Maybe there's something in him that's flirting with coming out. If Gerry Studds can come out and then run for re-election to Congress and win, why can't Byrd do it? Why can't he turn this into some kind of an advantage. Or crusade. It could be that, you know. It could be . . . relatively innocent. It can't be comfortable for him to have to sneak around, worrying all the time that he's going to be found out. I mean, the fifties are a long time gone. He's got to be at least tempted."

"Don't you think it'd lose him his audience?" McCracken asked.

"Not necessarily. It'd lose him a piece of it, but he'd maybe make it up with another group, maybe even with better demographics. Homosexuals spend a lot of money on themselves, after all. They don't have to save up for their kids' educations."

"So, what do I do? Even if you're right about his reasons for considering the idea . . ."

"You make your best pitch. You tell him that you know about Millwood. And then right away, you tell him you think he's doing the right thing. It's the public-spirited thing to do. It will help all those other people who have been caught in the same way. And you tell him you don't think he's going to lose much by it and you talk about Wanda Lathem and how confession is not only good for the soul but good for business. I mean, my God, it's the entertainment business! Who the hell cares?"

"What if you're wrong?"

"Then I'm wrong. There are other celebrities. There are other projects. I promised you I'd find something, and I will. Don't be so quick to give up on Byrd, though. Remember Yogi Berra's line. 'It isn't over until it's over.' Okay?"

McCracken laughed, thanked Castle for his time, and left the office.

Castle just sat for a few minutes, thinking about what he'd told McCracken. It had all been reasonable and cautious, and mostly sensible too, but it felt wrong. The stakes were too high and the outcomes were altogether unpredictable. Was Byrd dangerous? What was the worst that could happen?

Castle just didn't know. And that bothered the hell out of him.

He promised himself he'd go back to collecting names so that maybe he'd have another suggestion to make when this deal collapsed. The odds against success were very long, he thought, and it would be a good idea to have a couple of fallback possibilities.

Of course, that was why the women loved Byrd. He was one of those impossible objects of desire, all the more desirable because they were impossible, which also made them safe. It was like the passion French women of a certain class used to have for priests. If a guy was faggy in just the right way, and if he played it right, that could make him a national heartthrob.

It was unlikely that Byrd would want to screw around with a formula that had worked this well for this long.

Castle realized that in McCracken shoes he'd have quit. Right there, right then.

He thought about calling McCracken up to advise him to do just that, but couldn't quite bring himself to make the call. It just went against the grain to undo a deal that hadn't actually collapsed. Maybe Byrd admired McCracken's khaki-covered ass enough to cooperate.

"He's a big boy. He went to Harvard," Castle said aloud. He shook his head and went out to put up the coffee.

*

The tough thing was not expecting any particular turn of events. It was important to be alert and on top of things, but in order to do that, McCracken knew he had to be open to whatever signals Byrd was sending. That would be more difficult if he was on the lookout for any particular message. Anything was possible, after all. The only expectation he could allow himself was that this dinner would be decisive one way or another. He certainly hoped that Byrd would at least tip his hand and indicate how the relationship might go from here on.

Still, it was impossible in the intervening days not to propose to himself a few strategies he might try if it seemed appropriate to do so.

To ask a few direct questions, for instance—Byrd would expect him to do that. And if Byrd answered and they were able to make some kind of start, then maybe there wouldn't have to be any confrontation.

But McCracken wasn't prepared to bet money that it would turn out that way. The worst case was that there'd be a moment when he felt desperate and was ready to give up on the book and on Byrd. That would be the time to hit him with Millwood. Whatever Byrd did, at least there'd be a decision, and whichever way that decision went, McCracken figured he'd be better off than in this limbo.

The days passed. Byrd was as friendly as ever and as unforthcoming. On the morning of their date, McCracken checked with Pammy and confirmed that Mr. Byrd was planning on dining with him. She looked at the book and told him, "So far as I know."

"Can you find out where? And when?"

She promised she'd try. McCracken wondered whether Byrd would cancel. And if he did? Storm into his office? Send him a note? Or just quit and walk away from this idiotic enterprise?

He told himself one more time to take it easy, to keep cool and see what Byrd did and how he did it, and to take his cue from that.

The phone in his cubicle jangled later that morning and McCracken picked it up to hear from Pammy that the dinner was on, at eight o'clock at a little Hungarian restaurant on the Upper East Side.

"Why there? I wonder," he asked.

"I have no idea," she told him.

"Is it near where Mr. Byrd lives?"

"That must be it," she said. "I think it's just across the street, actually."

"I see. Well, fine, thanks. I'll be there."

A little dinner, a bottle or two of wine, Tokay or that Bull's Blood stuff, and then a casual invitation over dessert to come across the street and see his scrapbooks? It wasn't implausible.

McCracken showed up at the restaurant five minutes before eight, asked for Mr. Byrd's table, and declined the waiter's offer of a drink while he was waiting. He'd promised himself that he'd drink nothing stronger than wine and no more than two glasses of that. Byrd appeared just after eight, waved from the doorway, came across the room, sat down, and said he hoped McCracken hadn't been waiting long.

"No, no, I just got here myself."

"Good. They've got a terrific goulash here. It's the three-meat goulash, with beef and veal and pork. It's great. I think it's the fresh paprika."

"Sounds fine," McCracken said. "And then we get to talk a little?"

"That's why we're here, isn't it?"

"I don't know. I hope so."

"What's that supposed to mean?" Byrd asked. He was smiling but attentive, like an animal that catches a scent, either of quarry or predator.

"Well, we've got to start somewhere. I don't know your birthdate or your birthplace. I'm not even sure that Byrd is your real name. I don't know who your parents were or whether you have any brothers or sisters. Or where you were educated. Or, for that matter, whether you were educated. You do maintain your privacy."

"I guess so," Byrd said.

"Which is fine with me," McCracken said. "But it makes doing the book fairly difficult, unless you're contemplating a change in policy on this."

"I'm contemplating it."

"Good," McCracken said. "How about we start with your name. Is it really Byrd?"

"It is now. It used to be Bayer, but that sounded too German back in World War I, so my father changed it."

"What did he do?"

"He played the clarinet."

"For a band or an orchestra? Or what?"

"In movie-theater orchestras. Before sound came in, they had orchestras in big city theaters. And he was in one of them. Sound changed all that. In 1927, *The Jazz Singer* came out, and then in 1929 there was the Crash. So that was the end of a not particularly distinguished career in music."

"And your parents moved to Florida?"

Byrd nodded.

"Fort Myers, right?"

Byrd nodded again.

"And they did what?"

"They ran a trailer park. Or my mother did. My father helped her, more or less. And also ran moonshine. That was Prohibition time, remember."

"And?"

"And he got caught and went to prison for it. He died in prison."

"I'm sorry."

"It was a long time ago. I was six years old."

McCracken began to feel hopeful. Maybe a confrontation wouldn't be necessary, after all. He relaxed a little. Maybe it could at least be postponed for a few weeks. Or even months. Once they had established a pattern of cooperation and trust, it would be time enough to go into Millwood's charges.

"Is your mother still alive?" McCracken asked.

"Oh, yes. Alive and well, and living in New York."

"Any brothers or sisters?"

"No, I was an only child."

The waiter came to take their orders and they busied themselves with their menus. When that was done, McCracken more or less expected Byrd to return to the subject and make further comments about his family and his childhood, either filling out the general pattern or else adducing new details. But instead Byrd was charming. It was a part of his routine from the show, and McCracken recognized some of the tricks. Byrd had a way of bouncing questions back, so that McCracken felt prompted to talk about his own family, his own boyhood and young manhood . . . But that wasn't the subject of their book.

There was also small talk, pleasant anecdotes about celebrities and what they'd said and done, about parties Byrd had been to and places he'd visited. It was witty and amusing and would no doubt fill a few pages. But McCracken had the feeling that all this was just Byrd's way of keeping him at arm's length, even while seeming to be cooperative. After all, Byrd had found time in a busy schedule for an evening with McCracken and the book. And in another couple of weeks, there might be another evening. At this rate, in two or three hundred years, McCracken would have enough for a rough outline of what the chapters might be if they ever actually got around to working on the material.

Over dessert of fresh raspberries and cream, Byrd was talking about boats and the way they reflected their owners' personalities. It was a kind of parlor game to categorize celebrities and decide which were obvious sail people and which were speedboat types. It was a clever enough bit of business, but not the business they were there to transact.

To hell with this, McCracken thought. He took a sip of the Bull's Blood they'd ordered, waited for an opening, and asked, "Did you ever marry?"

Byrd looked mildly pained by this resumption of dreary interrogation. "Yes, once. But it didn't last."

"Oh?"

Byrd thought about it, nodded, and said, "It happens that way sometimes."

"What way?"

"That marriages don't last."

"That's terrific," McCracken said. "I ought to write that down."

"Why don't you do that?"

"A good idea," McCracken said. "You want to tell me about it first? Or do I have to find out for myself what must have happened? From people like Alex Millwood, for instance?"

He took it pretty well. No gasps, no sudden blanching. He was an experienced enough performer to keep his balance. But clearly he'd been hit.

"And where did you find him?"

"I bumped into him. He used to work for you, right?"

"And I suppose you believe everything he said?"

"Not necessarily. But it's a place to start. It's more than I've had from you, isn't it?"

"I don't know whether it's a start or an end. I'll be frank with you. It's that kind of thing that has kept me from doing a book like ours before. And maybe will keep me from doing it now."

"Even if what he said is all true, I don't see how that necessarily follows," McCracken said. "After all, people are more accepting now than they were twenty years ago, or even ten. Think of what Hollywood did to Ingrid Bergman because of her affair with Rossellini . . . and that's unimaginable now. It's out of medieval Spain! Nobody gives a damn any more."

"That's your wisdom on it, hunh?"

"That's my wisdom, yes. That's what's going on these days. What are you worried about? Your audience? They'll love you anyway. More than ever."

"You're living in fairyland," Byrd said, and then he caught himself and started to laugh.

It was the most likable thing he'd done since McCracken had met him.

"You think it's all cut-and-dried, a dead issue . . . But it isn't," Byrd said. "In New York and L.A., and with your Harvard friends, maybe it is. But there's the rest of the country out there, and they still get excited about things like faggotry, which isn't the worst thing they call it."

"Those people don't watch you anyway. How many stations have you got in Texas?"

"I'd lose even more. I'm telling you, it's crazy. If we talk about it honestly, I'm dead. And if we don't, the book will be wooden and fake, and I'm dead anyway."

"I don't think so."

"You're not taking the chances. I am."

"Maybe," McCracken acknowledged. "Maybe you're right. But it seems to me that we're sharing the risk. Which is only fair."

"What are you talking about?"

"What we're risking is time, at this point. Why don't we give it a couple of months, but a real shot this time? And then you'll see whether you're comfortable with it. Your decision, absolutely. If you like it and feel okay, we stay with it. And if not, then we drop it, and there are no hard feelings and no problems either way. Is that any better?"

"Let me think about that," Byrd said. "Coffee? A schnapps?"

"Sure, why not?" McCracken agreed.

"Or I've got some great cognac at the apartment. I live across the street you know."

"I know."

"If you're not full of shit about this willingness to share risks, maybe you'll come up for a while," Byrd said. He delivered the line as if it were an offhanded, spur-of-the-moment idea. McCracken realized, however, that the entire evening had been orchestrated to lead up to this question, and that the success or failure of the book depended upon the answer he now gave Byrd.

It would not have been difficult to decline the invitation. And there would have been other projects, other names and faces Leonard Castle could have found. But here was a live one, a naked soul, with the terms of his struggle quite clear and dramatic. Here was a public issue —the most fundamental question of individual liberty and where that ended and where society's interests began—that could pretty well ensure success when it was joined with a face and personality as widely recognized as Byrd's.

It was a hell of an admission price, McCracken thought, but, to be honest, he was just a little curious. As the sailor said, to try it once is to be a philosopher; it's the second time that makes you a faggot.

Maybe he'd known all along. Maybe that was why he'd felt that antipathy to Byrd back at the beginning, before they'd ever met.

"It's up to you," Byrd prompted.

"It might be interesting," McCracken said.

"It could be," Byrd agreed, signaling for the check. "Let's go, then."

*

Castle hurried back toward Susan's building, thinking as he walked that he wasn't God. He was only an agent, a facilitator, a helper along of people and projects. If he'd made mistakes, they were mistakes of optimism, hoping that men and women of intelligence and goodwill could find ways to accommodate one another. And there's some goodwill and intelligence even in the meanest and most unprepossessing specimens.

Better to light a candle than curse the darkness, the saying goes. And that was what he'd been trying to do, wasn't it?

Or giving matches to kids who were going to play with dynamite?

The main thing was that he was okay, that he'd managed to elude his pursuer, at least for this evening.

Tomorrow, if he had to, he could go to the police.

He reached Susan's vestibule. Without hesitating this time, he pushed the button to sound the buzzer up in her apartment. And he heard the answering buzz that let him in.

13

Five months later, with the first crispness in the air to suggest that summer might not after all be endless, the 450-page typescript was centered on the table in the conference room of Overbrook & Granger, Inc. At opposite sides, halfway down, Byrd and McCracken faced each other. Next to Byrd was Gerald Oliphant, his lawyer. McCracken had brought his lawyer too, Ken Ahora, a Japanese classmate from Harvard who had gone on to Harvard Law School. Castle was down at the foot of the table. Up at the other end, Roger Granger presided over the meeting. At his right hand, Jasper Quinlan twiddled with a gold mechanical pencil.

The question before the group was simple enough. Byrd wanted to back out. Having agreed one way or another at various times and at several stages, he now objected to the book and wanted to buy McCracken out, which meant getting the book back from Overbrook & Granger.

The only question, everyone agreed, was whether a buy-out on the basis of the publisher's advance would be sufficient. "There are, after all, further moneys that the book could be expected to earn," Ahora said.

"When the publisher puts out money, it is in the expectation of making a profit on his investment," Quinlan agreed.

"No argument," Oliphant said. "The difficulty we have is with the figure . . ."

"Jesus, a million dollars!" Byrd said. "You guys are out for blood!"

Quinlan pointed out that once the advance had been repaid and the interest on the advance had been calculated, the remainder would be

divided between the publisher and the author—who deserved to keep
what he'd already received and what he could have anticipated as
recompense for his labor, which had been considerable.

"Nobody's criticizing his workmanship," Oliphant said.

"It's the book itself. The very idea of it . . ."

"Which you knew up front . . ." Ahora said. "None of this was a
big surprise to you."

"I got talked into it. I got persuaded. I went along. But if my
mother reads this, it will kill her," Byrd said. "And the question here
seems to be whether you guys want to kill my mother or disembowel
me. It's a hell of a choice, I'll be frank to say."

"I think you're selling your mother short," Castle said. "I think
she's smarter and tougher than you give her credit for. And I think
she loves you more than you realize."

"You don't know my mother."

"I know people. I know human beings. Think of those mothers of
mass murderers, or of people like Lee Harvey Oswald. Do they start
hating their kids? No, sir! The one thing you can rely on in this world
is that your mother is going to stand up for you, no matter what. My
bet would be that she's more or less guessed anyway. How old are
you? Fifty?"

"Fifty-three."

"And she's how old?"

"She's eighty-two."

"Well, she wasn't born yesterday. She must have guessed. Why
don't you have a talk with her? Face to face. And then this book won't
be such a terrible prospect. For a million dollars, for God's sake . . .
More than that, because you'll be in for a profit instead of a huge
loss."

"It's something to think about," Granger said.

"I can't. I haven't even been able to face this meeting, which I've
been putting off now for weeks—and look where that's got us. It's
cowardice, I admit . . ."

"Go and talk to her," Castle advised. "Today. Now. If you like,
we'll wait for you. Or we'll meet again this afternoon or tomorrow
morning."

Byrd sat there, unable to speak, his mouth opening and closing like
that of a great carp.

Ahora said, "You can't afford a million dollars. Neither can I. And
if you can't afford that, then the book goes ahead. Or we haul you into
court and everything that you want to keep hidden comes out in the

tabloids, in which case you might as well have gone along with the original deal. You don't have any choice, Mr. Byrd. Face up to it."

"I wish I could tell you something different," Oliphant said.

Byrd managed to croak out, "Okay."

"Okay, you'll talk to her?" Granger asked.

"Okay, we'll go ahead. I withdraw my objections," Byrd said.

"Good," Granger said, getting up from his chair.

"I just hope to God you're right," Byrd said, glaring at Castle. "This isn't going to be easy."

"I never said it would be. But it's the right thing to do. And your mother will come through for you, just as she always has. I'm sure of it."

Later on, as they walked back toward Castle's office, McCracken said he wished he'd never got involved with this.

"You came to me, my friend," Castle said.

They came to a corner where McCracken and Ahora said goodbye and went off in another direction.

Castle had his doubts too, but they were only doubts. On the other side of the scale, there were hopes, as there always were. Maybe it would all work out. Sometimes, some things did that.

*

Minna Handelman was annoyed but not frightened. A levelheaded woman, she realized that almost anything could have happened to keep Thelma from the regular Thursday-afternoon outing—lunch, a little window-shopping, and then a trip to the grocery store and a shared cab ride back to the apartment house. It would have been nice, though, if Thelma had thought to call. But maybe she'd tried. Maybe she'd called a couple of times. The night before, Minna had been on the phone, first talking to her son, Dennis, in Rochester and then to her daughter, Harriet, in San Antonio.

Of course, it was also possible that Thelma had been taken ill, or that her son was ill. Emergencies come up, and it doesn't do to get aggravated until one has heard the other person's story. Maybe even something good had happened . . .

That was a possibility, but not a likely one. After a certain age, untoward events tend to be dreadful. A misunderstanding, then, or maybe Thelma had forgotten? Or maybe her phone was just out of order.

Still, she could have come downstairs. A trip in the elevator isn't such a big deal!

It was Thursday evening. Minna had had a hamburger for lunch and had done her shopping. She'd been back in her apartment for three hours now and hadn't heard a word from Thelma. She had called, hoping to find that Thelma was all right, but there had been no answer, even after twenty rings. She'd dialed the number again, very carefully, and listened for another twenty rings, but there'd been no answer.

The son's number was of course unlisted.

Minna told herself she was making a mountain out of a molehill and that she shouldn't be a meddling neighbor. She tried to put it out of her mind, but it kept coming back, like the itch of a mosquito bite. She went downstairs to the lobby, looked in through the perforations in the metal cover of Thelma's mailbox, and saw that she hadn't picked up her mail.

She told the doorman, a new one, a Cuban named Raúl, that she was worried. He had a passkey, didn't he?

But Raúl said he couldn't go into an apartment just like that. It would have to be the super who did that, and the super was out of the building for the evening.

"But I'm a friend of hers. You know that. You know who I am!"

"You should call a policeman. If you're really worried, I could go in with a policeman."

"I'll think about it," she said. She went up to Thelma's apartment, stood outside the door, listened, rang the bell, listened again, and even sniffed. No, this was ridiculous, she told herself. But it was also ridiculous to do nothing. She wasn't a meddling neighbor. She was a friend. She would want Thelma to call someone if the situation were reversed, God forbid!

She was still not worried. But if she didn't call, she knew she'd become worried later on and wouldn't be able to sleep. So, to get it over with, then, and to prove to herself that it had just been some small emergency or maybe just a misunderstanding, she called the police department and explained the situation to the desk sergeant on duty. He listened, and the machine listened too—every thirty seconds there was a beep to let you know you were being recorded—and Minna felt like a fool. But the damage was already done. She'd given her name and address. She was already entered in their records as a crank.

"Okay, we'll send somebody over," the sergeant told her.

"I'll be downstairs, waiting in the lobby," she promised, and she thanked him and hung up the phone.

Then, because an ache always subsides the minute you call the doctor, she tried Thelma's number again, but there was still no answer. And at first she felt vindicated, but then she realized that she was worried, really afraid for her friend now. She went downstairs to sit on the uncomfortable brocade sofa in the lobby and wait until that patrolman showed up.

It didn't take them very long. In ten minutes, a squad car pulled up in front of the building. A uniformed poiceman came inside and Minna identified herself as the woman who had called. She went over the same ground she'd covered with the desk sergeant, explaining once more that she and Thelma Byrd were friends, that they went out to do their shopping every Thursday, that Thelma hadn't called to cancel and hadn't shown up. And she hadn't picked up her mail from that morning either.

The policeman looked at the mailbox, then asked Raúl to come upstairs and open the door for him. Minna came along. Nobody told her not to. She would actually have preferred to wait down in the lobby, but she felt she owed it to them—to Raúl and the policeman—to be there so that she could apologize when they found that nothing was wrong, that nothing was even out of the ordinary. Please, God, let it be all right, let *her* be all right . . .

But it wasn't all right. She was on the floor next to the chair by the window. The policeman knelt down, put his hand on Thelma's neck, feeling for a pulse. Or feeling the chill of a cooling corpse. He shook his head. "I'm sorry. She's gone," he said. "Is there a phone?"

Minna showed him where the telephone was. He called the coroner's office. She stood there waiting while he made the call.

"They'll be here in a few minutes," the patrolman said. "It looks like she had a stroke or a heart attack or something. She must have been sitting there, reading that book or whatever it is, and she just died."

Thelma looked at the blue cover of the spiral-bound galleys of *Byrd: An Autobiography.*

"Why, that's her son's book. She's Dickie Byrd's mother, you know. The television star! And that's his book. She told me about it a couple of days ago, when it arrived. She was so proud . . ."

She picked up the open book and looked at it.

*

Like most of the rest of the population of New York, McCracken heard the news from television. He turned to another channel, and they too were reporting the same story. He did not hesitate. He began packing instantly. Within the hour, he was heading north out of New York and into Connecticut. He figured on reaching Rhode Island before he stopped to eat. And he'd make Maine before he stopped for the night.

He did call Castle, from a pay phone at one of the service stations on the Connecticut Turnpike. Castle's office was closed, and he tried the home number, where he got the answering machine. He waited for the beep and then blurted out the message: "This is Pete McCracken. Listen, I've just heard the news. I'm hoping you've heard it too. Byrd's mother has died. With the galleys of the damned book in her lap. I've taken off. And I'd watch my ass if I were you. He's not likely to take it very well. Thanks for everything. I'll call you in a week or two."

*

Byrd's first thought had been to go after McCracken. He'd been the one. He'd written it. More important, he'd talked Byrd into opening up that way, against his better judgment and ignoring all his deepest instincts. But McCracken wasn't an easy man to get hold of. He wasn't at his apartment, and there was no way of predicting whether he'd be gone for ten minutes or ten days.

But to do nothing was intolerable. So Byrd had settled for Castle. Settled for him and on him. Castle had put the deal together in the first place and had kept it from coming unglued at the end. McCracken might have been the Doberman, but Castle had been the handler, the one to unleash the animal and set it on Byrd's trail. Castle was also an easier target in a number of ways. He had a more or less predictable schedule, going from his apartment to his office and back in a routine way. And he was a fellow of some size. He'd be hard to miss, even with a handgun, at any reasonable range.

Byrd had waited for Castle outside his office building and had followed him home, watching his quarry and enjoying the smug feeling of stalking prey. But he'd misjudged the distance, and somehow he'd missed with that all-important first shot. Castle had then dodged among the parked cars with surprising agility and had disappeared into the lobby of an apartment house.

Presumably he knew who was after him. Which was also, in its way, a satisfaction. Better that he should have some time to think about what he'd done, to repent of his arrogance and stupidity, and to know that punishment was about to catch up with him: the sudden searing pain, and then the oblivion the son of a bitch deserved.

Byrd had waited for him to come out, as he'd have to do sooner or later. But he'd also begun to consider other scenarios. What if Castle called the police? One of the disadvantages of being recognized by everyone in North America was that it was tough to hide. Byrd wanted to be the pursuer, not the pursued. He flagged a cab, got in, gave the cabbie twenty bucks, and told him to park, turn his lights off, and just wait. Keep the meter running but just sit there.

"For how long?"

"I don't know."

"Whatever you say," the cabbie said. And the meter clicked up another unit, as if in punctuation.

It wasn't long before the doorman came out, flagged a cab, and brought it to the marquee. Byrd watched Castle hurry out and dive into the back seat of the waiting taxi.

"Follow that cab," he said.

"Just like in the movies?"

"That's right. Just like that."

"I never did this before," the cabbie said. "But I guess there's a first time for everything."

"Keep back about half a block," Byrd told him.

"Yeah, yeah. I've seen the same flicks you have. I know the drill."

It wasn't difficult. They followed Castle across town to the East Side. "Keep going," Byrd ordered, and then they followed him downtown, down Fifth, across to Park, down to the ramp around Grand Central, and then uptown again.

"Clever!" the cabbie exclaimed.

"Not so clever," Byrd said. "He didn't lose you, did he?"

When Castle's cab slowed again, Byrd ordered his driver to keep going and to pass him. Then he looked back through the rear window and watched Castle get out and dart from his cab into the lobby of one of the small apartment houses.

Byrd paid his driver, waited a moment, and then went to a pay phone on the corner. He dialed the number of Jim Pennybaker, the producer of *Byrd Calls*.

He listened to the ringing, hoping Pennybaker would be home. If not, Byrd had no idea where to turn or what to do next. He closed his eyes and tried to will the interruption of the mechanical chirring— and, yes, Pennybaker answered.

"Dickie? Are you all right?"

"I'm okay," Byrd said. "But I need some information. You mentioned a couple of months ago some girl Len Castle was seeing. You remember? One of Ditson's people on *Periscope?*"

"Yeah? So?"

"Do you remember her name? Can you call Ditson and find out?"

"You mean now? Right away?"

"I need it right away, yes."

"Jesus, I guess. No, wait a minute. I know it. It's on the tip of my tongue. Sawyer. Sanders. Or, no, it was the first name that started with an *S.* I met her at some party. I can see her face, I swear! Cute. Susan something. Susan or Suzanne. Susan . . . Flower! Or, no, plural. Flowers. Susan Flowers. That's it, I'm sure."

"Thanks."

"You're sure you're okay? You want me to come over?"

"Maybe later on. Right now, I've a couple of things I've got to take care of. I'll be talking to you."

He wrote the name down. Now all he had to do was find a Susan Flowers. He was sure she'd be somewhere on the block and that he'd find her. He felt as if he were flying, as if he could do nothing wrong. It was okay. It was all going to come out fine.

*

It was from Susan that Castle first heard the news about Byrd's mother and how she died.

"No!" Castle groaned. "I don't believe it!"

"Would I make up a thing like that?"

"My God! I told him . . . I promised him it would be all right. I told him she'd stand by him."

"I thought it was a book you'd represented. I just had that feeling. Or that fear."

"Byrd was worried that his mother would never talk to him again. And I told him he was underestimating her. With the book on her lap, for God's sake?"

Susan nodded.

"Well, that's it, then," he said. "I wasn't sure who it was."

"You mean there are others? You have a whole list of people who'd want to kill you?"

Castle thought for a moment. There were a few, here and there. Dan Lucid, maybe. Jill Morgan's long-lost son, Drew Fontaine, was a lively possibility. Lila Love's mother, Darlene, was not at all out of the running. Each of them, at the right moment, might have grabbed a gun and come after Castle. It was frightening, but even more it was depressing. "It happens," he said. "It comes with the territory."

"Some territory," Susan said.

He nodded.

"What are you going to do? Call the police?"

He shook his head.

"But you have to!"

"If I have to, I guess I will. But not yet. I've already done enough to the poor bastard, haven't I?"

"I don't see that you've got much choice."

"If I stayed here tonight and slept on your couch," Castle began, making clear that his intentions were simply to hide in her apartment, "I could call his office tomorrow and let them know what he's doing. They could come after him and have him put away for a while. Tranquilizers or whatever, and proper medical care. For his own good. For *his* sake. If I call the police, it's all over the front pages . . ."

"It's there already."

"But it stays there. And it's a hell of a lot worse than what's happened so far. You know that."

She nodded. "I guess you're right."

"It's okay, then?" he asked. "For me to stay?"

"Of course," she said. "Have you eaten?"

He shook his head. "But I'm not really hungry. I could do with a drink, though. Brandy, maybe."

"A glass of soda on the side?" she offered. She was smiling.

"Yes, thanks. Bless you!"

                                    *

Byrd stood there in the vestibule, looking at the names, and he figured that if Susan Flowers was in 3F, then the people he wanted to talk to were in 4F or 5F. He took down those names and was about to go back to the pay phone to call them when someone came out of the lobby. Byrd was able to get to the door and grab it before it swung closed and locked.

Golden. Perfect. He took the elevator up to the fourth floor and rang the bell of 4F.

"Mrs. Wheeler?"

"Yes?"

"You know me, don't you? I'm Dickie Byrd from television."

"My goodness, yes. What on earth are you doing here in the building?"

"It's a surprise for Susan Flowers, your neighbor down below. A few of her friends from *Periscope* have dreamed up this little gag. And what I need is to come down her fire escape and climb into her bedroom window. I'm the surprise, you see. It's silly, but I promised a friend of hers I'd do this. You don't mind, do you?"

"Well," she said, "if it were anyone else, I certainly would. But with someone like you . . . I'm sure it's all right. Why not? Go ahead!"

"Thanks, you're a great sport. I appreciate it."

She led the way through her front hall and into her bedroom and even helped him open the window. He climbed out onto her fire escape, blew her a kiss, and then carefully descended the metal steps to the floor below and Susan Flowers' bedroom window. He took the pistol from his pocket and used it to smash the pane of glass next to the window lock. He reached in, unlocked the window, and then tugged a couple of times until he'd raised the sash enough to be able to climb inside.

*

They froze.

"What was that? Glass?" he asked.

She started toward the bedroom but Castle grabbed her. He held his finger to his lips, commanding silence, and he shook his head. He mouthed the words "It's Byrd," and looked around. There was a closet behind her. He considered trying for the front door but he was afraid there might not be enough time. He settled on what was quickest and closest and pushed Susan into the closet, once more enjoining silence as he closed the door behind her.

How in hell had Byrd found him? And what could he do?

But there was no question in his mind about what had made the noise in the bedroom. It was too much of a coincidence for Byrd to be coming after him on the same evening that Susan should just happen to have a burglar break into her apartment.

He looked around for some weapon. There was a set of fireplace tools beside Susan's mantel, and he grabbed the poker. Then he went for the phone. He'd picked up the receiver and had dialed the first 9 when he heard the expected voice tell him, "Hang it up."

Byrd was standing there with a gun in his hand, pointing rudely. Castle replaced the receiver.

"Where is she?" Byrd asked.

"She went out for food."

"Good. This has nothing to do with her anyway."

"That's right," Castle said. "I'm sorry about your mother."

"I expect you are. Now that you're looking at this gun, I'm sure you are."

"That's not the reason."

"No? Tell me another."

"The gun doesn't frighten me."

"No?"

"Not at all. You'd be doing me a favor."

"Sure, I would."

"Go ahead, then. Shoot," Castle said. "But get it over with before she gets back. As you said yourself, this hasn't got anything to do with her. You can kill me and get away clean."

"Not exactly. The woman upstairs recognized me. That's why she let me come through her apartment and out onto the fire escape. I'm a dead man too."

"As I said, I'm sorry. About your mother. And about you too. But as for me, it's a quick way to go. I'd just as soon check out now as later. Get it over with."

"You're full of shit, you know? You're just talking to save your ass."

"Then shoot. Call the bluff, if that's what you think it is. Why would I lie? Two dead men talking to each other? If there's ever a time for honesty, this is it."

"You wouldn't know honesty if you fell in it."

"It's rare, maybe, but I can still recognize it. I was hoping you could too."

"Why?"

"So you'd believe me about my regrets. If it was the book . . ."

"Jesus! Don't give me that. Just . . . don't! It was the book, all right. The book was next to her on the floor. She dropped it as she died."

"Yes, that's what happened. But if she'd been reading the New York Times and she'd dropped that, would you assume necessarily that the Times had killed her?"

"I might," Byrd said. "If there was a headline on the front page about 'Thelma Byrd's Son Revealed as Homosexual,' I damned well might. And I'd go shoot the reporter too. Just the way I'm going to shoot you."

"When I set up this deal, do you think I knew? You really think I had any idea?"

"Not at the beginning, no. But at the end, at the last meeting, when

I was trying to buy McCracken out, you knew then. And you said it
would be all right. You promised."

"I thought it would. I promised you your mother wouldn't cut you
out of her life . . ."

"She cut *herself* out of her life. Don't you see? She stopped living. I
was afraid she'd never speak to me again, and she won't, will she?"

"Why didn't you speak to her? You were going to tell her. That's
what you said you'd do. That would have been the decent way to
break it to her."

"I tried. I must have tried a dozen times. I . . . . I just couldn't."

"Is that my fault?"

"Partly. You set it up. This terrible situation I was in was your
doing. Your fault."

"You should have told her," Castle insisted.

"I shouldn't have been put into that position. I shouldn't have been
forced to do an awful thing like that. And that damned book, your
book, was at the bottom of it. I killed my mother, and that's a terrible
thing, but as long as I'm a killer, I don't see any reason to stop with
her. I might as well take out a few other sons of bitches, kill a few
people I hate along with the one I loved. Like you, for instance."

"Go ahead, then, for God's sake! Do it and get the hell out of here,
before Susan gets back."

"You put on a good act. I'll say that for you," Byrd said. "But why
would you be so eager for me to kill you?"

"You think you're the only one with a secret? You think that makes
you special? Everybody's got something he's ashamed of, some skeleton rattling around in his closet. And I've got mine. It's not the kind
of thing anyone would have guessed—or I'd have gone off some deep
end years ago, drinking, or into a mental hospital, or maybe out to
some leper colony to do good works. There are all kinds of ways of
running away."

"And what is this dark secret?" Byrd asked. "Make it good. Maybe
I'll shoot you in the head instead of in the gut, the way I'd planned."

"Incest," Castle said.

"I don't believe you."

"Fine. Pull the trigger, then. Or squeeze, I think, is what you're
supposed to do. Do you know how to use that? They kick up, you
know."

"Incest with whom?"

"My sister. Half sister, actually, but that doesn't change anything.

We still live together, more or less, in the two halves of what used to be the family apartment. We can hear each other, through the walls."

"You're making it up."

"What on earth for?"

"I don't know. Maybe to see if you can gross me out. To see if you can persuade me that it's worse to let you live than to kill you. Worse for you, I mean."

"No, not worse. About the same. I really don't care. I realized, years ago, that I was stuck. That we both were, my sister and I . . . Lisa Barr, the columnist. She's the one. My sister, I mean. And there's just no place to go, no way to escape."

"Why not?"

"All that pop psychology you spout on your program all the time, and you have to ask a question like that? I'm surprised at you, Byrd. Your childhood is what you are, for God's sake. You don't need Freud for that. The Jesuits knew. 'Give me the first few years of a man's life and we have him forever.' That kind of thing. It's . . . arrested development. As far as she and I are concerned, the rest of the world is just a charade. She and I are what's real. Nothing else. All *you* can do is kill me, which would free both of us. Go ahead. Or put the gun down and go. Shit or get off the pot."

Byrd nodded. "Well, I give you credit. It's pretty good. I don't believe it for a minute, but I'd option the script. It's got heart."

"Which one of us are you making fun of, me or yourself? You've got other choices, you know. There are other ways to handle anger besides picking up a gun. You ought to see somebody. In six months, you'll be able to accept what's happened . . ."

"But that's exactly what I don't want to do. I don't want to accept it. I won't accept it, now or in six months or ever. It's unacceptable. What you did, and McCracken, and that fucking Alex Millwood, and what I did myself—and most of all, I blame myself—is just not acceptable."

"To whom?"

"To me! To me, for Christ's sake! I'm the judge and the jury and the executioner as well as the defendant, and all of us say 'Guilty!' It's just not acceptable to go and get my head shrunk or my mind straightened out, and go on as if nothing had happened. Something has happened. Something very bad has happened. And the only decent thing to do is punish the people who are responsible."

"I know how you feel," Castle said. "It'd be neater that way. If you could figure out what made you bisexual, or if I could figure out what it was that happened between Lisa and me, and blame somebody, it'd be a hell of a lot easier to live with. But it just doesn't work that way. These things just happen. Go shoot the cop who arrested your father when you needed to have him around. That'd make as much sense as shooting me or any of those others."

"You talk a great game. You've got a hell of a mouth on you, Castle. It's a shame to make it stop."

"But you know what I'm telling you is true. It feels true. You can't tell me it doesn't. Your father went to jail for bootlegging when you were six or seven years old. That had as much to do with your turning out AC/DC as anything else. And I still say that your mother knew. I think she knew all along, only the two of you never talked about it. And she just happened to have that heart attack while she was reading your book. You don't know what page she was on, for God's sake."

"It doesn't matter."

"Of course it does. You know damned well it does."

Byrd didn't say anything. He stood there, pointing the gun at Castle, but he was shaking his head slowly, no, no, no.

"Put the gun down, Byrd. You're not a killer. You didn't kill her and you're not going to kill me. And you don't want to kill yourself, which is what this is really about. I'm telling you, I know how you must feel. You get to a point where you realize it just doesn't make any difference. But that's no reason to kill yourself. It's a reason not to. It's just another stupid and extravagant thing to do that's easy for you and messy for whoever has to clean up after you. Put the gun down. Go home."

Byrd lowered the gun.

"You might as well try to kill whoever it was who invented sound movies. Or whoever was responsible for the crash of '29. The quarrel we've got is with God. I'm telling you. Nothing less! And you can't kill God. Or if you do, it doesn't matter, because He pops back up like one of those rubber clowns. All you can do is keep on going from one day to the next and try not to hurt people or make the mess any nastier than it already is . . ."

Byrd put the gun into his pocket and walked toward the door. He put his hand on the knob, stopped, turned back, and said, "You're a fast-talking son of a bitch, and I don't believe you for a minute."

"You don't have to believe me. Believe what you feel. Believe what you know in your guts is true, which is what I'm telling you. You didn't kill your mother. It's sad that she died, but you didn't kill her. And you can't even know for sure that the book was what killed her.

She died. That's all. And that's bad enough, my friend. That's bad enough. I know."

Byrd looked as though he was going to say something else, but he changed his mind. He opened the door, shook his head once more, and went out into the hall. As soon as the door had closed behind him, Castle ran to throw the bolt.

Susan came out of the closet. "My God, Len, is that all *true?*"

"What do you think?" he asked. He had a restrained grin that she recognized as his poker face.

"It was certainly convincing," she said.

He didn't say anything.

"And it would explain why we were always here rather than at your place."

He still didn't say anything.

"You'd rather not talk about it?"

"I don't mind," he said. "It's just that I'm a little confused about where we are now, you and I. I came here to hide from somebody coming after me with a gun. And you took me in on that basis—for which I'm grateful. But I don't have that excuse any more. The gunman's gone."

"You don't need an excuse. You never did."

"Didn't I?"

"Well, maybe. I've been difficult too. But you were terrific back there. By instinct, which is the best way. There's nothing fake about what you did."

"What I did? What did I do?"

"Protecting me. Shoving me in the closet that way."

"Oh, yes, well . . . It wasn't your problem. And I'd never have come here if I thought he was following me. I thought I'd shaken him."

"You want that drink?" she offered.

"We'd been on the verge of a brandy, if I remember. I could do with that now."

She nodded. "On the cart there. You know where it is. Help yourself. I'll be back."

She went into her bedroom to inspect for damage. The windowpane was smashed and there were glass shards all over the carpet. It wasn't so much the damage to the windowpane, which was trivial and fixable, as the sense of having her private space violated . . . It made her angry. And she felt hurt and . . . tired. She forced herself to pick up the larger pieces of the broken glass and drop them into the wastebasket. She even found a yellow evidence pad on her writing table, ripped off the cardboard back, cut it to fit the pane, and Scotch-taped it in place. But it was as exhausting as if she were doing heavy manual labor.

She went back out to the living room. Castle was sitting on the couch, a cognac in his hand and the bottle on the table next to him.

"I'll be all right in a minute or two, and then I'll go," he promised.

"Would you mind if I came with you?"

He was surprised. "Not at all."

"I can't sleep here," she explained. "I just couldn't. Tomorrow, after the window is fixed and there's a better lock on it, then maybe I'll be able to go back in there. But right now it's hateful. Soiled."

"Sure."

"I could go to a hotel, if you'd rather."

"No, no. By all means. Come to my place. Nothing would please me more."

"Or we could both go to a hotel. Together, I mean."

"No, my place is fine. I'd prefer it."

She went back into the bedroom to throw a few things together, toothbrush, makeup, underwear, and a change of clothing. She didn't take an overnight case: between her oversized purse and her briefcase, there was plenty of room for everything she needed.

She paused when she caught sight of herself in the bathroom mirror. She looked . . . fair. Not terrific, but not bad, considering. A little pale, maybe. She put on some lipstick, a little rouge, and some powder. That was better, a bit less haggard. Considering what she'd been through, she was in good shape, she thought.

And him? Was she pushing him too hard? Asking too much? She supposed she was, but she didn't care. If he couldn't handle it, she'd be rid of him for good and all and would recognize the rightness and necessity of the relationship's end. And if not?

Who could say how far it might go?

All she knew was that she hadn't felt so close to anyone in a long time. And if he felt that way about her, having gone through this thing together, then it was the kind of opportunity that she'd always dreamed of, even back when she was a kid who didn't know anything except what she wanted.

Which was, come to think of it, rather a lot.

Besides, she'd given him all kinds of outs. And he hadn't taken any of them.

She clicked the compact closed and switched out the light.

*

On the way, they decided they were hungry, after all. Ravenous, actually. Castle told the cabdriver to take them on to Broadway, where there was a good Chinese restaurant that did take-out. They sat at the bar waiting for their order to appear and Castle had another brandy. This time, Susan had one as well.

She thought of several possible topics of conversation just to keep the silence from looming too large, but none seemed quite right. She hadn't ever been in his apartment and was curious about that. But it seemed indelicate to refer to this, under the circumstances. She was also wondering what Byrd might do now, how dangerous he really was, either to himself or to other people—McCracken, in particular— but she didn't want to go back to that. And any neutral topic was so artificial, so obvious an avoidance of the relevant questions each of them knew the other was thinking about, that it was hardly worth the effort to pretend.

So they just sat there, drinking and looking at the fish in the tank behind the bar, and Susan found that she was less and less uncomfortable as the time passed. It was okay.

The headwaiter came out with a large bag and handed it over to Castle. They grabbed another cab and went to the Dakota. He led the way through the gate to his courtyard, into his entranceway, and up the stairs to his door.

"Go ahead," he said, standing aside for her to enter first.

She crossed the threshold. He switched on the lights and went into the kitchen to put down the bag. She looked around at what she could see from the hall. The living room was spartan, with uncarpeted parquet floors and bare white walls. On a table near the window there was a collection of succulents, cacti and other such plants that didn't require much care but that didn't give much back either—every now and then a rare blossoming, and then back to prickly somnolence.

Yes, that was right. That was like him.

There was a pair of good speakers and an expensive hi-fi rig, and one wall was lined with records, tapes, and compact discs. There were no books on display. They'd be in another room, a study or the bedroom. That was right too.

"Go ahead, look around," Castle called from the kitchen. "I'm heating up the soup. I hate lukewarm soup."

"Thanks, I will," she called back, starting down the hall, which led, she assumed, to the bedroom.

There was a thud as though something had dropped onto the floor.

"You all right?" Susan called, hurrying back to the kitchen.

"I'm fine," he said. "That was from next door." He pointed. "Lisa's heard us. And she's letting us know."

"I see," Susan said.

"You want to get the plates? They're in the cabinet behind you."

"Sure," Susan said. She fetched a couple of plates and bowls. She wasn't making any particular effort to rattle the dishes but neither was she trying hard to be secretive. Still, it was odd hearing an answering noise of dishes being handled. Or, after a moment, smashed.

"Spooky," Susan said.

"A little."

"Does this happen often?"

"No. Not this way. Never this way."

It took a moment before she realized what he was telling her—that he'd never brought anyone here.

They ate in the kitchen, the hot and sour soup, the cashew chicken, the orange beef, and the shrimp with snow peas and water chestnuts. Then they went into the bedroom, where she was surprised to see that his bed was a narrow single bed with ship's wheels carved into the headboard. The bed he'd had since boyhood.

"That's ridiculous," she said.

"Yes, I know."

It was, in a number of ways, still a boy's room, except that the toys were more elaborate now. There was a computer in the corner where he played games, and there were chess books and bridge books on a shelf next to the computer setup.

"She seems to have subsided," Susan said as she unbuttoned her blouse.

"For the moment. But we'll be hearing from her again."

"And she from us, maybe."

He blushed. But he was taking off his shirt and then his trousers.

Was it the experience of having faced down Byrd with the gun in his hand? It hadn't freed him yet, or not altogether, but it had opened the gate of his cage. She could lead him out.

What was novel for her, arousing her tenderness along with her desire, was her realization that he needed her and trusted her. It was perfectly clear to her that if she didn't rescue him now, he'd be condemned to this room and this bed for the rest of his life. And he was no fool and understood that just as clearly as she did.

"Maybe the radio would be a good idea," she suggested.

He nodded and switched on the little bedside radio on his night-stand. He found some Vivaldi on WNYC and turned up the volume. Then he took off his socks and his boxer shorts and got into bed.

She unhooked her bra, leaned forward, and let it fall away. She stepped out of her briefs and climbed into bed beside him. On the narrow bed, it was a tight fit, but they managed.

"Just barely," he said.

"The best way," she said, nestling close in his arms.

Even over the energetic sawing of Vivaldi's violins, they could hear bumping from the other side of the dividing wall. But it didn't seem to bother Leonard. Which gladdened Susan.

Then the phone rang.

"Ignore it," Castle said.

And the wonderful thing was that they could.

CODA

In the morning, Susan surprised herself and Castle as well when she said, "You can't go on here. You ought to move out of this place and this . . . situation. Move out and move on. Move in with me, maybe."

"That's quite a step."

"Yes, I guess it is."

"For both of us."

"Yes," she agreed.

"What if it doesn't work?"

"What if? There are no guarantees, ever. We'll play it by ear, I expect. But we've as good a chance as most couples. Better than most, in fact."

"I don't know what to say," he told her.

"That's not so important. What's important is what you want to do."

He nodded.

She waited. She didn't want to plead with him, but if she had to, then, for his sake, she supposed she would.

It never came to that. "Yes," she heard him say. "Yes, that's what I want. I mean . . . Yes."

"Good. I want that too," she said. "Up. Dress. Pack."

"I'll put up coffee," he said. "Then I'll pack."

"I can do coffee," she said.

She grabbed a robe and padded out to the kitchen. The roasted beans from Zabar's were in the refrigerator. The Braun grinder was on top of the cabinet. The coffee filters and the filter cone were in the little cabinet over the sink.

Hardly thinking, she switched on the little black-and-white television set he had on top of the refrigerator in time to see the *Today* show cut away for the five-minute insert of local news.

The suicide of prominent television personality Dickie Byrd was the lead item.

"Len!" she screamed. And then she listened as the newswoman read the story about how Byrd had been found outside his apartment late last night, having jumped to his death after leaving a suicide note. "The television interviewer made no reference to his mother's death two days ago of a heart attack which she sustained while reading an advance copy of his autobiography," the newswoman said.

"He really did it!" Castle said. He was standing in the doorway with a towel around his waist. Rivulets of water were dripping down the hair of his legs and onto the floor. "I'd thought maybe he was just trying to scare me," he said. "I'd hoped that's all it was. Maybe we should have called the police, after all."

"Either way," she said, "his life was over. It wouldn't have done any good."

"Maybe. Who knows?"

"You can't blame yourself. Who could have predicted that his mother would die that way? I mean, that's . . . crazy!"

He nodded.

"It could have been worse," she said. "He could have shot you first and then shot himself."

"All over your carpet!"

"That's not what I meant," she insisted.

"I know," he said. "I'll go back and finish my shower now."

Susan waited until the kettle began to whistle. Then she picked it up and poured the boiling water through the ground coffee. When it had dripped through, she poured two cups and brought them into the bedroom.

"Thanks," he said.

"Need any help packing?" she offered.

"No, no, I can manage," he said. "I'll be coming back here, after all. To pick up more of my things. And the cacti will need attention. Maybe I'll bring them down to the office."

"A good idea," she said. "How do you feel?"

"A little nervous, maybe, but good."

"Me too."

"If you change your mind, you can always throw me out," he said. "You're not stuck with me."

"That's always true. On both sides," she said. "You'll need a key. I'll get one made and I'll drop it by at your office."

"Or are you free for lunch?" he asked.

"I think so."

"Fine. I'll get it from you then," he said.

"Okay."

"As simple as that?" he asked.

"It always was."

*

When she'd gone, he went to the big closet where the suitcases were stored way up high on a series of shelves of diminishing size. "You can come out now," he said.

Lisa emerged from the closet.

"You were in there all night?"

"Most of it."

"What in hell for?"

"Actually, my dear brother, I came to kill you. I figured I could kill the both of you, which seemed a pretty neat idea."

"Neat?"

"Oh, yes. They'd have tied it to Byrd, wouldn't they?"

"Would they? Why?"

"He was at my apartment last night. This is his gun." She displayed the all too familiar revolver.

"What happened?"

"What do you think happened? He was at Susan's apartment, wasn't he? And you told him about us?"

Castle nodded, stunned. She couldn't be guessing.

"And then he came over to ask me whether it was true or not," she explained.

"Just like that?"

"Just like that."

"How did he get in?"

"The doorman announced him. He said it was Dickie Byrd, asking to see me. I said to let him in."

Castle sat down on the edge of the unmade bed.

"You told him about us," Lisa said reproachfully. "I couldn't believe it."

"He had a gun. It was the only thing I could think of to save my life. It was the only thing that kept him from killing me."

"If I'd been there, if the situation had been reversed, I'd rather have died."

"Why? What difference does it make? He's dead now, isn't he? So it doesn't matter . . ."

"But she knows."

"Susan? Yes, she knows. But I think I'd have told her anyway. Sooner or later."

"I know," Lisa said.

"You were going to kill both of us?"

Lisa nodded.

"And then yourself?"

She nodded again. "Not right away. Not for a week or so. I was curious to see if I'd get away with it. His gun, after all. And an obvious motive. It was just so elegant, so . . ."

"Neat, I think, is what you said."

"Yes."

"When did you know he was dead?" Castle asked.

"I hadn't slept, as you can imagine. I was listening to one of those round-the-clock news programs on the radio. And they announced that he'd killed himself."

"So you had a free ride."

"That's right."

"And why didn't you? Why didn't you do it while you had the chance?"

"I don't know. Because I love you. I'm jealous as hell, and I'm angry, and I feel betrayed. And I hate her. But I still love you. I couldn't do it. I had the safety off, and I had it pointed at you. Sometimes at you and sometimes at her, and sometimes at myself. But I couldn't do it."

"I'm glad. For your sake, I mean. I love you too, you know."

She nodded.

"If things had been different, and if we hadn't been brother and sister . . ."

". . . or if we'd been Egyptians like Ptolemy and Cleopatra," she said, chiming in with a very old routine.

". . . it would have been great. But it wasn't different and we aren't Egyptians."

"I know," she said. There were tears streaming down her face. She put the gun down. And then, next to it, her key to his apartment, the one he'd given her for emergencies.

"You better finish packing," she said.

He nodded. "You keep the key," he said. "You can have the whole apartment."

She made a kiss into the air and walked out of the room.

*

Over the course of the next week or so, he made a number of trips back and forth until he'd moved everything that was important. Some of his things, that absurd bed for instance, he put into storage. Some he threw out. The cacti, he made room for in the conference room of the office, just as he'd said he might.

It was a couple of days after he'd moved when he saw the item in the *Daily News* about a body that had been discovered in an apartment in Greenwich Village and just been identified—as that of Alexander Millwood.

That was the name Byrd had mentioned in Susan's apartment, the man who'd told McCracken his secret. From what Castle was able to gather from the paper, Byrd had beaten Millwood to death. And then he'd gone home, written his note, and taken the high jump. It couldn't have been a coincidence. Byrd must have regretted leaving the gun with Lisa. There was no suggestion of any connection between the two deaths in the newspaper article, but . . . it had to be.

A terrible thing! Castle's first impulse was to tell Susan all about it, but then he caught himself and asked what good that would do. If she hadn't seen the article, why burden her with it? It would only upset her. And there was nothing she could do about it.

She'd already done more than enough. And was continuing to do, wonderfully and well, whatever he needed.

In return, he could do her this favor, and himself too. He could still keep some things secret, after all.